STAGECOACH TO PURGATORY

STAGECOACH TO PURGATORY

The Violent Days of Lou Prophet, Bounty Hunter

Peter Brandvold

PINNACLE BOOKS
Kensington Publishing Corp.
www.kensingtonbooks.com

PINNACLE BOOKS are published by

Kensington Publishing Corp.
119 West 40th Street
New York, NY 10018

ISBN-13: 978-0-7860-4346-0
ISBN-10: 0-7860-4346-6

First printing: September 2018

10 9 8 7 6 5 4 3 2 1

Printed in the United States of America

First electronic edition: September 2018

ISBN-13: 978-0-7860-4347-7
ISBN-10: 0-7860-4347-4

In Memory of
Miss Sydney
200(?)–April 9, 2016
Gone but Never Forgotten

CONTENTS

LAST STAGE TO HELL

From *The Life and Times of Lou Prophet, Bounty Hunter*
by HEYWOOD WILDEN SCOTT

I'd been a tough-nosed newsman for nearly sixty years, yet it was with more trepidation than I like to admit that I knocked on the big, old rebel's door.

I'd heard the stories about him. Hell, I'd printed many of those yarns in the various newspapers I'd written and edited in that grand old time of the Old West gunfighters, larger-than-life lawmen, and the much-maligned, death-dealing bounty hunters, of which he'd been one.

Yes, I'd heard the tales. I'd printed the tales. With feigned reluctance (I was a journalist, after all—not a reader or writer of dime novels!) but with unabashed delight, if the truth be known. With admiration and even envy. Imagine such a man living such a life at such a time, hoorawing badmen of every stripe, risking life and limb with every adventure while the rest of us suffered little more than festering galls to our posteriors while scribbling ink by the barrel onto endless rolls of foolscap in dingy, smoky, rat-infested offices off backstreet alleys, the big presses making the whole building rock.

I'd never met him.

I'd heard from those who had crossed his trail that he was a formidable, mercurial cuss, by turns kindhearted and generous and foulmouthed and dangerous, and he'd grown more and more formidable, unpredictable, and recalcitrant with age. The years had not been kind to him. But, then, what would you expect of a man who had lived such a life and who, it was said, had sold his soul to the devil, exchanging an eternity of coal-shoveling in hell's bowels for a few good years after the War Between the States "on this side of the sod, stomping with his tail up," as he was known to call what he did between his bounty hunting adventures?

In fact, I once heard that he'd hunted only men with prices on their heads in order to pay for his notorious appetite for whiskey, women, and poker.

He'd seen so much killing during the war, out of which he'd emerged something of a hero of the Confederacy, that he really wanted only to dance and make love and swill the Taos Lightning to his heart's delight. But he was not an independently wealthy man, so it was only with great reluctance, I'm told, that after such bouts of manly indiscretions he took up his Colt .45, his Winchester '73 rifle, his double-bore, sawed-off, twelve-gauge Richards coach gun, and his razor-edged bowie knife, and stepped into the saddle of his beloved but appropriately named horse, Mean and Ugly, and fogged the sage in pursuit of death-dealing curly wolves prowling the long coulees of the wild and woolly western frontier.

He usually had a fresh wanted circular or two stuffed into his saddlebag pouches, carelessly ripped from post office or Wells Fargo bulletin boards.

Now, as I rolled my chair up to his room, I'd recently seen for myself that he was every bit the colorful albeit formidable old codger I'd heard he was. It had been only within a week or so of this recounting that the old warrior had shown up at the same Odd Fellows House of Christian Charity in Pasadena, California, that I, too, after several grave illnesses had broken me both financially and spiritually, had found myself shut away in, whiling away the long, droll hours until my own annihilation.

He'd been working as a consultant in the silent western flickers, I'd heard, until a grievous accident involving a Chrysler Model B-70, a couple of pretty starlets, and several jugs of corn liquor caromed off a perilous mountain road in the hills above Malibu. Now he prowled the halls on crutches—a big, one-legged man with a face like the siding of a ruined barn, at times grunting and bellowing blue curses (especially when one of the attendants confiscated his proscribed cigarettes and whiskey) or howling songs of the old Confederacy out on the narrow balcony off his second-story room, his raspy voice ratcheting up out of his tar-shrunken lungs like the engines of the horseless carriages sputtering past on Pacific Avenue.

As I was saying, I knocked on his door.

I shrank back in my chair when the door was flung open and the big bear of the one-legged man, broad as a coal dray and balancing precariously on one crutch, peered out from the roiling smoke fog inundating his tiny, sparsely furnished room.

"What?" he said.

At least, that's how I'm translating it. It actually sounded more like the indignant grunt of a peevish grizzly bear prodded from a long winter's slumber.

Out of that ruin of a face, two pale blue eyes burned

like the last stars at the end of the night. At once keen and bold, flickering and desperate.

Wedged between my left thigh and the arm of my wheelchair was a bottle of rye whiskey. On my right leg were a fresh notepad, a pen, and a bottle of ink. I hoisted the bottle high, grinned up at the old roarer scowling down at me, a loosely rolled cigarette drooping from a corner of his broad mouth, and said, "Tell me a story, Lou!"

Chapter 1

Something or someone peeled Lou Prophet's right eyelid open.

A female voice, soft as tiny wooden wind chimes stirred by an April breeze, said as though from far away, "You've ruined me!"

The bounty hunter's rye-logged brain was only half registering what his optic nerve was showing it, what his ears were telling it.

A face hovered over him, down close to his own, in fact, but the features of that face were a blur. He could better make out what he was not looking at directly. The head that the face belonged to owned a pretty, thick, long mess of light red tresses curling down onto slender shoulders as white as new-fallen snow on Christmas Day in the north Georgia mountains of Lou Prophet's original and long-ago home.

The girl released Prophet's lid, and she disappeared behind a veil of darkness. The accusatory words had stirred him somewhat, despite that his brain was a sponge still soaked in last night's tornado juice. He had no idea what had been meant by the accusation, and, while vaguely curious, slumber tugged at the ex-rebel bounty hunter like a heavy wind, albeit a wind that owned the inviting aroma of lilac water and natural, bed-fermented female musk.

Down, down, Prophet fell . . . until his other lid was tugged open, and the face appeared again, even closer to his own this time, so that he could see a gunmetal blue eye staring into his own left one. "Did you hear me? You've utterly and completely ruined me! *Ohh!*"

That nudged Prophet closer to full wakefulness. What in the hell was this girl, whoever in hell she was, talking about?

Ruined?

While Prophet had a somewhat wide-ranging reputation as a hard-nosed man hunter, he'd never been anything but gentle with women. Unless said women were running on the wrong side of the law and had tried to kill him, of course. (One of the first things he'd learned when he'd first turned to bounty hunting after venturing west after his beloved South had been whipped during the War of Northern Aggression was that not all hardened outlaws were men.) But those women were the exception rather than the rule, and he doubted that any of them would say he'd "ruined" them.

Prophet tried to say the word but, just as his brain was not yet hooked up to his eyes, it was not attached to his mouth, either, so that what he heard his own lips say as they moved stiffly against each other was: "Roo-hoom . . . d . . . ?"

"Ruined!" the girl said, louder, heartbroken. "Purely *ruined*!"

The half squeal, half moan was a cold hand reaching down into the warm water of the bounty hunter's slumber and plucking him into full wakefulness. He bolted upright in bed, blinking, heart thudding, wondering if he'd done something untoward during his inebriation.

Untoward, that was, beyond the usual transgressions of gambling himself into mind-numbing debt, drinking himself (as he'd obviously done last night) into a coma, frolicking with fallen women, brawling, fighting with knives, pistol-shooting shot glasses off neat pyramids arranged on bar tops, howling at the moon, swinging from the rafters, herding chickens, stealing bells from courthouse cupolas, singing to his horse, getting beaten up or thrown in jail or both, and, as per one occasion, asking a fallen woman to be his bride and actually going through with the ceremony. (Fortunately, the union had been rendered null and void when it was revealed that the minister had been defrocked due to his having had carnal knowledge of his organist.)

Prophet turned to the girl sitting naked beside him, not having any recollection of who she was or where he had met her but vaguely amazed at her sparkling, Christmas-morning beauty, and wrapped his left arm around her. "Oh, honey, I'm sooo sorry if I did *anything* last night that . . . that—"

"Oh, Lou—you've ruined me for all men hereafter. Last night was . . . well, it was absolutely *magical.* I've never been treated that way before . . ."

"Honey, who is your pa, anyway? Apparently, he knows me . . . ?"

"Oh, Lou," she said, rubbing against him and

purring like a kitten, "stop fooling around, would you? You know very well my father is Richard Teagarden, governor of Colorado."

Prophet's heart hiccupped. He jerked his head up as a rush of disconnected images from last night battered his tender, sodden brain. As disjointed as the images were, they told the story of Prophet recently riding into Denver with the body of Lancaster Smudge draped over the saddle of the horse Prophet had trailed behind his own hammerheaded dun, Mean and Ugly.

Over the past year and a half, Lancaster Smudge and his gang of five other owlhoots had become the bane of the territory not to mention of the Denver & Santa Fe Railroad, whose trains they'd preyed on without mercy, threatening to run the company into the ground and leave Colorado where it had been ten years before—relying on stagecoach services and mule trains for transport and commerce.

Many lawmen had been sicced on the gang, and a goodly portion of those few lawmen who'd gotten close to their quarry had ended up turned toe-down and snuggling with the diamondbacks in a Rocky Mountain canyon. The Smudge Bunch, as the papers had cheekily called Smudge's gang, were as elusive as Arizona sidewinders.

Prophet, however, working in cahoots with his sometime partner, Louisa Bonaventure, had proven the equals of the Smudge Bunch, and taken them down in their hideout up near the little mining town of Frisco, when the boys had let their hair as well as their pants down to enjoy a romp in Mrs. Beauchamp's House of the Seven Enchantments.

After Prophet had turned Smudge into the federals

for the two-thousand-dollar reward, the jubilant governor had insisted on inviting the bounty hunter out to the Larimer Hotel for a meal on the state's tab. There, Prophet had met the stately, smiling but distracted-seeming Mrs. Teagarden as well as the governor's pretty, precocious daughter, Clovis.

Clovis! Her name was Clovis Teagarden! Whew!

Prophet had never been given such grand treatment before. Bounty hunters were more or less considered vermin on the frontier, not all that higher on the human ladder than the men they hunted for the bounties on their heads. So Prophet was more accustomed to being treated like dog dung on a grub line rider's boots when he wasn't being ignored altogether by those of a more prestigious link in society's chain.

He certainly had never been invited out to dinner by anyone as important as a governor.

However, it had turned out that Governor Teagarden, being of a romantic turn of mind as well as a frequent reader of dime novels and the *Police Gazette*, was a secret fan of both Prophet and Louisa Bonaventure, whom the pulp rags had dubbed "the Vengeance Queen." Teagarden had apparently followed the duo's bounty hunting careers in the western newspapers, including Denver's own *Rocky Mountain News*.

Prophet suspected that the dapper little gray-haired man, who wore a gold ring on his arthritic little right finger and a giant, gray, walrus mustache on his lean, pasty face, had wanted to meet the comely blond Louisa far more than he'd wanted to dine with the scruffy Prophet. When Lou had informed the man that Louisa would not be joining them, as she'd decided to light out after a trio of outlaws they'd learned about near Leadville rather than accompany her partner back to Denver with a dead man, Teagarden had acquired a fleeting but poignant expression of deep disenchantment.

His sprightly and precocious daughter, Clovis, however, had kept her eyes on Prophet all through dinner, till he thought her smoldering gaze would burn a hole right through him. Still, the bounty man had been more than mildly taken aback when she'd slipped him a room key as he'd shaken her hand after dinner. It turned out the girl often spent nights in her father's private suite in the Larimer Hotel—under the strict supervision of a female chaperone, of course—because she attended a finishing school only two blocks from the hotel.

It also turned out, to Prophet's incredulity, that the girl's chaperone, Mrs. Borghild Rasmussen, who supposedly resided in the hotel, did not, in fact, exist, and that the bank drafts the governor wrote her were, in fact, never cashed. The governor's private secretary, a male no doubt under the mesmerizing influence of the carnal Clovis, kept it all a secret from the doddering fool.

So Clovis was pretty much running off her leash in the burgeoning and colorful cow town of Denver, inviting bounty hunters—well, one, at least—to her room.

Prophet rubbed the heels of his hands against his temples. "Clovis, I, uh . . . don't know what to say."

"You did remember my name!" the girl said.

"How could I forget a girl like you? It was a wonderful night, Clovis, but I tell you, honey, I never realized you were only sixteen. Hell, I thought you were at least twenty-one pushin' forty-five!"

Prophet scuttled over to the side of the bed that was, he saw now, enormous. It was easily the largest bed he'd ever seen let alone slept in.

"Oh, Lou—where are you going? You can't go yet! The day is just getting started!"

Prophet scowled over his shoulder at her, trying to ignore the fact that she was naked, not an easy task even in his whiskey-logged state. "You best get ready for school, little girl."

"Oh, phooey," Clovis said, leaning back on her elbows, pooching her pink lips out in a pout. "I'm going to skip school today. I often do. Father doesn't care. Neither does Mother. She'll be busy with her tea parties and such. Father's so busy with affairs of state he doesn't think about much of anything but work, work, work . . . and getting reelected, of course."

She rolled her eyes then beamed at Prophet. "That's why we can spend the whole day together, Lou."

"Doesn't your father ever check up on you?"

She only tittered an ironic laugh and wrapped her hands around her ankles, pulling her feet back toward her shoulders, giving him a haunting but unwanted eyeful.

Between love bouts the previous night, she'd told him a lot about herself, but he'd drunk so much whiskey, having gone without any skull pop for the past month he'd been hunting owlhoots in the mountains with the teetotaling Vengeance Queen, that he could remember only bits and pieces.

Clovis was a talker, though—he remembered that.

He'd made a mistake when he'd tramped up the Larimer's broad, carpeted stairs to find the lock that fit the key Clovis had given him.

Having entered a celebratory frame of mind the second he'd hit town, he'd gotten drunk before he'd dined with the governor's family, so his judgment had been off. And, if the truth be told, Prophet was far too weak a man to be able to ignore the fact of a pretty young woman handing him her room key with a coquettish dip of her chin and alluring glint in her eye.

In such a situation he was not now nor ever had been the type of jake who could shake his head and say, "Sorry, ma'am, but I'm not that sort of fella," and walk away. Just as he was having trouble averting his attention to what she was teasing him with now . . .

And some day he'd likely be fed a couple loads of buckshot for just that failing . . .

Or . . . maybe that day was here now, he amended the unspoken warning to himself as someone hammered on the room's door and a man's angry voice said, "Clovis? Clovis, are you in there?"

Chapter 2

Clovis gasped and drew her knees together.

The knock came again—two knocks, in fact, much louder than the previous ones. "Clovis? Clovis, I know you're in there, damnit!"

Prophet turned to the girl staring in wide-eyed shock at the door. "Who in the hell is that?"

The man on the other side of the door must have had the ears of a jackrabbit. "Who in the hell is *that*?" he yelled.

Clovis drew her hands across her mouth and said just loudly enough for Prophet to hear, "That is Miles Swarthing . . . son of the lieutenant governor . . . and"—she rolled her terrified gray eyes up to Prophet—"my betrothed!"

"*Betrothed?*" Prophet said, aghast.

Three more hard knocks came on the door. They were like three quick belches of a Gatling gun, and they made the stout walnut door bounce in its frame. The reverberation nudged an empty whiskey bottle off a table by the bed to drop to the carpeted floor with a dull thud. "Clovis, I will not ask you again. Who is in your room?"

"He is supposed to be in military school," Clovis said in dull shock behind her hands, which she'd steepled to each side of her nose. "He's supposed to be in *Pennsylvania*!"

"Oh, for Pete's sake!" Prophet grabbed his longhandles that were hanging off the carved arm of an upholstered chair. As he did, he looked for an escape route but found none.

It didn't matter. He wouldn't have had time to skin out through one, anyway, because just then the angry Miles Swarthing bellowed, "Clovis, damnit—what in hell is going *on in there*?" With "there," the door exploded inward to bang against the lavender-and-gold-papered wall, knocking an oil painting of ships jouncing on a rowdy sea from its nail over a distant fainting couch.

Prophet had only just grabbed his longhandles but had not yet started to draw them on when a clean-shaven young man in a dark blue military uniform complete with a gold-buttoned cape and leather-brimmed forage hat stormed into the room like a bull through a chute. He wasn't very tall but he was stocky, and his head sat like a large red roast set atop broad, thick shoulders.

"Oh my God," Clovis squealed. *"Rape!"*

"Wait," Prophet said, turning his incredulous scowl to the girl on the bed. *"What?"*

Clovis clawed up one of the several twisted sheets on the bed and drew it over her nakedness and, shuttling her terrified gaze from Prophet to her betrothed standing crouching in the open doorway, facing the bed, screamed louder this time, "Rape!"

"*Rape?*" both Master Swarthing and Prophet said at the same time, in the same tone of voice.

"Oh God, Miles," the girl squealed, kicking her bare legs to scoot toward the far side of the bed, as though to put as much distance between herself and the big man standing naked before her, "I just woke to find this . . . this *animal* in my room!"

"Oh, you did, did you?" Miles said, stomping toward Prophet, his beet red face bunched in anger, raising his balled fists. "We'll just see about that!"

Prophet dropped the longhandles and raised his hands, palms out. "Now, just hold on there, kid. I didn't do any such—"

Clovis held several sheets up to just below her wide, glistening eyes.

The uniform-clad younker, who was a good foot shorter than Prophet's six-four, came at Lou like an angry mule, swiping at the air with both fists before swinging his right fist hard at Prophet's face. The bounty hunter jerked back into the night table, and the kid grunted as his fist whistled through the air where Prophet's head had just been.

Prophet took a step back, holding up both placating hands. "Kid, it ain't what you think!"

The kid shuffled up to Prophet, moving his feet like a practiced pugilist, and sent a left jab toward Prophet's jaw. Lou raised his right arm, deflecting the blow. "Kid, it ain't what she said, and if you don't get your neck out of a hump, I'm gonna hurt ya!"

But then the kid landed a solid right to Prophet's bare belly. It wasn't much of a blow, really. It might have been for some men, but Prophet had been injured worse throwing the wood to the younker's girl the previous evening. The punch did, however, bring a hot ball of anger up from the base of Prophet's spine.

As the kid tried to land another similar blow to the bigger man's belly, Prophet rammed his right fist into the younger man's right temple—two short, swift, hard hammering blows that made resounding smacking sounds.

The kid stumbled backward, bringing a hand to his injured forehead and saying, "Ohhh!"

He dropped to a knee, blinking, holding his hand to his head. "Ohhhh!"

"Rape!" screamed Clovis from the bed.

Prophet scooped his balbriggans off the floor and turned to her. "Clovis, will you knock that nonsense off?"

He shook out the twisted garment before him and stepped into one leg. He tried to step into the other leg, but the determined and fiery Miles Swarthing bolted off his heels and came storming at Prophet like a bull at a red cape.

"Oh, fer Pete's sake!" Prophet stepped to one side, grabbed the young man by the collar of his cape, and, pivoting on his hips, thrust him into the wall behind him.

"Ohhh!" cried Master Swarthing, crouched with his forehead kissing the wall, pressing his hands to both sides of his head. "Ohhhhh!"

His legs buckled and his knees hit the floor, where he knelt, head down, as though in fervent prayer. "Ohhh . . . ohhhh . . . *boy*!"

"Someone, please help me!" Clovis bellowed, the

sheet drawn up to just below her eyes. She lowered it to her chin long enough to mouth the words, "Sorry, Lou, but I have a reputation to think about! I'm the governor's daughter, after all!"

"What about *my* reputation, Clovis?"

"Lou, you're a bounty hunter!" Clovis jerked the blanket back up over her nose and cut loose with another, "Oh, someone, please help me-*ee*!"

"Oh, fer chrissakes!" Prophet complained, wrestling with his longhandles once more. Before he could get his second leg covered, a middle-aged woman in an early-morning wrap and hairnet poked her head into the room.

Her eyes found Prophet in all his masculine nakedness, dong swinging as he wrestled into his underwear, and added a chorus of her own screams to those of Clovis.

"Ah, Jesus!" Prophet cried as the woman's screams drifted off down the hall.

Prophet got his longhandles on and then hustled crazily around the room, grabbing his boots, socks, denim jeans, buckskin shirt, and his gun belt and six-shooter.

As he did, Clovis thrust the bedcovers aside and scrambled off the bed. She grabbed his hat off the upholstered chair near the still-kneeling Miles Swarthing and handed it to Prophet as he headed for the door, saying under her breath, "Please forgive me, Lou, but my honor is at stake! That said, if you're ever back in town, do please look me up!"

She winked, blew him a kiss, and then shrank back in horror and screamed, "*Rape!*"

"Crazy lady," he groused, setting the hat on his head and then poking his head out the door to cast cautious looks both ways along the hall. "I'd love to see you again, Miss Clovis . . . and beat your bottom with a willow switch!"

He glanced at the girl once more. She was hunkered down beside Miles Swarthing, who was still kneeling against the wall by the chair, saying, "Boy . . . oh, boy . . . jeepers, that hurts!"

Seeing no one in the shadowy hall, Prophet clutched his clothes in a unwieldy ball before him and ran out of the room, heading toward the stairs at the far end. He'd almost reached the wide mouth of the staircase bleeding gray light up from the lobby, when two silhouetted figures appeared, taking the stairs two steps at a time.

Prophet froze as both figures, reaching the hall, turned toward him. One Prophet recognized as the Larimer Hotel's concierge, Stephane St. Germaine, a neat, bald, well-groomed Frenchman whom Prophet often played poker with in one of Denver's livelier parlor houses—between mattress dances with one of the doves, that was.

The other man was the house investigator, Harry Boyles, a tall, beefy gent with a thick mustache. A pugnacious, hard-bitten former railroad detective whom Prophet had never cared for, Boyles was holding a .41 caliber, silver-chased pocket pistol in his beringed right fist.

Both men stopped abruptly eight feet from Prophet, snapping their eyes in shock at the big bounty hunter cowering in the shadows near the wall.

"Lou—is that you?" Stephane said, scowling incredulously, raking his eyes up and down Prophet's balbriggan-clad, barefoot frame.

Boyles curled his mustached upper lip into a sneer

as he said, "Someone up here's been yellin' 'rape.' That don't have nothin' to do with you, now, does it, Proph?"

Prophet shook his head. He knew there was no use trying to convince Boyles, who didn't care for Prophet any more than Lou cared for him, so the bounty hunter turned to his friend Stephane. "No, it sure don't, though I didn't realize what a bailiwick I was stumblin' into when . . . when . . ." He let his voice trail off as he turned toward the gray light marking where Clovis's open door bled light into the otherwise dark hall.

"Oh, Lou—you didn't!" Stephane said in disgust. "The governor's daughter? You accepted her key?"

Prophet didn't know how to respond to that. Feeling like an utter fool, he managed only to move his lips and shake his head, wishing like hell that some unseen door would open in the floor beneath his feet and give him release of this horrific, embarrassing, and potentially lethal situation.

Stephane jerked his head to indicate behind him. "You see that door that says 'Private'?"

Prophet saw the door just beyond the mouth of the stairs, with the word PRIVATE sketched in looping cursive into a gold plate in the door's upper panel. He nodded.

"Go through it, you crazy loon. It's the housemaids' rear staircase. There's an outside back door at the bottom. The police have been summoned. They'll arrive any minute. Take that door and do yourself a favor."

"What's that?" Prophet asked, feeling like a chastised schoolboy.

"Stay away from crazy young women in general

and *that one* in particular unless you want the governor hanging you by your unmentionables from the nearest cottonwood along Cherry Creek!"

"Obliged, Stephane," Prophet said, sheepish.

"And for God's sakes, man," Stephane added as he began striding on toward the girl's room, giving a caustic laugh, "get some clothes on. You're not decent!"

"Hold on," Boyles said, hovering near Prophet with the peashooter aimed at Lou's belly. "I think I should—"

"Forget it, Harry," Stephane said, slapping the detective's arm with the back of his hand. "She probably raped *him*!"

And then they continued off down the hall, albeit with Boyles giving Prophet the woolly eyeball over his left shoulder.

Prophet slinked off past the top of the stairs to the door with the gold plate, opened it, and slipped into a narrow, dingy stairwell that smelled like breakfast cooking in a kitchen somewhere on the first floor. As Prophet descended the stairs, his stomach rumbled and his mouth watered at the delectable aromas of fresh coffee, scrambled eggs, and bacon.

He dropped down two flights of stairs and stopped at a junction with two doors, one in the outside wall straight ahead and one to his right. The breakfast smells were pushing through the door to his right, so heavy and intoxicating that he had to almost physically resist the temptation to push through it and scavenge around for a few strips of bacon and a sip or two of coffee.

He had to get out of there, though. Not just any girl but the governor's daughter was screaming "rape" upstairs, and he supposed he could be charged with assaulting her beau, as well, though he'd been trying only to defend himself, for crying in the king's ale!

Standing by the outside door, he grabbed his socks from the bunch in his hands and dropped the rest of the clothes on the floor. Footsteps sounded beyond the door to his right. Someone—probably a maid bearing room service—was heading toward him.

Quickly, Prophet swiped his clothes off the floor, opened the outside door, peered out, and, seeing no one near, slipped out into the back alley abutted by the rear ends of several large, brick buildings and littered with all manner of sour-smelling trash.

He eased the door closed as he heard the kitchen door click open.

Turning to the alley, he dropped his clothes on the coal-and-gravel-littered ground, and began plucking individual garments from the pile one and two at a time, until only his cartridge belt, Peacemaker revolver, and sheathed bowie knife were on the ground between his right, booted foot and a large coal pile.

He kept a wary watch around him, seeing sleepy-eyed pedestrians, carriages, horseback riders, and the occasional coal wagon pass on the cross streets to his right and left. On the opposite side of the alley, a man in the ragged suit of a traveling drummer sat slumped against the rear of a building Prophet knew to be one of the lesser whorehouses in this neck of Denver.

The man's legs were stretched wide before him, and his chin rested on his shoulder. He'd vomited down his arm sometime during the night. An empty bottle lay beside him, near where a wild, charcoal-colored cat was foraging around a pile of food scraps likely tossed out of a restaurant, and casting feral, proprietary glances toward the big man dressing hastily at the rear of the Larimer Hotel.

"No need to worry, Mr. Puss," Prophet said, strapping his gun belt around his waist. "I'm hungry but not *that* hungry."

Tugging his hat brim down over his eyes, he headed south along the alley, ignoring the cat humping its back at him and giving an angry whine. At the cross street, he stopped. Pressing his left shoulder against the building to his right, he looked up and down the cobbled street and froze when three men in the blue, gold-buttoned uniforms of the Denver police ran toward him from the street's far side.

Damn.

Chapter 3

Prophet took one slow step backward, not wanting to make too hasty a retreat and draw attention to himself. As the trio of blue-clad men with copper shields pinned to their wool tunics angled across the street toward Prophet's right, one of them turned toward him.

The policeman—whom Prophet recognized as Finnegan Walsh, another card-playing, whiskey-swilling crony—slowed to a near-stop and said, "Hey, Lou—didn't know you was in town!" He slowed his pace as his two partners turned the corner of Larimer Avenue and hustled off to the hotel. Walsh's accent was as thick and green as a peat bog. "You should've dragged your mangy arse into Kenny O'Brien's. We had us one hell of a stud game a-roarin', big money fillin' pockets, and Minnie Winstead brought a couple of her Chinese doves over for a frolic!"

The gray-bearded Irishman grabbed his crotch, grinned, and yelled, "Gotta be off—some depraved fools is pluckin' a cherry off an unwilling bush over to the Larimer, don't ya know!" He shook his head in sadness. "The world gets more and more depraved every day I'm alive to bear witness to it."

Turning and jogging after the others, he called, "See you around, Louie-oh!"

"Yeah—maybe in about twenty years," Prophet muttered, relieved to see his old friend sidestep to avoid a young Mexican selling hot burritos wrapped in newspaper from a wooden cart, and disappear around the corner of a hat shop. "That'll be about when I'll be able to show my ugly face in Denver again—thank you very much, Miss Clovis!"

With that, he ran out of the alley, crossed the street, and jogged south toward Cherry Creek. He crossed the creek via a wooden bridge and then ran across an empty lot to Roy Stover's Cherry Creek Stable and Livery Barn on the corner of Front Street and Second Avenue, so close to Union Station that he could smell the cow pens and hear the panting of the big Baldwin locomotives and the echoing clang of coupling cars out in the rail yard.

Stover was greasing the hubs of a leather-seated, red-wheeled phaeton when Prophet jogged into the barn, huffing and puffing and sleeving sweat from his forehead.

"Rope and saddle Mean an' Ugly for me, will you, Roy?"

The overall-clad liveryman, bearded and smoking a corncob pipe, glanced over his shoulder at Prophet, and grinned. "What's her name, Lou?"

Prophet leaned forward, hands on his knees, trying to catch his breath. "Huh?"

"The name of the girl with the jealous boyfriend."

Prophet's heart quickened. But then he realized

didn't know where he'd end up hanging his hat for a night or two until the time came. And when it came, he was more often than not three sheets to the wind and hardly in any condition to care for his gear.

Besides, hauling his trail possibles around all night would have put one hell of a crimp in his spine and made it damn near impossible to enjoy whatever dove he ended up settling in with.

So he always stowed his gear in a corner of Stover's office, and it was from this corner that he retrieved it all now—saddlebags, rifle scabbard, bedroll wrapped inside his greased-canvas rain slicker, and the Confederate gray war bag he'd owned since he'd signed up to fight with the Old Man. Slinging the Richards over his head and right shoulder by its wide leather cartridge lanyard and resting his rifle on his shoulder, he turned to leave the office, and stopped.

Men were talking out in the barn.

Prophet's heart hiccupped. He recognized Stover's raspy wheeze caused by the corncob pipe he always smoked. He also heard the sonorous Irish rhythms of Sergeant Finnegan Walsh!

Blood singing in his ears, Prophet stepped back into the office and drew the door partially closed.

"No, I ain't seen hide nor hair of that miscreant, Sergeant," Stover said.

"I thought ole Proph usually stabled his horse with you, Roy," Walsh returned, the rebuttal tinged with skepticism.

"Not usually, Sarge. *Sometimes.* When he's feelin' partial toward them French girls Ma Anderson has up the creek a ways, he stables that hammerheaded cayuse of his in her stable—you know the one behind her cribs? Ma lets Lou stable that broomtail for free as long as he stays a coupla nights, don't ya know."

Prophet imagined the wink Stover sent up to Walsh, who was likely sitting a horse out front of the barn. The bounty hunter could hear several horses snorting and blowing in that direction.

"That's just fine with me, too," Stover added. "Proph named that horse right when he named him Mean an' Ugly. Someone must not've told that beast he's gelded. Whenever he gets in my corral, he stomps around with his tail up, picking fights with any stallion in sight and harassing the mares somethin' terrible. And you can't turn your back on him less'n you want him to tear the seam out of your shirtsleeve. Oh, he's a devil, that one!"

Prophet couldn't help snorting at the correctness of the liveryman's observation but he wished to hell the man would stop flapping his lips and send Walsh and the other local constabularies on their way.

"All right, then, Roy-o," Walsh said, "I'll leave you to it. We'll check out Ma Anderson's place. If you see that catamount, you tell him to turn himself in to me. That's the only way we're gonna get this mess cleaned up, and the sooner the better!"

There was the stomp of hooves telling Prophet the policemen were about to ride away, but the stomping stopped when Walsh, to Prophet's tooth-grinding dismay, said, "Say, what did that rascally ex-reb do, anyways, Sarge?"

Walsh hemmed around for a minute then said, "Let's just say it's a little matter concerning the governor's daughter."

Prophet heard Stover suck a sharp breath. "Ah,

nah—Prophet didn't walk into her trap, now, too, did he?"

"'Fraid so, and she's howlin' up a storm, and the lieutenant govna's son is, too, which makes this all one hell of a big mess. So, you tell that ugly Southern rebel to haul his arse over to headquarters so we can get the matter cleaned off the books before the newspapers have a heyday with it."

Hooves thudded.

As the policemen rode away, Walsh must have yelled back over his shoulder, "You tell him the sooner the better, too, Roy-o!"

"I will, Sarge," Stover called. "You can bet the seed bull on that!"

When the hooves had dwindled to silence, Prophet stepped out of the liveryman's office, grunting under the weight of his gear as well as the anvil-like heft of his dilemma.

Walsh stood staring out the open barn doors. He turned as Prophet approached and said, "You dunderheaded fool!"

Prophet stopped to scowl at the bearded old-timer sucking once more on his pipe. "She's done this sorta thing before?"

"Of course she has! Don't you know that? Hell, most of Denver knows about Miss Clovis's reputation—everyone but the governor himself, most like! Him and the missus see that hydrophobic polecat of a daughter of theirs with rose-colored glasses. She invites all breed to that room of hers up in the Larimer, and if all don't go exactly the way she wants, she starts screamin', 'Rape! Rape! Oh, he's rapin' me! Please help!'

"Last time it was some army lieutenant one of the

hotel maids caught her with. She tried that on some poor shotgun rider for the local stage company who didn't know who she was till he found himself bendin' her over some rain barrel out behind the hotel, and a coupla drummers happened on 'em an' recognized Miss Clovis for the governor's daughter. 'Rape! Rape! Oh, this ugly cur is trying to have his way with me!'

"That poor fella ended up spendin' several months in jail, and the lieutenant was court-martialed. Of course, it was all taken care of right quick, without either case ever even goin' to a jury, and, of course, without the name of the accuser being shared with the newspapers. All so the little miss's reputation wouldn't get soiled and the governor and his wife wouldn't be embarrassed!"

"Well, hell," Prophet griped, indignant, "why in the hell didn't you warn me about her, Roy?"

Stover took his pipe in his hand and opened his mouth in exasperation. "I thought every man within two hundred miles any direction from Denver would have done heard about Miss Clovis and taken heed. Hell, ever'body's heard about the governor's daughter—randier'n a she-griz with the springtime craze! Stalks the streets around the stockyards where the gov can't see, flouncin' around like an alley cat in heat!"

"Well, I never heard nothin' about that!"

"Only because you're a damn fool!" Stover raged, his raspy voice cracking on the high notes.

With a disgusted chuff, Prophet hauled his gear through the side door into the corral. Mean and Ugly stood ground-reined, facing Prophet, an eager look in his dark copper eyes though he was twitching his ears curiously, pondering no doubt the nature of its rider's argument with the liveryman and likely wondering if the tiff had something to do with what he, Mean and Ugly himself, had done.

Which it usually was only this rare time it was not.

"Besides," the liveryman said, following Prophet into the corral to continue the squabble, "who in the hell would ever think a reprobate like yourself would ever get that close to a girl like that, anyways?"

Prophet had draped his saddlebags across Mean's hind end and was now lashing his bedroll to the cantle of his saddle. "Just so happens the governor and his wife invited me to sup with 'em last night." He gave a curl-lipped jeering glance at Stover, who was bent slightly forward at the waist and pointing the stem of his pipe at Prophet, as though it were a cocked .44. "You ever have the opportunity to sup with the governor, Roy?"

"Pshaw!" Stover said, his ears red with enmity. "Wouldn't accept such an invitation. What in the hell would I have to talk to the governor about?" His thin brows curved down over dark, withered sockets as he grew fleetingly pensive. "Say, what in the hell did *you* have to say to him, anyways—an ex-rebel bounty hunter gassin' with the governor of Colorado? Must have been one hell of a short conversation."

"Hell, no!" Prophet shoved his rifle down inside his wool-lined saddle sheath strapped over the fender of his right stirrup, butt jutting up within easy reach of a quick grab. "He asked my opinion about several things. Laws and policies an' such, and he seemed right interested in what I had to say, too. I'd love to tell you all about 'im, Roy, but since you didn't warn me about his randy polecat of a daughter, I best be on my way before the sergeant heads back in this direction."

He swung up into the saddle. Stover lifted the loop of rusty wire over the end pole of the corral gate and swung the gate wide. "Damnit, Lou—you best stay away from Denver for a long damn while. If you get caught, it's gonna be your word against Miss Clovis's, and I don't care what kind of a high-up chin session you had with her pa, you're liable to do some serious time in the state pen . . . you sorry son of a bitch!"

"Ah, hell, I reckon I know that by now." Prophet felt real regret. He didn't know what he'd been thinking—accepting that key and tramping off to the girl's room. The room of the daughter of the governor of Colorado! How was anything good going to come of that?

But then he gave a wry snort, remembering the good that had come of it—at least the good that had come before young Miles Swarthing came knocking . . .

"Damn, she must've been a sweet ride," Stover said, shaking his head as he gazed up at the sheepishly grinning bounty hunter. "You done been run out of Denver, but you're still lit up like a sunset!"

"I reckon it just hasn't sunk in yet," Prophet said, flipping a silver cartwheel to the liveryman for services rendered. "There you are, Roy. Keep the rest. Buy yourself a noon ale over at Paddy St. John's and bid the fellas a long farewell for me, will you?"

He neck-reined Mean into the street.

"Oh, mule fritters—say, Lou!"

Prophet drew back on Mean's reins. "I don't got time to swap any more insults with you, Roy. I—"

Stover held up a white envelope that glowed golden now as the morning's buttery light hit it. "The postman Ernest Myers brung me this damn near two weeks ago, knowin' how when you're in town you usually stable that mean ole hay burner of yours with me. I plumb forgot about it until I rolled out of the hay this mornin' and seen it on my desk."

Chapter 4

Prophet looked skeptically at the envelope flopping around in the liveryman's arthritic brown hand. He didn't normally get mail. "What is it?"

"What does it look like, ya damn fool—it's a letter!"

"I can see it's a—" Prophet cut himself off, casting an anxious gaze in the direction that Walsh and the other policemen had gone, looking for him. "Well—fork it over and I'll look at it later!"

He snatched the envelope from Stover's hand, stuffed it into a pocket of his vest, and nudged Mean with his spurs. "See you when I see you again, Roy!"

"Good luck, Lou. Try keepin' your pecker in your pants for a change!" The man's voice faded as he added, "You'll live a lot longer that way!"

Stover laughed as Prophet galloped straight south along a dirt street. It wasn't long before the stables and ancient, sagging shanties of Denver's outskirts gave way to rolling, brush-covered prairie. On his right Prophet could see a locomotive chugging on a route parallel to his own, the giant, diamond-shaped black stack issuing a large dark banner of wood smoke trailing off over the tender car and passengers and freight cars rumbling along behind.

Prophet wished he were on that train, heading south toward New Mexico. Then, again, when Walsh realized he'd been led astray, he might figure that Prophet had indeed hopped that very Denver & Rio Grande flier. He might send telegrams southward toward Pueblo and Trinidad, putting the authorities down there on his trail.

The bounty hunter shook his head as Mean lunged through the prairie brush. Another fine fix Prophet was in. This one was even finer than most. He'd been accused of rape by a governor's daughter. A governor's daughter! Denver had always been a destination for him when he had no other—a general hub, a home of sorts where he rested up and frolicked between bounty hunting jobs. Now there was no telling when, if ever, he could return.

And in the meantime, his ugly mug would no doubt be plastered across the West on wanted circulars!

As Denver became a smaller and smaller smudge on the prairie behind him, he became more and more aware of the direness of his situation. He was a hunted man, little different from the men he'd made a career of hunting. Also, he had a thousand dollars in his wallet—half of which belonged to Louisa—but would he ever see the Vengeance Queen again? He'd likely have to hole up in the Indian Nations with the other owlhoots on the dodge from the law, or change his name and take up some other occupation. His infamous mug would likely be recognized on the trails he usually haunted.

When he figured he was a good five or six miles

south of Denver, Prophet swung north, following what appeared to be an ancient Indian hunting trail meandering across the near-featureless prairie. He rode slumped in the saddle, weary and sad as well as frustrated and angry.

For a brief time he considered riding back to Denver and trying to clear his name with the local police, even if it meant going to trial, but then he realized what would likely happen if he pitted his word against that of the governor's daughter . . .

Ten or twenty years of hard labor in the Colorado State Pen.

For a crime he hadn't committed.

As Stephane had said, if anyone had been raped last night, it was him!

But then he realized that self-pity and general moroseness were not going to get him out of his current tight spot. Besides, he had no one else to blame but himself. How long did he think he could keep living the lifestyle he'd been living, hunting badmen for enough money to carouse carelessly to his heart's delight, before that life would turn into a coiled diamondback and sink its teeth into his backside?

Well, that time had come. The snake had bit him hard. Dark poison surged in his veins. Now he had to confront the cards his own careless betting had dealt him and figure out a new way of life as a wanted man.

Self-pity wasn't going to help, but he rode for the rest of the day, slumped in the saddle, licking his proverbial wounds. He continued to follow the old Indian trail on its leisurely course generally to the northeast. Having followed such trails many times before, he knew they usually led to rivers. This one would lead to both forks of the Platte. Probably also to the remains of some ancient tipi town. Round indentations in the sod would be all that remained of the hide tents that had been erected to form a hunting camp from which the braves would ride out each day, stalking the buffalo herds that had once blackened this vast, blond, cerulean-capped prairie bordered by the majestic, ermine-tipped Rockies in the west.

Lou Prophet liked it out here. He liked the space and the silence punctuated by the rasping breeze and piping meadowlarks. Maybe he'd put too much stock in stomping with his tail up in towns like Denver, bedding down with questionable women . . . and governors' daughters. Maybe he was better off out here.

What he didn't like, however, were the ghosts of the dead that haunted this remote prairie. He was reminded of them when, late in the shadowy afternoon, crossing a dry, shallow gully, he came across several human bones embedded in the sand scalloped by many spring floods.

He recognized one such bone as a human arm to which a few blue wool remnants of a cavalry uniform still clung. A little beyond the gully he found an Indian spear with a moldering gray shaft. A few bits of feather remained attached to the bottom of the shaft, near the obsidian spear point.

Some likely nameless, long-forgotten skirmish had been fought out here many years ago, probably even before the War of Northern Aggression. Due to circumstances that would forever be lost to time, at least one dead from each side had never been recovered. There were many more bones strewn around this slice of the Colorado prairie. Prophet had seen his share. The Utes, Prophet knew, believed that when their dead had not been given a proper send-off to the Land Beyond, the spirits of those dead warriors inhabited living coyotes and gave voice to their grief in the yips and yammers that haunted the western frontier on any given night.

The thought caused gooseflesh to ripple across Prophet's shoulders, when, later that night, sitting around a crackling fire along the banks of another shallow wash, he heard the first coyote give its ululating cry. The sun just then teetered over the Rockies, and heavy black shadows spilling out away from those mountains engulfed the plains like stygian floodwaters released by some giant, broken dam.

The green sky darkened. A star winked to life. Then another.

Another coyote added its yammer to that of the first.

Prophet had enough ancient Appalachian superstition in his Confederate bones to hear the cries of the dead in those mournful wails. He fumbled his whiskey flask out of a saddlebag pouch, twisted off the cap, and added a goodly portion of the firewater to his coffee. He capped the flask, set it at his feet, drew the collar of his mackinaw, which he'd donned against the growing night chill, up tighter around his jaws.

Still, he shivered.

"Damn scaredy-cat," he told himself, and gave a dry snicker.

He sipped the coffee. A breeze lifted, making

rasping sounds in the brush, causing the limbs of the gnarled, old cottonwood flanking his camp to squawk like rusty door hinges. A crinkling sound caused him, in his anxious state, to give another jerk, causing some of the coffee to dribble over the rim of his cup. He turned his head to find the cause of the noise and saw the pale envelope lying over a small grass clump near his right boot.

The letter Stover had given him must have fallen out of his vest pocket when he'd pulled his coat on. The breeze tugged at it, lifted it over the grass clump, slid it along the ground so that it made a sound like a small rattler. Prophet reached down and with a grunt plucked the envelope off the ground. He held it to the fire's flickering orange glow, studied the loopy, feminine writing on its face.

It was addressed to Mr. Lou Prophet, c/o General Post, Denver, Colorado.

The return address was Mrs. Margaret Knudsen, Jubilee, Dakota Terr.

"Margaret Knudsen?" Prophet didn't know any Margaret Knudsen, much less anyone else in Jubilee, Dakota Territory.

Apparently, however, someone up there in that land of the brutal winters and mosquito-feasting summers knew him . . .

Prophet slid his bowie knife from its sheath and used its razor edge to slice open the envelope. Returning the knife to the scabbard, he shook out the folded piece of lined notepaper and awkwardly peeled open the folds with his thick fingers.

The date written at the top of the single sheet told Prophet that the missive had been written nearly a month ago. He adjusted the sheet to the dancing flames and crouched low over the writing, so he could get a better look at the purple-inked cursive that filled a little over half of the sheet.

He fidgeted atop the log he was sitting on, a nettling chagrin warming his ears as it did at such times he was presented with the need to dredge up his limited reading skills. It wasn't that Prophet hadn't had the opportunity to go to school now and then back in the north Georgia mountains, it was just that nearly every time he had, he'd chosen to go fishing instead.

Holding the breeze-nibbled paper up before him with his left hand, he used his right index finger to point out the words as he sounded out each one in turn.

Hello my Dear Friend,

Do you remember me? I am the former Margaret Jane Olson whom you once knew by my show name—Lola Diamond. Lou, I am in terrible need of your help. The problem is too long and complicated for written words. This letter may not even reach you. Just know that if you get this, I am in dire need of the assistance only you can provide, so won't you please visit me here in Jubilee, in the Dakota Territory? If you remember me at all you probably remember me well enough to know that I would not ask such an enormous favor unless I was in desperate need.

I hope this letter somehow finds its way to you posthaste, and finds you alive and well and in better spirits than I—

Your friend,
Lola

Prophet recited her name again, "Lola," as he lowered the paper. A smile of fond remembrance touched his lips. "Of course I remember you, girl."

Longer ago than he wanted to remember, he'd met the showgirl Lola Diamond in Montana Territory. She'd witnessed a murder, and an old lawman friend of Prophet's, Owen McCreedy, had deputized Prophet. He'd also armed him with a subpoena that he was to use to fetch Lola from where her traveling acting troupe, Big Dan Walthrop's Traveling Dolls and Roadhouse Show, had been playing in the little mining town of Henry's Crossing. McCreedy had wanted Prophet to escort the showgirl back to Johnson City, where she'd witnessed a murder, so that she could testify against the accused—the notorious brigand Billy Brown.

It had been supposed to be a routine favor that Prophet was doing for a friend for very little money, but, because Lola had not wanted to testify and incur the wrath of the infamous Brown, Prophet and Lola had not started off on the right foot. In fact, on their initial meeting in the hotel where she and her troupe had been holed up, she'd tried to shoot him with a .41 caliber pocket pistol. When that hadn't worked, she'd buried her right foot so deep in Prophet's crotch that he could have sworn he'd felt her toes tickle his windpipe!

The bounty hunter chuckled at that now, though it had been nothing to chuckle about at the time. His oysters had been sore for days. Finally, however, he'd gotten her away from her angry troupe, including Big Dan Walthrop himself, and on the trail headed to Johnson City . . . and things had gone from bad to worse.

Billy Brown had sent his henchmen after Prophet and Lola. They'd been under orders to do everything in their power to keep the showgirl from testifying at their boss's trial. Brown had sent wave after wave of kill-crazy men until, for a time, alone and on the run in the middle of nowhere, it had seemed that Prophet and Lola were pitted together against the entire world.

There had been no way that a perilous journey like that wouldn't bring two people close together. In more ways than one. Even two people who couldn't have started out any farther apart than Prophet and Lola had. But by the end of the trip, Lou was sure that he'd tumbled for the snooty but beautiful, blond, blue-eyed actress, and he had a feeling that she'd tumbled for him, as well.

Of course, they couldn't have remained together. They'd had no future. He'd been, as he was now, a rough, ex-Confederate frontiersman. A bounty hunter. Margaret Jane Olson, hailing from an upper-class family from Utica, New York, had not only been a rare flower to look at—she'd had the face and eyes of an angel and the body of the most ravishing, irresistible temptress ever to corrupt a red-blooded rebel bounty hunter—but she'd aspired to the greatness of the world's largest stages.

Apparently, something had happened to prevent her from fulfilling her dream. Otherwise, she wouldn't have ended up in the tall-and-uncut country of the Dakota Territory. She wouldn't have become Margaret Knudsen now residing in Jubilee, about thirty miles west of Deadwood. For whatever reason she'd ventured so far off her original path, her luck in Dakota had obviously soured.

Now she needed Prophet's help.

And in light of his current situation, on the run from a rape accusation in Denver, which would no doubt spread beyond Colorado Territory in days if it hadn't via telegraph already, his old friend Lola had unknowingly flung him a lifeline.

Sure, he'd ride up to Dakota. He couldn't think of a better place for him to be right now. Surely, no one would expect him to flee that far to the north. South, maybe. New Mexico or Arizona or Old Mexico, for sure. But not Dakota Territory, where even the summers could be chilly and the opportunity for licentiousness and debauchery, two of the bounty hunter's favorite pursuits, were few and far between. Dakota was still relatively unsettled. Civilization was slow to stretch its tentacles up that close to Canada. Hell, pockets of Sioux still ran wild up thataway . . .

Making it the perfect place for Prophet to cool his heels.

He neatly folded Lola's note but not before giving it a sniff and detecting the remembered raspberry scent of the girl, and giving another smile of fond remembrance. He returned the missive to its envelope and stowed it for safekeeping in his saddlebags.

He spent the rest of the night sipping coffee laced with cheap whiskey, nibbling jerky, and building and smoking cigarettes. He stared out across the starlit prairie to the north, remembering his bittersweet time with Lola Diamond, wondering what kind of a woman the former Margaret Jane Olson and current Margaret Knudsen had turned out to be . . . and what brand of trouble she was in now.

"I'll be there soon," he said after he'd kicked dirt on his fire and rolled up in his soogan, laying his weary head down on the woolen underside of his saddle. "Don't you worry your pretty head, Miss Lola Diamond. Ole Lou will be there soon."

He yawned and drifted asleep with remembered images of the pretty young actress dancing behind his eyelids.

Chapter 5

A day and a half later, tired and dusty but armed with the ticket he'd just bought from the Cheyenne and Black Hills Stage and Express Line office, Prophet slacked onto a bench on the broad front veranda of the Inter-Ocean Hotel in Cheyenne, Wyoming Territory.

He'd decided to take the stage to Jubilee for two reasons—speed and safety. He could make better time riding a coach than he could riding his horse, which he'd stabled at the Big Horn Livery and Feed Company flanking the Inter-Ocean. Also, while most of the Sioux had been subdued after their rout of Custer at the Greasy Grass, there were still several bands running off their leashes, and, knowing their days were numbered, they could be more dangerous than hydrophobic wolves.

When the Indians were not making for hazardous travel up in northern Wyoming and across into western Dakota Territory, small gangs of non-Indian cutthroats were. Judging from the urgent tone of Lola's letter, Prophet had to make it to Jubilee sooner rather than later, and that meant that he could not take time to shoot it out with either Red Cloud's embittered braves or the brand of curly wolf that haunted the Black Hills and farther north these days, there not being much law in that country to cull the outlaw herds.

Besides, the bounty hunter had a thousand dollars burning a hole in his saddlebags (though half of it was Louisa's) and he saw no reason not to travel in relative comfort and style—if you could call comfort and style traveling through rough country in a rocking, pitching Concord coach, on a barely cushioned seat and with horsepoop-laced dust roiling in through the windows. Not to mention the stench of human as well as horse sweat fermenting in the summer heat assaulting your nostrils.

But at least he'd have a pillow, albeit a bedbug-infested one, on which to rest his weary head for the two nights it would take him to reach Jubilee by stage, in relay stations peppering the northeasterly route. On Mean and Ugly, it would be a good four-day ride.

When he'd bought his ticket, the ticket agent had informed him he was just in time, as this would be the last time the stage would roll through the remote Jubilee, the last stop before Deadwood. Jubilee was a little too out of the way for the line to continue service to it, and not enough folks were making it their destination. Apparently, most folks had already left town. Avoiding the town would shorten the trip from Cheyenne to Deadwood by thirty miles.

Wondering again what Lola Diamond could possibly be doing in such a backwater, Prophet took his time building a quirley on the Inter-Ocean's veranda.

He pondered the possibility of taking time for an ale at one of the several saloons residing on the far side of the bustling main street. The board-and-batten-fronted watering holes jutted wooden signs on peeled log posts into the street, muddy from a recent passing thundershower.

Each sign—bearing names from THE PARSON'S BLUSH and THE SUDSY BARREL to THE FAT LADY and THE DRUNKEN SKUNK—was gaudier than the last. Fallen angels, unmistakable in their brightly colored gowns and ample samplings of exposed flesh, loitered out front of such places, accosting passing menfolk with ribald invitations, occasionally grabbing one such gent and giving him a good feel of what he could be feeling so much more of, if he'd only spring for a half hour's tussle in one of the back-alley cribs.

Forget it, old son, Prophet silently chided himself, licking his freshly built quirley closed. *You done wore your pecker out the other night and were run out of town for your trouble. Besides, there's no time. The stage to Jubilee is due any minute now.*

He struck a lucifer to life on the sole of the boot resting atop his left knee and was about to touch the flame to the quirley, when a red-wheeled, leather-seated chaise pulled up in front of the Inter-Ocean, a fancily clad, opera-hatted gent with thick mutton-chop whiskers sitting straight-backed on the driver's seat. It wasn't unusual to see such a rig carting the obviously moneyed around Cheyenne, for plenty of rich folks lived in these parts now. They were mostly associated with the mining boom in the mountains or the proliferation of large, mostly foreign-owned ranches sprawling across the high plains between the Rawhide Hills and the Big Horns.

What you did not often see among such folk, however, was a full-blooded Indian. At least, not a full-blooded Indian who seemed to be one of them. And certainly not a beautiful, full-blooded, young Indian *girl* dressed in the silks and taffetas of a very un-Indian debutante.

But that was whom Prophet found his eyes riveted on now.

As the chaise driver set the brake, wrapped the reins around its brass handle, and scrambled down from the buggy to help the girl and her matronly, white, gray-haired traveling companion down from their perches, Prophet became so distracted that the lucifer burned his fingers.

"Ouch . . . goddamn—!"

Prophet let the match drop to the porch floor. As he did, the girl, having heard his clipped exclamation, cast him a fleeting, expressionless glance just before she stepped down from the coach and into the waiting hands of the driver. During that brief time when Prophet's eyes met hers, he felt a hard male pull in his overworked nether regions.

The girl was a slender, long-limbed, full-busted beauty with coarse, blue-black hair piled into two neat, tightly woven buns atop her regal head. A silly straw hat adorned with fake berries was pinned askance atop the coiled hair. Her face was round and chocolate-eyed, her mouth wide, the dark red lips rich and full. Her nose was long and fine. Her smooth, dark skin owned the copper-cherry sheen of the finest, varnished wood.

Prophet had become familiar with Indians from many tribes on his wanderings across the frontier, and he guessed that this girl hailed from one of the Plains tribes. Sioux, most likely. Something, maybe the heart-shaped face with not overly severe cheekbones, told him Hunkpapa, but she could have been Lakota or Wahpeton, as well.

It was startling to see such an obvious pedigreed American native, a veritable if not literal Indian princess, clad in the attire of a white girl. A rich, blue-blooded white girl, no less, dressed in a fine, spruce green traveling gown and shirtwaist with a ruffled white collar and matching waistcoat. An amethyst-encrusted cameo locket dangled from her fine, brown neck on a gold-washed chain.

She couldn't have looked more out of place in such a getup than Prophet would have appeared clad in an eagle feather headdress and beaded buckskins from head to toe, a drum in one hand, a rattle in the other. He found himself feeling sorry for the girl. Not only because she seemed so out of place in such attire, but because her much older traveling companion was ordering her around in a voice many reserved for ill-behaving dogs.

"Here, take your carpetbag . . . no, no, not that one—that one's mine . . . now, go stand here on the porch while I get our tickets. But stay out of the sun. You certainly don't need to be any darker. And please stop chewing your finger, Mary! Is that what they taught you at Mrs. Devine's—to stand around chewing your finger?"

The girl dropped the finger in question to her side. She'd started nibbling it once she and the carriage driver had piled a legion of matching leather bags and several accordion carpetbags atop the porch, about ten feet to Prophet's left, near the Inter-Ocean's stout, oak double doors. The doors were propped open to allow the breeze, fresh from the recent rain, to filter through the closed double screen doors.

The poor Indian princess with the unlikely name of Mary looked uncomfortable and out of place and it didn't help that several other people milling on the porch were staring at her, as well, as though she were some rare, exotic captive animal traveling with a circus.

The older woman paid the carriage driver, relinquishing the coins as though they were the last silver she'd ever see again. While the driver climbed back onto the chaise and drove away, the woman adjusted her flowered velvet hat atop her turtlelike head and allowed a gentleman smoking a fat stogie on the porch to open one of the screen doors for her. She acknowledged the expected politeness with a curt dip of her spade-shaped chin and wobbled into the lobby, grunting and sighing as though her hips grieved her.

The old woman had just gone inside when two more women, both middle-aged and attired in similar fashion to Mary's traveling companion, were deposited in front of the Inter-Ocean by another chaise. They had likely come from the Great Northern Depot at the south end of Main Street, just as Mary and the old woman had, Prophet idly speculated, puffing his quirley.

The women, a little breathless from their journey and looking anxious, as most such folks did when they were far from the security of their tailored gardens and nattily appointed parlors, gave Mary quick, darting glances, muttering to each other in shocked, disapproving tones, as though they feared the circus animal might spring from its cage and tear them limb from limb.

When they seemed to have exhausted the topic of Mary, they turned their attention to their luggage, consulting each other again through worried mutters. One of the women—they looked strikingly alike, both skinny and rat-faced—turned to Prophet and said, "Excuse me, sir, would you mind—?"

"No, no, Dorothy—not *him*!" the other woman scolded her companion, nudging Dorothy's arm with her own.

Regarding Prophet with a look of sour distaste, she muttered into Dorothy's left ear, and then both women turned to the portly gent wearing a three-piece suit and beaver hat and smoking a stogie by the door. They asked him to keep an eye on their luggage. When he assured them he wouldn't let it out of his sight, he opened the screen for them, and they flounced into the Inter-Ocean's shadowy interior.

Prophet returned his gaze to the Indian girl, who stood in the shade of the porch roof, staring sullenly out at the street, hands crossed on her belly. A beaded reticule dangled from her slender right wrist. She must have felt his eyes on her, because she turned her head ever so slightly, glancing at him out of the corner of her right, chocolate-colored eye.

When her gaze met his, he quickly turned away, sheepish. He was just another ogler. Castigating himself, he took the last drag from his quirley, flipped the cigarette over the porch rail and into the street, then sagged back against the hotel's front wall. He tugged the funneled brim of his battered Stetson down over his eyes. He'd try to snatch a few winks before the stage rolled in.

Shortly, he was awakened by a woman's loud voice carrying out to him from inside the hotel: "You don't mean we'll be riding in the same coach as that *savage*!"

A voice Prophet recognized as belonging to the ticket agent Ralph Fenton said something in placating tones too low for Prophet to hear. The woman returned with: "Oh no, she won't! Surely the stage line has rules about giving passage to Indians. I don't care how she's dressed—she's still one of them! And I simply cannot and *will not* share a coach with those people!"

"Certainly not," said another woman's voice. There was a sharp stomping sound. "I put my foot down, as well. Dorothy and I had nearly our entire family wiped out by those animals back in '71. You cannot ask us to share a stagecoach with someone capable of something so depraved!"

"Besides, they're heathens!" intoned Dorothy. "They don't belong in a Christian carriage . . . among good Christian people!"

"Now, ladies, please," said Fenton in a whining, anguished tone. "I can't just—"

Another woman's voice—this one belonging to the old woman with Mary—cut him off with, "Mary is not a heathen! She has spent the last two years at a Christian boarding school in Denver. They taught her to wash and bathe and eat and dress in appropriate clothes—just like civilized people. True, she was born a savage, but she was orphaned early and my brother adopted her. Vance has always been a bleeding heart, taking in all manner of injured or orphaned critter. However, let me assure you ladies that Mary grew up in a Christian house, on a Christian ranch up in Dakota, and, like I said, she's been taught by the good teachers at Mrs. Esther Devine's Christian Academy for Wayward Girls. Why, last night I watched Mary say her prayers down on her knees by her bed, and she bathed in good, clean, hot water before we boarded the train in Denver. I guarantee you that she does not smell any different than you or I!"

"There is no taking the savage out of a savage!" Dorothy returned.

The argument continued, but Prophet didn't bother listening to it anymore. He knew how it would go. He watched Mary. If she heard—and she must have heard because she was standing nearly directly in front of the door—she didn't let on but continued to stare stonily into the sunlit street.

Prophet's heart swelled for the girl as he imagined how she felt, standing there and listening to such haughty blather. Hearing such talk about yourself, how could you not feel that you were any better than a mongrel, scrap-chewing dog? Well, the girl—Indian or not—was better than a dog, by God. She was probably far better than the two old, pinch-faced fools laying down judgment on her.

Feeling the burn of rage ameliorate the sympathetic ache in his heart, Prophet reached down to where his own traveling gear was piled to his right. He shucked his Winchester repeater from its leather sheath, stood, rested the long gun on his shoulder, and strode toward the screen doors.

The well-dressed gent, still puffing his stogie inside a thick cloud of aromatic smoke, looked him up and down, a wary cast entering the man's gaze. He took two steps to the right, scuttling aside from the big bounty hunter, as Prophet opened the screen door and walked into the lobby's cool shadows.

Chapter 6

The stage line's ticket cage was to the right of the hotel counter.

Ralph Fenton had come out from behind the counter to arbitrate the argument, which was continuing, the two rat-faced women standing to Prophet's left, Mary's traveling companion facing them on his right. Fenton sort of stood between the two factions, holding up his hands, demanding a silence he had not yet managed to obtain.

The three biddies were going at one another like crows fighting over the same dead, sun-seasoned squirrel.

Prophet gave his best imitation of a heavy-footed, wobbly-kneed drunk as he shambled into the lobby before stopping about fifteen feet from the trio, and shouting, "Fenton, what in the hell kind of raggedy-heeled operation you runnin' here, anyways?"

That commanded the silence that the bespectacled, mustached Fenton had failed to obtain in a less dramatic manner. The old biddies' lips stopped flapping and their picture-hatted heads swung around as though their necks were all attached to the same marionette string.

The ticket agent's glasses glinted in the light pushing through the screen doors flanking the bounty hunter.

Prophet shifted his weight from one boot to the other, bringing his Winchester down off his shoulder and setting the rear stock against his hip, angling the barrel toward the ceiling and curling his right index finger through the trigger guard.

"I asked you a question, Fenton. What in the hell kind of backwoods confidence game you got here, fer doin' your bizness in the nuns' privy? The stage was due in fifteen minutes ago, and I'm gettin' a mite tired of waitin' on it. Don't you people know how to keep a schedule?"

Fenton suddenly looked constipated. His lower jaw sagged as he thumbed his spectacles up his nose and grimaced. "Lou . . . what in the hell's gotten into . . . you know there ain't no stagecoach west of the Mississippi that's ever on time. Fifteen minutes ain't late!"

Prophet pretended to notice the two rat-faced biddies for the first time, and shaped a lusty grin. "On second thought, who cares if the stage is late?"

He stumbled toward the two rat-faced women. They stared at him warily, eyes growing wider with every toe-dragging step he took closer to their position fronting the ticket cage.

"Looks like I got me somethin' purty to look at now, anyways! Say, you two ladies look so much alike, you must be twins. Sisters, anyways—ain't that right?" He used the barrel of his Winchester to shove his Stetson up off his forehead. He continued to slur his words as he said, "I love me a pair o' twins—I purely do! Say, how about you two an' me go on across the street to the Parson's Blush an' have us a coupla drinks?"

Prophet winked and arched his brows with unbridled, albeit 100 percent feigned, lust.

Fenton, apparently having caught on to Prophet's ploy, choked back a laugh and brushed his fist across his nose to cover it.

Both women backed away from the tall man in the sweat-stained, dust-caked buckskin tunic leering down at them. Mary's traveling companion had edged wide around the big bounty hunter, as well, eyeing him dubiously.

Dorothy looked at Fenton and said, "My God, who is this beast? Don't tell me he'll be on the stage, as well!"

"Say, you two takin' the stage?" Prophet made his face light up like that of a child on Christmas morning. "Well, don't that beat all! We'll have us a good long time to get to know each other, then, won't we?"

He lifted his head and loosed an ear-assaulting rebel yell at the high, arched ceiling.

Dorothy's sister turned to the ticket agent, grabbed the lapel of the man's wool coat, and gave it such a hard tug that Prophet thought she was going to rip the coat plumb off the poor man's back. "Mr. Fenton, we'll be making other arrangements for our trip to Mandan. Good Lord—the people you allow to travel on your coaches!"

"Indeed!" exclaimed Dorothy, raking her horrified gaze across the grinning Prophet once more. "Savages and brigands! And here we heard the frontier was becoming civilized!"

"Civilized, my foot!" intoned her sister.

Arm in arm they hustled off to the hotel's front counter, waving at the clerk and pleading for a room and a porter to fetch their bags.

Prophet glanced at Mary's traveling companion, who stood watching him warily by the door. He regarded the two biddies standing at the hotel desk, chirping like angry grackles, and shook his head. "Don't that beat all? I've never been so insulted in all my days!"

He shot a wink at Fenton, who smirked then wandered back behind his ticket cage, chuckling to himself and shaking his head.

Resting his Winchester on his shoulder again, Prophet walked to the doors and held one screen open for Mary's traveling companion, giving a courtly bow. "Age before beauty, ma'am."

The woman pursed her lips and eyed him dubiously again as she stepped out onto the porch.

Prophet followed her out. The well-dressed gent with the stogie gave him a knowing smile inside a wreath of billowing cigar smoke. Prophet slacked back onto his bench with a weary sigh and glanced at Mary standing where she'd been standing before.

She swung her head around to regard the tall man, her expression vaguely quizzical, then, dismissing him with a slow blink of her chocolate eyes, turned her dark, regal head back to stare sullenly into the busy street.

The flashy and relatively new stagecoach, manufactured by the Abbot-Downing Company of Concord, New Hampshire, pitched and rattled into town only thirty-five minutes late. The jehu made a show of the impressive contraption as well as his matched six-horse team, proudly standing in his driver's boot and bellowing loudly while popping a blacksnake over the team's lathered backs.

Pedestrians as well as horseback riders and ranch supply wagons made haste to get out of the lumbering team's way, and the grizzled jehu grinned with pride. His name was Mort Seymour. Prophet had brushed elbows with Seymour as well as the shotgun messenger, J. W. Plumb, in the past.

Adding to the hubbub surrounding the red and yellow Concord's arrival, several dogs ran out from alleys in which they'd no doubt been dining on discarded café scraps or dead chickens, and nipped and barked at the wagon's large, churning, iron-shod wheels. One old-timer who'd been snatching thirty winks on a loafer's bench fronting the mercantile was so aroused by the impressive contrivance's dramatic arrival that he rose from his seat, shucked an old Remington revolver from the holster on his hip, and snapped off three shots, bellowing, "Stage is here! Stage is here! Stage is here!" with each shot.

Young boys seemingly materialized out of the dirt to chase after the rolling carriage and then mill around as the dusty passengers destaged, brushing two or three layers of talcumlike dust from their clothes and hats. Most were soldiers from Camp Collins in the foothills of the Front Range mountains, likely on their way to another post. When the team had been switched to another matching six-hitch of frisky, glass-eyed, tail-arched thoroughbreds, Prophet helped the old woman traveling with Mary into the carriage, and then Mary herself.

The only other passenger was the portly gent in the three-piece suit, who dropped the one-inch stub of his stogie into the dust and held out his hand to Prophet, saying, "I'm Max Beermeister. Figured we might as well get to know each other since we'll be smelling each other's sweat for a while."

"Lou Prophet. Pleased to make your acquaintance, Max. I can tell we're gonna get along just fine."

"How's that?"

"Your name. I'm partial to anything having anything to do with beer!"

Prophet winked at the man and then gestured for Beermeister to climb in first. When Prophet had said how-de-do to both Seymour and Plumb, he stowed his gear in the rear luggage boot and climbed into the coach, which rocked like a small fishing boat on its leather thoroughbraces. He took the rear seat, facing forward as well as toward the pretty, exotic visage of the enigmatic Mary, who quickly slid her own gaze out the window beside her.

The old woman sat to Mary's right, facing Beermeister, who sat across from her, to Prophet's left.

When the jehu and shotgun messenger had climbed back into the driver's boot atop the coach, Mort Seymour did his best imitation of a train conductor, shouting, "All *abooo-ard*! First stop the Rawhide Buttes, folks!"

He released the brake with a sudden jerk and began haranguing the team in earnest, popping his blacksnake over their backs. Prophet knew the team needed no encouragement. A fresh hitch was always ready to air out its lungs and tear up some trail. The hoorawing was all part of Seymour's show.

Prophet smiled at that, sharing the smile with Mary, who gave him a brief, vacant stare, as though looking right through him, before shifting her gaze once more to the window and the main street of Cheyenne quickly dancing past beyond it.

In less than a minute, they'd left the last shacks and outlying stables of Cheyenne behind and were heading straight north across pancake-flat sagebrush country broken here and there by haystack buttes and shelving mesas the color of wet adobe. Gradually the terrain began rising and more and more chalky, eroded buttes appeared along both sides of the trail.

The coach's first stop for a new team was the Rawhide Buttes Relay Station, nothing more than a chinked-log shack, unchinked-log barn, windmill, stone water tank, and unpeeled-pole corral. Prophet and Beermeister got out to stretch their legs while the two women remained in the coach, quiet as dusty moths on a windowsill.

When the fresh team had been hitched up, the coach pulled out once more, heading north. This time Seymour forwent his raucous bellowing, for the only ones to hear out here were the grim-faced station manager, his two hostlers—both tongue-tied bashful from too much isolation—and a yellow mongrel dining on a dead rattler in the barn shade.

There were several more stops—Bear Springs, Wheatland, Chugwater, Chug Springs, and Eagle's Nest—before the coach stopped for the night at the appropriately named Rustic Hotel at Fort Laramie, a hundred miles northeast of Cheyenne. Here Prophet and the other passengers dined on antelope stew. The two women, neither of whom had said more than two words to anyone since the stage had left Cheyenne—and those two words had been offered only by Mary's traveling companion—drifted upstairs to bed around sunset.

Prophet, Beermeister, Seymour, Plumb, and the hotel manager, a man named Hodges who had had one eye burned out by the Sioux and also wore the scar of a near-hanging when he'd been mistaken for a stock thief some years ago in Montana, sat out on the front porch, playing stud poker for nickels.

When the mournful wails of "Taps" drifted in from the fort's parade ground, the men, including Prophet, called it a night and headed upstairs to their flea-infested, sour-smelling beds scratchy with corn husks protruding from the mattress ticking.

Though the country traversed by the Cheyenne-to-Deadwood stage was notoriously perilous, Prophet had seen no signs of trouble so far. For that he was grateful. He wanted no delays in reaching the fondly remembered Lola Diamond and helping her out of whatever entanglement she'd found herself in.

Trouble, however, reared its ugly head the next day.

Chapter 7

Heads, rather.

There was more than one ugly head that showed up the next day, not long after the coach had pulled out of the Robber's Roost Station, where it had stopped for the noon meal.

Prophet, habitually on the scout for trouble, had spied the silhouettes of at least four riders keeping pace with the stage from about three hundred yards off the trail's southeast side. He soon lost them behind an outcropping of rock and pines but picked them up again twenty minutes later. Only now there were clearly five riders riding in the same general direction as the coach, and they were on the northeast side of the trail.

They were also less than a hundred yards away now, apparently not much caring if they were seen or not. Prophet couldn't see them clearly, for they were still a ways off and the coach was rocking and pitching through a jog of pine-clad, rocky badlands, steep ridges occasionally closing on either or both sides of the trail. But he could see the frequent glint of sun flashing off guns. Something about the way the riders were staying close to the trail without following it themselves, told him they were something other than benign range riders looking for bogged beeves.

He soon lost them again. He had a feeling he'd pick them up again when they wanted to be picked up again.

Automatically, he unsnapped the keeper thong from over the hammer of his .45 and slipped the revolver from its holster. He hadn't meant to rile the others, but of course all three had spied the movement and turned to see him open the Colt's loading gate to check the loads.

The old woman traveling with Mary was Aunt Grace. Prophet had learned her name on the rare occasion he'd overheard Mary addressing the woman. Aunt Grace acquired an anxious look, as though she thought, as she'd probably suspected in the first place, that Prophet was a road agent. Now, showing his true colors, he was about to rob the stage and probably rape both her and Mary!

Mary, however, looked at the bounty hunter with the customarily sullen, skeptical expression he'd come to know too well over the course of the one and a half days he'd traveled facing her from three feet away.

"Trouble?" asked Beermeister sitting to Prophet's left, arching a brow as he watched Prophet slip a fresh brass cartridge from his shell belt and push it into the chamber he normally kept empty beneath the hammer.

"Probably nothin'." Prophet gave Aunt Grace a reassuring smile. "Probably nothin' at all."

He shifted the look to Mary, who stared at him almost as vacantly as usual, but now she was slightly wrinkling the skin above the bridge of her long, fine nose. Her gaze did not waver from his.

"Nothin' at all," Prophet repeated.

She turned her head to stare out the window. As she did, she nibbled the nail of her right index finger.

Prophet turned his own attention to the rugged country sliding past the coach, spying nothing more of the men he had to assume were following the stage, possibly looking for a place to strike. He didn't think the stage was carrying a strongbox, however, so unless the coach's shadowers assumed otherwise in error, they must have been after the horses or whatever valuables they could find on the four passengers.

Or they might have been after the women. They might have spied Mary from a distance and decided she was worth hitting the stage for. Prophet never underestimated the desperation of men this far off the beaten track. One pretty girl out here could drive a man to a rare savagery.

Stages had been hit for a lot less.

Prophet wasn't surprised that trouble had shown itself. Earlier that day they'd crossed into Indian Territory. Or, what Prophet still knew as Indian Territory because it had been called that for as long as he could remember. It had been officially changed to Dakota Territory in 1861, during its official organization. But most of the old salts still called it Indian Territory, so that's how Prophet knew it, as well.

The name still seemed right. The area might be

officially organized and under the jurisdiction of the U.S. marshals, but it was a savage place, a no-man's-land of sudden death or slow torture. Official laws might exist here, but those were just for show. The real law that reigned supreme in these parts was the Law of the Gun.

Prophet kept a close watch as the stage continued wending its way through the tawny buttes. There were only two more stops before he'd reach his destination—Jubilee—and he wanted to beat trouble to the end of the line. Soon, the stage dropped down a gradual slope, and the humble brick adobe buildings of the Cheyenne River Station slid around it on both sides.

When Prophet and the other passengers had stepped out of the carriage, Prophet turned to Mort Seymour, who was supervising the changing out of the team by the station's two hostlers. He asked the jehu if he'd seen the gang of riders, and Seymour said he had.

"Just checkin'," Prophet said.

"I don't like it."

Prophet had turned to head into the small, low-slung station house, but now he turned back to Seymour, who was shaking dust out of his sweat-damp neckerchief while the hostlers led the sweat-lathered team away to the barn. Seymour looked at Prophet warily and slid his pale blue gaze toward the cabin.

"Mrs. Van Camp's boy, James, was found dead two weeks ago. They found him between here and Lacrosse's trading hut down by the river. There's a partic'lar nasty brand of curly wolf running among these coulees, Lou. Folks around here think they're the ones who beat James to one helluva bloody pulp. For fun, most like."

Prophet headed around to the coach's rear luggage boot and pulled out his sawed-off Richards twelve-gauge. He slung the mean-looking popper over his head and shoulder and headed into the cabin.

Mrs. Van Camp ran the Cheyenne River Station with the help of her daughter, Lydia, and, until last week, her son, James. James hadn't been right in the head but he'd been good at horse wrangling and general maintenance of the place. Mrs. Van Camp's husband, Ezra, had died two years ago when, not in good health in the first place, a frisky team had slammed him against the side of the adobe brick barn, breaking his back.

Mrs. Van Camp had run the place alone with her two children ever since.

She was a small but stalwart woman who was ladling stew into bowls when Prophet walked into the cabin. Lydia, a much younger version of her rawhide-tough mother, who appeared old enough to be Lydia's grandmother, was taking the bowls to where Mary, Aunt Grace, and Beermeister were sitting at separate tables in the crude but well-scrubbed, earthen-floored shack.

Mrs. Van Camp acknowledged Prophet with a single dip of her chin, which was all the acknowledgment she ever gave anyone. He sat down across from Beermeister, mostly to make for less running for Lydia, and pegged his hat on a hook on the wall to his right. He lifted the coach gun's lanyard above his head and set the shotgun on the edge of the table.

Mary and Aunt Grace sat against the opposite wall, to Prophet's left.

He'd just glanced at Mary, who was hunched over her soup, when he spied movement out the window flanking her. A man crouched to look into the window, pressing his face right up against the warped but freshly scrubbed glass. Long, curly, chestnut hair fell to his shoulders. He looked from Aunt Grace to Mary, pressing his nose against the glass, and ogled the girl, bug-eyed.

Aunt Grace glanced toward the window and jerked back in her chair with a terrified shriek. Mary lifted her head, saw the man in the window, and slapped a hand across her open mouth with a hushed gasp. The man in the window laughed, turned, and strode toward the front of the station. Another man walked past the window, following the first man.

Prophet reached under the table and unsnapped the keeper thong from over his Colt's hammer. He loosened the big popper in the oiled holster then returned his right hand to the top of the table, where Lydia had just set a bowl of steaming antelope stew down before him when Aunt Grace had screamed.

Now the girl stood staring toward the front door, where the man from the window just now ducked into the shack, grinning.

"Hi-dee, folks!" he said. "How's everybody today?" He turned to where Aunt Grace sat, still recovering from the start the man had given her. "Sorry to frighten you, ma'am." He lifted his hat by the crown then set it back down on his curly head as he nodded to Mary. "Miss."

As the second man stopped beside the first man,

Mrs. Van Camp, standing by the range, where several pots were pushing steam up into the shack's humid air, pointed a long, arthritic finger at the newcomers and narrowed her eyes angrily. "Out! Out! Get out!"

The curly-headed gent looked hurt. "Say what? *Out*? But we just got here." He glanced at the man standing to his right—a big, freckle-faced man in a wool coat and billowy red neckerchief. "Ain't that right, Moon Face? We just got here—am I right?"

The appropriately named Moon Face shrugged his heavy shoulders. Two pistols bristled on his shell belt, positioned on each hip for a cross draw. A Green River knife jutted behind the holster on his right hip.

"We was just wantin' to buy a bowl of that stew off'n ya, is all. We could smell it all the way from the next ridge over, and, who-eee . . . we're a mite hungry—aren't we, Moon Face?"

The curly-haired gent had been speaking to Mrs. Van Camp, but he'd kept his eyes on Mary, who stared straight down at her wooden stew bowl. Aunt Grace stared up at the two hard-bitten newcomers, her face twisted into a mask of horror. Mrs. Van Camp continued to glare at him, narrow eyed, hard jawed, fuming.

Prophet glanced out the window flanking Mary and Aunt Grace. Mort Seymour and J. W. Plumb were standing over by the barn. Their backs faced the cabin. Apparently the station's two hostlers had noticed a problem with one of the coach wheels. They'd removed the wheel and all four men were staring down at the felloe, smoking and talking it over.

Obviously, they hadn't noticed the two newcomers.

Prophet wondered where the rest of the gang was, and what their intentions were. That these two were part of the pack he'd spied from the coach he had little doubt.

The curly-haired gent pointed at Mary and said, "Say, lookee there, now. You ever seen the like o' that, Moon Face? A purty li'l Injun gal all dressed up like—"

Prophet, whose anger was burning up into his ear tips, cut him off with: "You gents are botherin' us who's tryin' to eat, so you'd best run along now. I think I hear the rest of your gang callin' for you."

Both the curly-haired gent and Moon Face swung around toward Prophet, looking shocked and befuddled at having been addressed so disrespectfully.

"Well, excuse me all to hell," said the curly-haired gent, "but who the hell are you, friend?"

"Lydia!" cried Mrs. Van Camp, who grabbed her daughter's arm and pulled her out of the line of fire, where she'd been standing, frozen in fear.

"I'm not your friend—that's for damn sure," Prophet said casually.

The curly-haired brigand looked at the sawed-off shotgun resting on the table near Prophet's right arm. Prophet was spooning stew into his mouth. He glanced up at the two brigands now as though they were pesky flies buzzing around his head.

"You the shotgun guard?" asked Moon Face. His voice was several notches lower than the curly-haired gent's.

"Nope," Prophet said, spooning another mouthful of the delicious stew into his mouth. "I'm the fella who just asked you two to leave, seein' as how

Mrs. Van Camp don't want you here and you're bein' impolite." He took another bite of the stew and glanced up at the pair once more, curling one half of his upper lip. "And, if you'll forgive me fer sayin' so, you stink to high heaven."

The newcomers shared a quick glance, faces coloring with rage.

"*What* did you just say?" asked the curly-haired gent.

Moon Face slid one of his three pistols from its holster. As he began to level the long-barreled .44 at Prophet, clicking back the hammer, Prophet picked up the Richards with his right hand, swung the barrel out away from the table, angled it toward the floor, rocked one hammer back, and squeezed the eyelash trigger.

The blast sounded like angry thunder from a sudden storm.

Moon Face's right boot turned dark red.

Moon Face triggered his Colt into the hard-packed earthen floor near his bloody boot, then dropped the gun.

"Oh! Oh! *Ohhh!*" he screamed as he hopped back on his good foot, falling backward into the curly-haired man.

He screamed shrilly as he looked down in horror at blood oozing through the shredded leather of his boot. Beyond him, Prophet saw another man step quickly into the doorway. The man was silhouetted against the bright noon light, but Prophet saw him cross his arms on his belly and start to draw two revolvers.

Prophet extended the Richards at him, triggered the second barrel, and blew him out the door.

The man was dead so fast, he didn't have time to scream. There was just a heavy thud as his body hit the ground outside the cabin.

"*Jesus!*" Beermeister cried, half rising then falling back into his chair, him and the chair tumbling backward and hitting the floor with a crash.

Chapter 8

Prophet set the smoking shotgun on the table. As the curly-haired gent flung the howling Moon Face away from him with a shrill curse and reached for his pistols, Prophet leveled his Peacemaker on him and ratcheted back the hammer.

Lou gave a challenging half grin.

The curly-haired gent dropped his half-drawn Remington back into its holster and slowly raised his hands. "Now," he said, taking a step backward. "Now . . . just . . ."

"Take them pistols out and drop 'em on the floor. Every one you got, includin' any aces in the hole."

Out the window behind the curly-haired gent, Prophet could see Seymour and Plumb and both hostlers running toward the cabin. The jehu and the shotgun messenger had their pistols drawn. Keeping his tense gaze on Prophet, the curly-haired gent slowly slipped both his visible pistols from their holsters and tossed them to the floor.

"Aces, too," Prophet said, pitching his voice threateningly.

The curly-haired gent reached into his duster and

withdrew another revolver from a shoulder holster. When he'd tossed it onto the floor, he lifted his right foot and pulled a small-caliber, pearl-gripped over-and-under pocket popper from the well of his boot. He dropped that down with the others.

"Anything else?" Prophet asked, again with threat.

He had to speak loudly enough to be heard against Moon Face's wails. The moonfaced brigand was flopping around on the floor near the curly-haired gent's feet, blood from his ruined right foot pooling on the floor. He was the only one making any noise. The others in the cabin were frozen in place, staring in shock at the wounded outlaw.

Beermeister sat on the floor near his chair, also staring in shock at Moon Face's bloody foot. The shredded leather of the man's boot made it apparent that he was now missing most of that foot's toes.

The curly-haired gent reached up over his head and pulled an Arkansas toothpick from a sheath strapped to the back of his neck. He tossed that down with his guns.

"Who you ridin' for?" Prophet asked him.

Before the curly-haired gent could respond, Seymour ran into the cabin. Plumb ran in behind him, stepping over the dead man lying outside the front door.

"What the *hell* . . . ?" Seymour said, scowling above his long, tangled beard. Stepping sideways around the curly-haired gent, he looked at the howling Moon Face then pointed his cocked .44 at the curly-haired gent and said, "Why, Jimmy Wells . . ."

"Who's Jimmy Wells?" Prophet asked.

"No-account peckerwood," Seymour said, flaring his nostrils. "Hind-tit calf who grew up in the badlands, took to the long coulees when he was still knee-high to a short-legged lizard."

"Drop dead, you old buzzard!"

Seymour raised his pistol at Wells's head and narrowed one eye.

Wells lurched back in terror, raising his hands higher and yelling, "I ain't armed, you old fool!"

"Old fool, am I?" Seymour railed, and began tightening his right index finger around his Schofield's trigger.

"Hold on, hold on," Prophet said. "Don't kill him just yet, Mort. I wanna know who he's ridin' with."

"He's ridin' with the bunch who killed my brother!"

All eyes turned to Lydia standing by her mother, steam wafting up from the range behind them. She glared at Wells, brown eyes glistening with anger. "I saw you skulking around here that day. Stalking the trail, just like you always are, lookin' for folks to rob . . . or worse!"

She screamed that last. Her mother grabbed her and pulled her against her, and Lydia sobbed, "Oh, Mother, he killed James!"

Mrs. Van Camp held her daughter's head taut to her chest and glared at Jimmy Wells, who laughed and said, "I don't know what she's talkin' about. Why, she's as cork-headed as her fool brother!"

Lydia jerked around and bolted toward Wells, her fists clenched, but Mrs. Van Camp grabbed her and pulled her against her once more.

Wells laughed. "She's crazy. Look at her. Crazy as a rabid skunk!"

Prophet had risen from his chair. Now he walked up to Wells. As Wells turned toward him, laughter still in the outlaw's eyes, Prophet slammed the barrel of his Colt against the man's left temple. Wells yelped and fell, howling.

"Get him outside," Prophet told Seymour.

While the jehu and J. W. Plumb half carried and half dragged the raging, cursing Wells out the door, Prophet slung his barn blaster over his shoulder and dragged the wailing Moon Face outside by his shirt collar. The hostlers were standing around the dead man, looking baffled and worried. Seymour told them to get back to work on the coach's wheel, and when both men had jogged back to the barn, where the stage was now parked, Prophet, Seymour, and J. W. Plumb looked around warily.

"The rest of their gang is likely skulkin' around here somewhere," Seymour said.

Wells was on his hands and knees, one hand clamped to his bloody left temple. He laughed jeeringly as he looked up and slid his glance from Prophet to the jehu and the messenger. "You fellas is sooo dead for what you just done to me an' Moon Face. I mean, you're so dead the coyotes that's gonna feed on you might as well break out the forks and knives right now!"

Prophet looked around. The sun-splashed relay station yard was eerily quiet. There was no movement in the chalky buttes surrounding the place, nor in the scattered, stunted cottonwoods standing hunched at their bases, the breeze making the leaves flash silver and gold.

Lou turned to Mort Seymour. "What're you carryin'?"

"Not a damn thing except you, Mr. Beermeister, and the ladies."

"No strongbox?"

"Nope," said Plumb, shaking his head.

Prophet turned to Wells. "That's what you were wondering, weren't you? That's why you and your two friends came skulking around. You were scouting the coach and passengers to see if there was anything worth hitting the stage for, farther on down the line, most likely."

"A pox on you!!" Wells raged, climbing awkwardly to his feet. He'd lost his hat inside the cabin, and his curly chestnut hair hung in his eyes. Blood glistened on his torn left temple. "You had no cause to pistol-whip me like that. No cause at all." He pointed at Prophet. "You're gonna pay for that, big fella!"

Prophet raised his Colt once more as he lunged at Wells.

Wells gave a yelp as he stumbled backward. He tripped over the groaning Moon Face and hit the dirt with another shrill curse.

Prophet turned to Seymour. "That's what they were doing. They were scouting us. The rest of the gang is likely on the lurk in them buttes yonder. They're probably glassing us right now."

"No doubt," Seymour said.

"Really? You think so?" Plumb stomped around, lifting both hands and waving his middle fingers at the buttes. "There—take that, you son of bitches!" He laughed caustically. "There you go—them birdies is for you!"

Prophet looked at the shotgun messenger skeptically.

Seymour looked down at Wells. "What're we gonna do with him?"

"We'll take him," Prophet said. "Maybe the gang won't hit us if we got one of their own aboard. Of course, they probably don't care if he lives or dies any more than we do, but it's worth a shot. No point in lettin' him go. We'll use him for leverage and then you can turn him over to the law when you get to Deadwood."

Plumb jerked his chin at Moon Face. "What about him?"

Prophet looked at Moon Face just as the big man was lifting his right fist. The barrel of a little gun flashed between his fingers.

"He's got an ace!" Plumb yelled, leaping a foot in the air.

Prophet still had his Colt in his right hand. He whipped it up toward Moon Face and drilled a neat, round, .45 caliber hole in the man's broad forehead. Moon Face's head jerked back. His eyes rolled up in their sockets, showing only the whites. His hideout popper dropped in the dirt.

Moon Face sagged slowly backward till he lay flat on his back, quivering crazily.

"Jesus Christ!" Wells said, staring incredulously at his partner.

Prophet lowered his smoking Colt. "That takes care of that." He looked at Wells. "Let's find some rope and tie this son of a bitch up."

"There's some in the barn," Plumb said. "I'll fetch it."

He walked away.

Something moved in the shack's open doorway.

Prophet turned to see Mary staring out, nibbling speculatively on her right index finger.

"Mary, come away from there this instant!" Aunt Grace yelled from behind her.

Mary's flat, expressionless gaze met Prophet's. After a few seconds, she removed her finger from her mouth, turned slowly, and retreated back into the shack's murky shadows.

Seymour looked down at the two dead men. "What're we gonna do with the fresh beef here?"

Prophet was staring cautiously off toward the buttes rising in the west. Something told him they were being glassed from that direction. "Let's send 'em back to where they came from."

"How we gonna do that, Lou? As you can see, they're in no condition to walk very far."

"They must have horses." Prophet looked at Wells sitting on his butt in the dirt, between the bounty hunter and the old jehu. "Where are they?"

Wells sneered up at him, squinting against the sunlight. "Go to blazes, you rebel devil!"

Prophet stepped forward and smacked his pistol against the brigand's left temple again, making the cut a little deeper and bloodier. The outlaw howled.

"Now, where were they again?" Prophet asked.

Pressing the heels of both hands to his bloody head, Wells jerked his chin to the south, toward where three dusty cottonwoods separated a narrow dry wash from the base of a broad-based haystack butte. "Over there! Over there, for chrissakes! *Oh, Jesus hell, you're gonna die slow and hard!*"

"That's where I thought you said," Prophet said. "I reckon my hearin' ain't as good as it used to be." To Seymour, he said, "Stay with him, Mort."

Prophet went into the shack to retrieve his shotgun. The passengers sat in shock at their tables. They had eaten only half their food but they no longer seemed hungry. Mrs. Van Camp and Lydia had retreated to a back room, behind a curtained doorway. Prophet could hear Lydia sobbing back there.

He walked back outside, breaking open his gut-shredder and replacing the spent twelve-gauge wads with fresh. Plumb had returned from the barn and was down on both knees, tying Wells's hands behind his back while Seymour aimed his old Schofield at the brigand's head. Wells was cursing like an Irish gandy dancer on Monday morning.

Prophet snapped his shotgun closed and said, "Tie him good and tight. His ankles, too, but leave enough slack between his feet so he can walk."

Plumb glared up at Prophet. "You wanna do it?"

Prophet didn't take offense at that. Everybody's nerves were frayed, his included. Taking one more glance toward the western buttes, which were hard to look at with the harsh sunlight reflecting off them, he started walking south, resting the Richards atop his right shoulder. He shuttled his glance carefully around him, wary of an ambush.

He found all three horses just where Wells had indicated, in the wash behind the screen of cottonwoods and a few pale boulders. He looked carefully around the wash and then into a notch in the haystack butte, making sure none of the rest of the gang was sneaking up on him. Then he untied the horses' reins from the spidery branches of the cottonwoods and led them back to the cabin.

Looking toward the barn, he was glad to see that the hostlers were now back-and-bellying the wheel onto the coach's axle. They'd be on their way soon.

Wells lay belly down in the dirt beside Moon Face. Plumb had craftily hog-tied him.

Prophet chuckled and, dropping the horses' reins, said to their prisoner, "You sure walked into one."

Wells gave his customary response.

Prophet, Seymour, and Plumb hefted the two dead men over two of the horses and tied them in place. Prophet led both horses to the west side of the yard and fired his pistol over their heads. They galloped straight west, noses in the air, likely sniffing the horses of the other riders hidden away in the buttes beyond.

The crack of Prophet's Peacemaker echoed around the station yard and off the surrounding bluffs. The other curly wolves were out there somewhere. They'd likely heard the shot. Prophet hoped they'd taken the pistol shot as a warning. If they came calling, they'd get what their friends got.

It was probably too much to hope for. Men of their apparent stripe weren't deterred by much, and they'd likely want to avenge Moon Face and the other gent whom Prophet had nearly cut in half with his gut-shredder. Maybe Prophet's having taken Jimmy Wells hostage would be another deterrent.

Maybe not.

Probably not.

The bounty hunter stared up at the rise of buttes before him. The horses ran out away from him, through a thin, ragged stand of trees and brush. They disappeared for a moment and then reappeared a moment later, lunging up a crooked crease angling between the formations, heading west.

He could see no sign of men up there. But the

others were watching him. He could sense it. His senses had been honed to a razor's edge over the years.

He walked back to the cabin. The new six-horse hitch had been buckled into place in the Concord's harness, and the coach was drawn up in front of the shack. Seymour called the passengers out, and Aunt Grace, Mary, and Beermeister boarded. They all looked weary and edgy. Prophet shoved Wells into the coach and thrust him onto the rear seat where Prophet had been riding.

Prophet sat down beside him, between Wells and Beermeister. Wells faced Mary, and already Prophet saw that the brigand was ogling the girl.

"Knock it off," Prophet told him.

Seymour cracked his blacksnake over the team, and the coach lunged forward, throwing Prophet, Wells, and Beermeister back in their seat and the women slightly forward.

"Knock what off?" Wells said. He smiled at Mary, lasciviously ran his tongue across the underside of his upper lip.

"Oh!" cried Aunt Grace. "You're an animal!"

Mary merely dipped her chin and curled her upper lip at the devil.

Prophet smashed his .44 against Wells's ear.

The brigand yelped and cursed and then fell silent, cowering against the outside wall when he saw Prophet's look of arch-browed, imminent threat.

Prophet glanced at Mary. She'd been looking at him, but now she jerked her eyes away from his and let fade the half smile that had touched her lips.

As the stage rocked and pitched, Prophet settled his coach gun against the padded wall behind him and rested his Winchester across his thighs. He looked out the window, at the passing terrain, and waited for the trouble that he could feel brewing in the rolling hills around him.

Nasty luck, running into Wells's brigands.

Prophet just wanted to get to Jubilee and find his old pal Lola . . .

Chapter 9

Prophet leaned over his prisoner's legs to gaze out the coach window. He turned his head to glance out the opposite window, past where Beermeister sat, looking nervous, then he turned to stare out the window by Wells again, blinking against the dust roiling into the carriage.

Nothing out there but trees and bluffs, occasional flat patches of buckbrush and rocks.

He turned to see Wells smiling at him.

"What's the matter, big man?" Wells said. "Nervous?"

"You're the one that should be nervous." Prophet pressed the barrel of his Winchester against Wells's belly and gave a cagey smile. "If your friends attack the stage, you're gonna get a .44 bullet to your guts. You ever have to swallow a pill that size?"

"Uff!" said Aunt Grace, shaking her head. "Such vile men. Both of you. Vile!"

Mary turned to her aunt and said, "Mr. Prophet isn't bad, Aunt Grace. He's trying to help us."

Prophet stared at her in surprise. Until now, he hadn't heard her utter more than a handful of words and maybe two clipped phrases beneath her breath.

But now she'd said two entire sentences out loud. Her voice was deep and, while her English was unaccented, it owned the flatly lilting rhythms of the Native people.

She turned to Prophet with her customary expression of nonchalance but he could see a faint glitter in the depths of her chocolate eyes. Then she glanced at Wells, flaring a nostril distastefully, and continued turning her head until she was staring out the window.

Wells looked at Prophet. "You're a real hero, ain't ya, big man?"

"Shut up."

Wells smiled. "You're just tryin' to get into the Injun gal's bloomers."

"Oh!" Aunt Grace intoned, shaking her head again with exasperation.

Mary glanced at Prophet then returned her stony gaze to the window.

Prophet rammed his Winchester's barrel deeper into Wells's belly, until Wells gave a yelp and doubled over. Gritting his teeth, Prophet said, "Keep it up, and you're gonna ride all the way to the next station with my Winchester kissin' your liver. You like that idea?"

Grimacing, red-faced, Wells shook his head.

"You gonna be nice?" Prophet asked him.

Wells bobbed his head.

Prophet pulled his Winchester out of the man's gut. Wells tipped his head back and drew a deep breath, groaning, "Damn . . . that hurt!"

"Next time it's gonna hurt a whole lot mo . . ." Prophet let his voice trail off. He'd just spied movement out the window beyond Wells. He began to raise his rifle but stayed the motion when he saw a mule deer dashing off through the brush.

He slid the Winchester barrel back down against Wells's belly. He rode like that, hunched forward slightly in his seat, casting his gaze out both sides of the carriage. Tension was a large hand pressed tight to the back of his neck. The gang could strike at any time. There was plenty of cover along the trail. The Concord's panels were maybe a half-inch thick.

They wouldn't stop rifle bullets any better than pasteboard would.

The miles ticked off, however, and nothing happened.

The coach rocked and swayed, lurched and bounced over the occasional chuckhole. Dust roiled through the windows. The heat of the midafternoon hung heavy. The coach slowed as it plodded up inclines and speeded up as the team caromed downhill. They crossed a wash sheathed in berry thickets and started up the opposite bank, slowing to a near standstill as the team negotiated the steep incline.

Prophet's hands sweated inside his gloves. Here's where Wells's bunch would hit them. Here, for sure. Rifles would start belching at any time, and bullets would punch through the coach's ash housing . . .

Prophet whipped his head from one window to the other.

Sensing his tension or maybe realizing the danger, Aunt Grace gave a sob. Beermeister just sat stiff-backed in his seat, staring out the window on his side of the carriage, his cheeks and heavy jowls mottled red. He kept wiping sweat from his face with a soaked handkerchief. Mary looked out her window and chewed her finger.

But then they were off on another straight swath of open ground, the team leaning into their collars and stretching their strides, and Prophet heaved another sigh of relief, easing his grip on his Winchester's neck.

Fifteen minutes later, the coach slowed.

Prophet looked out the window by Wells to see weathered log buildings pushing up along the trail's south side. A sign over the main shack read PORCUPINE RELAY STATION, *Diego Bernal,* MGR.

Again, Prophet heaved a relieved sigh.

They'd made it to one more station.

The next stop was Jubilee. That's where Prophet would destage and turn Wells over to Seymour and Plumb, and the stage would continue with a fresh team to Deadwood. He'd learned from direct as well as indirect conversation that Beermeister, who sold roulette wheels and other gambling paraphernalia, was the only passenger continuing to Deadwood. Aunt Grace and Mary's trip was ending at Jubilee, as well. From there, they'd travel to the ranch where Mary had been raised, in the shadow of the Black Hills.

"Whoaaaa!" Mort Seymour bellowed from the driver's boot, the stage slowing. "Whoaaaa, there now, you broomtailed cayuses!"

The carriage drew to a stop in front of the log shack with a gullied sod roof and a front porch resting on stone pylons.

Leaning forward, Jimmy Wells started to rise from his seat. Prophet pushed him back. "Hold on. You ain't goin' nowhere. Not yet, anyways."

Wells glared at him. "I need to stretch my legs."

"I'll consider it once everyone else is off."

Prophet rose from his seat and opened the coach's door. He stepped out into the yard and, holding the door open, looked back into the carriage. Aunt Grace was waving a white-gloved hand at the dust billowing inside the coach, shaking her head and blinking her eyes in disgust.

"This is my last stage," the woman complained. "My last stage—do you hear? I will never, ever board another coach again." She glanced at Mary. "If your father thought it so important that someone fetch you from Denver, I for the life of me don't understand why he didn't go himself. Instead, he sends a woman ten years his senior and in very poor health!"

She looked at Mary.

"How many times do I have to tell you to stop chewing your finger?" Aunt Grace pulled Mary's hand down away from her pretty, full-lipped mouth. A little spittle clung to it. "All that money for nothing!"

Seeing that the women were going to take their time destaging, Beermeister pushed past Prophet, doffing his bowler hat and swiping it against his broadcloth-clad thighs. "I'm with the old bat," he muttered to Prophet. "I hate these goddamned contraptions. Make me feel like a craps dice."

He chuffed as he headed around to the rear of the coach.

Prophet leaned into the carriage, offering Aunt Grace his hand. "Come on, ma'am. The air's fresher out here."

Aunt Grace looked distastefully at the big, gloved hand that had been offered. Reluctantly, she rose from her seat, placed her hand in Prophet's, and allowed him to help her down out of the coach. She stood near a stock trough, shading her eyes as she looked around.

"Where in the hell is everybody?" yelled Mort Seymour.

Prophet just then realized that he and Plumb had been yelling for a while now, calling for the hostlers. Now both men stood up near the head of the six-horse team, staring toward the barn, stable, and unpeeled-pine corral to the east. The stable doors were open, and a good dozen or so horses milled inside the corral, but there appeared to be no men around.

"Nash? Coates? Quit playin' with yourselves and get out here and fetch this hitch!" shouted Seymour while Plumb stood beside him, staring toward the stable, gloved fists on his hips.

Plumb turned toward Seymour and chuckled.

A high-pitched whine rose in Prophet's ears. At first, he thought a bluebottle fly must be on the prod near his head. But then he realized that the sound stemmed from his growing apprehension.

He'd offered his hand to Mary, and she'd taken it and was now rising from her seat. Prophet turned to her and, frowning, said, "Hold on."

Her head frozen in the coach's open doorway, she frowned. "What is it?"

Prophet released her hand and turned toward the cabin.

As he did, the cabin door opened with a menacing squawk of dry hinges.

Beermeister was on the porch steps, heading for the front door with a small carpetbag in his right hand. As he gained the top of the porch, a man stepped out of the rectangle of shadow made by the door. Sunlight winked off gunmetal.

A blast from the rifle in the hands of the man in the doorway kicked Beermeister two feet up in the air and then punched him back down the steps to hit the ground behind the stage with a resolute thud.

"Dear Lord!" yelled Aunt Grace.

A quarter second later, more rifles began belching from the direction of the barn. Seymour and Plumb began shouting. There was the nasty metallic rasp of the rifle in the cabin doorway being cocked, and Prophet yelled to Mary, "*Get down!*"

Aunt Grace howled.

As the man on the porch cut loose with his rifle, Prophet hurled himself straight back into the coach, smashing into Mary. He bulled her over as he fell to the floor between the seats. Bullets sliced into the side of the coach and stitched the air around his head. He could feel Mary squirming around beneath him. The coach jerked ahead, stopped, jerked again.

Beneath the cacophony of rifle fire—there were four, maybe five, shooters, he vaguely surmised—he could hear the left-front wheel grinding against the brake blocks as the frightened team tried to bolt.

Prophet cast a quick look out the door beyond his boots. Aunt Grace faced him, seemed to be shuffling toward him. It was an odd, paganlike dance.

The old woman jerked wildly, like a scarecrow beaten with a club. Bullets smashed into her back and exited her pillowy bosom with little jets of splashed blood and viscera. A couple of large drops splashed the toe of Prophet's right boot.

Behind and above the old, dying woman, standing atop the porch and out in the sunlight now, where

Prophet could see him, a tall, broad-faced man with a mustache and red neckerchief was cutting loose with a Colt's revolving rifle. He was trying to hit him, Prophet, the bounty hunter could tell, but Aunt Grace stood between them, taking all the bullets.

Meanwhile, the screaming horses were dragging the coach herkily-jerkily across the yard. Prophet's shotgun lay beneath him—between him and the writhing Mary. He reached beside him for his rifle, which he'd hurled into the coach ahead of him. As he reached for the long gun, a face came into view in the right periphery of his vision.

The face belonged to Jimmy Wells. Wells's eyes stared at him, blinking rapidly. Blood oozed out of Wells's open mouth to dribble over the side of the deerskin-upholstered seat and onto Prophet's rifle lying on the floor beneath Wells's body. As the coach continued to jerk, turning sideways now as the horses danced and pranced, in frantic need to flee the shooting, the coach wheeled first to one side, then the other.

Three wheels were moving but the left-front one was gripped motionless in the jaws of the surprisingly effective brake blocks.

As the coach was jolted sharply sideways again, Wells rolled off the seat to Prophet's right. The body landed atop the bounty hunter. The hot, yielding, bloody body jerked as more bullets punched into it. Prophet knew a January chill as he became aware that Wells had, without a moment to spare, just saved the bounty hunter from taking those bullets himself.

And then the coach careened from side to side just before the left wheel dug into the ground. The coach pitched beneath Prophet like a rowboat being thrust up from below by a swell in a storm-tossed lake.

"Jesus!" Prophet heard himself cry out as he watched his boots, framed by the open coach door, rise higher, higher, until his legs and ass and then his back, too, were hurled up off the coach's floor.

Mary screamed beneath him.

Then their bodies and Wells's body were entangled, and Prophet felt the raw punch of his own shotgun's stock against his right jaw as the carriage careened onto its side. Prophet watched his legs climb up over his head until he and Mary and Wells were turning backward somersaults. Prophet grunted and Mary groaned as they landed on what was now the bottom of the carriage but which had been the left side only a second before.

Prophet felt the door handle grinding against his right kidney.

Mary lay against his left side, half on top of him. Wells was beneath him. He could see the man's right leg beside his own.

The carriage kept sliding along the ground. Dirt poured in through the windows. Prophet could hear the thudding of the horses' hooves, the team's shrill whinnying.

Suddenly, the carriage stopped sliding. The hoof thuds died. The whinnies settled to whickers. A man was cooing to the team, as though trying to calm the frightened beasts.

Otherwise, an ominous silence had descended on the now-still coach.

Dust billowed.

Chapter 10

Mary lifted her head, shook it.

She blinked against the billowing dust.

Her hair had fallen from its bun and hung in a dirt-caked mess around her shoulders, a large, brass pin hanging from it, off her left shoulder. Her eyes met Prophet's. He touched two fingers to his lips then felt around for his shotgun. He saw the butt jutting up from beneath Wells, who was curled against Prophet as though he were a young child taking a nap with Daddy.

Outside, several pairs of crunching footsteps sounded.

Wincing against the various aches and pains in his battered body, Prophet reached over Wells and grabbed the stock of the Richards with his right hand. Wincing again, not wanting to make any sounds, he slid the shotgun out from under the dead outlaw, tightening his grimace as the stout steel barrels raked against the coach's wooden shell.

His heart lurched, and Mary gasped, when there was a loud, hollow thud above him. Then another.

He stared straight up toward what was a minute ago the coach's opposite side and not its top, which it was now.

Two men, both holding rifles, stood on either side of the closed door, squinting into the coach's dusty shadows. Prophet had frozen when he'd heard the men leap onto the coach. Now he stared up at the hatted outlaws staring down at him, turning their heads this way and that, trying to see if anyone below them was moving.

Prophet could feel Mary's heart beating an anxious rhythm against his left arm. He held the shotgun in his right hand, barrel down, stock up. The man on the right staring down at him must have just now seen that Prophet's eyes were open, and that the gut-shredder was in his hand.

The man jerked with the recognition and aimed his Winchester down through the window to the right of the door. Prophet flipped the big popper in his right hand, clicked a hammer back, rammed his right index finger through the trigger guard, and squeezed.

The blast was deafening inside the coach. Flames spat from the Richards's right barrel toward the man aiming his Winchester through the window. The man's head turned bright red as it was torn off his shoulders and thrown a good five feet straight up in the air.

The man's headless body triggered the Winchester into the coach. The bullet tore into the left arm of Jimmy Wells, causing the dead man to jerk once more.

The other man, on the coach door's left side, widened his eyes and thrust his own Winchester through the window to the left of the door. Prophet tripped the gut-shredder's second trigger and made both men who'd come to investigate the coach's contents a matching pair of headless, blood-spewing, Winchester-wielding corpses.

Only, the second man did not fire his own Winchester. As his head blew high toward the cobalt blue of the sky, his hand opened and the Winchester dropped down into the coach to land on Mary's left knee.

The girl grabbed her knee, groaning.

Prophet dropped the Richards, grabbed his Winchester, which lay on the other side of Mary, and, jacking a round into the chamber, heaved himself to his feet to poke his hatless head through the coach's door. Two men stood out in front of the coach, between the coach and the barn. The heads of the two dead men lay on the ground between the coach and the two outlaws like strange plants growing out of the finely churned dirt of the station yard.

The headless bodies of the two men lay near the belly of the overturned carriage, in growing blood pools.

The men were staring down at the heads in wordless revulsion.

As they were jolted out of their stupors by the appearance of Prophet's own head jutting out of the coach doors, they sprang forward, shouting and bringing their Winchesters to bear. They didn't get a single shot off, however, before Prophet pumped a round from his own rifle into each, sending them spinning.

Another man who'd been holding the team's lead mount, now ran toward the coach, swinging wide of the team and sliding two pistols from holsters on his hips. Prophet ejected his second spent shell casing, seated fresh, aimed over the coach's door, and fired.

The bullet puffed dust from the man's shirt, just beneath a billowy blue neckerchief with white polka dots. He kept running toward Prophet but lifted his head abruptly, the cords standing out from his neck as he gritted his teeth, triggering both his six-shooters into the air. He took one more running lunge then hit the ground and rolled up on top of one of the two headless corpses, where he howled with the agony of his wound.

Prophet used his elbows to hoist himself up out of the coach. He jumped to the ground, looked around quickly, ready for another onslaught. But none came. Nothing now moved in the sun-splashed station yard. He looked down at the last man he'd shot, who was trying to reach a pistol holstered on the left hip of the headless corpse he'd fallen upon.

Prophet gave a caustic chuff, dropped the barrel of his Winchester, and sent the fifth man packing with a single shot to his right ear.

Lou ejected the smoking cartridge, seated fresh, and held the rifle at port arms, looking around, still wary. The team stood looking back over their shoulders at him, twitching their ears. They were still hitched to the overturned coach. Their harnesses were badly tangled, and one horse was down on his knees, whickering anxiously.

Prophet swept his gaze back toward the cabin.

Seymour and Plumb lay bloody and twisted where they'd been ambushed.

Aunt Grace lay beyond them, facedown in the dirt. Her silk and taffeta traveling gown was a large, bloody rag. Her picture hat, also blood-splattered, lay several feet away, the breeze plucking at the ostrich feather plumes.

Beermeister lay sprawled on his back several feet straight out from the steps rising to the shack's porch.

A knock sounded from inside the coach behind Prophet. A thud and a scrape. Mary poked her head and arms out the door, spreading her arms and placing her elbows against the door and the frame to hoist herself up out of the overturned rig. She hardened her jaws and winced, grunting as she heaved herself up through the door.

Prophet leaned his rifle against the belly of the coach then reached up, grabbed Mary around the waist, and settled her onto the ground. She winced again, favoring her left knee.

"You all right?" Prophet asked her.

She didn't say anything.

She looked around, dazed. Prophet knew how she felt. He was disoriented and dizzy, and there was a dull ache in his head. He and the girl had been rattled around pretty good inside the coach, likely had their brains scrambled.

Mary turned toward the station cabin and froze, shoulders tensing. She'd discovered Aunt Grace.

She started walking toward the dead woman. Prophet reached out to stop her but then lowered his hand. Who was he to intervene?

Mary strode slowly over to stand staring down at Aunt Grace. She dropped to her knees and placed her hand on the dead woman's shoulder. Prophet thought he heard her sob, and was surprised. He hadn't seen her show any emotion at all, or even much expression, for that matter.

"Aunt Grace," she said in her odd, Indian-flat tone.

She rolled the old woman over onto her back. Prophet saw her shoulders tighten as she gazed down at the old woman's eyes staring up at her, glassy in death.

"Aunt Grace," Mary whispered, as, sitting back on her heels, she drew the old woman's head onto her lap and cradled the woman's torso in her arms, ignoring the blood that nearly covered the corpse.

Mary's shoulders jerked as she lowered her head and sobbed quietly.

Prophet turned away, allowing the grieving girl some privacy.

Finally, trying to clear the cobwebs from his brain, pondering his next course of action, he strode over to the front of the shack. After checking to make sure Beermeister was dead, he walked up the porch steps and looked through the cabin's open door.

"Anyone here?" he called.

There was little inside but wooden tables and chairs and a range and cupboards built from old shipping crates. A couple of pots were smoking on the range. The windows were steamed. The rank, pungent odor of burned beans permeated the place.

Prophet walked inside. As he strode into the kitchen area behind a makeshift bar of pine planks propped on beer barrels, he saw a fat, dark, mustached man in an apron lying on the floor near the dry sink.

Diego Bernal ran the place. *Had run* the place, Prophet corrected himself. Lou hadn't known him well, but he'd known that a wife and daughter had once lived here with Diego, helping him run the station for the stage line, but the wife had met another man and run off. Not long later, the daughter had met another man and run off, as well.

Well, Diego was gone now, too. The gaping hole in his back was where a bullet had exited his husky body, likely after shredding his heart. The man's fat, brown left hand still held a wooden spoon crusted with dried bean juice.

Prophet cursed and with his rifle barrel nudged the burning pot off to the side of the stove.

He headed back outside.

Mary was still cradling her dead aunt's head on her lap, rocking slowly while she very quietly, almost under her breath, recited the Lord's Prayer. Her dirty hair hung in thick tangles around her head, screening her face.

". . . Thy will be done on earth as it is in heaven . . ."

Prophet dropped down the porch steps, crossed the yard to the barn.

He found the two drovers lying dead in the corral, likely where they'd been getting the fresh team ready for the stage when the outlaws had struck. They were Bobby Nash and Tom Coates—both good men though Coates could get mean when drunk and even meaner when he was drunk and losing at stud poker. The horses stood statue-still on the far side of the corral from the two dead men, who lay about ten feet apart, one on his belly, one on his back, ankles crossed, staring through half-open lids at the sky.

Prophet walked back outside and stood pondering the overturned carriage and the horses. The right wheeler was still on its knees. Prophet tramped over to the coach, shucked his bowie knife, and went to work cutting the tangled ribbons and unhitching the team. The wheeler gained its feet and cut loose with what sounded like an exasperated whinny.

"Yeah, me, too, feller," Prophet grunted, patting the horse's rump.

When he had the team freed, he led them by pairs into the corral and removed their harnesses, hames, and collars. Before they'd died, the hostlers had filled the stock troughs with fresh water and forked hay into the crib fronting the corral, so the tired, jittery horses were taken care of.

Now, the coach . . .

Prophet walked back out into the yard. The sun was teetering over the western buttes, and long, heavy shadows were beginning to consume the hollow in which the station sat. Mary was still slumped over her dead aunt. She must be getting stiff and cold, kneeling like that in the dirt with the sun going down. Prophet considered going over and ushering her into the cabin, but decided to leave her alone with Aunt Grace for the time being.

He considered the coach.

If he could get it back on its wheels, he and Mary could ride the rig on to Jubilee the next morning, with the bodies of Aunt Grace, Beermeister, Mort Seymour, and J. W. Plumb strapped to the roof. He'd leave the bodies of Diego Bernal and the two hostlers in the barn. The stage line could decide what to do with them. Prophet didn't have time to bury them. It would be dark within the hour, and he had to get Mary into the cabin and see to her comfort, maybe get some food into her, if she felt like eating after what she'd seen and been through.

A strange apprehension still held its chill hand

against Prophet's sweaty back. The gang was dead. He didn't have to worry about them anymore. Still, a concern nagged at him:

What had they been after?

What had they been after that had been worth dying for?

The stage hadn't been carrying a strongbox, and its four passengers couldn't have been worth the trouble the gang had gone to, even with one of the passengers being a pretty girl. If they'd been desperate for a woman, they could have found one in Jubilee or farther east in Deadwood, only a half-day's ride away. Prophet knew there were hogpens, low-rent parlor houses of a sort, not far from here in Wyoming.

It didn't make sense.

The bounty hunter looked around at the buttes that appeared more menacing now as the early-evening shadows slid across them, filling in their gaps and fissures and long, meandering erosions. A breeze rose, moaning around the bluffs, making the darkening cottonwoods whisper foreboding secrets, picking up a few handfuls of dust here and there about the yard and swirling them.

The water bucket hanging under the porch roof swung to and fro, its chain squawking shrilly.

The dead lay where they'd fallen—the grisly result of the sudden violence in the wake of which a thick silence hung with burgeoning menace as the night threatened. Old superstitions and Southern-born hoodoo anxieties stirred Prophet. He had to drag the dead out of the yard. He didn't like to think he was afraid of ghosts, but he was.

First, the carriage.

He walked over to where the coach lay on its side, near the two headless corpses and the last man Prophet had shot. His gaze caught on the carriage's yellow-painted, blood-splattered belly, which faced him. He frowned, studying what had drawn his attention—an irregularity in the otherwise smooth, slightly convex housing.

He moved still closer to the coach, squatted before it, and ran his hand down the belly and over the steel handle protruding from it. He gave the handle a tug. It didn't move. He brushed some of the splattered blood and dried mud away from the panel around the handle and found a lock.

He stared at the small, round lock beneath the handle, soundlessly moving his lips, pondering.

Finally, he walked over to where J. W. Plumb lay and went through the man's pockets. From the dead shotgun messenger's right pants pocket he withdrew a two-inch-long key connected to a length of braided rawhide. He walked back over to the coach, poked the key in the lock, and turned it.

There was a faint click. Prophet pulled the handle. Out came a steel drawer.

It slid at an angle about seven inches down from beneath the carriage's belly and then straight out, parallel with the belly's housing. Prophet stared, lower jaw hanging in surprise, at the three canteen-sized canvas pouches that slid out with the box, nestled inside it like little, fat pigs in a manger.

The box kept sliding out from the compartment built into the undercarriage. Prophet was so intent on the canvas pouches that he didn't see the end of the drawer until, leaving the compartment, it dropped to the ground with a heavy, clanging thump. The drawer was constructed of solid steel. It was roughly two feet wide and four feet long—about the same size as your average strongbox.

That, apparently, was what this was.

A hidden strongbox.

Chapter 11

A hidden strongbox made sense.

The trail from Cheyenne to Bismarck was notoriously treacherous, teeming with robbers of every stripe. Most strongboxes rode atop the coach, in plain sight. Someone was using their thinker box when they came up with the idea of building a hidden compartment beneath the coach's floor for carrying the box, which had become a drawer.

Obviously, Seymour and Plumb had lied when they'd told Lou they weren't carrying a box. Which was understandable. You don't go to the trouble of a hidden box and then tell everyone it has money in it.

But when had they picked up the three coin sacks? Had they carried them all the way from Camp Collins, which was the southern end of the line, or had they picked them up at the train depot in Cheyenne, before rolling on to the hotel to pick up Prophet and the other passengers?

Wherever it had come from and whomever it belonged to, Wells and the other outlaws must have found out about it. Had they known what this box was carrying, or had they just learned about the stage line's new trick and assumed this coach was carrying something of value in the box?

Prophet heard a shoe crunch gravel behind him.

He jerked with a start to see Mary standing there, holding a pistol in her hand. The barrel was aimed at Prophet. She stared down at the drawer containing the three sacks that probably contained specie, judging by the clanks they'd made when the box had hit the ground.

Sliding her dark eyes to Prophet, she said, "What's that?"

Prophet looked at the gun. His throat had gone dry. He reached up and wrapped his hand around the gun, angling the barrel away from him, and gently pulled it out of Mary's hand.

"Hidden strongbox," he said, scowling up at the girl. He hefted the .45 in his hand. "What about this?"

"It's a gun."

"I know it's a gun. What were you doing with it?"

Staring dully at the box, Mary hiked a shoulder. "It was on the ground near Aunt Grace. I picked it up. I don't know why. What's in the box?"

Prophet looked at Mary, looked at the gun, then opened the loading gate, shook out the cartridges while spinning the wheel, and tossed the pistol away. He picked up the pouches, hefted them in each hand.

"Money, looks like. A good bit, judgin' by their weight."

"Do you think Aunt Grace will go to heaven?"

Prophet looked at Mary again, incredulous. She had turned to look back at where her aunt lay by the cabin porch, not far from Beermeister. The breeze was nipping at Aunt Grace's gray hair, blowing it around the old woman's head, like dry corn silk.

"She was good," Mary said. "Deep down . . . in her heart . . . she was good."

"Well, I reckon she will, then." Prophet cast the puzzling, obviously worried girl a reassuring smile. "If that's where she's headed, she's already there."

Mary stared at Aunt Grace as though pondering what Prophet had said.

"Wait here," Prophet told the girl, placing both hands on her shoulders.

He went inside and dragged the body of Diego Bernal out onto the porch. Prophet paused to catch his breath. Bernal was a big man. The bounty hunter saw Mary sitting on the porch's bottom step, looking off toward Aunt Grace. She'd pulled a dress out of one of Aunt Grace's several bags; she'd used it to cover the old woman's bullet-chewed body.

Now Mary just sat there on the step, leaning forward as though chilled.

Prophet went inside and found a blanket in a back room of the shack. He walked back outside and draped the blanket over Mary's shoulders.

"Cold and gonna get colder," he told the girl. "Why don't you go on inside? Can you build the fire up in the range?"

Mary turned to him, nodded.

"Are you going to be all right, Mary?"

She stared at him. "Who are you, Mr. Prophet?" She canted her head toward the dead outlaws. "Are you a man like them?"

Prophet pursed his lips. It was a fair question. He probably looked much like the men he'd killed. At least, he dressed similarly, and his features had been seasoned by the western sun and wind. Now, Mary's aunt was dead, and she was alone with a strange man out here in the middle of nowhere.

She might have looked the wild savage, but she'd been raised a civilized white girl.

"No, I'm not one of them."

"Will you help me take Aunt Grace home, so she can be buried in the family plot?"

"You bet."

Mary nodded. She rose and, frowning pensively, holding the blanket taut about her shoulders, walked into the station and closed the door against the chill. Prophet heard a scraping sound and then a dull thud as she dropped a locking bar into place across the door.

Prophet dragged Diego Bernal into the barn.

Then he dragged Aunt Grace into the barn.

And then Seymour and Plumb.

He left the dead outlaws where they lay. He'd dumped the bullet-riddled body of Jimmy Wells into the yard with the others. The stage line could decide what to do with them. Such craven killers didn't deserve a burial, decent or otherwise. They deserved to have their carcasses chewed on by whatever predators that were lured in by their stench during the night.

That grisly task completed, Prophet back-and-bellied the coach back onto its wheels. It wasn't all that heavy though he cursed a little and noted a hitch in his lower back. He cursed again when he saw that the left-front wheel was badly twisted, the felloe broken, the brake blocks snapped off and lying on the ground.

He pushed the carriage into the barn, found a new wheel, and wrestled it onto the axle, and lubed it before replacing the hub. He didn't bother with the brake. He didn't think there were any steep hills between here and Jubilee. He hoped he was right. He'd find out tomorrow.

If someone from Jubilee rode out looking for the stage, he wouldn't have to find out. Men from the stage company could then decide what to do about the coach.

He stowed the three money sacks in his saddlebags. He wanted to keep it close to him tonight, in case anyone else came looking for it. Mainly out of curiosity, he also wanted to count it.

By the time he had Aunt Grace, Seymour, and Plumb wrapped in blankets and strapped to the top of the coach, the sun had gone down. A stiff, chill wind had risen and a rainstorm had blown in. He closed the barn door and, hefting his rifle and shotgun, adjusting his saddlebags on his left shoulder, he jogged across the rain-pelted yard to the cabin. By the time he'd made it up the porch steps, he was soaked to the bone, rain sluicing down the funneled brim of his hat onto his face.

He flipped the door latch, pushed. The door wouldn't budge. He remembered that Mary had locked it. He moved over to the window to the left of the door, and, crouching, lifted his right fist to knock on the glass.

He froze.

His eyes widened and his lower jaw loosened as he stared into the shadowy cabin where Mary was standing naked in a corrugated tin washtub, not far from the window.

A lamp flickering on a near table caressed her smooth, wet, brown skin that owned the luster of varnished walnut. Mary was brushing her damp hair, tilting her head from side to side and raking the thick, coarse, blue-black mass from the inside out.

The girl's body belonged to no girl. It was the body of a young woman in full flower.

His heart skipped beats as, ears warming with shame, he continued to stare, riveted, through the window.

"Holy hell on the devil's stick," Prophet wheezed.

Mary owned the body of a beautiful young squaw ripe for childbearing . . .

The girl suddenly turned her head toward him, as though she'd glimpsed him out of the corner of her eye. Both eyes snapped wide in shock and fury. She flung a hand toward the table, where a pistol lay beside the flickering lamp.

"Oh, tarnation," Prophet yelled. "Oh, wait, now . . ."

The girl pivoted on her beautiful hips, taking the pistol in both hands and gritting her teeth as she thumbed back the hammer. She aimed hastily. The gun cracked. Flames lapped from the barrel. There was a tinny ping as the bullet hurled through the glass just as Prophet slid his head away from the window.

He winced as a sliver of glass dug into his left cheek, just beneath his eye.

"Hold on, Mary, it's me—Lou!" Prophet yelled as another crack sounded inside the shack and another chunk of the window was blown onto the porch floor. "It's Lou! Lou Prophet!" He plucked the sliver of glass from his cheek and yelled at the window beside him. "I was just wantin' in—that's all! I saw the door was locked!"

Running footsteps sounded inside the shack. There was the scrape of the locking bar being removed from the brackets. The door opened.

Mary looked out. "I'm sorry! I didn't know it was you! I thought . . ." She let her voice trail off. "Come in."

As she stepped back, Prophet walked into the cabin. She stood before him, wrapped in a towel, her damp hair hanging down past her brown shoulders. Looking up at him, seeing the blood running down his cheek, she sucked air through her teeth. "Did I do that?"

"Don't worry about it." Prophet hung his shotgun on a wall peg and leaned his rifle against the wall beside the door. He dropped his saddlebags onto the floor. He removed his wet hat and tossed it onto the bags.

Mary closed and locked the door. "You're soaked!"

"Yeah, well, it's rainin'."

"Don't be mad at me. I'm sorry!" Mary rose onto her bare toes to look up at his bloody cheek. "Does it hurt?"

Prophet pressed his soaked neckerchief against the cut. "Like I said—don't worry about it."

"Sit down."

"Huh?"

"Sit down!" Mary pushed him into a hide-bottom chair at the long table running along the front of the cabin. She cupped his chin in her right hand, and tipped his head back. She lowered her head to get a look at the cut. "I can stitch it. Do you think it needs stitches?"

Prophet brushed her hand away. "Hell, no, it don't need stitches."

"It might—sit still!" Brusquely, she grabbed his chin in her hand again and tipped his head back once more. She crouched to one side, angling his head to the light of the flickering lantern.

Suddenly, she looked into his eyes, scowling suspiciously. "Were you looking in at me?"

"Huh?"

Mary stepped back, drawing the blanket more tightly around her. Her breasts strained against it—two large, rounded mounds. Prophet tried hard to keep his gaze off the girl's frisky bosoms but they were like magnets to the steel balls of his eyes. "You were—weren't you?"

Prophet's ears warmed again. "Well, hell, I didn't mean to. I was just tryin' to get your attention, and . . ."

She arched an accusing brow. "And then . . . ?"

Prophet averted his eyes in shame. "And then . . . I seen you in here, an' . . . I don't know . . . you was naked an' just standin' there, an'—"

"And you decided to get an eyeful, didn't you?"

"Ah, hell—I didn't know what to say!" Prophet shifted around in his chair, shame burning in him.

"Well, did you get an eyeful?"

"What?"

"You seem awfully tongue-tied, Mr. Prophet. This whole trip I've never heard you at a loss for words."

Prophet looked up at her glaring down at him. He was indignant. "Well, hell, ain't you suddenly the chatty one! For a long stretch of this trip I thought you was a mute. Now I can't get you to stop talkin' long enough for me to look around for a bottle. I'm powerful thirsty, and if you don't mind, I'd appreciate it if you'd accept my heartfelt apology for ogling you through the window. It ain't every day a man sees somethin' like that, if you'll forgive me for sayin' so, and I reckon, yeah, I had me a good look. I apologize. Now, can we get on with the business at hand?"

Mary gazed at him. Her eyes lost a little of their incrimination. She stepped forward and grabbed the handkerchief out of his hand. "Here, give me that. Let me see how deep this is."

"I told you—it ain't that deep."

She dabbed at the cut with the wet handkerchief, pulled it away. "It's already starting to clot. You'll live, though it's more than you deserve for ogling a girl through a window. I thought you told me you weren't like one of those men outside."

"I'm not! Ah, hell . . ."

Mary tossed the rag down on the table and stepped back, looking him up and down. Her eyes seemed to linger as she took in his chest and the width of his shoulders, and her voice was a little softer when she said, "You're soaked."

Prophet felt the cold from the rain penetrate him. He shivered. "Tell me about it."

"I'll heat water for a bath, but I have to get dressed first."

"I'll just sip whiskey in front of the range."

He started to rise but Mary pushed him back down in his chair. "No, you won't. Just stay there. I'll add wood to the fire and heat you some water, but

I'm going to get dressed first, so you don't get any ideas about me. I am not a savage."

She gazed down at him, defiantly, as though to drive her words home.

"I didn't say you were."

"I was raised in a good home, by a good man. Aunt Grace ruled with a switch and she could be short with me at times, but I needed it. I was born a savage, but I had it raised out of me."

Prophet stared at her, shivering. "Mary, fer chrissakes—I don't think you're a savage!"

She stepped back. A flush darkened her cheeks, deepened the red in them.

Prophet frowned. "What's wrong?"

Mary's bosom rose and fell sharply as she breathed. "I feel . . . strange." She paused. A look of terror slackened her face. "Noo!"

She turned away sharply, chewed on the nail of her right index finger. Her shoulders rose and fell as she breathed. Her thick, black hair hung straight down to the middle of her back.

"Mary, are you all—?"

She swung around. Tears glazed her eyes. "What's wrong with me?"

"What the hell do you mean?"

"I'm not a savage!" she exclaimed, pressing the heels of her hands to her temples. "I am not wanton!"

"Hell, I didn't say—!"

"I am not a craven heathen!"

Prophet just stared at her, mouth ajar. He began to understand that those were the things she'd been called—maybe by her foster father and Aunt Grace, maybe by her teachers and the other girls at school.

Maybe by everyone she'd known since she'd come to live in the so-called civilized white world.

Mary stared at him, chocolate eyes glazed with tears.

She reached up and untucked the towel from over her bosom. She let it fall to the floor at her feet.

Chapter 12

Prophet's heart hiccupped as Mary stood naked before him.

Her swollen lips were parted. She shoved her face up close to his, pressed her mouth to his lips.

Prophet was so startled by her sudden change that he sat frozen. But then as she kissed him, desire rose in him, hot and heavy, chasing out the chill, and he held her in his arms and returned the kiss.

Before things could go any further, Mary said, "They were right about me."

"Who was right about you, darlin'?"

"Aunt Grace. Pa. The preacher from our church. The preacher's wife."

"What were they right about, darlin'?"

Mary squeezed her eyes shut and bawled as she yelled, "That I'm a whore!"

Prophet stared at her in shock. "What're you talkin' about? You ain't no whore. They do it for money!"

Mary turned to gaze up at him through tear-filled eyes. "Back at the ranch . . . I knew a boy. Son of one of Pa's hands. We did it in a barn stall, on a horse blanket.

"Pa caught us the third time. That's when he called me a whore. Aunt Grace, too. They made me see the preacher and the preacher's wife. They called me a whore, too. Not in so many words, but I could see it in their eyes. I was a savage heathen whore!"

Mary sobbed for a time and when she could catch her breath again, she said, "That's when Pa and Aunt Grace and the preacher said I should go to Mrs. Devine's Christian Academy for Wayward Girls!"

Again, she sobbed. Prophet let her cry. He just lay beside her, running his big right paw slowly through her hair.

She turned to look at him again in anguish as she said, "That was two years ago. I spent two years there in that place around those good Christian girls and those good Christian teachers, and still they couldn't school the savage out of me. I'm just what they said I was and always will be what they said—a savage strumpet. Oh, how can I go back to the ranch knowin' I'm no better than before I left, and that Pa wasted all that money on tryin' to set me straight?"

"Easy, darlin', easy," Prophet cooed into her ear.

She turned to him again. "The first time I looked at you, big, tall man that you are, I had an unclean thought. It popped right into my head—I tried so hard to cleanse my mind of the thought. I stared and I stared out the stage window, and I prayed for salvation from such awful thinking, but I couldn't do it."

Prophet said, "Your pa and Aunt Grace and the preacher and the preacher's wife had it wrong. They shouldn't have called you a whore just for bein' with a boy.

"Especially when they were as old as you were when you frolicked with that boy. You just had the rotten luck of gettin' caught in the act. The most natural act in the world, I might add. Every girl and boy in the world feels the need to do just what you done. It's nothin' to be ashamed about, and I'm sorry they made you feel ashamed. If they was here right now, I'd take the strap to the backside of each one in turn!"

Mary stared into his eyes. Her upper lip no longer trembled. "You're sayin' . . . you're sayin' that—"

"There ain't nothin' wrong with you. You're a pretty girl who enjoys life."

Mary's eyes brightened.

Prophet slid a lock of tear-soaked hair away from her right cheek and tucked it behind her ear. "I bet your pa and Aunt Grace and the preacher and the preacher's wife didn't enjoy life half as much as you do. That's their problem. Not yours. From now on, darlin', you don't listen to what small-minded people say about you. You're pretty and good and kind and you're sharp as a tack. Don't you ever let anyone make your shoulders slump ever again just because you enjoy life—do you hear me, Mary?"

"I—I think so, Lou."

"Good."

Chapter 13

Prophet woke early the next morning.

Fatigue lingered.

He groaned at the aches and pains from having been shaken like dice in a cup when the Concord had rolled, and from his and Mary's prolonged tussle in Diego's bed. He was sore, but at least he was clean. When they'd taken a break from the night's festivities, Mary had thrown together a supper of beans and bacon and baking powder biscuits, and Prophet had taken a bath.

Then they'd gone back to bed to make love once more and to cuddle and listen to the rain lighten and the storm drift away, leaving only the relaxing sounds of water dripping from the eaves. The horror of the ambush had seemed a million years away.

Together, they drifted into deep, dreamless slumber.

Now Prophet blinked as sleep was slow to release him. Gray touched the windows. It was time to rise. He had a lot to do—namely, get a fresh team hitched to the coach and get himself and Mary as well as their cargo of cadavers up the trail to Jubilee.

He walked naked into the main room, where his clothes hung from chairs near the now-cold range. He dressed quietly, moving around stiffly, so as not to awaken Mary. He'd let her sleep a few more minutes, until he got a fire going. As he stepped into his boots, he wondered why no one from the stage station in Jubilee had come looking for the stage. Obviously, it was overdue. There was no telegraph line on this stretch of the trail.

Maybe he'd meet a posse on the trail this morning.

As he got a fire started in the range, he remembered the money he'd found in the coach's hidden compartment. He lit the lantern on the table then hauled the three money pouches out of his saddlebags. He started a pot of coffee on the range, and while the firebox ticked and snapped and the cabin heated and the coffee began chugging and sighing, he emptied the bags onto the table.

Freshly minted gold eagles and silver cartwheels glinted up at him in the lantern's buttery light.

"I'll be damned," he said, running his hands through the coins.

He got up and poured himself a cup of piping-hot mud, then retook his chair at the table and began counting the coins. Mary came out, yawning and blinking sleep from her eyes. She was dressed in a simple wool traveling skirt, cream blouse, short leather jacket, and high black boots. Her clean, freshly brushed hair shone radiantly in the lantern light, purple highlights threading the black.

Prophet marveled at her beauty as well as their

good time together in Diego's bed, wishing it hadn't had to end.

Despite her aunt's death, Mary looked good. Vibrant. Not necessarily happy, but strong and ready to confront what could be another challenging day.

When she'd poured herself a cup of coffee, she sat down at the table and helped Prophet count the coins.

Fifteen minutes later, they'd returned all the coins to the three bags, and the bounty hunter sat back in his chair, shaking his head. "Thirty thousand dollars."

"What do you suppose it's for?" Mary asked. She was at the range now, stirring the pot of beans and bacon she was reheating from the night before.

"I got no idea."

"Do you think the money is what the outlaws were after?"

"Must be." Prophet sipped his coffee and frowned over the rim of the cup at Mary stirring the beans. "But how did they know about it?"

Mary looked at him and hiked a shoulder. "Does it matter? They're dead. I suppose we'll find out who the money belongs to when we get to Jubilee."

"Yeah, unless the money's going to Deadwood or on to Bismarck."

"Yes," Mary said. "Deadwood. That's probably where it's going."

"Well, we'll get ourselves and the coach to Jubilee, and we'll let the stage line worry about getting the money on to wherever it's going." Prophet sipped his coffee. "Your pa is probably worried about you. We should have been to Jubilee last night."

"Stages are notoriously slow around here," Mary

said. "He'll probably be there, waiting for me." Her voice dropped an octave and she frowned as she spooned the beans into a couple of tin bowls. She was thinking about Aunt Grace, Prophet knew. Just as he'd marveled at her beauty, he marveled at her heart. Despite how wretched her aunt and father had been to her—at least, regarding her tryst with the ranch hand's boy—she still obviously loved them both.

To think they'd called her a savage . . .

Inwardly, Prophet shook his head. People never ceased to puzzle and disgust him.

When they finished eating, Mary put the kitchen in order, scrubbing the pots and bowls they'd used with water she'd hauled from the well and putting everything back in its place. Prophet headed out to the barn and hitched the team to the Concord. He closed the barn doors, saying a solemn good-bye to poor Diego Bernal and his hostlers.

When he had the team buckled into place, Mary walked out from the cabin. The morning was cool. She wore a hooded wool cape over her vest, and black gloves. She'd drawn up the cape's hood. Strands of her long hair slithered out of the hood to dance around her head in the chill breeze that was still damp from last night's rain.

Prophet adjusted the harness on the right wheeler then walked out to meet Mary as she approached the coach. "You wanna ride inside or up top? Kind of bloody inside, what with all Jimmy Wells's rollin' around in there. But up top is Aunt Grace and Seymour an' Plumb. It ain't gonna be a pleasant ride into Jubilee, I'm afraid, no matter where you ride."

"I didn't figure it would be, Lou," Mary said. "I'd

like to ride up top with you. Despite Aunt Grace." A tear shone in her right eye. She smiled and flicked it away with her finger.

"Up top it is." Prophet took her hand and held it, steadying her, as she stepped onto the iron rung by the front wheel. He released her hand as she climbed from the rung into the driver's boot.

Prophet walked around to the opposite side of the coach and climbed into the boot. Then they were off, the team jogging free and easy, leaning into their collars and hames, stretching their necks, the chill breeze making them toss their heads friskily, their manes dancing. Prophet saw Mary glance over her left shoulder at where the bodies of Aunt Grace, Seymour, and Plumb were tied in tightly wrapped and bound bundles, shivering a little as the stage rocked and rattled its way along the trail.

She turned her head forward, drawing the corners of her mouth down slightly.

"We'll be to Jubilee in no time, Mary," Prophet said. "Then you and your pa can take Aunt Grace back to the ranch and bury her."

"I hope he doesn't regret calling me home, after all that's happened."

"What do you mean—calling you home? Weren't you finished back at Mrs. Devine's?"

Mary shook her head. "I wasn't going to be finished until Christmas."

Prophet looked at her. "Do you know why he called you home so early?"

Mary shook her head, hiked a shoulder. "I assume—maybe it's just wishful thinking—that my letters convinced him I didn't need to be there. While I valued my lessons and appreciated learning how to play the piano and the violin, and I came to like Mrs. Devine herself, I felt I'd learned all she could teach me. I wanted to go home. That's where I belong. I feel out of place around most people."

She turned to Prophet. "I love the ranch. I was raised there around the men and the horses and the open spaces. I suppose that's still the savage in me, though I don't remember anything of my life before Father adopted me. The ranch is where I want to be. That's where I'd like to live my life."

"I reckon I must have some savage in me, too, then," Prophet said, staring straight ahead at the gauzy black mounds of the Black Hills humping up along the eastern horizon.

"How's that, Lou?"

"I like horses and open spaces my ownself."

She gazed at Prophet, soft-eyed. "I'm going to miss you, Lou."

"I'm going to miss you, too, Mary."

"What brings you to Jubilee?"

"An old friend wrote me a letter." Prophet frowned as he turned to her. "You wouldn't know her, would you? The name's Margaret Knudsen."

Mary shook her head. "Sorry, Lou. I don't know the name. I've been gone from Jubilee for two years and even when I was growing up out at the ranch, I rarely got to town. My father and Aunt Grace were very protective and didn't think that towns and young girls mixed."

"I see," Prophet said, turning his head to stare over the team's twitching ears once more. "Worth a shot."

They rolled through a jog of low hills peppered with cedars and post oaks, the gullies between the hills choked with juneberry, chokecherry, and hawthorn from which white-tailed deer bounded at the thunder of the approaching coach. When they'd climbed to the highest point in the hills, Prophet could see Jubilee on the prairie below though he wouldn't have spotted the town if he hadn't been looking for it, hadn't known it was there.

Jubilee wasn't much. Never had been. It had started out as a watering and overnighting spot for freight and immigrant trains and army patrols as well as a hiders' camp back when buffalo were still plentiful on the plains around the Black Hills. This had been dangerous country for white buffalo hunters and, later, for gold prospectors. The Sioux had been bound and determined to keep out the white hordes. Prophet couldn't blame them, knowing now how rooted into this country they'd been, how dependent they'd been on the buffalo, and how badly the Great Father back in Washington had double-crossed them.

Jubilee, named after Jubilee Springs bubbling up in the rocks at its southern edge, had been a dying town since the first time Prophet had ridden through it. The last time he'd visited, maybe three years ago, there had been only around thirty remaining residents inhabiting the fifty or so remaining shacks and log cabins and sod-roofed mud huts. Most had been over the age of forty.

One of the more colorful residents, an elderly black man named Charlie Royals who ran the town's only hotel and sported only one leg, courtesy the Sioux, had claimed there'd been thirty-five and one half residents and three coyotes. The half resident had been the bun in the oven of one of the three remaining whores.

Prophet wondered idly how many fewer folks there would be now. He wondered again what had brought Lola there, to a dying town. The former Margaret Jane Olson, presently Mrs. Margaret Knudsen.

He didn't run the team overly hard, just enough to let them stretch out their strides before checking them down. He wasn't in any hurry, as he had no timetable to keep. He might as well make the last leg of the trip as pleasant for himself and Mary as possible. He'd been expecting to meet searchers for the stage along the trail but had given up hope until, dropping down out of the hills, he spied riders galloping toward the trail from the north.

They were four men coming hard and fast, crouched low over their horses' necks.

Prophet didn't like the hard-driving, determined way they were coming at him. They could be a worried group sent out by the stage station. On the other hand, they could be men like those rotting in the yard of Porcupine Station.

Prophet glanced at Mary. She'd spied the riders, as well, and was gazing at them apprehensively as they galloped across the prairie, pulling a thick dust cloud above and behind them.

"Don't worry," Prophet said as he slid his Winchester from its sheath and rested it across his thighs. "Probably just men from town looking for the stage."

"Yeah," Mary said almost too softly for Prophet to hear above the thunder of the team. "Probably."

Chapter 14

The four riders reached the trail about fifty yards ahead of Prophet and checked their mounts down, their dust catching up to them.

They turned their horses toward the stage, blocking the trail. Prophet cursed under his breath and caressed the repeater resting across his thighs. As he slowed the team gradually, he sized up the four men facing him.

Clad in dusty trail clothes, including brush-scratched chaps, they were obviously range riders. Only one man was holding a gun—a Sharps carbine—but he didn't look like he was eagerly anticipating using it. The other three were content to leave their pistols and rifles in their scabbards.

Prophet left his rifle in his lap as he continued pulling back on the team's ribbons until the horses finally stopped and the coach creaked to a halt, silence settling over the trail.

The four riders sized up Prophet, their gazes flicking to the dark-skinned girl sitting beside him. Prophet returned the men's interested stares. Dust sifted. Red-winged blackbirds screeched in the brush off both sides of the trail. The team blew and switched their tails.

"Mr. Leonard?" Mary said, leaning forward, frowning. "John Leonard?"

One of the four men nodded. He appeared to be the group's leader, as the other three cast frequent, deferring glances at him. He was tall and mustached, with dark brown eyes set in deep, shaded sockets. Around forty, Prophet judged, he wore a low-crowned black hat, and black beard stubble carpeted his craggy, hollow cheeks.

He dipped his cleft chin cordially. "Hello, Miss Mary." He tipped his head a little to one side, glancing over Prophet and Mary at the grisly cargo tied behind them. "We were expecting you last night out at the ranch. Your father sent a buggy for you. When you didn't show, your father grew worried. We were heading out to locate you."

"We ran into trouble," Mary said in a regretful tone, glancing at the coach roof behind her. "Aunt Grace is dead."

"What kind of trouble?" Leonard had directed the question at Prophet, as though he were somehow better qualified to answer it.

"A bushwhack at the Porcupine Station. Bloodbath, more like it. Me an' Miss Mary here are the only survivors. Mort Seymour and J. W. Plumb are resting behind us with Mary's aunt."

"You two are the only survivors, eh?" said Leonard, as though he were skeptical of the information. "Who were the bushwhackers?"

Prophet didn't like Leonard's tone. "They didn't introduce themselves," he said in a curt tone of his own.

"What did they take?" Leonard asked.

"Beside lives? Nothing."

Leonard looked mildly relieved by the response.

"Who are you?" asked one of the others flanking Leonard. He was younger than Leonard, and he had a confrontational cast to his gaze. He held a gloved hand over the grips of the Schofield riding in its holster strapped to the young rider's right thigh.

"Prophet."

"Prophet, huh?" said the younger rider in a disbelieving tone, cutting his gaze at Leonard.

"Lou saved me," Mary said, placing her left hand on Prophet's forearm. "If it hadn't been for him, I'd be dead like Aunt Grace."

"Lou," the younger rider said in a sneering tone to Leonard, wrinkling a nostril. "You hear that?"

Leonard ignored him.

"I see," the lead rider said, his tone lightening and his grave expression brightening somewhat though Prophet doubted that John Leonard's granitelike features ever cracked a real smile. "The good news is, you're alive, Miss Mary. Your father sent us for you. Why don't you climb down from there and climb up here with me? We'll get you back to the ranch. Your father has been worried."

"Oh," Mary said, glancing uncertainly at Prophet. "All . . . right. But what about Aunt Grace?"

"Your father will likely send a wagon for Aunt Grace and your luggage," Leonard said. He held out a gloved hand. "Come, now, Mary. Your father is worried."

The girl rose from her seat. Prophet grabbed her

arm. "Are you sure you want to go with these men, Mary?"

Mary hesitated, but then she turned from Prophet to the group's leader and said, "Yes. I know Mr. Leonard. He's my father's foreman." She smiled at Prophet, dark cheeks turning a little darker as she obviously reflected a little sheepishly but not without fondness, as well, upon their previous night at Porcupine Relay Station. "Good-bye, Lou."

"All right, then," Prophet said, releasing the girl's arm. "I'll help you down."

"I can manage."

Mary carefully stepped down from the stage. She glanced again at Prophet as she walked up alongside the team to where Leonard was extending his hand to her. She offered the bounty hunter another fleeting smile then accepted the foreman's hand. John Leonard drew her up onto his horse, and she settled her weight behind the man's saddle.

"Are you comfortable, Mary?" Leonard asked her.

"Reasonably," Mary said, looking over the man's shoulder at Prophet. To the bounty hunter, she said, "Please pay me a visit before you leave Jubilee, Lou. My father will want to thank you for saving my life."

Prophet smiled as he pinched his hat brim to the girl. "I might just do that."

Leonard gave Prophet a cordial nod as he turned his horse, nudged the mount with his spurs, and galloped off to the south. The three other riders galloped their own mounts after him, the younger rider casting several sneering looks behind at Prophet before the bunch disappeared over a hogback.

Their hoof thuds dwindled to silence.

Prophet sat staring after them. They reappeared a minute later, riding up over the crest of another, higher, more distant hogback before disappearing down the far side of that rise, too. A nettling apprehension walked cold fingers along the back of his neck.

But she'd recognized the foreman, he told himself.

Disregarding his foreboding as merely a reluctance to have Mary part ways with him so suddenly and unexpectedly—he'd taken a liking to more than just the girl's bewitching ways in the mattress sack—he clucked and shook the ribbons over the horses' backs. The team lunged forward, and then they were trotting eastward along the trail, following a long curve, Jubilee taking shape a half a mile ahead.

Prophet frowned as he stared out over the bobbing heads of the team. More riders were riding toward him, trotting their horses along the trail.

"Now, what?" Prophet muttered, brushing his right hand across the Winchester still resting in his lap.

The riders kept moving toward him. They were roughly two hundred yards from Jubilee and heading toward Prophet at a slow but purposeful clip. There were five of them. Each held a rifle as though ready to use it. Prophet kept the stage moving but he slowed the team to a walk. The nettling apprehension walking cold fingers along the back of his neck grew more nettling, the fingers colder.

Something was out of whack here. He had no idea what, but something . . .

When the riders were within thirty yards of the coach and made no move to yield the trail but kept riding straight toward the stage, grim, vaguely challenging looks on their five faces, Prophet drew back on the team's ribbons.

The coach squawked and rattled to a halt.

Again, the horses stomped and blew. They were close enough to town now that they could probably smell the hay and water awaiting them. The off-front puller lifted its head and loosed a protesting whinny. Its hitch mate angrily shook its head.

Twenty yards beyond them, two of the five riders stopped their horses in the middle of the trail. One rider rode off the trail to Prophet's left. Two others rode off the trail to his right.

One of the two men facing him on the trail said, "Where's the girl?"

Prophet hesitated. He wasn't sure how to answer the question. Trouble had come to call, but it wasn't showing its true colors so he had no idea how to address it.

"What girl?" he said, though he wasn't sure why. Maybe he was just trying to buy enough time to find out what all this—two sets of riders stopping him before he reached town—was about.

"What girl?" exclaimed the man on the trail, rising up in his saddle and shoving his gray-mustached face toward Prophet, wielding his heavy chin as though it were a weapon. His frosty blue eyes blazed beneath the high crown of his cream Stetson. "What girl, my ass!"

He turned to one of the riders just now approaching the stage on Prophet's right. "Kendrick—who's inside?"

Kendrick leaned out from his saddle, peering into the coach from roughly ten yards away. "I can't see no one in there, boss!"

"No one!" shouted the gray-mustached gent, by at least twenty years the oldest man of the five. "Check the money drawer!"

Prophet's heart drummed. He rested his right hand on the stock of the rifle in his lap. The middle-aged man sitting a black horse on the trail straight out in front of him loudly racked a cartridge into his own Winchester, snapped the rifle's butt to his shoulder, and aimed at Prophet, yelling, "Get your hands off the long gun, you son of a bitch!"

"Looks like three dead bodies on the stage roof, Boss!" shouted the rider riding up to the coach on Prophet's left. He was positioned over the bounty hunter's left shoulder, so that Lou could see him only in the far periphery of that eye. "None of 'em looks the girl's size, though."

Staring down the barrel of his cocked Winchester, "Boss" shouted, "I told you to take your hand off that rifle, mister!"

Prophet stared back at him. He had him dead to rights. He removed his hand from the neck of the Winchester.

"Check the slide box in the undercarriage!" Boss ordered.

The man slipped off his horse to Prophet's right, and, keeping a hand on one of the two six-shooters bristling on his hips, and one eye on Prophet, he strode over to the side of the carriage and dropped down out of Prophet's sight.

Prophet's heart slammed harder against his ribs as he stared down the barrel of the cocked Winchester aimed at his head. Sweat trickled down his back beneath his shirt. The money wasn't in the strongbox. After he and Mary had counted it, Prophet had put it back in his saddlebags. He'd placed the saddlebags in the rear luggage boot, where he intended for it to remain until he found out who it rightfully belonged to. It would have galled him no end to turn the money over to owlhoots.

Prophet couldn't see the man from his position atop the coach, but he heard a clinking sound as the man rattled the strongbox's handle. A sudden blast caused the coach's team as well as Prophet to lurch with a start. There was a heavy, metallic thud. The man to his right had shot open the hidden drawer and pulled out the strongbox.

Prophet looked at the older man aiming the rifle at him. "If you gents'll just identify yourselves, we could probably iron all this out. There wouldn't be no cause for shootin' irons or harsh words."

"Shut up!" Boss ordered.

"Now, see?" Prophet said. "There wouldn't be no need for that kinda talk!"

"I know who he is, Boss," said the man to Prophet's left, pointing up at the bounty hunter. "That's Delmer Cates. One of Creighton's riders!"

Prophet looked at the man who'd just wrongly identified him. "The hell I am!"

"Cates, eh?" Boss said, curling his mustached lip back from his long, yellow front teeth. "Where's the girl, Cates?"

"I am not Delmer Cates!" Prophet yelled, incensed. "The name's Prophet. Lou Prophet. I am not nor ever *have been* Delmer Cates. Wouldn't know Mr. Cates from Adam's off-ox!"

"The money ain't here, Boss!" The bellowing yell had risen from Prophet's right, where he'd heard the heavy thud of the strongbox hitting the ground. When the man on that side backed away from the coach, Prophet saw him drawing both his pistols. "Strongbox is empty!"

"Cates, you son of a bitch!" shouted the older gent.

The rifle belched smoked and flames. Prophet had anticipated the bullet. He'd jerked sharply left just in time for the bullet to miss him by a hairsbreadth. He'd felt it curl the air off his right earlobe. A half second later, he heard it spang off a rock back along the trail behind him.

Prophet snapped his own Winchester to his shoulder, cocking it, and fired just as the old gent's black thoroughbred curveted sharply, causing Prophet's bullet to cleanly miss the man and puff dust along the trail beyond him. The stage's two lead horses loosed sharp whinnies and reared at the rifle blasts, scissoring their front hooves in the air above their heads.

In the corner of his left eye, Prophet saw the man who'd called him Cates raise his own rifle. Prophet twisted around in the coach's seat, levering another round into the Winchester, and hastily lined up his sights on the man bearing down at him.

He fired one blink ahead of his opponent, his bullet punching through the left side of the man's neck, causing the dead man's rifle to swing forward of Prophet and send his own bullet into the upper-right chest of the man sitting his horse on the trail by the older gent.

The man who'd taken the stray bullet yelped like a coyote caught in a trap. His horse whinnied and pitched.

At the same time, the coach's two lead horses slammed their front hooves back to the ground and wheeled sharply right. Since there was no brake securing the left-front wheel, the carriage sprang forward without resistance. Prophet flew backward, pivoting left, as men ahead of him and to his right shouted furiously and triggered lead into the air around him.

The bounty hunter threw his left hand out to grab something with which to break his fall but clutched only air. That's probably what saved him from taking one of the bullets still stitching the air around where he'd just been. He bounced off the coach's left panel, twisting around to face the carriage itself, and fell nearly headfirst toward the ground.

Chapter 15

Prophet watched the trail slam toward him in a yellow-brown blur.

He avoided a painful meeting with the backside of the front wheel by the width of a chin whisker but that did not mean his landing was without pain.

He hit the ground on his right shoulder. His right temple followed his shoulder. And then all went gray and fuzzy, bells ringing in his ears. When his vision clarified, he saw a pair of glassy eyes staring at him.

The eyes blinked once, twitched.

They were the eyes of the fast-dying man Prophet had shot in the neck.

Blood geysered from the hole in the man's neck as he continued to stare in horror at Prophet, his body jerking convulsively, as though he were trying to fight off the devil tickling his toes.

"Good luck," Prophet groused, pushing himself onto hands and knees and looking around, wondering why bullets weren't chewing into him.

Then he saw why.

The stage was barreling off to the south behind the runaway team. The three remaining riders were galloping after it, firing their rifles from their saddles. Two were, that was. The older gent just now got his thoroughbred settled down and was galloping far to the rear of the other two, slapping his horse's rump with his rein ends.

In the chaos of the shooting and the pitching horses, they must not have seen Prophet tumble off the coach. He watched the stage and the three riders dwindle into the distance. He blinked and wagged his head, trying to shake the cobwebs from his brain. The riders wouldn't be fooled for long, he had to assume. Soon, they'd realize their mistake and head back.

His pulse quickening with the urgency of his predicament, Prophet looked around. Slight relief touched him. His Winchester lay only a few yards away. It, too, had tumbled out of the driver's boot. The Richards was still hanging from his right arm, as he'd had it slung behind his back, as usual, when the bullets had started to fly.

He might be on foot, but at least he was armed.

Prophet pushed heavily to his feet. His neck and shoulder ached brutally. His right arm felt heavy and numb, his fingers tingling. He walked over, bent down with a grunt, feeling as though his lower spine were going to snap and poke through his battered hide, and scooped his Winchester out of a clump of buckbrush.

He brushed off the rifle with his gloved right hand.

He looked around. He knew from previous trips to the area that there was an ancient river canyon among the buttes rising in the north. He couldn't see the cut from here, but he remembered it was only a half a mile or so from the trail.

Casting a backward glance at where the stage and his pursuing attackers had disappeared, he began striding north. Limping, rather. His hip had taken a good bit of the tumble, and it squawked now like an injured dog.

The hip loosened up a little the more he moved so that about fifty yards away from where he'd started, he was able to jog. It wasn't a fast jog, but a slow one, and he still favored his right leg, but at least he wasn't a sitting duck and he had a chance of making it to cover before the riders came back to finish him.

He cast frequent quick glances over his shoulder. Ominously, it was still and quiet to the south. All he could see were rolling prairie and distant, cone-shaped buttes. The sun beat down.

Ahead he could see only buttes and blond prairie grass for another five minutes of jogging. Then he saw the cut. It began as a thin, dark line—sort of like a giant black snake laid out on the ground ahead and slightly right. Prophet quickened his pace, cursing at the increased hitch in his gait.

Ahead, the dark line grew wider until it became a broad, serpentine gash in the earth. The gash grew wider and wider as he approached. The far slope appeared, vertically streaked with erosions and pocked with large rocks and a few boulders.

He stopped at the cut's southern lip and found himself staring down at the deep ravine that some ancient river had carved through the prairie longer ago than Prophet could begin to imagine, to drain the Black Hills. The old canyon curved away to both sides of the aching, winded bounty hunter, meandering along the bases of several chalky, badly eroded, rock-strewn buttes on its south side.

Where Prophet stood, the cut was about seventy yards wide, but he could see that its width varied widely to both the east and west.

Distant hoof thuds sounded behind him. He whipped his head around to see the three riders galloping toward him from a quarter mile away, hunkered low over their horses' necks.

Prophet stepped over the lip of the ravine and hunkered down on the steeply declining slope. He doffed his hat, set it beside him, and snaked the barrel of his Winchester over the ravine's tablelike edge. He rammed a fresh round into the chamber and aimed toward the men galloping toward him.

They were spread out in a ragged line. He recognized the older gent by his high-crowned Stetson and his black thoroughbred. He lined up his sights on the bobbing, jerking image of the older gent.

Cut off the head of the snake, kill the snake. He took up the slack in his trigger finger.

The Winchester lurched in his hands. Roared. Flames lapped from the barrel.

The older gent jerked back in his saddle, whipping up his reins.

His horse slowed, curveted, bucked. The older gent tumbled out of his saddle with a yell that Prophet could hear above the rataplan of the other two riders, who continued racing toward the ravine. They raised their Winchesters. The long guns sprouted smoke and flames. The bullets thumped into the tableland near Prophet, pluming dust and ripping up grass as the reports reached his ears.

Prophet winced as he racked another round, lined up his sights once more, and fired. The bullet sailed wide of its mark. The two riders checked down their mounts, slipped out of their saddles, lay belly down in the grass, and commenced firing at Prophet.

The bullets thumped into the ground around him. One scratched a burn across his right cheek. He sucked a sharp breath through gritted teeth.

He could maybe hold them off from here, but he was getting low on ammunition.

Time to pull out . . .

He pulled his head and rifle down into the canyon, grabbed his hat, and started moving down the slope. It was a steep decline. To keep from falling, he descended at an angle across the slope's shoulder, holding his rifle in his right hand, gouging his heels into the chalky alkaline soil in which little grew except sparse patches of short, wiry yellow grass. From above he heard the shouts of his pursuers. They were running toward the canyon.

Prophet quickened his pace. He was a sitting duck here on the slope with no cover. With each downward stride, his right hip felt as though a spike were being hammered into it. His neck was sore. It felt like a warm hand was gripping it, occasionally giving it a painful squeeze.

"Crazy damn trip," he told himself aloud, hearing three men shouting now on the rim. "Last stage to Jubilee, my ass. Last stage to hell, more like. And I ain't even found Lola yet!"

"There!" a man shouted from above.

Prophet whipped a look over and above his right shoulder. A hatted head and pointing finger appeared on the lip. Prophet recognized the high-crowned Stetson of the older gent, whom Prophet had not put out of commission as he'd intended. Probably only winged him.

The older gent angled a rifle down toward Prophet, who lurched into a run. The rifle cracked. The bullet screeched over Prophet's left shoulder and gave a nasty squeal as it hammered into the floor of the canyon now about thirty yards below him, kicking up dust.

Prophet lurched slightly with a start. His right boot got tangled up with the left one.

He fell forward, hit the slope, and rolled.

More rifles cracked above him. Bullets plunked into the slope around him.

He rolled wildly, unable to break his fall. The Richards, slung over his right shoulder, beat him about the head and back. He'd dropped his rifle when he'd hit the slope, and it slithered down the slope behind him like a large, metallic snake bearing down on him.

He struck the canyon floor with a heavy thud and a grunt, dust rising around him. His rifle slid down to smack him in the chest then fall to the canyon floor to his left.

"This just ain't my day," Prophet said.

Above him, the rifles continued to crack. Bullets continued to screech around him, thumping into the slope above or onto the canyon floor to his left. He looked up, grateful to see that the slope itself, which he was lying snug against the bottom of, shielded him from the shooters. As long as he didn't lift his head more than a foot or stretch a body part out more than a foot to his left, he'd be all right.

For now.

He didn't have long to savor his slight good fortune. While the shooting suddenly stopped, above him came the sounds of footsteps and a man's grunts. Gravel clattered and dirt and sand made soft ticking sounds.

Prophet glanced cautiously up over the cutbank, which had been eroded out of the bottom of the slope, to gaze up the incline. Two of the shooters were running toward him, following his own route across the canyon wall, loosing dirt and gravel in their wakes, chaps flapping against their legs. Neither was the older gent. The two young firebrands were separated by about twenty yards.

The nearer one was getting close to Prophet. Damn close.

Prophet drew his head down beneath the cutbank.

He grabbed the Richards, whose pummeling had left him further scratched, scraped, and bruised. He closed both hands around the gut-shredder, held it close against his chest, slowly thumbing one of the rabbit-ear hammers back to full cock.

Above him, the grunts and boot thumps and spur chings grew louder. A stone tumbled down over the cutbank, dropped past his face to land on the canyon floor six inches off his left shoulder.

Lou jerked to a sitting position, raising his shotgun.

The man pursuing him stopped ten feet away, straight up the cutbank. His eyes snapped wide as they found Prophet and the savage-looking two-bore.

"Dang!" the man screamed with a start, bringing up his Winchester.

Prophet gave a grim half smile as he squeezed the Richards's trigger.

The buckshot tore into the man's chest and flung him up and back against the canyon slope. He scrunched up his face, lost his hat, and dropped his rifle.

As the man began to roll down the slope toward Prophet, dead or fast dying, the bounty hunter grabbed his Winchester and took off running down canyon, hearing the thump of the dead man's body hitting the canyon floor where he himself had been lying only seconds before.

"Son of a bitch!" bellowed the other man on the canyon wall.

Prophet stopped and whipped around, sliding the Richards back behind him. The second man was near the bottom of the slope, still awkwardly hot-footing it down the canyon wall. Prophet raised his Winchester to his hip and fired three quick rounds.

The man on the slope stumbled, fell, regained his feet, and kept coming, cursing.

The older gent opened up from the canyon's rim. The bullets hammered the canyon floor around Prophet. One blew his hat off. He wheeled again and, scooping the battered topper up off the ground with a curse, resumed his run down canyon. A couple more slugs plunked into the ground around him, one cracking into a sun-bleached chunk of ancient driftwood.

The gunfire fell silent after that.

Still Prophet ran, following the course of the ancient riverbed as it doglegged to his left. He ran hard, scissoring his arms and legs, the Richards jostling down his back. He needed cover, but, looking around, he saw none. As he continued to run, however, another, smaller canyon opened before him, in the middle of the main canyon floor.

A second canyon inside the first one?

When he got to the edge of the second cut, he saw that that was exactly what it was. A secondary canyon roughly twenty feet wide and with chalky, crenelated walls. Its eroded floor was roughly ten feet below Prophet, who looked for a way down, as the secondary canyon appeared to continue to follow the main one, possibly offering better cover.

Voices rose behind Prophet, echoing. He looked behind to see two men running toward him along the canyon floor—the older gent and the last young one. The older gent held back a little, running stiffly, limping.

"There he is!" the younger man shouted, pointing.

Prophet lunged into another run along the lip of the secondary canyon. He cast his gaze ahead, looking desperately for an easy way into the second cut.

Rifles bellowed behind him, the reports echoing shrilly off the main canyon's walls. A bullet screeched off a rock to Prophet's right. Suddenly, he felt as though he'd been smacked in the right temple with an iron fist. He staggered left, toward the secondary cut.

The ground dropped away beneath him. He fell, rolled, dropped freely for maybe one second, and landed on something solid with a deep grunt as his breath was punched out of his lungs.

He lay in grinding agony.

Then, as the cobwebs began to clear a little, he realized he'd just tumbled into the second canyon.

He heard himself groaning, writhing. Remembering the two men pursuing him, he forced his eyes open. Each lid weighed ten pounds. A dark crevice shone in the wall beside him. Instinctively, like a wounded animal, he crawled toward the assumed safety of the gap.

He had no choice. There was nowhere else to go.

He crawled into the gap, desperately clawing at the ground with his hands, gouging at it with the toes of his boots. The top of the narrow gap raked his head and shoulders. Cold dirt and pebbles rained down on him, slithered under his shirt collar and down his back.

He squeezed his eyes closed against it. It was too dark to see anything, anyway.

A snug fit. Damned snug. Probably snakes in here. He was in no condition to investigate. He was probably a dead man, anyway. His thoughts were quarter-formed. Only his animal instinct for survival was working now though the raw fear of death in a tight, dark place made his heart hammer.

He could smell cool earth and roots and stone.

He could also smell the copper smell of blood. Taste its coppery taste on his tongue.

Consciousness bled away, as though a heavy hand had been placed over his face, pinching off his wind.

He rested his forehead on his left forearm.

Darkness.

Chapter 16

When he awoke he wasn't sure if he were awake or dead.

He couldn't be dead because it was doubtful that dead people felt this bad. Did they feel anything at all?

That's not how he'd heard it was. He'd heard you didn't feel anything. At least, you didn't feel pain.

Unless you'd made a pact with the devil, as Prophet himself had done. Then you felt hot, right? Hot and overworked.

He'd sold his soul for a good time in his remaining years, as a reward of sorts for all the hell he'd endured during the war. In hell, you suffered deeply, but it was supposed to be hot there, and Prophet wasn't hot here. He couldn't smell the burning tang of butane, either. He couldn't hear the screams of his fellow condemned swimming or treading water in that burning butane, either.

Wouldn't there be the bright orange of leaping flames?

Wouldn't he have a shovel in his hands? That had

been part of the deal. In return for Ole Scratch giving him a good long time to drink and screw and gamble and generally stomp with his tail up on this side of the sod, Prophet was supposed to shovel coal throughout eternity, keeping the giant stoves stoked that boiled the propane that the poor devilish souls were condemned to swim in until hell froze over or time ran out—whichever came first.

Shoveling coal had been part of the bargain. A foolish bargain, maybe, but then, Prophet hadn't been in his right head in the years following the war. He probably still wasn't, but that was another matter . . .

No, dead folks didn't feel the kind of physical agony he was feeling now.

Dark here. Could be his grave. If so, he'd been buried alive!

His heart lurched at the possibility of that. He'd dreamt such nightmares. But then he remembered the fall and the abrupt landing that had crushed the air out of him, and his crawl into what he'd hoped was the safety of a gap. Probably a notch cave that had revealed itself at the base of the secondary canyon's wall.

He lifted his head from his forearm, which, he realized, was slick and sticky and also crusty. With his own blood. His own partially dried blood that had leaked from the bullet crease in his forehead.

He turned his head to his left. It was dark all around him but it seemed to be a little less dark in that direction. Cool air breathed at him from that direction, as well. He drew a lungful, wincing at the ache in his battered ribs and elsewhere, but feeling minimally refreshed by the air.

But why was it dark? How long had he lain here? Long enough for night to have fallen while he'd been out?

The earth pressed against him from above and below. He felt as though he were in the jaws of a cold, black, giant snake. The earth pressed against his right side, as well. But not from his left. That's where he'd come from.

He saw that his rifle lay against that side. He'd instinctively dragged it into the notch with him. He could feel the Richards rammed taut against his back, between his back and the ceiling of the narrow cave he'd sought safety in. The jaw of the Richards was digging into his back, on the right side about halfway between his shoulder and belt.

He groaned.

Damn, that hurt . . .

He stared toward the notch's opening, fresh air pushing against his face. If it were truly night, and that's what it looked like out there from here, then his two pursuers—the older man and the younger one—must have long since given up on him. If they were out there waiting for him, they'd been waiting a long time.

Nah, they'd most likely given him up for gone or dead.

Only one way to find out.

Prophet dug his fingers into the floor of the notch cave and pushed himself back and sideways, slithering along the ground. The Richards dug deeper into his back, twisting like the knife of a hateful opponent. Prophet grunted again, pushing, crawling, slithering out from his tight confines, loosing dirt and gravel as he did.

His leg came free. Then his waist. Then his shoulders and, finally, his head. He slid the Richards around from his back and breathed a sigh of relief to be rid of that nagging discomfort. He rolled onto his back and took a deep breath of the fresh, cool night air.

Night. It sure was. Prophet lay staring up at a black sky salted with twinkling stars. Just over the rim of the canyon toward what he thought was the southeast kited a sliver of waxing moon. The cool breeze raked across the canyon between the steeply sloping walls.

Somewhere, an owl hooted. From somewhere else came the soft notes of . . . what?

When the breeze lessened a little he heard it again.

The melodic notes of a distant piano.

A piano. He'd be damned.

He lifted his hat, gritted his teeth against the agony in his head. In his right temple, more specifically. He must have caught a ricochet. He touched fingers to his head, felt the crusty blood. Some of it crusted, some of it gooey. Just beneath his hairline. His head felt as though a hammer were inside it, trying to smash his brainpan flat against an imaginary anvil.

He groaned again, gritted his teeth again as he heaved himself to a sitting position.

"What the devil have I got myself into now?" he said, taking his head in his hands.

Who in the hell was the second bunch of riders?

Why in the hell had they tried to kill him?

He tried to remember. To recall all the bits of his conversation with the older gent, all the incidents leading up to this, his sitting here in dire agony. But it was all a jumble in his mind.

He knew only that he couldn't stay out here all night. He wasn't going to do any healing out here. He needed to get the gash in his head tended. He needed a couple of good, stiff shots of whiskey if not the whole bottle. He also needed, if he could hold it down, a plate of food. He hadn't eaten since breakfast.

Steeling himself against the increased agony in his head, he heaved himself to his feet. He picked up his rifle, brushed it off, and looked around. The secondary canyon stretched away on both sides. The southern slope of the primary canyon loomed darkly above, blotting out the stars halfway up to the zenith.

Two slopes to climb. One a good two hundred feet high.

He sighed, looked around again for a relatively easy way out of the secondary ravine. Finding none, and having no idea where one existed . . . *if* one existed . . . he strode off to his left. He supposed he chose left merely because from the right was where trouble had been. He'd walked only a few yards when he saw his hat clinging to a branch poking up out of the sand.

He hadn't thought of the hat. He was glad to have it back, though. He groaned as he bent forward, plucked it off the branch, and then set it gently on his aching head. He shouldered his rifle and continued to walk heavily, stumbling often, along the secondary wash.

When he'd shambled sixty yards or so, he was relieved to see that the floor rose gradually, so that there was only an easy, gradual climb required to reach the base of the primary canyon. He just had to make his way around large chunks of clay and adobelike sand and a few boulders that littered the tonguelike inclination and that had probably washed away from the steeper slopes on both sides of the canyon when the original floor had eroded away and dropped, forming the secondary canyon.

When he reached the base of the primary cut, he sat on a large rock for a breather. He could have sat there all night, but the pain in his head wasn't going away even with the lack of motion, so he again heaved himself to his feet. He looked up at the slope towering above him with dread.

He cursed, moved forward, and began climbing.

By the time he reached the top, he was understandably even more miserable than before. Crawling over the canyon's lip onto the tableland, he slumped against the ground, raking air in and out of his battered lungs, his shirt sweat-basted to his torso. He wasn't sure how long he'd lain there like a dead man, before the piano's melodic notes drifted to him once more.

He hadn't heard the music since he'd started making his way out of the canyon. It must have stopped for a time. Now it was starting again. He lifted his head, somehow buoyed by the sound not just because it meant people and possibly whiskey and general physical comfort but because it was damned pleasing to the ear . . . even though he was hearing beneath the clang of cracked bells in his ears.

He lifted his head, stared off in the direction of the ragged melody.

The moon was higher now. It shed its wan, milky light on the rooftops of Jubilee, which was a murky collection of small, bulky shadows gathered on the prairie maybe two hundred yards straight southeast of him. The piano strains were the only sounds emanating from the town. He couldn't see any flaming oil pots or lamplit windows. But, then, he was looking at it from its northern flank. When he got closer he'd no doubt spy signs of habitation.

And, hopefully, signs of a bottle of whiskey, a plate of food, maybe a sawbones, a comforting doxie, and a warm feather mattress . . .

All right, maybe the doxie and the feather mattress were too much to hope for. But he'd find the tangleleg and some food, by God . . .

Of course, as he dragged his boot toes toward the dark town, following the continuing strains of the soft piano music, it occurred to him that he might very well find his assailants in Jubilee, as well. The thought didn't deter him, however. He needed a sawbones, whiskey, and food, and he'd just have to find a way to elude the wolves while pursing those three needs.

Shouldn't be too hard, it being night . . .

He walked for what seemed a long time but probably wasn't much more than fifteen or twenty minutes. Abandoned shacks and shanties and falling-down stock pens shoved up around him. There was an old windmill and several privies. The windmill's two remaining blades creaked like a dying old witch when the breeze picked up.

No lights shone in any of the shanties. The only sounds were the piano, the windmill, the breeze, and rodents rustling around in the knee-high grass.

Several times Prophet stumbled over unseen trash, old planks, and discarded tools, including a hay rake hidden in the brush beneath his boots.

Distantly, coyotes yammered.

He continued to follow the piano chords to the rear of a bank of large buildings. The buildings doubtless fronted Jubilee's main street, predictably called Jubilee Street. The structures were mostly built of log with a few of board-and-batten and one of stone. The stone one was the bank, Prophet remembered. Aside from the bank, all of the structures he could see looked rickety and abandoned, weeds growing tall and ragged along their foundations. Even a few small trees.

He stole up the badly trash-littered gap between two of the buildings and stopped, finding himself staring out onto Jubilee Street, as he'd expected.

"Christ," he said, shunting his gaze from right to left along the broad thoroughfare.

Or what had once been a thoroughfare. Now it resembled the deserted canyon he'd just left. The buildings on both sides of the street were dark and haggard. Weeds grew up between the rotted slats of the boardwalks fronting the old business establishments. Windows and doors were boarded up. Some windows had been broken out. Awning roofs sagged severely.

Jubilee Street resembled the main street of a ghost town, which it obviously was.

Prophet walked a few paces to his right, surveyed the front of the bank. The large front window was also boarded over. Even the bank was closed.

The piano music had faded but Prophet turned now to stare east along the street. That's the direction from which the music had come. There was a light up that way. It came from an oil pot set out on the street before one of the businesses. There also appeared to be a light in the window of the building the oil pot fronted. A lone horse was tied to a hitchrack.

Prophet pressed two fingers to his head, trying in vain to quell the ceaseless throb of the bullet burn. His feet were getting heavier. His knees weaker.

He stumbled along like an old drunk as he made his way along the street. The smell of the burning oil laced the breeze. Smoke fluttered around the pot and on the boardwalk fronting the Lazy Day Saloon.

At least one saloon was still open. Nothing else appeared to be. The last time he'd ridden through Jubilee, the Lazy Day and the Three-Legged Dog had been the town's two remaining watering holes. Now there was only the Lazy Day, it appeared. There was no light on up the street where the Three-Legged Dog had once been.

Prophet stumbled up past the oil pot and the lone horse toward the covered boardwalk, saw the large, badly faded sign mounted above the boardwalk's sagging awning which read LAZY DAY with *Day* tilted at an angle. A bullet had punched a ragged hole through the tail of the *y*.

The horse gave a curious whicker as Prophet shambled up onto the boardwalk and stopped to peer over the batwings. A couple of lanterns offered a watery amber light that couldn't compete with the saloon's inky shadows.

The bar ran down the room on Prophet's left. There were a dozen or so tables and chairs to his right. One man sat at one of the tables, his head on his arms. He was snoring softly. At the rear, a staircase climbed to the second story. A piano sat near the base of the stairs, and just as Prophet focused on it, gentle notes began to ebb once more.

That's when he saw that someone was sitting behind it. He could barely make out the player in the weak light angling that way from the lanterns. The player's head bobbed slowly as the notes drifted gently, melodically through the air. Prophet recognized the tune, "The Willows of Old Ohio."

Prophet smiled as the notes soothed him.

He stumbled forward through the batwings and into the saloon, trying to walk lightly so as not to startle the piano player. He wanted the song to continue. He took another step, then another, setting each heavy boot down carefully. He took one more step, vaguely angling toward the sanctuary of a near table and a chair, but then his right knee buckled.

Then the other one buckled. Both knees hit the floor with a thunderous *boom!*

"Oh!" said the piano player with a start, sending a loud, resounding off-key note bolting about the room.

"Who's there?" a woman called, frightened.

Prophet sagged forward on hands and knees, the saloon's dark floor pitching around him. He heard the bark of chair legs scraping across the floor. Sharp heels stomped toward him. He smelled her before he saw her. He thought he recognized the scent—a hint of raspberry blossoms and lime.

She stopped before him, a safe six feet away. He saw only the billowing folds of her dark green gown, the hem edged with white lace. He saw the toes of her high-heeled, gold-buckled, black patent shoes.

"My God, what's wrong?"

The voice was familiar.

No. Couldn't be.

Prophet lifted his head, wincing against the hammer smashing incessantly against his brain. He stared up at her, squinting, trying to make her out.

"L-Lola?"

Chapter 17

"Oh my God," the woman said, shocked, taking a quick step forward. *"Lou?"*

"Lou who?" came a man's voice, slurring the words. The question had come from the man who'd been slumped across a table to Prophet's right, against the far wall.

Lola dropped to her knees before Prophet. She sandwiched his face in her hands, shoved hers up close to his until he could see the watery light glinting in her soft, blue eyes. "Oh, Lou!" she cried half in joy, half in anguish.

"Lou who?" said the drunk again, more persistently this time.

"Oh, shut up, Buster!" Lola said, keeping her eyes on Prophet, raking her eyes across his bullet-torn temple. "Lou, my God, what happened to you?"

"Had a little trouble . . . out on the trail." Prophet stared at her in amazement. "Lola . . . it is you. My God!"

It was Lola, all right. Whoever she was now, she was still Lola Diamond to him. She looked very much the same as when he'd last seen her several years ago. Still beautiful despite a slight tightening of the skin around her eyes and mouth. Maybe the eyes were a little less sparkling than before, a little more jaded. Maybe she was even prettier for time's tempering of youth's raw blush.

"It is me, Lou. It is me. Come on. We have to get you upstairs."

Prophet smiled as he gazed into her eyes. "You're even more beautiful than before, Lola. I didn't think it possible, but, by God, girl . . . er, woman . . . you sure are!"

Despite his physical agony, he couldn't help taking a peek at the well-filled, low-cut bodice, which she wore over a ruffled, equally low-cut white blouse.

Lola gave a throaty chuckle. "You've taken a right big blow to your head, Lou. Obviously." She chuckled again and then turned to where the only other person in the place was now sitting up in his chair, watching them. "Buster, if you're one bit conscious, get over here and help me get Lou upstairs. He's a mite more man than I can handle on my own."

"You managed before . . . a time or two, as I recall." Prophet grinned at her, winked.

Lola blushed. She gave a grunt as, wrapping Prophet's right arm around her neck, she hoisted him to his feet. Prophet couldn't offer much help. His knees were weak. Likely the result of pain, blood loss, overexertion, and lack of food. But it was whiskey he craved the most.

"Whoever runs this dump," he said, glancing toward the bar, "you think they'd sell me a bottle?"

"Since I'm the one who runs this dump, I reckon I would."

Prophet blinked. "You?"

"Yep." She turned toward where the drunk was stumbling toward them. "Buster, hurry!"

"This is all the better I can do," Buster said, walking like a knock-kneed, old, long-legged horse ready for the glue factory. He was as tall as Prophet but he was whipcord thin with a pronounced forehead and chin and bulging, drink-bleary brown eyes. His brown patch beard was liberally sprinkled with salt.

He stumbled over a chair, nearly fell, then came around to Prophet's other side and wrapped the bounty hunter's left arm around his neck. "What'd you say your name was?" Buster asked as he and Lola began leading Prophet to the stairs at the back of the room.

"Lou Prophet, Buster. The pleasure's mine."

"Lou Prophet. Damn, I think I've heard that name," Buster said, tripping over another chair.

"Buster, be careful!" Lola cajoled him.

"Lola, how do you know this big fella here?" Buster asked her as they made it to the bottom of the stairs.

"Long story." Lola gave Prophet a sidelong, conspiratorial smile. "Long, long story—eh, Lou?"

"Ain't near long enough for me, girl," Prophet said as he put one foot on the bottom step and, with Lola's and Buster's help, began climbing.

He gave Lola a wink and she returned it. He cast a glance down her corset, into the deep, dark cleavage.

"You still have a brazen eye, bounty hunter." Lola's eyes danced with amusement.

"A brazen eye for beauty."

Lola laughed. So did Buster. They almost fell back down the stairs but then Lola got serious and, grabbing the banister to her right and scolding both men profusely, got them back on an upward climb that, after another near-catastrophe, had them stumbling through the first door on the right of the second-floor hall.

The room was large and well appointed in a feminine manner, with ornate wallpaper and lacy curtains over the two large windows. A thick oriental rug graced the floor, and a wine red canopy anointed the four-poster bed, which was covered with a black, silk, gold-embroidered comforter and large pillows also swathed in silk.

"Holy Christ," Prophet mumbled as Lola and Buster led him to the massive bed. "I didn't know the queen of Merry Ole England was livin' in Jubilee now."

"This is my room," Lola said.

"You sure you want this big ole reprobate in your room, Lola?" Buster sounded astonished.

As they sat Prophet down on the edge of the bed, he narrowed one eye at the drunkard. "Buster, have we met before?"

"I don't think so. I've heard the name before but I don't think we've ever met."

"Then how did you know I was a reprobate?"

"Don't let it make you feel bad," Buster said. "I'm the town drunk."

Prophet snorted.

"Lou, you hush now, and lay back." Lola was pulling the covers down. "You lay here and rest while I get some brandy and heat water so we can stitch that wound in your head before you bleed out."

She reached into a closet, grabbed a man's shirt off a hanger, and laid it on the pillow near Prophet.

"That's so you don't get blood all over my bed, you old reprobate."

She cupped her hand under his jaw and stared down at him with concern. "What happened to you, Lou?"

"I'll tell you about it after you fetch that brandy." Prophet smacked his lips. "Damn, I'm thirsty!" He frowned as he kicked out of his boots and shifted his position on the bed, scooting up to lay his head back on the shirt-covered pillow. "Who'd you say was gonna stitch my head?"

"Me an' Buster are."

"You an' Buster *qualified* to stitch my head?"

"Not tonight, I ain't!" Buster said. He was holding on to one of the posters holding up a corner of the canopy, as though it were the mast of a ship he was clinging to lest he should get swept overboard.

"Buster's an old ranch cook. You know how they are. They're doctor and lawyer and mother and father and peace officer and even sometimes a judge and jury, when it comes to that. He's been Jubilee's only doctor for the past year and a half, since old Doc Baldwin kicked the bucket just down the hall with one of the girls who used to ply the old trade here."

"He died with a smile on his face, though, I'll give him that," Buster said, chuckling but looking peaked.

"Go on downstairs and have a cup of coffee," Lola told the man. "Have two. I'll be down in a minute."

Buster negotiated the gap between the bed and the door as though it were the deck of the ship threatening to toss him into the cold, dark drink. "I think I'd better have three."

"Yeah, I think you'd better," Prophet called to him.

Lola turned to Prophet, who lay staring up at her, deeply puzzled. "Lola . . . ?" He shook his head, so confused that he wasn't sure which question to ask first.

Lola placed two soft fingers on his cracked lips. "You're wondering what I'm doing here—the great actress, Lola Diamond, who had her hat set for the New York stage. What could I possibly be doing in this boil on the devil's backside, running a watering hole? I'll explain it all to you soon, Lou. As soon as we get you stitched up. And I'll tell you why I summoned you here, as well."

"Yeah," Prophet said, letting his heavy lids flutter closed. "All that . . ."

He fell helplessly into a deep, dreamless sleep.

He woke believing he must have fallen asleep in a raspberry patch. He opened his eyes. Lola stood beside the bed, running a cool, wet sponge across his naked chest.

He couldn't feel a stitch of clothes on him. Sliding his gaze down his body he saw that, sure enough, he was naked. Naked and damp, his body glistening dully in the faint, rippling lamplight.

"Shhh," Lola whispered. "All's well, Lou. I'm just giving you a little bath. Make you feel better, cool you off."

Chapter 18

Prophet awakened with his bladder on fire.

He imagined it swelling to the size of an overfilled gut flask, straining its seams. He had to piss like a grizzly bear that had drained a rain barrel before nodding off and had held it all winter.

He tossed the covers aside, dropped his feet to the floor, and looked around. The room was in a shadowy red glow, as though a massive wildfire were raging just outside the room's windows. He wasn't even sure where he was, for his mind was still fogged with sleep. He knew only that he had to drain the dragon before it drained of its own accord.

He leaned down and reached under the bed. His hand found a porcelain pot. He dragged the pot out by its handle, rose from the bed, aimed, and let go.

He lifted his chin to the ceiling and gave a long, ragged sigh as his stream hit the pot with a ping and then a steadily deepening zinging sound as the pot filled.

The door latch clicked. Prophet jerked with a start but kept the stream going. He flung his right hand out, instinctively reaching for a gun though he had no idea where his Peacemaker or Winchester were, then lowered the hand when Lola came in.

Seeing her, it all came to him in a rush. The stagecoach, Mary, the ambush at Porcupine Station, the notch cave . . .

"Sorry to interrupt," Lola said, setting a food tray on the dresser by the door then walking over to him as he continued to fill the thunder mug. She smiled down at his workings.

"A lady would avert her gaze," Prophet said.

"I'm no lady," Lola said.

"Is that the sun setting out there? Have I slept all the way since *last night*?"

"Last night?" Lola snorted. "You slept all through yesterday, last night, and today!"

His head no longer ached. At least, not near as badly as before. He could feel the pinch and rake of the stitches that Buster had sewn into his temple, closing the notch. He only vaguely remembered that—both Buster and Lola crouching over him while Buster, bright eyed from coffee but still a mite tipsy from tangleleg, had sutured closed the wound. Prophet had slugged down half a bottle of brandy and passed out.

"You sit back down," she said. "Are you hungry? I brought you some bread and stew. I also have coffee and brandy."

Prophet rubbed his belly. "Yeah, I reckon I could eat a bite. Now that I think on it, I'm right hungry. As empty as a dead man's boot, in fact."

Lola set the tray on his lap. On the tray was a wooden bowl filled with steaming beef stew swimming in thick, brown gravy showing the whites of chopped potatoes, the orange of carrots, and the green of beans. A plate containing two slices of grainy brown bread sat beside the bowl. There was also a tin cup filled with coffee and a corked whiskey bottle.

"Holy cow," Prophet said. "I didn't know you could cook. Didn't know that was in the actress's bag of talents."

"I had to learn, after coming here," Lola said, popping the cork on the bottle and splashing a goodly portion into the coffee. "I have a garden out back. It's so dry around here it's tough to keep it growing without hauling water from the rain barrel two, three times a day. But Roy always liked his vegetables, so I tended the garden for him."

Prophet dug into the stew, dipping the bread into the gravy as he ate with his fork, following up each forkful with a bite of the bread. Lola sat on the edge of the bed beside him.

"Who's Roy?" Prophet asked her.

"My husband."

He jerked a wide-eyed look of shock at her.

"Don't choke, Lou. Yes, I married."

Prophet glanced at the door, a pang of consternation joining his other various miseries.

Lola chuckled. "Don't worry, he's not about to kick the door in, Lou. While I'm sure you're accustomed to that sort of thing, he's totally incapable."

Prophet gave a sheepish shrug while arching a quizzical brow.

"Roy is dead."

"I'm sorry, Lola." Prophet swallowed a mouthful of stew and said, "Hearin' that you got yourself hitched is even more surprising than finding you here in hell. Er . . . Jubilee, I reckon it's called, though back along the trail I found myself feelin' like I was headed fer hell."

"Hell is a good name for this place now. I'm one of the last few folks still residing here. There's me and Tad Demry, who runs the stagecoach station, and Demry's lone hostler, Buster O'Brien."

"A hostler and a sawbones," Prophet said. "Buster's right talented." He shoved in another forkful of food, chewed. "How did you come to marry this Roy feller?"

Lola looked off for a time, sighed, then walked over to where a small liquor cabinet hung on a wall. Glasses lined the two upper shelves, and three cut glass decanters lined the lower one. The decanters were empty, but Lola grabbed a glass off the shelf, returned to the bed where Prophet continued to eat, watching her, and poured whiskey into her glass.

He'd seen that look on a pretty woman's face before. The look of a run of bad luck and broken dreams, hopes unfulfilled.

Prophet's heart ached for the girl. Woman, rather. She was a girl no longer, but a woman who was running out of options.

She sat back down on the edge of the bed, sipped from the glass, and set the glass on her thigh.

"I was working in Cheyenne." She glanced at Prophet, giving a wan smile. "Never quite made it to San Francisco or New York."

"Few do, Lola," Prophet said, setting his fork down. He'd had enough. Besides, he wanted to give his old friend his full attention. "Those are faraway places. Ain't no shame in not makin' it to the top. Few are cut out for it. I reckon I should know that much."

"I'm not complaining," Lola said. "Nothing quite so unattractive as a failed actress whining about not being ushered around on the arms of royalty. I met Roy there, in Cheyenne. He'd come to a few of my shows. He traveled to Cheyenne every couple of months on business. He took me to dinner a few times.

"His wife had died a couple of years ago, and he was living here in Jubilee, running the Lazy Day, and he was lonely. He offered his hand and, realizing I wasn't as talented as I'd once thought I was, and had become the age when I was probably soon to be culled from the saloon's herd of dancers, I accepted."

She looked at Prophet quickly. "Not that that's the only reason I married Roy. He was a good, sweet man. Very kind. Very gentle. And he gave me a good home here . . . until he died eight months ago. Stroke, Buster thought. Roy hung on for a day and then he died quietly in my arms."

"I'm very sorry, Lola."

She shrugged. "I reckon I've become accustomed to hard luck. Anyway, I've stayed on here, not having anywhere else to go. Hardly anyone lives here anymore, but business is still good enough now and then, with passing trail traffic, to keep me going. It's not to my advantage that the stage line is pulling out, of course, but I'll make do. My overhead is low."

Prophet reached up and caressed her shoulder with his big right hand. "Why did you call me here, Lola?"

She sighed, turned her head to kiss his hand on her shoulder. She looked at Lou again, and her eyes were cast with fear. "Trouble, Lou. The kind I was hoping you could solve, but now . . . now I know who you tangled with. It should have occurred to me when you came in later that same night as Vance Dunbar came through with a bullet in his arm, but . . . for some reason I didn't put you and him together."

Prophet squeezed her shoulder gently. "Lola, what is it?"

On the street outside, a horse whinnied. It had seemed to come from outside the saloon.

"That's strange," Lola said, frowning at the curtained window that had turned dark now since the sun had finished setting. "I don't usually get any business on weeknights. None besides Buster and maybe the men from the—"

"Help me!" a girl's pleading cry rose from the street. *"Someone . . . please, help!"*

Prophet jerked his head up.

"Oh my!" Lola said, rising from the bed. "That's a girl. I didn't think there were any girls left in Jubilee."

Prophet slid the tray onto the bed beside him. "I recognize that voice."

As though she hadn't heard him, Lola strode quickly to the door. "You stay where you are, Lou. You're in no condition to be getting out of bed. I'll see to the girl . . . whoever she is," Lola added as she left the room.

"Someone, please help me!" Mary called again from the street. "Is anyone there?"

Her voice was filled with anguish.

Heart thudding, Prophet dropped his feet to the floor, heaved himself out of bed. His head swam, the pain in his temple kicking up again. He felt disoriented and weak, a little sick to his gut. But he had to get outside and help Mary.

Stumbling around, he found his clothes neatly piled

on a shelf in a large, oak armoire standing against the wall opposite the bed. His guns were in there, too—the Peacemaker and shell belt, his Winchester and scattergun.

He stepped into his balbriggans then shrugged into his shirt and drew his freshly washed and dried denims up his legs. He could hear Lola striding across the wooden floor downstairs, heading for the batwings, but now only silence rose from the street.

Prophet stomped into his boots and then, strapping his pistol belt around his waist, headed out of the room, sucking a sharp breath through gritted teeth when pain lanced through his head from the bullet tear in his temple.

The narrow, murky hall pitched around him.

He steadied himself with one hand on the wall and then hurried over to the stairs. As he dropped down the steps, holding on to the railing, he could hear Lola's voice outside. It was accompanied by the thuds of several horses and the loud voices of angry men.

As Prophet gained the bottom of the stairs and headed toward the batwings, a man outside loudly ordered, "Just leave her where she is, Mrs. Knudsen. She's goin' with us and there ain't no ifs, ands, or buts about it!"

"Oh, there's a few, I think!" Prophet said, pushing through the batwings and cocking his .45.

Chapter 19

Prophet stepped forward to the edge of the boardwalk as Lola dropped to a knee beside Mary, who was on both knees in the street, beside a lathered, saddled horse that had obviously been ridden a long ways at a full gallop. The horse gave an anxious whinny and, frightened by the three riders riding up behind it, sashayed hard to its left, then scampered away, trailing its reins along the ground.

Now Prophet had an unobstructed view of the three riders as they sat their horses about ten feet behind Lola and Mary, who lifted her head toward Prophet and said, "John Leonard no longer works for my father, Lou! He works for Sand Creighton now!"

"That's neither here nor there, Miss Dunbar," said Leonard, who sat his own lathered horse in the middle of the three-man pack. He held a Winchester carbine across his saddlebow. "The fact is, you belong to Mr. Creighton, and we're taking you back." He jerked his chin at Prophet. "Stay out of this, mister! This ain't none of your damn business, so just stay out of it! You, too, Mrs. Knudsen!"

"I will not!" Lola said, straightening to face the three riders, shielding Mary with her body. "You are not taking this girl anywhere she doesn't want to go. You can tell Mr. Creighton to go to hell. Mary Dunbar is not some pot to be won or lost in a poker game!"

Prophet had no idea what they were talking about. He had no idea the nature of the conflict he found himself at the center of. But he did know whose side he was on.

He stepped down into the street behind the two women and aimed his cocked Colt at Leonard. "Lola, take Mary into the saloon."

Leonard shook his head determinedly and began to raise his carbine's barrel. "That *ain't* gonna happen, old son!"

Prophet took quick aim at Leonard. His Colt roared, flames lapping from the barrel.

Mary cried out. Lola leaped with a start. John Leonard sagged back in his saddle, howling, dropping his Winchester to grab the bloody hole in his upper right arm. The other two riders turned in shock to their wounded leader, all three horses uneasily shifting their weight, looking wide-eyed-wary and ready to run.

"You son of a bitch!" Leonard wailed.

"Lola!" Prophet said.

Lola snapped out of her shocked daze, wrapped an arm around Mary's waist, and pulled the girl to her feet. Mary walked gingerly, limping on her left foot, as Lola led her past Prophet, onto the boardwalk, and into the saloon.

Prophet waved his cocked Peacemaker at the three men sitting their nervous horses before him.

John Leonard was gritting his teeth painfully and glaring at Prophet as he clutched his bloody arm. "Do I need to make it any plainer?" Prophet asked.

Leonard looked from Prophet to the two men on either side of him. They stared in frustration at Prophet, who held his smoking Colt on them.

"Shoot him!" Leonard ordered. "Shoot him right now!"

The man on Leonard's right cursed sharply and jerked up his rifle. Prophet blew him out of his saddle. He hadn't even hit the ground behind his shrieking horse before the man to Leonard's left dropped his own rifle and threw up his gloved hands, palms out.

"No!" he cried. "No! I'm done!"

"You coward!" Leonard barked at him.

The rider glanced once, sheepishly, at Leonard, then turned his horse and galloped off along the street to the west, the dark night quickly consuming him.

Leonard shouted at him, cursing. Leonard's frightened horse turned sharply to follow the other horse to the west, pitching Leonard from the saddle. Leonard gave a shrill cry as he threw up his right arm as though to regain his balance. It didn't happen. As the horse galloped after the other horse and rider, Leonard bounced off his own mount's left hip and plunged into the street.

He rolled several times before piling up against the boardwalk fronting a boarded-up barbershop.

Prophet strode into the street, stared off toward where the last of the three riders had disappeared. He couldn't see the man but he heard the faint rataplan of his galloping horse growing fainter.

Lightning flashed to the north. Thunder rumbled—an especially ominous sound, given the circumstances.

Prophet turned to the saloon, where Lola and Mary had disappeared. Mary's sobs caromed over the batwings. They were drowned by another, louder thunderclap. Prophet looked at where Leonard lay against the boardwalk fronting the barbershop. He was groaning and clutching his arm. He turned to Prophet, began to slide a pistol from the holster on his right thigh.

Prophet aimed his Peacemaker at the man, clicked the hammer back.

That stopped the pistol's slide. Leonard removed his hand from its grips. "I need tendin' here. Get Buster!"

"Shut up."

Prophet walked over to him. "Get up."

"Diddle yourself!"

"I said get up!" Prophet grabbed the man by his wounded arm. Leonard yowled as he gained his feet. He cursed loudly. "Goddamnit, that hurts!"

Prophet grabbed the man's pistol from his holster, shoved it behind his own cartridge belt. "Get inside."

"I need Buster!"

"Get inside or you'll get another bullet. This one to your belly button. See if Buster can doctor that."

Leonard opened his mouth to give a retort but closed it when Prophet poked the barrel of his cocked Peacemaker against his belly button. Leonard looked down at the gun then began staggering toward the saloon. Prophet came up behind him, grabbed the back of his shirt collar, and threw him through the batwings.

Leonard cursed and went shambling through the

door. He hit the floor and rolled twice. He came up on his back, glaring at Mary, who was sitting across from Lola at a table right of the bar.

Mary had been crouched forward over her entwined hands. Lola had given her a blanket; it was draped over her shoulders. Now Mary looked at Leonard, and said, "How could you deceive me like that? How could you take me to him when I thought I was going to my father? We used to be friends—you and me."

"I do what I get paid to do!" Leonard barked. "I was friends with you because your father wanted me to be. To make sure the other, younger men stayed away from you. I quit him because Sand Creighton offered me more!"

Mary shook her head. Tears ran down her cheeks as she gazed befuddledly, heartbroken, at Leonard. "I don't understand any of this."

"That makes two of us," Prophet said. He looked at Lola. "Is this . . . situation . . . why you asked me to come?"

Lola nodded. "I didn't know that you and Mary would be riding the stage together. If I'd known that, I would have explained more in my letter, so that you knew what you were getting into."

"I'd like to know what he was getting into, too," Mary told Lola. "Since I seem to be the one who caused it."

"It was your father who caused it, Mary. I know we haven't met until now, but I run this place. I used to run it with my husband, Roy. I'm Lola Knudsen. I was here the night that your father, Vance Dunbar," she added for Prophet's benefit, "and Sand Creighton sat here drunker than skunks and gambled for three nights in a row."

She looked at Prophet standing just inside the door, his Peacemaker still in his hand, aimed at Leonard, who sat now with his back against the bar. "Mary's father and Creighton have been rival ranchers here for at least as long as Roy could remember. Creighton ranches to the north, Dunbar to the south. They've pretty much crowded out all of the smaller operators. There is only those two, and that's partly why Jubilee has dried up."

Lola returned her gaze to Mary, whose eyes were riveted on the older blonde. "As I was saying, they gambled right here, at this very table, for three nights in a row. The third night, Creighton got on a lucky streak. By eleven o'clock, he'd relieved your father of over six thousand dollars in cash. Then the stakes got even higher."

Lola glanced at Prophet then turned to Leonard, who sat grunting and clutching his arm but also apparently listening to the conversation.

"Oh, for chrissakes, go ahead and tell the girl. What're you waiting for?" Leonard barked.

"Tell me what?" Mary asked.

"Tell her what?" Prophet said, hearing dark dread in his own voice.

"They bet their own ranches," Lola said, keeping her voice low.

Rumbling thunder with occasional, sharp peals punctuated her words. Lightning flashed over the batwings behind Prophet. Fresh, chill air pushed in behind him. It smelled like rain, which he could hear plunking into the thick dust of the street.

"Your father lost his ranch," Lola told Mary, who

sat there staring at the older woman as though she couldn't quite make out what she was saying.

Lola looked down at her lap for a moment, then licked her lips and said, "But your father didn't stop there. He said . . . he said . . ."

"Said what?" Mary urged, leaning across the table, her voice becoming shrill.

"Oh, fer chrissakes," Leonard intoned. "Tell the girl. She has a right to know." He looked at Mary. "Since your pa didn't have nothin' else, he threw you into the pot, to boot. But he put a condition on it. That Creighton accepted you in lieu of the ranch . . . but he had to pay Dunbar thirty thousand dollars."

Leonard laughed cynically, blood running through the fingers of his left hand and dribbling down his arm. "See, Dunbar knew Sand had an interest in a mine up in the mountains. He also knew that interest was worth right around thirty, thirty-five thousand dollars. Another thing he knew was that Creighton didn't really want the Three-Box-D. He put far more value on somethin' else. For several years, even when you was a little girl, Sand Creighton had his eye on Dunbar's li'l Injun princess. Some men—their taste just runs toward the dark-skinned girls."

Leonard laughed caustically. "Dunbar lost the hand but kept his ranch. That's why your father sent your old aunt down to fetch you . . . and thirty thousand dollars from Creighton's Denver bank."

Prophet stared incredulously down at Leonard.

Then he looked at Lola. "Is that true?"

Lola looked at Prophet. Then she looked across the table at Mary, who sat with her head down, hands in her lap, quietly sobbing. Lola reached over and placed a hand on Mary's shoulder while turning again to Prophet and nodding.

"Yes, it's true," she said, tears glittering in her own eyes. "I'm so sorry, Mary."

Leonard turned to Prophet. "Creighton and several other men—all he's got up at the home ranch—are probably on their way here right now. We was all together when we left the ranch, chasin' this polecat who stabbed Sand in the belly, just when he was gettin' ready to bed her, and rode out on a horse. We lost her trail and split up. My group came to town. The others headed toward Dunbar's Three-Box-D. I'd bet the seed bull that by now Sand realizes he's on a cold trail."

Leonard grinned savagely. "He and the others are headed this way, all right. When they get here, you'd best be prepared to turn this girl over to Sand, or there'll be hell to pave and no hot pitch!"

Mary whipped around toward Prophet, her wide eyes bright with terror. "Lou, you can't let them take me. I'll kill myself before I let myself go back to that fat, sick, old Sand Creighton!" Her face crumpled. "How could my father *do* that to me?" She bawled into her hands.

Prophet was about to walk over to her but stopped when hooves thudded in the street behind him.

Mary lifted her head with a horrified gasp.

Leonard laughed.

"Oh, Lou!" Lola said.

"Quick," Prophet said. "Get her upstair—!"

A man's deep, resonant voice rose from the street above the ticking rain and rumbling thunder. "Mary? Are you here, Mary?" A pause. "Mary, it's your father!"

"Oh, Christ!" John Leonard grunted.

Mary stared in silent shock toward the batwings, her lower jaw slowly loosening. Numbly, she lowered her hands to her knees.

Prophet stared out over the batwings as four riders rode up in front of the saloon. He recognized one as the older man who'd stopped the stage the second time and who he now realized was Mary's father, Vance Dunbar. Dunbar's left arm was in a sling, compliments the bullet Prophet had gifted him with. Prophet recognized the other, younger survivor of the original group, who'd helped Dunbar chase Prophet into the secondary canyon.

The other two were new to him—a short, stocky gent with a spade beard and a big half-breed with black hair tumbling down his back in twin, hide-wrapped braids.

Dunbar and the others were talking among themselves as they stared down at the Creighton rider whom Prophet had left dead in the street. The rain was falling steadily now, making silver puddles in the mud. Dunbar and the others wore greased canvas rain slickers, which shone wetly in the weak lamplight emanating from the saloon.

Prophet turned toward Mary. "Your call. What do you want to do?"

"What are my options?" Mary said, though it wasn't a question. It was really more of a statement of fact that she had only one course of action, and that was to confront her father and let the chips fall where they may.

Dunbar turned toward the saloon and called his daughter's name again.

"Here," Prophet said, and pushed through the

batwings. He stepped out onto the front boardwalk, holding his Colt down low by his side.

Dunbar rode straight up to Prophet and stopped. He stared at Prophet from beneath the broad brim of his tall, cream Stetson. The man's face was mostly in shadow but the light shone in his eyes and delineated the gray mustache mantling his thin mouth.

"You again," Dunbar snarled, lifting his Winchester from his saddle pommel.

"Slide that Winchester into its boot," Prophet said. "That's the price of gettin' in here out of the rain."

"What about my daughter?"

"She's in here."

"How do I know that?"

Prophet turned to Mary. She sat twisted around in her chair, half facing him. She stared at the floor in mute shock, her dark eyes round and flat.

Prophet shuttled his gaze back to Dunbar. "You're just gonna have to take my word for it."

He stepped to one side of the batwings.

Chapter 20

Dunbar glanced at the men sitting their horses to each side of him. He looked at Prophet then swung down from his saddle. The others began to dismount but froze when Prophet said, "Only Dunbar. You two are welcome to wait out here with your horses."

"To hell with you," said the man on Prophet's right, and stepped to the ground.

"Yeah, you, big man," said the half-breed, swinging down from his saddle and pointing an angry finger at the bounty hunter. "You put the hogleg down and we'll fight man to man. I'll break you in half, send you home in a bag!"

"Stand down, Curly," Dunbar ordered.

"Maybe some other time, Curly." Prophet wagged his pistol at the rancher. "Leave the Winchester in its sheath."

Dunbar wrinkled a nostril at him then reluctantly slid his rifle into the scabbard strapped to his saddle. He stepped up onto the boardwalk, looked at Prophet disdainfully. "If you're not a Creighton man, who are you?"

"A friend of your daughter."

Dunbar gave a frustrated chuff then peered over the batwings. "Mary!" he said, and pushed through the doors.

Prophet returned the glares of Curly and the other Dunbar rider, both men standing in the rain beside their horses, then followed the rancher inside.

"Mary," Dunbar said again, striding haltingly toward his daughter.

Mary still had her eyes on the floor, as though stricken.

Dunbar looked at John Leonard, who'd heaved himself to his feet and was leaning back against the bar, holding his wounded arm. Dunbar glanced at Prophet, who stood wide of the bar so he could keep everyone inside the saloon in sight while also keeping an eye on the batwings.

"What in hell is going on here?"

"Leonard took your daughter off the stage," Prophet said. "She didn't realize he no longer worked for you."

Dunbar stared at Leonard. Leonard stared back at him, hatless, his chest rising and falling heavily as he breathed.

Showing his teeth like a demented dog, Leonard said, "I was just doin' my job. The deal was Mary went to Sand. For thirty grand. It seems you didn't tell Mary, so she was a little surprised when we got to the Jinglebob. She'll get used to it in time. He's a rich man, Sand is. Far richer than you, Dunbar. He'll likely be showin' up here any ole time now."

Dunbar turned to yell over the batwings, "Keep an eye out for Creighton!"

The rancher turned back to Leonard. "So that's why we saw him headed toward the Three-Box-D." He turned to Mary. "He was after M-Mary. We were headed to town. I figured you'd eventually end up here, Mary. At least, I hoped. We heard riders comin', turned off the trail, watched 'em pass. It was Creighton and four others, all right." Dunbar scrubbed his weathered face with a battered hand. "Christ!"

Mary was staring up at him, her eyes a mixture of rage, despair, and disbelief. "So it's true, eh, Pa? What they told me you did. You lost me in a poker game to Sand Creighton."

Dunbar gave a deep, animal-like groan then whipped the sling from his shoulder, setting his left arm free. He stumbled forward and dropped to his knees before his daughter, doffing his hat and tossing it onto the floor beside him. "Oh God, Mary—please forgive me!"

"It is true . . ."

"It's true, but it was the act of a desperate man!"

Mary shook her head as she gazed at him through tear-shiny eyes. "What are you talking about—a desperate man?"

"I'm losing the ranch, Mary. Three hard winters in a row have crippled me financially. Creighton has better protected range in those canyons to the north. As far as hands, I am down to those four men out there. They are the last of my role, because I can't afford to pay any more!"

"So rather than lose the ranch, you sold me to . . . your worst enemy?"

"I couldn't relinquish the ranch. My father built it! Your aunt and I grew up there!"

"Aunt Grace is dead."

"I know that. I saw the body on the stage . . . after the horses broke away and dumped it in a ravine." Dunbar convulsed with a mewling wail, raked his big hand down his face, swallowed. "I've taken her home, buried her." He turned to Prophet. "Who killed her?"

"A pack of outlaws at the Porcupine Station. They must have got word you were haulin' that much money here on the coach. And your daughter . . . to sell." Prophet put extra emphasis on *sell*, showing his disdain for the man on his knees before him.

Dunbar flushed sheepishly. He turned to Mary. She stared at her foster father, tears still streaming down her cheeks, upper lip quivering. Dunbar crawled forward, placed his hands on her knees. "There is something more. I'm dying. I have a cancer. A doctor in Cheyenne diagnosed it. I have three, maybe four months left."

Mary didn't respond to that. At least, not on the outside.

"The thirty thousand was to keep Grace in the house until she passed, and to keep a couple of men around to try and hold the wolves at bay."

"You sold me for thirty thousand dollars," Mary said, voice pitched with both awe and exasperation.

"For thirty thousand and the ranch, Mary!" Dunbar cried. "Thirty thousand and the ranch. Don't you see? It was in your best interest. Creighton has money. He's a rich man. While I may not like the man, our enmity stemmed from business. It wasn't personal.

He raised a family at his place, lost his wife a few years ago. He lost his little girl just after she was born; both boys died in a stampede. But he treated his kids and his wife well. They were well provided for. He would have treated you well, too. He would have provided for you.

"He's old, Mary. Nearly as old as I. He won't live that much longer. And then . . ." Dunbar shook his head in wonder. "And then all that land would have been yours. By then, Grace would likely also have died, and you could have had the Three-Box-D, as well. Combined the two ranges. You could have had an empire out here!"

Mary leaned forward, placed her hands on her father's hands, atop her knees. Her hands were small, brown, smooth, and young. His were as large and red as roasts. They dwarfed hers. She dug her fingers into his flesh. "Did you ever think to discuss this diabolical scheme with me—your daughter?"

Dunbar frowned, as though perplexed by the question.

Mary wrinkled a nostril at him, shook her head. "No. You didn't. Why? Because I'm Indian? Because, since I *am* Indian—though you did your best to raise me white—maybe you see me first as property and then as your daughter . . ."

"Mary, no."

"That's it, isn't it, Pa?"

"Mary, sweet Mary—you could have had an empire!"

"Well, I'm sorry you didn't ask me. If you had, I would have told you that I didn't want an empire. There is no way in hell you're ever going to get me to live with Sand Creighton!"

"Don't worry. I realize what an awful mistake that was. Mary, I was drunk that night. And desperate. But believe me when I tell you that I realize what a mistake I made. I'm here to take you home. For good!"

"Yeah, well, Creighton himself is gonna have somethin' to say about that," John Leonard said, sneering.

Dunbar turned to him, rose with a grunt, knees popping. He squared his shoulders at the grinning Leonard then jerked his right hand down to his holster. He whipped up his Bisley .44 and sent two deafening blasts rocketing throughout the saloon.

Mary jerked in her chair and screamed.

The bullets slammed Leonard back against the bar. The man looked dumbfounded. Blood geysered from the twin holes in his chest. He twisted around, grabbed for the edge of the bar, but there was no strength in his hands.

He hit the floor on his knees then turned again and piled up at the bar's base on his back, legs twisted, jerking and bleeding as he died.

"My God!" Lola said, leaping out of her chair and slapping a hand to her chest in astonishment.

Outside, more guns popped.

"Mr. Dunbar!" a man shouted. "We got trouble, Mr. Dun—!"

He was cut off by another blast. Horses whinnied shrilly. Men shouted.

As more guns popped, Prophet ran to the batwings and pressed his shoulder against the wall left of the doors. He shoved the left batwing open with his left hand and peered out.

Dunbar's four men lay belly down in the street. Their horses were fleeing in opposite directions as six riders galloped up in front of the saloon, their horses kicking up mud from the growing puddles. They were led by a portly gent in a yellow india rubber rain slicker and a broad-brimmed, bullet-crowned, cream Stetson with an Indian-beaded band, the thong jostling beneath his chin.

All six turned their horses to face the saloon, smoking rifles resting butt down against their thighs.

Lightning flashed in the sky above them. Thunder clapped. The rain came straight down. Not a torrent by any means, but a steady summer squall.

"You in there, Dunbar?" shouted the portly gent—Sand Creighton, Prophet assumed. "We made a deal—you and me. You send the girl out here or we're gonna come in and drag her out kicking and screaming!"

Dunbar had moved up behind Prophet, his pistol in his hand. He canted his head to the right, to see out the open batwing.

"Creighton!" he raked out. "*Christ!*"

Prophet glanced behind and jerked his head toward the saloon's far wall. Quickly, Lola grabbed Mary's arm, pulled the girl out of the chair, and ushered her out of the line of fire from the door.

Dunbar glanced at Prophet. "I'll try to reason with him."

"Might not be possible. He looks a mite het up."

Dunbar brushed Prophet, pushing out the right batwing as he stepped onto the boardwalk. When the echo of another thunderclap had passed, he said, "I know we made a deal, Sand. But I'm reneging on it. I did an awful thing. I can't turn Mary over to you. You can take your money back." A brief pause. "And you can take the ranch, as well. It's yours. Just leave Mary alone."

"Where's the money?" Creighton yelled above the rain.

Prophet stepped out to stand beside Dunbar. "It's in the coach. In my saddlebags in the rear luggage boot."

"The coach is piled up in Bull Creek north of town," Dunbar added.

"Good to know," Creighton said. He lifted his left hand. Prophet saw that he held a bottle in that hand. He raised the bottle to his lips, took a long drink, set the bottle back down on his thigh.

He wiped his mouth with his sleeve and grinned inside his wet, sandy-colored beard. "But I want the girl, too, Vance. She stabbed me in the belly. Nothin' too serious. I'll get over it. But I'll be damned if I ain't mad!" He gave a dry chuckle. "The little squaw needs a lesson taught her, and since you weren't man enough to do it at home, it's gonna be up to her husband. That's *me*!"

"No!" Dunbar shouted. "I told you—you can have the ranch! Take your money back! But Mary is off the table!"

"No, she ain't! She's mine! I been wantin' that little squaw for years! Now she's mine, and I ain't goin' home without her!"

Dunbar bounded forward. "You drunken devil!" As he raised his Bisley, Creighton snapped his rifle to his own shoulder and fired.

Dunbar lunged back, stunned, and triggered his Bisley into the boardwalk.

"Get inside!" Prophet shouted, grabbing the wounded rancher by his arm, twisting him around and shoving him through the batwings.

As the bounty hunter turned around to face the six horseback riders, he was met with six separate gun flashes and a hail of hot lead storming toward him.

Chapter 21

As bullets tore into the front of the Lazy Day Saloon, cracking through the batwings and shattering the glass of the big front window, Prophet dove behind the stock trough fronting the boardwalk to his left.

He snaked his Peacemaker up over the trough and fired three shots, all missing their targets as the riders' horses danced around in front of the saloon. He was just wishing he had his Winchester when Lola yelled through the broken-out window behind him, "Lou!"

He shot her a look. She hurled his Winchester through the window. Prophet dropped the Peacemaker and caught the rifle over the boardwalk. "Thanks, but get your head down!"

He pulled his own head down behind the stock trough as more bullets chewed into it and screeched through the air around him.

The shooting stopped.

Prophet looked over the trough. The six riders were in the midst of dismounting their leaping horses.

Sand Creighton dropped his right boot to the ground but his left one got caught in the stirrup. His horse wheeled. Creighton screamed and flew sideways. His boot jerked free and he hit the muddy street and rolled.

The other riders dropped to their knees, raising their rifles toward Prophet.

The bounty hunter cursed and cut loose, the Winchester roaring savagely. He dropped two men right away, punched them back onto the boardwalk on the opposite side of the street. The three others hammered the front of the stock trough with lead. Prophet jerked his head down to keep it from getting blown off. He crawled to the stock trough's right side, snaked his rifle around it, and dispatched two more Creighton men.

The fifth man leaped to his feet and ran for cover.

Prophet blew his legs out from under him. The man screamed and piled up in a big mud puddle. He stretched an arm out for his rifle. Lifting his head, he cast his gaze toward Prophet, his eyes reflecting the yellow light flickering out from over the batwings and through the broken window behind Lou.

The bounty hunter drew a bead on the man's broad forehead.

The Winchester roared.

The fifth man's head jerked back on his neck then dropped straight down to the mud puddle. Prophet saw little bubbles forming around the man's face in the puddle as he died.

Prophet racked a fresh round. He looked around for Creighton. The fat rancher was not where Prophet had last seen him.

Prophet rose to his knees, frowning.

Creighton rose up in front of him. He'd been crawling toward the trough, dragging his belly through the muddy street. The fat, round-faced, bearded rancher wasn't wearing his hat. He was nearly bald save for a few strands of sandy gray hair. His mouth formed a savage grimace as he extended a long-barreled Smith & Wesson at Prophet. Prophet whipped his rifle around and squeezed the trigger.

It clicked, empty.

A gun popped behind the bounty hunter. A round hole appeared in the rancher's forehead. Creighton triggered the Smithy over Prophet's right shoulder and into the boardwalk running along the front of the Lazy Day. His eyes rolled back into his head as he dropped forward to hang his head and arms into the stock trough, like a drunk heaving up his guts.

He shook his head and then just hung there, dead, his head in the trough.

Prophet glanced over his left shoulder. Lola stared through the broken-out window, wide-eyed, a smoking, pearl-gripped .41 caliber Colt in her hand.

"Thanks," Prophet said.

Lola stared at the dead Sand Creighton. She looked at Prophet. "Are there any more out there?"

Prophet shook his head.

Lola gave a wan half smile as she lowered the smoking pistol. "Why don't you come in out of the rain, then, Lou?"

Prophet nodded, rose heavily to his feet. "Yeah. Why don't I?"

The saddlebags were where Prophet had placed them in the stagecoach's rear luggage boot.

The coach itself had broken free of the runaway team and had landed on its side in Bull Creek, a shallow dry wash about a half a mile southwest of Jubilee. Prophet reached into the boot, dragged out his bags. He settled them onto the ground between his knees and opened the flaps. He'd placed two of the money sacks into the left pouch, the other sack in the right one.

All three were where he had left them.

He held one of the bags up to show Lola and Mary. The two women were on hands and knees, gazing down over the lip of the cutbank at him. Lola smiled. Mary's face remained expressionless. The bright morning sun touched their hair, and the breeze, warm now after last night's rain, tussled their hair about their faces.

"It's all here," Prophet said.

He carried it up onto the cutbank and stood before Lola and Mary. Mary's father, Vance Dunbar, was resting in the box of the wagon parked on the trail about fifty yards to the east, a white-socked black gelding in the traces. The bullet he'd taken last night had only grazed the top of his left shoulder, but the past twenty-four hours had taken a lot out of him, as weak as he already was from the cancer.

He sat in the box, his back resting against its front panel, wrapped in blankets. He stared forlornly straight out behind the wagon, toward the widely scattered, bullet-shaped northern buttes. He hadn't said a word since the last words Prophet had heard him say to his daughter the night before, which had been: "Please forgive me."

Three men from the stage station in Deadwood

were removing the blanket-wrapped bodies of Mort Seymour and J. W. Plumb from where Prophet had tied them to the top of the stage. They were just now carrying Seymour to where a small buckboard waited on the cutbank. This day marked a grave and somber end to the stage line's route through Jubilee.

"Thirty thousand dollars here," Prophet said, patting the saddlebag pouch hanging down over his left shoulder. "Creighton won't be needing it where he is. Why don't you take it, Mary? Sounds like you and your old man could use it."

Mary turned her head to stare at where her father sat in the wagon, wearing his high-crowned Stetson, blankets pulled up to his weathered cheeks. She turned back to Prophet, shook her head. "I want nothing to do with Creighton's money, Lou."

"Are you and your pa going to be all right, Mary?" Lola asked her, sliding an arm around her shoulders.

Mary nodded. "He asked me to forgive him, and I have. I'll try to make him as comfortable as I can in the time he has left. Then I'll bury him beside Aunt Grace."

"I reckon you'll figure out the next step when you come to it," Prophet said.

Mary smiled up at the tall bounty hunter. "Thank you, Lou. For all you've done for me an' . . . for Pa."

"Don't mention it."

Prophet wrapped his arms around her, gave her a good, long hug, and kissed her cheek. Mary gazed up at him, fondness sparkling in her eyes. She glanced quickly at Lola and then returned her gaze to Lou as she said, "Are you going to hang around here for a while? In Jubilee?"

Prophet glanced at Lola, who smiled at him a little sheepishly. His ears warming, he said, "Yeah, I reckon I will. I ain't fully recovered yet." He stretched his back, giving a maudlin wince and a grunt. "I'll probably spend a few days"—he glanced at Lola again—"*restin' up* before I see about heading back to Cheyenne and picking up my hoss."

"Will you ride out and see me at the Three-Box-D before you go?"

"I'd purely admire to do that."

"I'll make supper and you can spend the night." Mary's eyes flicked toward Lola once more.

"That sounds even better."

"Good-bye, Lou." Mary kissed his cheek. She turned and gave Lola a parting hug, and then, lifting her skirts above her ankles, began walking back toward the wagon. She climbed up into the driver's boot, released the brake handle, shook the reins over the horse's back, and began rattling off along the trail to the north.

She glanced back at Prophet and Lola, and waved.

They returned the gesture.

"She's quite a girl," Lola said, watching the wagon grow small in the distance. She gave Prophet a light elbow to the ribs. "But, then, you probably know that better than anybody—don't you, Lou?"

Prophet gave a guilty snort.

"What about the money?" he said as he and Lola began walking over to where their saddled horses stood ground-tied. "You might as well take it. Sounds like Creighton didn't have any family . . ."

"I don't want that money," Lola said. "Why don't

you take it? That much jingle should keep you off the bounty trail for at least a month."

Prophet made a face, shook his head. "I can't take money I didn't earn."

"Well, what are you going to do with it, then?" Lola stopped by her horse and frowned up at him.

Prophet looked around. He spied a small pile of jumbled rock nearby. He walked over to it, rolled back a couple of the rocks, then deposited the money sacks into the hollow. He rolled the rocks back over the sacks. The rocks looked as though they'd never been moved.

Turning to Lola, he said, "There. If at any time in the future you need that money, you know where it's at."

"I won't take that money," Lola said. "Not knowing what Creighton wanted to do with it. Besides, it's blood money now."

"Just in case," Prophet said.

"All right," Lola said, chuckling. "We'll call it Just in Case Loot. Only you and I know about it. It'll be our secret." She reached up and wrapped her arms around his neck, pressed her breasts against his chest, and kissed him.

She pulled her head back from his, tugged on his ears. "Now, why don't we head back to the Lazy Day? I think you still have some more *recovering* to do, don't you, Lou?"

Prophet kissed her. He made a face of mock misery. "Oh, Lordy, I think you're right. I been out in the sun too long. I think I need at least a couple of hours—maybe the whole rest of the day and night . . . maybe the whole day tomorrow, too—under the sheets!"

He had some time to kill. After all, Clovis Teagarden was probably still crying rape back in Denver . . .

Lola laughed.

Prophet helped her onto her horse, and they galloped toward Jubilee.

Devil by the Tail

From *The Life and Times of Lou Prophet, Bounty Hunter* by HEYWOOD WILDEN SCOTT

The old roarer and I became fast friends.

One session in his smoky room, sipping whiskey and smoking hand-rolled cigarettes while he recounted the tales of his life from the mountains of north Georgia to the western frontier and beyond, led to another night . . . another . . . and yet another, until we'd gotten a few weeks in and I'd filled up several notebooks, dulled a few nibs, and emptied several ink pots.

We stayed up too late on some nights and endured the remonstrations of the henlike harpy who oversaw the night-shift attendants. Yet, we soldiered on, keeping our voices down . . . our old-man coughing and guffawing (some of the tales were quite wonderfully bawdy and humorous) as furtive as possible . . . while Lou palavered on in his petal-soft, gentling rolling accent fairly dripping with a soft, Southern spring rain and rife with the perfume of dogwood blossoms.

As I said, his room was sparsely furnished.

There was the cursory small bed with a lumpy mattress and a single pillow of striped ticking. There was a small wooden table, two straight-back chairs, an electric lamp, and a small shelf trimmed with a single photograph. It was the only photograph displayed anywhere in the room. In fact, it was the only decoration of any kind in his dusky, smoke-hazy quarters.

It was an old ambrotype photo in a velvet-lined, hinged case with a clasp. The gilt-washed case was open and sitting upright, displaying the photograph of a beautiful young blond woman in a calico blouse, long hair twisted into sausage curls tumbling to her shoulders, rich lips set in a firm line, a fiery, warrior-like defiance in her eyes.

The young woman sat in an ornately scrolled and upholstered armchair, probably on a photographer's set in Dodge City or Abilene or some such, and she held a Winchester repeating rifle across her skirted lap. Her right finger, clad in what appeared to be a kid glove, was curled through the rifle's trigger guard, as though she were ready and raring at a moment's notice—at the first scream of a defenseless child, say, or a horrified mother's wail issuing from a near street—to snap up the long gun and commence firing.

Chapter 1

"Mean and Ugly, I got a question for you," Lou Prophet said as he and his appropriately named horse made their way along a dusty, meandering West Texas trail. "Did that jasper up there in them rocks see me just now? And, if he saw me, is he about to snuff my wick and plant my ass?"

Mean and Ugly gave an ambiguous snort, rippled a wither, and kept walking.

"You're a lot of help, old son," Prophet grunted, keeping his gaze straight ahead along the trail, not wanting the possible bushwhacker to know he'd glimpsed his shadow.

The short hairs were prickling along the back of the bounty hunter's neck. Having seen the shadow move in the rocks atop the spur he was just now riding around the base of, his impulse was to throw himself from his saddle and spare himself a lead-heavy heart.

Something, however, made him keep his seat.

Quickly, drawing a deep, calming breath, he pulled

a quarter from a pocket of his skintight, wash-worn denim trousers, and flipped it.

"Heads, he's about to feed me a pill I can't digest. Tails, he's gonna wait till I get around this rock where the sun won't be facing him, and he'll have a clearer shot at my back."

Prophet caught the coin in his right hand and placed it atop his left hand. He moved his right hand away from it.

"Heads," he said.

Still, Prophet kept his boots in the stirrups. They felt as heavy as lead. His back felt as though leeches were crawling around on it, under his sweat-soaked buckskin tunic.

He held his breath, wincing, waiting for the bullet to shatter his breastbone while praying it wouldn't. He wasn't ready to shake hands with the devil just yet and make good on his end of the deal they'd made about shoveling coal for all eternity in exchange for a few more years of stomping with his tail up on this side of the sod.

He wasn't ready for the coal shovel or the stench of forever-burning coal oil or whatever Ole Scratch filled his burning oceans with. Besides, Prophet might have been born and raised in the Deep South, but he couldn't take the heat, even a dry heat.

The bounty hunter's heart thudded.

Mean and Ugly kept walking along the trail that curved more sharply around the base of the spur now.

Birds sang. A dry breeze rose, lifted a handful of dust, and dropped it. Mean's hoofs thudded softly in the well-churned, powdery dust of the sun-blasted trail.

As the horse kept moving, the face of the spur slid around behind Prophet, covering him from the man in the rocks. He heaved a relieved sigh. The shadow of the tall outcropping slid over him, cool and dark and as safe as a baby's cradle.

In about fifteen more of Mean's strides, however, horse and rider would be in the open again. Prophet's back would be exposed to the man no doubt tracking him with his Winchester, ready to plant his sights between the big bounty hunter's shoulder blades.

Quickly, Lou wrapped his reins around his saddle horn from which his double-barreled, sawed-off twelve-gauge Richards coach gun dangled by its leather lanyard. He'd leave the gut-shredder right where it was. This was likely a job for a long gun.

He shucked his Winchester '73 from the saddle boot jutting up over his right stirrup, said, "Good luck, Mean. I hope he don't shoot you before he realizes I ain't on your back, but it wouldn't be any more or less than what you deserve, you cussed broomtail!"

He chuckled whimsically as he swung his right boot over the horn and dropped smoothly to the ground, lunging off the side of the trail and putting his back up against the escarpment's uneven rock face. The horse gave a start at the sudden and unexpected disappearance of its rider and trotted ahead for a few steps, glancing incredulously back over its left wither at the bounty hunter.

Despite his earlier comment, Prophet hoped the son of a bitch atop the scarp didn't shoot his horse. Mean and Ugly might have been appropriately named by Prophet himself, but they had a lot in common. And while Mean wasn't much to look at, and he could be as colicky as all get-out, which were two more things he had in common with his rider, he'd been a damned good horse who'd carried the big bounty hunter many a mile along many an owl-hoot trail on the wild and woolly western frontier.

Prophet ran ten yards back along the trail then turned and stepped into a gravelly notch carved into the escarpment's stone face. The notch curved steeply up. Prophet hoped it let out somewhere near the top . . . somewhere near the son of a bitch with the long gun.

The bounty hunter was a big man who didn't cotton to walking much less climbing, so he silently cussed his predicament. But he could move fast and relatively gracefully when he needed to. He covered the twenty or so feet of gravelly, twisting ground relatively quickly. As he poked his head above the crest of the escarpment, a rifle cracked near enough and loudly enough to rattle his eardrums.

He blinked with a start and saw a man squatting not ten feet away from him, aiming a smoking Henry repeating rifle over the escarpment's opposite side. At the same time, dust plumed just beyond where Mean and Ugly was walking along the trail, heading away from the escarpment.

Mean gave a shrill, indignant whinny, buck-kicked, and ran.

Prophet took his rifle in his left hand and shucked his Colt Peacemaker .45 from the holster thonged low on his right thigh, clicked the hammer back, and said, "You're lucky you didn't shoot my hoss, you lamebrained son of a bitch!"

The man who'd shot only the air above Mean's saddle, still expecting the bounty hunter to be in the hurricane deck, yelled in sudden shock. He twisted around, ejecting a smoking brass cartridge from his long gun's breech and pumping a fresh one into the chamber.

"Or I'd have gut-shot you and left you up here, howlin' for your momma!" Prophet bellowed, punching two quick rounds side by side through the man's chest.

The slugs killed him instantly.

Convulsing violently, he dropped the Henry, stumbled backward, got a spur stuck on an upthrust thumb of crumbling rock, and fell silently down the scarp's far side.

Silence.

A muffled thump as the carcass hit the ground.

Prophet leaped up onto the rise and walked to the edge of the scarp. He looked down to see the man's body lying on the trail, belly up, arms and limbs akimbo. His battered hat and rifle lay beside him. His mouth was wide open in a silent wail of shock. Blood puddled on his chest and frothed on his lips.

"You can thank me for killin' you quick. More than you deserve, ya chicken-livered bushwhacker!"

Prophet looked around for any more chicken-livered bushwhackers. He could see a good distance in all directions, as this was the West Texas desert, near the New Mexico line, and there wasn't much cover except for a few rocks and low, cactus-studded hills. Blue mountains rose in the far distance to the north and west. South and east there was only flat, pale desert and brassy sky in which the sun rode like a giant ball of molten gold.

Nothing but rock grew atop the bald scarp that Prophet stood on. He walked around, peering around rocks, aiming his Winchester straight out from his right hip.

Nothing. No one.

There was, however, a lone horse standing down the backside of the rise—a rangy, saddled claybank that had been tied to a picket pin. The horse peered up at Prophet from a gap between two stone shelves, and gave a curious whicker.

The son of a bitch had been alone out here, all right. Just him and his horse.

Prophet looked toward the south for his own horse. Mean and Ugly stood roughly a hundred yards away, off the winding trail's right side, pulling at a patch of wiry brown grass growing up from the base of a clay-colored boulder. Prophet stuck two fingers in his mouth and whistled.

Mean looked up at him, chewing with casual insolence.

"You heard me, you stubborn cuss," Prophet raked out. "Get your ass over here!" He whistled again.

The horse continued to stare at him, in no hurry to comply with the command. Then, as though it had weighed through its options carefully, it began to mosey back toward where its rider stood atop the escarpment. It stepped slowly, ploddingly, taking its time.

"Collicky cuss," Prophet said, then started back down the rise the same way he'd come up.

He stepped on a couple of fist-sized rocks, which rolled forward. Prophet cursed as his left boot slipped out from beneath him and he dropped to his ass. Cursing, he regained his feet, rubbed his sore butt then continued down the decline but taking it slower this time and being more careful about where he set his feet.

When he was back on level ground, he swung left and strode along the trail, curving around the base of the escarpment. He found the dead man lying on the trail about ten yards beyond where Prophet had dismounted his horse and left Mean and Ugly to his own devices.

Prophet stood over the man, realizing that by killing him he'd lost his chance of knowing why the lowlife had ambushed him. At least, the man himself wasn't going to say. He was about six feet tall, and he wore the gear of your average cowpuncher. His red hair was coarse and wavy. His eyes were blue. Prophet judged him to be in his late twenties, early thirties.

There was a two-or-three-day growth of red beard stubble on his sallow cheeks that did not take the sun well. The skin over the nubs of his cheeks was pink and peeling. Same with that on his blunt nose.

Prophet pulled the pistol from the holster on the man's right hip. A Starr .38 with a worn walnut grip. Nothing special about the piece. The Henry, on the other hand . . .

Prophet picked up the rifle, gave it a good looking over. It was a well-cared-for Henry sixteen-shot repeater. Despite the dust and sand it had accumulated in the fall from the scarp, it shone with a recent oiling. The stock showed the wear and tear of much use.

The Henry had belonged to a man who'd used it often. Depended on it regularly. Perhaps even made his living by using it . . .

Prophet went through the man's pockets, finding nothing except a cheap pocket watch, a hide makings sack filled with chopped tobacco and rolling papers, a small wooden box containing three Lucifer matches, a chewed pencil stub, and a small leather-covered notebook.

Prophet opened the notebook and frowned down at his own named scrawled in thick pencil on the notebook's first, lined page.

LOU PROPHET.

The handwriting was large and childlike.

"Well, at least you spelled my name right," the bounty hunter muttered to the dead man. "But why were you out to perforate my hide?"

He'd been a fool not to try to take him alive. But, then, taking alive a man who was bearing down on you with a Henry repeater was easier said than done. The dead man had likely had a grudge against the bounty hunter, as so many did. You weren't a man hunter for as long as Prophet had been without making some enemies.

This man had probably seen Prophet somewhere back along the trail down from Lubbock. He'd probably shadowed Prophet for a time then swung around ahead of him to affect his ambush. Prophet didn't recognize him, but he'd seen a lot of faces on the frontier in the years since the War of Northern Aggression. He didn't remember them all. Also, this man might have been a friend or family of someone Prophet had caused to serve time or swing from a gallows.

Maybe, if the dead man were from around here, Jonas Ford would know who he was. Ford was the town marshal Prophet was on his way to see, at Ford's own request, which had been wired to Prophet when Prophet had been turning in two stagecoach robbers to the law in Lubbock. Prophet wasn't certain why Ford needed his services, but he'd find out soon, as Ford's town, Carson's Wash, was just a few more miles east along the trail.

A snorting sound rose behind Prophet. He glanced over his shoulder to see Mean and Ugly standing about six feet behind him, regarding him owlishly. The horse shook its head and whickered.

"What—you're piss-burned 'cause I used you as a decoy?" Prophet chuckled. "Believe me, pal, you'd have done the same thing to me if you'd been in my position. Which you weren't and never will be. I'm a man. You're a beast. Time you accepted that fact."

Mean gave his head another acrimonious shake, almost freeing himself of his bridle and bit.

"Some fresh hay and oats once we get to Carson's Wash will make you forget all about that bushwhacker's bullet. In the meantime, stay here." Prophet strode around toward the backside of the escarpment, muttering mostly to himself, "I got another hay burner to fetch so we can take him on to Carson's Wash and, hopefully, find out who he is and why he tried to drop a coin in my bucket."

Chapter 2

Prophet rode into Carson's Wash one hour after he'd tossed the jasper who'd tried to air him out over the back of the dead man's horse.

The bounty hunter had ridden through the remote West Texas ranching supply town only seven months ago when Prophet and his sometime partner, sometime lover Louisa Bonaventure—who'd been dubbed the Vengeance Queen by some ink-stained, raggedy-heeled Eastern newspaper scribbler—had turned in a couple of prisoners to Jonas Ford in return for the Wells Fargo bounty on their heads. Prophet and Louisa had spent a few days in the town, waiting for the paperwork to go through and the money to be wired to the local bank, so they'd gotten to know Ford passably well.

What Prophet had seen of Ford, he'd liked. Ford hadn't shown the prejudice against the bounty hunting profession that many badge-toters did. Many didn't see bounty hunting as a profession at all, but a mere sport practiced by cutthroats, which was true in some cases. But Ford seemed to think that Lou and Louisa were doing him and other lawmen a service by bringing in killers they were too short-handed and too strapped by jurisdictional boundaries to go after themselves.

Prophet did, however, wish that in his telegram Ford had at least hinted at why he'd summoned the bounty hunter back to Carson's Wash. At least he *had* wished he'd known. Now he was about to find out, for he was swinging Mean and the dead man's horse up to the small, squat, mud-brick, brush-roofed building that was identified as CARSON'S WASH TOWN MARSHAL by the wooden shingle tacked to gnarled mesquite posts jutting into the street.

Prophet glanced at the horse already tied to the hitchrack fronting the hovel, glanced away, then swung his gaze quickly back to the mount—a brown and white pinto with a hand-tooled, brown leather saddle and a Winchester carbine jutting from the boot. The horse's braided leather bridle was studded with brightly colored Indian beads.

Prophet would have recognized that horse anywhere.

As it was, he recognized it here as the fine, unnamed mount of his infamous and notorious partner, Louisa Bonaventure, her own persnickety self. She'd purchased the bridle only last year when she'd traveled through Navajo country. The girl might have been a stone-hearted killer of men who deserved killing, but her tastes leaned toward the fancy.

Or gaudy, as some would say . . .

Consider her matching, pearl-gripped, nickel-washed pistols and their hand-tooled leather holsters she wore thonged low on her shapely thighs.

Ah, her shapely thighs . . .

Recalling in his mind's eye her sumptuous body, burnished by the umber light of some backcountry fire, the bounty hunter knew a moment's tug of desire. No woman stirred him like the hazel-eyed Vengeance Queen.

"Well, well, well," Prophet said, keeping his incredulous gaze on the pinto. *Had Ford called Louisa in, too?* Prophet hadn't known she'd been in the area. He hadn't seen her for nigh on a half a year now. While they often rode together and shared each other's bedrolls at night, they didn't get along well enough *outside* of those bedrolls at night to work together for more than a few weeks at a time during the day.

Prophet swung down from Mean's back and tied the two sets of reins to the hitchrack. As he tramped up the veranda's three steps, he heard voices issuing from inside the marshal's office.

A man's voice and a woman's voice.

Laughter.

Prophet rapped twice on the door then turned the knob, poking his head into Ford's neat office. "Am I, uh, interrupting anything?"

Immediately, a pang of jealousy pinched his loins.

Jonas Ford was sitting on the corner of his desk, near Louisa, who sat in a Windsor chair beside the neat and orderly desk outfitted with a green Tiffany lamp. They were sitting close enough to each other that Ford's left ankle was snugged up against Louisa's own left ankle, the denim-clad leg of which was crossed over her right knee. They each held glasses of what appeared to be whiskey. The boyishly handsome, brown-haired Ford had been smiling down at Louisa, and Louisa had been smiling up at Ford when Prophet had knocked, but now they both turned to the door and shaped amused expressions of surprise.

"Well, if that don't beat all," Ford said, rising from his desk, grinning, dimples cratering his smooth cheeks. He was a well-set-up, snazzily attired, forthright man in his late twenties, and he'd been born and raised around here, hailing from a prosperous local family headed by a now-deceased father who'd been a Yankee general in the War of Northern Aggression. "We were just talking about you, Lou!"

"That a fact?" Prophet tried to smile but he knew it probably looked as though his lips were glued together. "What was funny?"

Ford laughed again as he stuck out his hand. Prophet shook it.

"Oh, that," Ford said. "That was nothing . . ."

Remaining in her chair, Louisa swirled her glass of whiskey and said, "Jonas was just wondering where you were, as he knew it was only a two-day ride down from Lubbock, and I just said that you were probably holed up in some hurdy-gurdy house between here and there."

Queen's snooty tone chafed him as it usually did. "Well, not to worry—there ain't too many hurdy-gurdy houses between here and Lubbock."

He looked at the handsome local lawman, who was still smiling his winning, dimple-cheeked smile though at the moment those cheeks were faintly flushed with chagrin, causing Prophet to wonder what else Ford and Louisa had been saying about him. "I jumped on my hoss as soon as I could, Jonas.

I just had to wait for the paperwork to go through on a bounty request I turned in to Uncle Sam."

"I'll be ding-dong-damned—that's Tom Lowry!"

The exclamation had come from behind Prophet as he stood in the marshal's office's open door. He turned to see three men standing between Mean and Ugly and the dead man's horse. They'd rolled the saddle blanket up to the dead man's shoulders, revealing his red-haired head, the cadaver's freckled, sunburned, right cheek resting against the claybank's side.

All three men, burly sorts in calico shirts and canvas trousers stuffed into the tops of mule-eared boots—freighters, most likely—held frothy beer mugs in their fists. The Periwinkle Saloon sat on the far side of the street, and three or four men stood on the watering hole's front, blue-painted veranda, peering toward the marshal's office.

"What do you have out there, Lou?" Ford asked.

"Tom Lowry, sounds like," Prophet said, dropping slowly back down the veranda steps.

"Tom Lowry?" Ford said with nearly as much surprise as the freighter who'd been the first one to mention the name.

As Prophet walked between the horses, heading for the dead man, Ford brushed past him to stop before the freighters and say, "Henry, Calvin—why don't you fellas go back and do your drinking in the Periwinkle? You, too, Dutch. This is law business."

"Who shot Lowry?" one of the freighters asked. A big, middle-aged man with a large, round belly, he wore a thick, tangled, salt-and-peppered beard and his eyes were shiny from drink. He looked Prophet up and down and asked, "You?"

"Come on, Dutch," Ford said, giving the man a gentle shove toward the Periwinkle. "Move along now."

Dutch looked at Prophet and shook a rope-burned, sausage-sized finger at him. "If you shot Lowry, you best not let any grass grow under your feet in these parts, mister!"

"Dutch, damnit, what did I just tell you?" Ford barked. "If you don't get your ass back across the street pronto, I'm going to arrest you for vagrancy!"

"Jonas, that ain't no way to talk to your elders an' you know it!" Dutch retorted, vaguely sheepish, as he turned slowly, reluctantly away to follow the other two men back toward the saloon. Glancing over his shoulder at Ford, he said, "I was friends with the General!"

Prophet knew that Ford's father was known throughout West Texas not by his given name of Hannibal Ford, but simply as "the General." And pretty much everyone north of rubber pants was aware of who "the General" was, too.

"I know you an' Pa was friends, Dutch," Ford said, his voice vaguely wheedling, "and I know Pa would appreciate you giving me room to do my job."

Dutch merely threw up a thick, dismissive arm.

Ford sighed and shook his head.

Prophet just now consciously noted that the young marshal's left arm was hooked over his chest in a black flannel sling. But at the moment, Prophet had a more pressing topic of discussion: "This fella dry-gulched me back along the trail a ways, Jonas. Tried to shoot me out of my saddle. If I hadn't spied his shadow atop an escarpment and got the drop on him, I'd be crowbait."

"You just can't stay out of trouble, can you?" Louisa said from where she stood atop the veranda, holding her whiskey glass up against her shoulder. She wore a saucy expression on her full, rose lips, one boot cocked forward, one hand on the grips of one of her pretty, pearl-gripped Colts.

Prophet looked at the glass in her other hand. "Since when did you start drinkin' whiskey? Whenever I've offered you tarantula juice, you clouded up like I was offering you skunk stink. I thought you were strictly a sarsaparilla or cold milk gal."

Louisa glanced quickly at Ford, her cheeks flushing slightly. She lifted the glass to her lips. "This isn't the coffin varnish you drink, Lou." She took a small sip. "Very smooth."

Prophet gave a caustic chuff then turned back to Jonas Ford, who was sliding his gaze between the two bounty hunters skeptically. "Never mind her, Jonas. Gettin' back to this bushwhacker . . ."

"Yes, getting back to this bushwhacker, Lou—this is indeed Tom Lowry." Ford looked down at Lowry's pale face and half-open eyes. Flies buzzed around the man's coarse, wavy red hair. "We should probably have a coroner's hearing, just to make sure I don't leave any loose ends. But, under the circumstances, since only two men know what happened out there, and one of them is dead, I'll write up an affidavit, have you sign it, and file it with the sheriff in the county seat."

"Everything by the book—eh, Jonas?"

"'Fraid so, Lou. And I'm also afraid that . . ."

Ford's face acquired a constipated expression as he glanced around at the men and a few women looking on from both sides of the street, including the half-dozen men now standing outside of the Periwinkle. "I'm afraid what Dutch said is right about Lowry. He's got quite a few friends as well as family in these parts."

"Just who was this Tom Lowry, Jonas?"

"He was a hard tail. A no-account. His old man, Emmett, runs a ranch of sorts south of town with a half dozen of Tom's brothers. No-accounts, all. Tom's especially good with a long gun. He's known to hire it out from time to time though I've never been able to prove his guilt in any of the killings that occur from time to time out here."

"That Henry's his weapon of choice, eh?"

"That's right. Most men with money around here who also have an itch they can't scratch—meaning a man . . . or in one case even a woman . . . they want to see turned toe down—turn to Tom. I'm told he was relatively cheap and very effective from long range. Back-shooter, mostly."

"Yeah, well, somethin' in the back of my ugly head told me he might be a back-shooter. That's what did him in."

"The county prosecutor and I tried for two years to make a case against him, but we just could never get enough evidence. Anyone who has any doings with any of the Lowrys have enough healthy fear of the clan to keep their mouths shut unless they want that Henry . . . and the other Lowrys . . . turned on *them.*"

Prophet looked around the street, pensive. "I wonder who wanted it turned on me."

"Nothin' personal between you and Tom Lowry, Lou?"

"I've never met the man. Leastways, don't remember ever doin' so."

"So he was hired to bring you down."

"Who else in these parts knew you summoned me here, Jonas?"

Ford shrugged. "I might have discussed it with the mayor and a couple of city council members at breakfast one day last week. And, of course, the telegrapher at the Western Union office knows about it. Any one of them might have mentioned it, and . . ."

"Half the county might know by now."

"Could be anyone who has a grudge against you."

"Yeah." Prophet looked around again, scratching his chin and turning his mouth corners down. "And that breed's thicker than tics on a south Georgia coon hound."

Ford sighed. "Well, complications aside, I feel compelled to thank you for taking him down for me, Lou. I'm sure it was self-defense and all, but I will have to have your John Henry on an affidavit. I'll write it up later this evening."

"I understand, Jonas. You're a good lawman. I know you have to cross your t's and dot your i's. It's my word against Lowry's and, well, cat's got his tongue."

Both men looked down at Lowry.

"The Lowrys will learn of this soon, Lou. They're a bunch of bad apples from the same basket this one crawled out of. You'll want to keep that third eye in the back of your head skinned. I'd hate to have anything happen to you"—Ford smiled again and gave a wry wink—"since I'm the one who summoned you here."

"Yeah, what about that, Jonas?" Prophet hooked a thumb at Louisa. "And why is this she-cat here? Don't you know she carries the rabies?" Before Louisa could give a cheeky retort, he continued with: "And one more question—what in the hell happened to your arm, old son?"

Chapter 3

"Let's discuss my arm and why I called you both here in my office," Ford said.

He looked around the street then called to a one-armed man in a shabby suit coat and battered derby standing on the Periwinkle's veranda. "Danny, get Drucker over here, will you? Have him take Lowry over to his undertaking parlor and fit him for a wooden overcoat."

"What am I gettin' out of it?" Danny asked.

"Maybe a day less in jail when you go on your next bender," Ford said. "As long as you don't stab or shoot anybody or break any furniture!" Turning to Prophet, the young marshal jerked his chin toward his open office door. "Shall we?"

"How long you been here?" Prophet asked Louisa as they followed Ford into his office.

"I got here three days ago," Louisa said, striding toward the chair she'd been sitting in before. "I was just passing through, but Jonas asked me to stay and wait for you for a special job he has for us."

Prophet found himself instinctively disliking the

admiring smile Louisa had cast Ford as she'd spoken. He didn't know why he did. He and Louisa were partners, and sometimes to while away a few hours at night out on the trail and to bleed off some sap, they slept together. They had no more of a future together than did a mongrel dog and a blooded she-cat—a *wild*, blooded she-cat at that.

For years now Lou had hoped the Vengeance Queen would eventually leave the man-hunting trail, find a good husband, and settle down. Such a husband would be Jonas Ford—a good man from a good family. A man who, with his inherited political connections, would probably run for office soon.

Jonas Ford was the sort of polished, affable, and conscientious fellow who would make a good politician, if there were such a thing. He might even make a good territorial governor in the years ahead. Prophet could see Louisa shedding her trail duds and pistols and Winchester carbine for a frilly ball gown and beautifully as well as charmingly decorating the man's arm at some Christmas dance.

They'd fill a house with some fine-looking offspring, such a handsome pair would . . .

So why did Prophet feel a tad on the bitter side? Why did he feel as though a rusty dagger were poking his guts?

As Louisa slacked into her chair, Ford walked around behind his desk and sank into his leather swivel chair.

"Pull up that chair there, Lou," Ford said, gesturing at the old, creaky-looking ladder-back sitting up against the wall right of the door, a couple dusters hanging from a wall hook hanging over it. It looked about as substantial as a house of cards.

Lou doubted it would hold him.

"I've been sitting since Lubbock," Prophet said, leaning against a square-hewn ceiling support post. "I'll stand."

He watched Louisa lift the whiskey glass to her lips and take a sip. He thought he detected a slight wince as the tangleleg went down, but she did her best to make it look like she was sipping the sweetest nectar. She glanced at Ford, and they shared a vaguely conspiratorial smile.

Prophet inwardly rolled his eyes.

Christ, will you two stop acting like twelve-year-olds on a school playground? If not, I'm gonna have to rustle up a slop bucket to puke in . . .

"If you won't sit down, at least have some whiskey," Ford said, pulling out a desk drawer from which he produced a labeled bottle of bourbon.

"It's a sin to turn down whiskey," Prophet said.

Ford chuckled as he splashed bourbon into a water glass that he'd also hauled out of the drawer. Prophet held up the glass, sniffed. He threw it back, taking down the entire quarter glass—roughly two shots of liquor—in two swallows.

Smacking his lips, he set the glass back down on the desk. "Hit me again, will you, Jonas? That stuff's too expensive for what I use it for, but it cuts through the trail dust just fine."

He glanced at Louisa, who returned the favor and rolled her eyes with her own particular brand of haughty disapproval.

When the young marshal had refilled Prophet's glass, the bounty hunter picked it up and leaned against the ceiling support post once more, absently swirling the whiskey in his big right hand. "All right—

let's get down to brass tacks, Jonas. Why'd you send for us? Or send for me, anyways, as my comely partner was already here."

Ford sipped his own whiskey and sat back in his chair. "I have a warrant for a man's arrest here in my desk. Just last week, the day before Miss Bonaventure rode into town, in fact, I and my only two deputies tried to serve it. Both of my deputies were killed. They were good men," the young marshal added with bitterness. "I was winged, as you can see. This arm will be out of commission for a good two months. The bullet shattered my humerus, traveled over my shoulder, and lodged in my back.

"Anyway, I've requested help from the sheriff, but he's down with a leg wound of his own. He has three deputies, but two of them are also out of commission for various reasons, and for *that* reason, he can't spare the third. I've inquired with the U.S. marshals and they've assured me they'll send two or three men just as soon as two or three men become available. Same with the Texas Rangers. I've tried to form a posse out of the citizenry right here in Carson's Wash, to help me try to serve the warrant again, but no man in this town wants to ride against Charlie Butters."

"Butters," Prophet said as though the name were a curse.

"Ring a bell, Lou?" Louisa asked.

"Rings a couple," Prophet mused. "I rode him down last year up in Oklahoma. Butters is a bank robber and regulator with a half-dozen federal warrants on his head. He and another son of a bronzed bitch robbed a bank up in Alva. When his bandanna slipped down his face, revealing his ugly features, Butters shot everyone in the bank—all the bank personnel as well as all six customers, including a six-year-old boy and an eighty-year-old retired schoolmarm—to make sure no one could identify him."

"But one did," Louisa said, taking another dainty sip of her whiskey. "His partner. Roy Todd was wounded by a deputy town marshal while leaving the bank. Only Butters himself got away . . . until Lou rode him down." The Vengeance Queen arched a brow at her partner. "How did you ever manage to catch him without my help, Lou?"

She and Prophet had had another one of their verbal dustups the week previous to the holdup, when they'd been on the hunt for another pair of badmen, and had forked trails. Two days later, Prophet had ridden into Alva, Oklahoma, the day after Butters's visit to the Merchants Territorial Bank & Trust, and had gone after him.

To Louisa, Prophet quipped, "Amazing what a fella can do when no henpecking females are around to chew his ears down to fine nubs an' he can concentrate on his task." He turned to Ford. "What the hell is Butters doing out of the federal lockup, Jonas? The jury was out only twenty minutes and they came back with not just a guilty verdict, but a *guilty as hell* verdict! I thought they'd hanged the rat by now!"

Ford smiled without humor. "An appeals judge turned him loose. After the trial it was learned that the judge presiding over the first trial was a relative of someone Butters had been accused of murdering. The second judge decided not to retry Butters, believing that after the debacle of the first trial, there was no way Butters could get a fair second trial."

"A man like that don't deserve a fair trial!"

"I tend to agree with you there, Lou," Ford said. "At least when it comes to killers like Butters. But the law says different."

"So, now you're out two good deputies and an arm."

"There you have it."

"What got you on Butters's stinky trail in the first place, Jonas?" Prophet asked.

"The widow of a local rancher believes . . ." Ford let his words trail to silence as footsteps rose in the street, growing louder. More than one person was approaching the marshal's office.

Ford peered past Prophet to the window flanking the bounty hunter and said, "Speak of the devil," as he rose from his chair.

"What is it?" Prophet said, instinctively closing his hand over the butt of his Colt as he stepped to the window. More than one person was approaching in a hurry.

As Prophet peered out the window, seeing several rough-hewn men in trail garb climbing the veranda steps, there was a single, loud knock on the door. Ford was just moving out from behind his desk when the door latch clicked and the door was pushed open.

A woman in a purple, pleated gown edged with white lace strode resolutely through the door, collapsing the parasol she held in her right hand. "Hello, Jonas," she said, taking three of those resolute steps straight up to Ford's desk and swinging toward him as though she were about to challenge him to a fistfight. She swung the thick waves of her dark brown hair back from her olive cheeks and continued with,

"I thought I'd stop by to see what progress you're making, if any, on . . ."

She stopped talking as her glance slid toward Prophet standing by the window flanking her. She turned away from him, turned quickly back. Was it Prophet's goatish imagination, or did a small fire flicker briefly far back in her copper eyes?

A flush rose into her cheeks. For a second Lou thought she must have recognized him from somewhere, or thought she had, but then she gestured to him quickly with her open hand and said to Ford, "Who's this?"

Prophet wasn't given to cursory niceties, but this woman rocked him almost literally back on his heels. He doffed his hat and held it in both hands before him and said after clearing a sudden small knot in his throat, "Lou Prophet . . . Miss . . . ?"

His heart thudded as his eyes took her in quickly, not wanting to openly ogle the young woman but having a hard time not doing just that. She must have been all of twenty-one, possibly twenty-two, with a bosom half-exposed by the deep dip of her gown's corset. She wore a black silk choker around her long, fine neck, and it was trimmed with a square diamond set in gold.

While her breasts were full, they were not overly large. Her waist was narrow, her hips gently rounded. While she was dressed like a West Texas queen, and was probably the wife or daughter of a powerful man—a rich man, judging by the fineness of her attire—something told Prophet she felt just as at home in the rough trail gear Louisa was wearing, firmly in a Texas saddle.

Her face was delicately sculpted, almost doll-like,

but her eyes, nose, and chin were as resolute as her walk. Her jaws were set for hard commands, her gaze for cajoling.

"The bounty hunter," she said, fighting back the flush that had risen into her cheeks and was the only sign of unrestraint. She looked him up, then down, then up again, her gaze brushing across the Colt he had his gloved right hand on.

She glanced at Louisa. "Miss Bonaventure's partner. I see you're finally here."

"You see right, Miss . . . ?" Prophet tried again.

Since she didn't seem in any hurry to introduce herself, Ford did it for her. "This is Mrs. Dahlstrom, Lou. As I was about to explain, Mrs. Dahlstrom's—"

"Oh, call me Phoebe, Jonas," the young woman said. "We've known each other all our lives, for heaven sakes!"

Ford smiled stiffly, cleared his throat tolerantly. "As I was about to explain, Phoebe Dahlstrom's husband was killed recently."

"Murdered," Phoebe corrected for Prophet's benefit. "By George Hill."

"*Allegedly,*" Ford corrected the young woman for her own benefit.

"You're reading for the law, now, Jonas?" she snorted. Turning to Prophet, she said, "It is my firm belief that George Hill, a prominent businessman here in Carson's Wash, hired Charlie Butters to murder my husband."

"Just to play devil's advocate," Prophet said, "why would Mr. Hill do such a dirty low-down thing, and why do you think it was Charlie Butters who did it for him?"

"I seen him. I was there. I know what Butters looks like."

This from one of the five men who'd either followed Mrs. Dahlstrom into the marshal's office or were hanging back, as two were, arms crossed as they held up both sides of the doorframe. They were all dressed like ranch hands in wool shirts, billowy neckerchiefs, battered Stetsons, and brush-scarred chaps. To a man they wore at least two pistols.

The man who'd spoken was roughly six feet, with wide shoulders and a modest gut. He had long, sandy red hair and matching mustache and spade beard. His blue eyes were small and flat beneath thick, sun-bleached brows.

"This is my foreman, Melvin Handy," said Phoebe Dahlstrom. "He and Lars Gunderson were leading my father out to where a mountain lion had killed two steers. They'd stopped to drink from a spring when a man fired a rifle from a stand of mesquites."

"It was Butters," insisted Handy. "I know what Butters looks like. I seen him in Dodge City back a few years ago, and it was him, all right. Little pinched-up face, short, greasy yellow hair. Got a bull-horn tattoo on his throat, the name *Audrina* written inside it, and a silly braid hangin' down his chin."

"Charming," Louisa said, coolly ironic as always. "I've always wanted to have my name inside a bull-horn tattoo on a man's neck."

Ford chuckled as he and Louisa shared an amused glance.

Phoebe Dahlstrom was staring up at Prophet. She had to tilt her head back to do so. She held her lids ever so slightly closed, giving her an insouciant, vaguely sneering look, as though she were looking up at some barbaric creature of the wild but was doing her level best at lowering herself to make conversation with it. "There you have it, Mr. Prophet. Butters is why you are here"—she slid an accusatory glance toward the marshal—"since Jonas got himself shot by Butters. And two of his deputies killed."

"Now, Phoebe!" Ford said.

Not letting him continue, and returning her haughty gaze to Prophet, she hurried forward with: "I understand you captured that killer once before. It is my hope that, with Miss Bonaventure's help, you can do so again. I want Butters and George Hill brought to justice for murdering my husband."

"Why do I feel like a dog just sicced on a calf-killin' coyote?" Prophet said, smiling ironically, offended by her tone and demeanor and mesmerized by her eyes and a couple of other attributes he was in prime position, tall as he was, to have a full, downward-slanting view of.

She gave an ironic smile of her own, revealing even white teeth behind sensuous lips. "If you bring Butters to justice, Mr. Prophet, I am in a position to reward you most generously."

Louisa snorted.

Mrs. Dahlstrom looked at her sharply, with exasperation. "I meant a monetary reward!"

Louisa gave her an arched brow.

Mrs. Dahlstrom's entire face turned the red of an expensive French wine. Flustered, she said, "A monetary reward for *both* of you. Five hundred dollars."

"I accept," Prophet said. "After all, I do this for a

living." He glanced at Ford. "Although I'd do it as a favor to you, Jonas."

"As would I," Louisa said. "But I hunt killers for a living, as well, and I, too, accept your offer, Mrs. Dahlstrom."

The rancher's young widow gave her chin a cordial dip.

"Now, I'd like to repeat a question I asked before," Prophet said after throwing back the last of his whiskey and setting the glass on Ford's desk. "Why do you think George Hill wanted your husband killed, Mrs. Dahlstrom?"

Again, the conversation was interrupted by commotion from the street. The crunch of footsteps rose, and a man's deep voice yelled, "Ford? Marshal Ford? If you're holding a meeting concerning the murder of Max Dahlstrom . . . and his poor, grieving widow is present . . . how dare you not make sure I'm in attendance, as well?"

Prophet turned toward the open doorway, as did everyone else in the marshal's office. Between the two Dahlstrom men standing on the veranda, their backs now facing Prophet, Lou could see a beefy gent in an ice-cream suit, checked vest, and brown top hat moving toward them. He walked down the center of the dusty street inside an evenly spaced procession of four other gents—burly fellows armed with shotguns and what appeared to be hide-covered bung starters.

All four of the burly gents in the entourage were Prophet's size or larger. To a man, they looked like bare-knuckle fighters—the kind of men Prophet had seen on the waterfronts of coastal cities or rollicking river towns like Kansas City.

Prophet turned to Jonas Ford, who was making his way to the door, his expression that of a man who'd just eaten an entire lemon.

"George Hill, I presume?" Prophet said.

"Oh, nuts," was Ford's only reply.

Chapter 4

Prophet followed Jonas Ford out onto the veranda fronting the lawman's office.

"What can I do for you, George?" Ford asked the beefy man in the ice cream–colored suit now standing with his four even beefier men in the street just beyond the veranda's bottom step.

"You can answer my question, Jonas," Hill said, lifting a fat stogie to his mouth and taking several puffs.

He had a fleshy, darkly tanned face with a single, insinuating, flat brown eye. His other eye, the left one, had a black patch over it. His lips were thick and leering. A thatch of thin, dark brown air peeked out from beneath his top hat. "Why wasn't I informed a meeting was taking place?"

"The meeting doesn't concern you, Mr. Hill." This from Phoebe Dahlstrom, now stepping out of the marshal's office, as well. Standing to Prophet's right, between him and Ford, she glowered down into the street at the five brutish men staring back at her.

Goatish lust floated into the gazes of the four

toughs surrounding Hill, like thin clouds passing over the moon and tempering its light.

The pretty young widow continued with, "I was merely inquiring about the whereabouts of Mr. Prophet, whom I know Jonas . . . er, um, *Marshal Ford* . . . summoned here to track the man you hired to kill my husband."

Hill bunched his lips angrily but as though not noticing, Phoebe added, "I see that Mr. Prophet is here now, so I am confident that he and Miss Bonaventure will be running him down soon, and we'll get Mr. Butters's side of the story. Surely he won't wish to hang alone when it would be so much more comforting to have someone hanging beside him. Especially when that man is as culpable in his crime as Butters himself is. That man, of course, being you."

Prophet had to hand it to the woman. She wielded her pretty tongue as well as any border bandito wielded a razor-edged stiletto. He could almost feel the blade going in and twisting.

"You got no right to accuse me of Max's murder, young lady! No right at all! I'm tired of hearin' it, and if you don't stop, I'm gonna hire me a lawyer and sue your bloomers off!"

The men around him gave slant-eyed grins. Two chuckled dryly.

As Phoebe's men walked up behind her or to stand to either side of Prophet and Ford, their backs and shoulders defensively taut, she said, "Everyone in town knows that you two openly fought in your saloon the night before my husband was murdered. He accused you of stealing his beef and trying to convince the smaller ranchers to form a pool to stand against him. You knew of his plans to fence in his range, and several detestable nesters along with it—several deplorable nesters with whom you are in league to drive my husband off his land!"

"You got that backwards, just like you've always had everything else! It wasn't me that was tryin' to drive your dearly departed husband out of this country! It was your husband who's been trying to drive me out of this country by burnin' me out and jumpin' my minin' claims for years. And you know as well as I do it all started back nigh on twenty years ago, even before he cut out my eye!"

Oh, crap, Prophet mused. *Some bailiwick I've just been lured into.*

He glanced at Louisa who, returning his look, corroborated his sentiment by dipping her chin and arching her brows.

"Maybe we oughta just get this over with right here an' now, Mrs. Dahlstrom," said Phoebe's foreman, Melvin Handy, stepping forward and sliding his revolver from its holster. "Maybe Butters deserves to swing all by his lonesome."

Ford cursed and turned angrily to Handy. "Mister, you put that pistol back in its holster right now, or I'll throw you in the lockup!"

"Well, hell," Handy said, indicating Hill's men, who all stood taut and ready, nostrils flaring. "They're all armed!"

"Do it now, Handy!"

Handy glanced at Phoebe Dahlstrom, who gave him a slow blink.

Handy sighed and slid his hogleg back into its holster but did not snap the keeper thong back over the hammer, Prophet noticed.

Ford turned to Hill and the other men in the

street. "George, no meeting was taking place. At least, nothing formal. As you can see, no attorneys are present."

"Ain't that convenient?" Hill drawled, smirking.

"As Mrs. Dahlstrom just told you, she'd come over to see if Prophet had arrived. And he had. I'm sure he and Miss Bonaventure will be hitting the trail shortly. I hope to have Charlie Butters arrested and this mess cleaned up within a day or two. If you have no culpability in Mr. Dahlstrom's death, then you have nothing to worry about."

"Fancy talk, Jonas," Hill said. "The General would be right proud of your back-East learnin'. I don't care how much readin' for the law you do at night, on your own time. I know how things work out here. I know how many friends the Dahlstroms have. Everyone knows the General . . . and his son . . . was and *is* two of 'em."

Hill slid his oily gaze from Ford to Phoebe Dahlstrom then glanced around at his men and said, "Come on, boys. Let's head back. We got a saloon to tend."

"That's a good idea," Ford said.

Hill turned away then stopped and looked back. "You keep this in mind, Jonas. I don't care what Butters says. I did not hire him to kill Max. If he says I did, he's lyin'. Someone put him up to lyin'. If he killed Max, it wasn't for me."

"Spit it out a little clearer, George," Ford said.

"What I'm sayin' is this: If you come to arrest me, you'll be grabbin' the devil by the tail, an' you best be ready for the fight of your life."

His men all sealed the threat with a dull-eyed, smirking gaze at Ford and Prophet.

Hill gave a resolute dip of his chin and started walking east along the street, his bulky men lumbering after him.

No one on the veranda said anything for a full minute.

Then Phoebe Dahlstrom sighed and turned to Ford. "I've taken a room at the Rio Grande Hotel until this matter is cleared up, Jonas. Until George Hill swings from a gallows rope. So, you'll know where to find me to inform me of any new developments."

She glanced at Prophet, then at Louisa, then slid her oblique gaze back to Prophet once more, her eyelids closing slightly. "Good luck out there. Please take him alive. I want him to be able to say George Hill's name loudly and clearly . . . so there is no mistake."

With that, she glanced at Handy and the other men, opened her parasol, lifted her skirts above her ankles, revealing side-button, black patent shoes, and stepped gracefully down the veranda's three steps and into the street. Her men followed her in the direction of the hotel, to the east.

She had a long stride with her narrow back set straight, her nose high, like a prow determinedly cleaving the water of a turbulent ocean. Her dark brown hair danced across her shoulders, copper highlights glinting in the West Texas sun.

Staring after her, Jonas Ford said, "Imagine hating your father as much as that woman hates hers."

Louisa frowned at the town marshal. "What do you mean, Jonas?"

Ford glanced at her. "I didn't tell you? George Hill is Phoebe's father."

Prophet twisted a finger inside his ear. "Say that

again, would you, Jonas? I reckon my ears are packed with trail dust. I thought you said . . ."

"That George Hill was Phoebe Dahlstrom's father," Louisa finished for him.

"You both heard right." To Louisa, Ford said, "I'm sorry. I thought I mentioned it. I don't know how I could have left that out."

Prophet whistled and glanced west along the curving street, toward where Mrs. Dahlstrom and her entourage were just now approaching the Rio Grande Hotel—a humble, three-story, mud-brick affair with a large, shaded front porch. As the pretty widow climbed the veranda steps, one hand on the rail, she glanced back toward the marshal's office then turned her head sharply forward and, chin up, entered the hotel.

Prophet turned to Ford. "Why does she hate him so much?"

Ford sighed. "That's a long story. How 'bout if I explain it later? I have to make my rounds. I'm a bit shorthanded these days." He looked at Louisa. "Say, this evening at dinner? The Rio Grande has a fine dining room for a town so humble. Carson's Wash is a good stopping point for freight trains headed between El Paso and Abilene, and those freighters figure they need a good meal by the time they make it this far."

Prophet had a feeling he wasn't really the one being invited, which is why he hurried to beat Louisa to a response: "Why, thank you for the kind offer, Jonas. I'll be there!"

He slid his grin to Louisa, who returned it with a pasteboard one of her own.

"It's settled, then," Ford said, also smiling stiffly. "I'll meet you, uh, *both,* there!"

He pinched his hat brim to Louisa, dropped into the street, and began making his rounds.

When Ford was gone, Prophet glanced at his partner. "You fancy that boy, do you?"

"He's no boy," Louisa said, drawing out the word *boy* and staring after Ford with her mouth corners raised. "And what's not to fancy? He comes from a good family, is well educated, has good taste in clothes, is not one to frequent pleasure parlors, and takes a bath at least once a month."

"Still," Prophet said, "I think he's an all right fella."

He glanced at Louisa, who drew her mouth corners down. "Speaking of a bath . . ." She scrutinized her fellow bounty hunter's sweat-soaked, dirt-streaked buckskin tunic and his face covered with a couple layers of West Texas trail dust clinging to a two-day's growth of beard shadow. "There is a bathhouse behind the hotel."

"Well, thank you for that information, Miss Bonnyventure," Prophet said ironically. "I'll pass it along to the first person who asks. What time would you like to head out tomorrow after Charlie Butters? Do you think you can tear yourself away from your new beau as early as, say, first light?"

"No promises," Louisa said snootily. "If not, you go ahead and start without me. I'll just follow your stench and catch up to you before noon, I'm sure."

"You still mad about that whore in Witchita?"

Louisa jerked her head back. "What whore in . . . Oh, the little redhead who couldn't have been much over fifteen years old? I'd completely forgotten!" She laughed a little too shrilly.

"Good," Prophet said as he watched his comely partner drop down the veranda steps and pull her horse's reins off the hitchrack. "I'll be seein' you tonight in the Rio Grande, then."

"Whatever."

Louisa swung up onto the pinto's back and rode east toward the hotel. Prophet watched her go, regretting the whore.

But, then, he'd never hidden the fact from Louisa that he often lay with whores when times were good and he felt like stomping with his tail up. Meaning, when he'd taken down a sizable bounty, as he and Louisa had just done when they'd taken down the ex–riverboat pilot and serial kidnapper and rapist, Walt "the Sturgeon" Maloney, on the outskirts of Wichita.

An old friend of Prophet's had told him and the Vengeance Queen that he'd seen the wanted pervert whoring and gambling in several seedy dens near the warehouses along the Arkansas River. A whore had been murdered in that district, and Prophet's informant had believed the Sturgeon was the culprit.

Despite the Sturgeon's reputation for slipperiness as well as savagery, the two bounty hunters had taken him down without firing a single shot, as Maloney had been drunk as three Irish sailors on a Saturday night in Honolulu. That had been the easiest twelve hundred dollars Prophet had ever pulled down.

Why shouldn't he live it up?

When he and Louisa had split their winnings and parted ways, he'd tracked down a green-eyed, redheaded whore he'd been told about, and he'd paid ahead for three days. After the third day, he'd decided to take the girl, whose name was Camille, out and buy her a steak as a token of his appreciation. He'd tussled with prettier and more talented doxies in his time, but Camille had been sweet, and genuinely sweet whores—as opposed to the disingenuously sweet ones—were hard to find.

When Prophet and Camille had come up for a breather to play two-handed poker naked, legs crossed Indian-style on the love-mussed bed, she'd confessed that her heart had been crushed by a young man who'd promised to marry her. The young man from a good family had broken his and Camille's engagement because his parents hadn't approved of Camille's lowly upbringing on the wrong side of the Wichita tracks, despite Camille's intentions of using the money she'd saved working in a greasy café/butcher shop to attend a bookkeeping college in Kansas City.

When the boy had taken Camille's ring back, she resigned from the café and headed for Market Street, where it didn't take her long to find less taxing work that paid better. Pretty in the face and well proportioned, all Camille had had to do to secure the job was raise her blouse. Her madam had hired her on the spot.

So Prophet had felt a kinship with the girl. They were both lost souls, and they'd gotten along well for three whole days. Lou never got along with anyone, including Louisa, for that long! So he'd taken Camille out for a steak. Unbeknownst to Prophet, Louisa had been in the restaurant, a fact he had been made all too well aware of when she'd risen from her table, walked over to his and Camille's table, picked up Prophet's beer, and poured it over his head.

Then, without a word, she'd walked out, mounted up, and rode away.

Yep, she was mad about the whore, all right.

She had no right to be, but there it was. They were not married or even promised to each other. In fact, they didn't even get along that well!

Prophet figured that what had gotten the Vengeance Queen's bloomers twisted was that he'd hunted down Camille so soon after he and Louisa had spent a sublimely memorable night in each other's arms around a lonely fire on the Kansas prairie, whispering long-kept secrets and sweet nothings and such. For that long, sleepless and enchanting night, it had been as though they were the last man and woman on earth, and there were no more men to hunt or trails to follow.

They'd had everything they'd needed right there around that fire and in each other's eyes.

They'd enjoyed such nights in the past, just the two of them, their horses cropping grass a distance away, a coffeepot gurgling over the fire. Coyotes yammering in the surrounding hills.

But those nights never lasted. And they were growing fewer and farther between.

That's the way it always was with everything, Prophet thought now, watching Louisa lead her horse into the livery and feed barn that sat on the far side of the Rio Grande Hotel.

Nothing lasts. Everything changes. The good times grow fewer and farther between . . .

What's wrong with spending three days with a sweet whore now and then?

Chapter 5

Prophet sat on the veranda steps and rolled a smoke, smoking the quirley until Louisa walked out of the livery barn and into the hotel beside it.

Then he flipped the half-smoked cigarette into the street, mashed it out with his boot toe, mounted up, and rode Mean over to the livery barn. He had nothing more he wanted to say to her just now. Sometimes she was just too damn much . . .

He'd intended to hunt down a bathhouse before he'd even ridden into Carson's Wash. Louisa's jeers had made him reconsider. He hated being prodded. It usually made him do the opposite of what he'd been prodded to do, but in this case, after two hard days on the trail, his clothes sticking to him with an inch or so of adobe comprised of trail dust and his own sweat, he opted for the bath.

He would have settled for a whore's bath in his hotel room, splashing himself down with water from a pitcher. But since he was having dinner with the persnickety Vengeance Queen and her trimmed and tailored beau, he decided to let himself be goaded into a bona fide wallow in hot, soapy water. In contrast to the dimple-cheeked Jonas Ford, he looked rough enough even without wearing ten pounds of West Texas dirt.

So when he'd turned Mean and Ugly over to the livery barn's hostler, a towheaded, bashful, but good-natured kid named Charlie, he burdened himself with his shotgun, his rifle and scabbard, and his bedroll and saddlebags, and tramped around behind the hotel to SYLVUS TAYLOR'S BATHHOUSE & TONSORIAL PARLOR, as the humble adobe hut was proclaimed by a sign over its front door.

Another, smaller sign read—HAIR TRIMMING 10 SENTS.

Yet another offered TOOTH EXTRAKSHUNS AND MINER BONE REPLASEMENTS (whatever the hell that meant).

A fourth, tacked to the bathhouse's halfway-open front door, warned FULL-BLOOD INJUNS AND JIPPSIES NOT ALOWED ON THE PREMISSES.

"You Sylvus?" Prophet asked the small-framed old man sitting in a ratty, brocade-upholstered parlor chair abutting the cabin's front wall. The chair looked half-disintegrated, likely having been left out in the sun and wind and rain.

The old man, wearing a shabby bowler, woke with a jolt, snapping his eyes wide and giving a startled grunt.

"Mercy sakes alive!" he yowled.

"Sorry about that, partner. I didn't know how else to wake you."

"Christalmighty, you like to give me a heart stroke! Probably shaved a good three years off my earthly allowance!"

"Life ain't so good after you hit thirty, anyways," Prophet said, still in the bad mood that had come over him when he'd reflected on his three days with Camille and Louisa's grudge against same. He shifted the saddle and bedroll riding his left shoulder. "I ain't in no hurry to start shoveling coal into the devil's furnace, but Ole Scratch can pluck me from this swampy mire anytime he wants."

"Scratch, huh?" the old man said, rising.

He appeared to be a humpback, the hump rising from the base of the back of his neck and shoving his head slightly forward, chin down. He had a lean, sallow face. Almost skeletal, with sunken cheeks and colorless beard bristles. His eyes owned an ironic, humorous gleam, however.

The hump made him appear to be in a perpetual shrug. He wore overalls over a red-and-black-checked flannel shirt, and his cloying stench made Prophet opine that in comparison he himself didn't smell all that bad.

"You one o' them devil worshippers, are ya?" he asked. "I hear some Injuns in Mexico do that—worship Ole Scratch."

"Nah, I just made him a deal, is all. My note's gonna be called in one of these days, likely sooner rather than later."

"Christ, you're a gloomy cus, ain't ya?"

"Ignore me, Mr. Taylor. I just had a long ride in the hot sun, almost had my head blown off, shot the man who almost blew my head off, and been mocked by an uppity blonde."

"Was the blonde pretty?"

"Oh yeah."

"That makes it worse."

"Tell me about it."

"You sound like a hard-luck character. Me—I'm superstitious. I'm not sure I want you on the premises."

"Well, I'm neither Injun or Gypsy. Just sour luck and a bleak mood, but I reckon I'll feel a little better after I scrub some of your proud state off my person." He looked around for a sign concerning baths but not seeing one, asked, "How much for a hot soak?"

"Six bits includes a bucket each of cold and hot water. Each bucket after that is three more bits."

"Why so steep?"

Taylor glanced at the mud-and-wood-frame hut to the right of the one proclaiming to be a bathhouse and tonsorial parlor. A thin tendril of gray smoke issued from a rusty chimney pipe. All manner of trash lay around the place. "I keep the stove goin' all day and you've likely seen the dearth of trees in these parts."

"Give me your standard bath."

"What about your duds?"

"What about 'em?"

"For another fifty cents I can take 'em over to the Chinaman who runs a laundry on the other side of the wash, and he'll scrub 'em for ya."

Prophet thought about it. He didn't want to wait that long. It was late in the day, and he wanted a couple more belts of whiskey before he met Ford and Louisa, to help stem his ill humor. "I'll just soak my longhandles in the tub. Would you hang them over a branch? Shouldn't take them long to dry in this West Texas furnace."

"I can do that." Taylor nodded.

"Could you hang the rest of my duds somewhere and beat 'em with a stick? I'll pay you an extra fifty cents."

"Does a man in my pathetic state look capable of that maneuver?" Taylor snarled, canting his head back as though to indicate the hump. "I'm liable to hurt myself, you insensitive lout!"

Prophet snorted. "Would you risk injury for an extra dollar?"

Taylor grinned. "Yep!"

Prophet gave another snort then reached into his pocket and tossed the man the coins.

While Sylvus Taylor ambled into his shack for the water, Prophet dropped his gear at the base of the bathhouse's front wall then walked into the hut's steamy shadows. There were two big, corrugated tin tubs inside. They were long and narrow, with headrests at the wider ends. They looked vaguely like coffins. A few tomato crates standing against the shack's walls served as shelves.

One of the tubs was occupied. Its occupant had his bare arms resting on the sides of the tub. His head was thrown back and to the right against the headrest, and his eyes were closed, lower jaw hanging.

Dead asleep and softly snoring.

His wet, dark brown hair was pasted to his broad skull. His arms were pale while his face was darkly tanned and etched with deep lines around his eyes and mouth. He wore a mustache that drooped down both sides of his chin.

It was hard to tell much about a sleeping, wet, naked man—you needed the eyes, Prophet vaguely realized, to complete the picture—but he thought he might be Mexican. That opinion was bolstered by the brightly colored clothes piled atop the chair beside the tub, on the man's right side. Also by the high-crowned, wide-brimmed, black felt hat hanging from the chair and the high-heeled, fancily stitched boots planted beneath it.

The man's tub was near full of sludgy, dark water, gray-streaked with used soap. He'd obviously shaved, because beard stubble like metal filings formed an oily slick atop the water, with here and there a creamy dollop of stubble-peppered shaving soap. Floating amidst the sludge was a quirley stub that had probably slipped from the man's slack mouth.

Prophet had undressed around enough men not to feel overly self-conscious. Besides, this one was asleep.

So he set his guns, including his shotgun and rifle, atop the ladder-back chair near his own tub then kicked out of his boots and skinned languidly, stiffly out of his filthy duds. He was still peeling out of his longhandles when Taylor returned with two buckets of water.

As Taylor poured the water into the tub, Prophet indicated the sleeping soaker and asked, "Who's that?"

Taylor shrugged—or at least bowed his head, which Prophet took for a shrug, given the man's impairment. "I don't know. Some tequila drunk. If he drowns in there, I'm charging him extra."

He chuckled.

Taylor waited until Prophet had washed his longhandles out in the water, then the bathman took the wet longhandles and dry, dirty clothes outside. Prophet found a cake of lye soap in a crate between his tub and that of the sleeping gent's, as well as a stiff brush, and went to work scouring his rugged, filthy, stinky hide.

He'd barely gone to work when his water turned black as ink. Oh well. He'd bathed in stock troughs before. This couldn't be any worse. A little stink might linger after the bath, but a man should smell like a man, by God, and not a French perfume factory.

Despite the dirty water he was lying in, his skin tingled with the feeling of clean.

He glanced at his bath partner. The man was still asleep, in the same position as before, face turned away from Prophet. His mouth hung wide, and he softly snored. His cigarette stub bobbed on the water, disturbed with each of the man's heavy breaths.

"Not a bad idea," Prophet muttered.

He sat back against the headrest of his own tub and closed his eyes. When he opened them again only a few seconds later, his bath partner was sitting up in his own tub, twisted around to face Prophet, his eyes and mouth wide in an expression of murderous lunacy.

In his right hand he held a razor-edged hatchet back behind his right shoulder.

"Time to shovel coal, amigo!"

Prophet snapped up his Colt Peacemaker, which he'd been holding down under the water and snugged up against his right thigh. His assailant saw the gun, and his eyes darkened. He gave a bellowing yell as he jerked the hatchet forward.

Praying that the metallic .45 cartridge residing beneath the Colt's hammer hadn't gotten wet, Prophet aimed quickly at the man's chest, and fired twice. The man grunted as he jerked back, sawing straight down with the hatchet and flinging it against the right-top edge of Prophet's tub.

There was a dull metallic thud as the hatchet ricocheted off the tub before clattering onto the floor.

As Prophet's assailant sagged back against the far side of his own tub, blood geysering from the twin holes in his chest, the quick thuds of running footsteps sounded outside the half-open front door. Prophet sat back in his tub, cocked the Colt again, and fired a third round as another man kicked the door wide and leveled a double-barreled shotgun.

As Prophet's slug tore into the man's throat, Lou dropped into his dirty water, hearing the dull, reverberating roar of his second assailant's shotgun being detonated. Wincing, waiting for the bite of buckshot and happy when it didn't come, Prophet lifted his head up out of the water to see the second assailant rolling around on the ground outside the wide-open door, thrashing wildly and clutching his bloody throat.

Both barrels of his barn-blaster had chewed into the ceiling. Wood slivers, dirt, and weeds were still raining down.

More footsteps rose from behind the bounty hunter.

Prophet turned as yet a third gunman kicked open the hut's back door. Prophet caught a glimpse of a black hat and a red shirt and of a Winchester bearing down at him a half second before his Colt roared two more times, bucking in his hand and stabbing red flames and gray smoke toward the third assailant, who screamed and stumbled back through the door.

The man triggered his rifle into the front of Prophet's tub, the bullet clanging shrilly.

And then he was gone.

But Prophet could hear him out there behind the bathhouse, cursing sharply. He was stumbling around, wounded. He stumbled into Prophet's view again, crouched forward and dragging his boot toes and trying to raise a revolver in his right hand.

Standing naked in his tub now, Prophet aimed carefully and shot the third assailant through the man's right temple. The man's head jerked back sharply. Prophet heard his neck snap. The man plopped onto his ass and then onto his back and lay jerking near a dusty mesquite.

Prophet stood in the tub, dripping.

His own powder smoke wafted around him.

He looked around, gun still raised, listening for more assailants.

Footsteps rose beyond the front of the cabin. Turning around in the tub, Prophet exchanged his empty Colt for his twelve-gauge Richards coach gun and clicked both hammers back as he squared his shoulders at the front door.

Someone was approaching, walking now.

The footsteps stopped. Louisa edged a look around the door's right side, peering into the bathhouse. She held a pretty, silver-chased Colt up high near her shoulder, hammer cocked.

Prophet depressed his shotgun's hammers.

Louisa looked at the dead man lying near her, outside the front door. She looked at the dead man lying half in and half out of his bloody tub beside Prophet. She looked past Prophet toward the third dead assailant lying just beyond the washhouse's back door.

Then she looked Prophet's naked body up and down, glanced at the black water at his ankles, curled one half of her upper lip, lowered her Colt, and said, "You clean up right well, Lou."

Prophet turned to the man who'd tried to give him a haircut. "I *thought* that hombre was sleepin' just a little too sound!"

Chapter 6

Jonas Ford came running toward the bathhouse that reeked of cordite and spilled blood just after Louisa had peeked in.

Several curious townsmen came, as well. The humpback, Sylvus Taylor, walked up cautiously from where he'd been beating Prophet's dirty pants and shirt with a willow switch to take a look around at the carnage.

He peered at the bounty hunter still standing naked in his tub, and said, "Holy jeepers, mister, looks like your day ain't gettin' a whole lot better, is it?"

At first, Prophet thought Taylor might have been in on the ambush. But he believed the man when he said the first time he'd seen the man with the shotgun was when the gent was running out of some brush toward the front of the washhouse, just after the man with the hatchet had screamed following the staccato bark of Prophet's six-gun.

Jonas Ford and several other townsmen, including the man from earlier whom Ford had called Dutch, recognized the three dead men as locals. The one who'd wielded the hatchet was—or, had been, rather—Ruben Ramirez. The dearly departed gent with the gut-shredder had been Mortimer Kinsley. The man with the rifle, now attracting ants and flies out back, had been one H. G. Holloway, whom some called "Bud" for reasons that blurred back into the murk of the man's childhood.

The three were not known as out-and-out criminals, just local louts who couldn't hold jobs longer than a few weeks at a time though they intermittently worked as market hunters for local restaurants and the Rio Grande Hotel, teamsters, ranch hands, woodcutters, general odd-jobbers, and anything else that would supply them with enough pocket jingle for a bender now and then. One townsman said he thought they were wanted for rustling down in Mexico but another townsman disagreed, saying, "Those three were too stupid to find their asses with both hands much less their way down to Mexico."

Jonas Ford remembered that the Mexican, Ramirez, had cut a whore while drunk and then tried to rob the whorehouse, but after a brief stint in the local hoosegow he'd been given probation.

The man called Dutch turned to Prophet, who had dressed by now though his balbriggans were still damp, and said accusingly, "All three was friends with Tom Lowry and Lowry's pa and brothers." Dutch spat to one side, wiped chaw from his lips with the back of one hand, and turned to Ford. "They was probably tryin' to kiss the Lowrys' asses by shooting your man Prophet here for Tom's sake. I told you there was gonna be a reckonin'!"

With that, Dutch cut a sneer to Lou, then, biting off another chunk of braided tobacco, turned and walked back in the direction of the saloon he and several others had poured out of when they'd heard the shooting.

Ford sent a man to fetch the undertaker again.

Then he turned to Prophet and said, "Well, Lou, I suppose you know this means—"

"Yeah, I know," Prophet said. "Another affidavit. I'm already getting writer's cramp." He sighed.

"If you stay on this track," Louisa told her partner, "you're going to be spending so much time fending off bushwhackers, you'll have no time to help me run down Charlie Butters."

"Help *you* run down Butters?" Prophet said with a caustic snort.

Louisa said, "You must have cleaned out your ears in there. Your hearing is just fine."

Prophet raked his indignant gaze from her to Jonas Ford then back to Louisa again. "It does me warm to see you two so worried about me," he said, donning his hat then leaning down to pick up his gear from where it sat against the front of the washhouse. "Are either one of you at all worried that the next passel of bushwhackers who come armed with croaker sacks in which to take my head to the Lowry clan, might just get 'er done?"

Ford looked down at the dead man lying a few feet from the washhouse's front door. Sylvus Taylor stood over the cadaver, admiring the man's relatively new Justin boots.

"You seem to be doing okay so far, Lou," the marshal said. "Just keep that third eye of yours skinned, and I reckon in time you'll whittle away so many badmen from these parts I can start taking a day off now and then and go fishing."

Ford and Louisa laughed.

Ford held his arm out to her as he swung around to face the heart of town. "May I chaperone you back to the Rio Grande, Miss Bonaventure?"

"Not if you're going to call me Miss Bonaventure, Jonas," she jokingly chided the man.

"All right, then . . . Louisa, may I . . . ?"

"Of course you may, Jonas," Louisa said, dipping her chin then beaming up at the handsome young lawman.

They walked away without so much as another glance at Prophet, who stood slumped beneath his gear, flaring his nostrils at them. "That's all right," he grumbled to the pair's backs. "No need to help me with my burden here. I'll get it just fine over to the hotel my ownself!"

He slumped after them.

Behind him, Sylvus Taylor asked sheepishly, "Uh . . . do you think it would be all right if I take Kinsley's boots? My heels are shot and Fred Simmons'll charge me an' arm an' a leg to sew another one on."

"Why not?" Prophet said, continuing toward the hotel. "I expect Kinsley's done all the walkin' in them boots he's gonna do."

When Prophet had secured a room in the hotel, he tossed his gear into a corner then stripped down to his birthday suit.

He hung his still-damp longhandles over a chair near an open window to let the desert air finish drying them, then lay down on the bed. He rolled a quirley and smoked it, leaning back against the bed's two pillows. All he wore was his hat, tipped down low on his forehead. He had his shotgun and Peacemaker on the bed beside him, in case any more owlhoots decided to try to kick him out with a cold shovel.

Prophet's nerves were normally like steel. It took a lot to shoot them. But they were shot now. Understandably, to his way of thinking. After all, he'd just ridden into this country around Carson's Wash and already four men had tried to blow his head off. At least, three had tried to blow it off. One had tried to cleave it in two, like a pumpkin, with a rusty hatchet!

Not only that, but he'd ridden into town to find his girl cozying up with a handsome young town marshal.

His girl?

Frowning, Prophet studied the coal of his smoldering quirley.

Now, you know she ain't yours, old son. Just like you ain't hers.

Got it?

"Yeah, I got it," he muttered, startled by the befuddlement he heard in his own voice.

He was glad when someone knocked on his door. That would be the bottle he'd asked the desk clerk to have sent to his room. Just in case it wasn't, he carried his Colt over to the door. He covered his privates with his hat and said through the door, "That my whiskey?"

When a high-pitched female voice said it was, Prophet set his gun on the dresser and opened the door, keeping his privates covered with his hat. A young girl, all of sixteen, her hair in braids, stood in the hall holding a labeled bottle of bourbon. Prophet had decided to go for a labeled bottle so he didn't feel so inferior to Jonas Ford.

He grabbed a quarter off the dresser, handed it through the door to the girl as a tip, then took the bottle. Her young eyes swept his bare chest and then dropped to the hat. They widened in shock.

"I'm, uh, dryin' out my balbriggans, little one," he said, sheepish, adding, "Much obliged for the jump juice," and closed the door.

The girl burst into self-conscious laughter and ran off down the hall.

"Old son, you don't have a damn bit of dignity," he muttered to himself, splashing bourbon into a water glass on the dresser. "Jonas Ford wouldn't go to the door in only his hat, you blasted fool. No wonder she fancies him more than you. And you can bet she wasn't just accidentally passin' through here, either, when the trouble with Butters erupted. She'd *come* here. To see Jonas."

He raised the glass, stared at it for a moment, said, "Ah, hell—so what?" And threw back the shot.

He refilled the glass, returned to the bed, and sat there and smoked and drank another few fingers of bourbon before he dressed, gave his hat a cursory brushing though it did little good—those ancient weather and crusted salt stains were there for the duration—and went downstairs. He walked into the dining room off the lobby, the carpet cushioning his foot thuds and muffling the ringing of his spurs.

He stopped a few feet inside the room, staring

toward the table at which Louisa and Jonas Ford were already sitting.

Again, that snaggletoothed demon, jealousy, nipped the bounty hunter's innards.

Louisa had brushed her hair till it shone. It spilled prettily across her shoulders, one side tucked behind her ear. Early-evening sunlight made it sparkle like spun honey. She wore a dressy leather jacket over her other customary attire, which never seemed as trail-worn as Prophet's duds.

Jonas sat across from her, dressed in his standard three-piece suit but this time with a paisley vest and glistening gold watch chain. The suit looked new and expensive. He'd recently combed his hair. It, too, shone in the light from the window, as did his thick mustache of the same chocolate brown.

Ford was leaning forward over the table, talking intimately with Louisa, smiling, showing his perfect teeth. They were drinking wine. Prophet could tell that Jonas was relating a humorous story. Suddenly the young marshal lifted his head and laughed, and Louisa did the same, throwing her head far back on her shoulders. Prophet could hear the music of her laughter. He realized suddenly how few times he'd ever heard her laugh.

It was a pretty laugh. As pretty as the rest of her.

Lou turned around. He'd find another place to dine this evening. Three would obviously be a crowd at Ford and Louisa's table. He'd nearly made it to the door when a female voice said, "You're leaving, Mr. Prophet?"

He stopped and turned to his left. Phoebe Dahlstrom stood at a near table, which, like the others, was covered in white satin. Her foreman, Melvin

Handy, sat at the same table, a napkin over his right, denim-and-chap-clad thigh. He was looking doubtfully up at Prophet. His sandy red hair had been neatly pomaded and combed. On the table was a bottle of wine and a basket of bread. Phoebe held a glass of red wine. A half-filled schooner of beer sat before Handy.

His hat was hooked over the back of a chair to his left.

"Oh, uh . . . Hello, Mrs. Dahlstrom," Prophet said, keeping his voice low so neither Ford nor Louisa would hear him. He didn't turn to look at them again. He hoped they hadn't seen him. He desperately wanted to leave the dining room before they did. "Uh . . . yeah . . . a change of plans."

He smiled cordially, pinched his hat brim, and took another step forward.

"Would you consider yet *another* change of plans?" Mrs. Dahlstrom said, halting Prophet once more. She glanced over at Ford and Louisa and then returned her gaze to Prophet, the twinkle of understanding in her eyes. A soft smile grabbed at her full, sensual lips. "One that involved dining with me this evening?"

Prophet frowned, a little taken aback by the offer. He looked at Handy, who returned his frown though Handy's was more like that of a dog with a bone.

"Melvin was just leaving," Phoebe said, a tightness in her voice, a just as tight smile on her lips. "Weren't you, Melvin?"

A flush rose in the foreman's cheeks. His frown turned to a hateful glare at Prophet, and then he tossed his napkin down on the table, slid his chair back awkwardly, and rose. "Sure. Why not?"

He doffed his hat and grabbed his beer. He

glanced once more, pugnaciously, at Prophet and then at his pretty employer as he stomped out of the dining room.

"That man ain't happy," Prophet said.

She gave a devious little smile then indicated Handy's chair with her open hand. "Please . . ."

Prophet dared another glance at Ford and Louisa, the dagger of jealousy twisting again in his gut. "Sure," he said, peevishness deepening his voice. "Sure. Don't mind if I do."

Phoebe followed his gaze to the marshal and the Vengeance Queen's table. "They seem to be quite involved," she mused.

"Don't they, though?" Prophet heard himself snarl, casting another glance across the room.

Mrs. Dahlstrom arched a brow. "I meant they seem to be quite involved in a *conversation.*"

"Call it what you like," Prophet said, his ear trips warming slightly with chagrin. He slid his chair up closer to the table. "I mean . . . that's what I meant, too."

She studied him until he grew self-conscious. Again, his ears warmed. "Would you like a glass of wine?" she asked. "Or are you more of a beer-and-bourbon man?"

Prophet hadn't quite heard her, for just then, as he'd glanced across the room again, he saw that Louisa had spotted him. She was looking toward him, a smile quickly fading from her lips. It was like a cloud passing over the sun.

Prophet knew that it was not to his credit that he suddenly felt a thrill of satisfaction. He slid his gaze from Louisa to Phoebe, who regarded him with both lovely brows winged curiously.

"I'm sorry," he said. "I was just a little distracted. What did you say, Mrs. Dahlstrom?" It was time to give the lovely woman before him his full attention.

"I said, please do call me Phoebe," she said, brightening, the fading, lemon-colored light from the windows dancing in her glossy brown eyes. "And let's get you a stiff glass of bourbon and some beer, shall we? Oh, waiter!"

Chapter 7

When Prophet's beer and double bourbon arrived, Phoebe Dahlstrom lifted her wineglass. "Let's have a toast, shall we?"

"A toast," Prophet said, lifting his bourbon glass. "To what?"

"To your bringing Charlie Butters to town in handcuffs." She arched a brow and dipped her chin, like a gently admonishing schoolmarm. "Sooner rather than later."

"I'll drink to that." Prophet couldn't help casting one more quick glance toward Louisa and Ford, who were now ordering, the dining room's single waiter scribbling on a small pad.

He clinked his glass to Phoebe's and sipped his bourbon.

"And how about if we make a little agreement, Mr. Prophet?"

"Only if you call me Lou, Phoebe."

"All right, then. Lou it is. Let's you and I agree to give each other our full attention this evening, shall we? I mean, it does look like we're all each other has." Phoebe gave a smoky half grin, glanced around, then leaned intimately forward. "And, if you won't think me too forward for saying so, I think I have the pick of the crop. At least, as far as this dining room is concerned."

Prophet smiled, feeling a flush in his cheeks. Now that he was giving this woman his full attention, having put Louisa where she belonged—on the back burner of the range in his mind—he saw again, as he'd seen in Ford's office, how pretty and sensual Phoebe Dahlstrom was. Every bit as alluring as Louisa, though in her own unique way.

Prophet followed the woman's gaze around the room. There were about twelve other diners, including Ford and Louisa. Most were men—businessmen and three or four fellas who appeared freighters. Maybe a stock buyer or two, whom you could distinguish from range men by their large, soft bellies and pasty complexions. Two of them sat with a gaudily dressed woman who Prophet assumed was a doxie. She laughed a little too loudly, and her late-middle-aged dinner companions didn't seem to care.

By far the handsomest man in the room was also the youngest—Jonas Ford.

"The marshal has me all beat to hell," Prophet said. "If you'll forgive my farm manners and blue tongue." He sipped his frothy ale, which was surprisingly cool for these parts. The hotel must have a deep cellar.

"If you like well-groomed men," Phoebe said. "If

you like men who have as good a taste in clothes as I do."

"You don't?"

"Nothing against Jonas," Phoebe said, a fleeting, deprecating smile twitching across her mouth. "He and I grew up together. I know him well. A nice man; a learned man as well as an ambitious man. But he's always had a bit of the dude in him. Maybe because of my own crude upbringing, I've always been attracted to large, masculine men. Men who could wield a filthy tongue when one was necessary, and know how to swing their fists when words won't settle the debate. That's the kind of man Carson's Wash needs for its lawman."

Prophet compared the woman's fragile beauty to her words, and the contrast was stark. As well as more than slightly arousing . . .

"You don't approve of Jonas's law-bringing skills?" he asked.

"I did before . . . well, before Butters murdered my husband and Jonas and his deputies did nothing to bring him in except to get two of them killed and Jonas with his arm in a sling."

Prophet didn't want to talk about Jonas Ford anymore. He felt funny about the topic, because he saw Jonas as a friend. He couldn't also help seeing him as competition, though he didn't want to see him that way. It was a nasty feeling. A boyishly immature one. If he'd been a few years younger, he might have thrown a punch or two by now and made a total ass out of himself.

No, he didn't want to talk about Jonas Ford.

By way of switching the topic of the conversation,

he angled toward the thing about Phoebe Dahlstrom that had been percolating in the back of his brain.

"Speaking of your so-called crude upbringing, Mrs. . . . I mean, Phoebe . . ."

"Yes?"

"Jonas told Louisa and me something earlier, outside his office, that I found a little hard to believe—given the circumstances, and all."

Phoebe gave a wry grin, pink lips parting just a little. She blinked once, slowly. "He told you that George Hill is my father." She dragged the words out as though she were confessing a secret she'd been keeping for a long time. One that she didn't like to even think about.

"So it's true."

"It's true."

Phoebe emptied her wineglass and set the glass back down on the table. As she refilled it, she said, "Let's order some food, shall we? If I'm going to tell you my life's story, I'm going to need some fortification beyond wine"—she set the nearly empty bottle down on the table and rolled her eyes—"though the wine helps."

Later, when their steaks and all the surroundings, including a steaming wicker basket of crusty bread, had arrived, and they were cutting into their meat, she said, "Yes, my father is George Hill. He raised me here in Carson's Wash—before there was anything *but* the wash. And the Apaches. There were plenty of Apaches. And rattlesnakes.

"My mother died when I was twelve. She and my father had had a terrible row, and my mother ran out. My father had slapped her while I cowered under the kitchen table. It was night. She must have lost her sense of direction and fell into a deep gorge. That was the Lord taking pity on her, saving her from my father's rough ways. God or whoever's up there took no such pity on me. George Hill was and is a coldhearted devil. I didn't realize it when I was much younger. Before my mother died. Before he *killed* her. He was a big, tough man who started the town when he built up a spring that made it possible to haul freight through this country. Then he built a saloon and a trading post that were the only ones within two hundred miles. He seemed to me a man who could do anything. To me, he *was* God!

"Only, this god had an enemy."

"Dahlstrom?"

"The man I came to marry."

"How did that happen? If I'm bein' overly curious, Phoebe, just tell this cat to lay down. I don't need to know any more than I already do to run Butters to ground."

"I have nothing to hide, Lou. All of my skeletons are right out in the open for all to see. I first fell in love with my husband Max's son, Erik. My father, however, forbade me to marry Erik. Max came into this country around the same time my father had, saw the future in that spring, and bought an old Spanish land grant on which he built his own ranch. He built several businesses here in Carson's Wash, and he partnered up with Hannibal Ford, or 'the General,' as everyone around here knows him, to establish a bank and trust as well as a land office and a stagecoach line, which is still running.

"All three men—Max, the General, and my father,

George Hill—were tough, belligerent, domineering men. They'd fought in the war back East and then the Apaches out here. All they really knew was violence. Naturally, they found themselves in competition with each other. Max and the General joined forces against my father. The two factions tried to drive each other out. Things got violent on both sides. Both sides hired gunmen. Men were killed in town and on the range.

"Through all this chaos, I fell in love with Erik Dahlstrom and saw him on the sly. When my father found out, he had Erik beaten to within an inch of his life. Erik survived, but, like a whipped dog, he was ruined. He headed for Mexico and died down there while running with a gang of ex-Confederate outlaws. My heart was broken. I turned against my father. I had nowhere to live, so Max took me in to keep house for him.

"A month after his sickly wife passed, Max and I were married. That was five years ago. On our wedding day, Max and I and his men came to town to celebrate and to stay here, in Max and the General's hotel, the Rio Grande. My father and his men came over from my father's saloon and mercantile and lumberyard to wreak havoc right here in this dining room. My father and Max fought mano a mano.

"They were a couple of splendid bulls fighting over past and current injuries. For their honor. For a *woman.* Damn near killed each other. When my father fell, beaten and exhausted, half his clothes ripped off his body, Max turned his left eye to pudding with a spur rowel. While my father screamed, clutching his bloody eye, I knelt before him and laughed in his face!"

Phoebe had lifted her chin proudly, defiantly, as she'd espoused this last in a voice buoyant with jubilation. Again, Prophet had the impression of the prow of a clipper ship cleaving a turbulent ocean. She smiled brightly over the rim of her wineglass.

Prophet had stopped eating midway through his meal. He'd been riveted on the girl's tale as well as on the passion with which she'd relayed it. He couldn't help being more than a little aroused, as well, by the half-crazed fervor in her eyes.

It was as if she were seeing it all again—that horrific mano a mano fight right here in the Rio Grande, and her father's eye turned to "pudding" by her husband on their wedding night. Her husband, who had likely been twice her age or more.

A man whom she had no doubt married for the sole purpose of defying her father.

"I believe the cat has your tongue, Mr. Prophet," Phoebe said, and laughed.

"It does indeed," Prophet said, clearing the frog in his throat and staring back at the ravishing young woman before him. He wasn't sure if it was the bourbon, but his brain was slow to absorb the information. Or the full impact of the violence and bloodshed that had occurred here. "Seems like such a nice, quiet little town."

"True, it's been a lot quieter here over the past five years. It helped when Jonas Ford came back from college in the East to take over as marshal. He'd returned a year before his father died. The General had always been respected in these parts, as he'd fought valiantly in the war, and that respect was passed down to his son."

"So why do you suppose your father waited until now to kill your husband?"

Phoebe cocked a brow and shrugged a shoulder as she resumed eating. Forking a large chunk of meat into her mouth, she said, "Evil. Wickedness. A malevolence he was born with. I knew that when things settled down they'd only really settled down on my father's part for one reason. He was biding his time. He was licking his wounds, savoring his pain. He wanted me and Max to have some time together, to come to love and respect each other. Which we did, in fact, despite the broad gap in our ages. Max might have been old, Lou, but I will tell you this"—she leaned forward to mutter with a devilish glint in her sexy eyes—"he had not only the right equipment but the skill to go along with it, to satisfy a woman."

Phoebe winked, gave a husky chuckle, and forked more bloody meat between her pretty, pink lips.

"I think that cat has got your tongue again, Lou!" she said with naughty delight, laughing as she chewed.

Prophet had never known a woman to make him blush as many times in one sitting, but Phoebe Dahlstrom wasn't just any woman. This was one whose mold had been broken across the knee of whatever laughing god had made her. Prophet had thought he'd had his hands full with Louisa. Here was another one who could tie a man's britches in a knot.

Prophet cleared his throat again. The last chunk of meat and potatoes he'd eaten had gotten turned cattywampus somewhere around his vocal cords.

While he was trying to pick some coherent words out of the confusion of thoughts running through his brain, Phoebe shoved her nearly empty plate aside, picked up her wineglass, and clutched it to her breasts as she leaned intimately forward and cast a furtive glance toward where Ford and Louisa were eating on the other side of the room.

"Tell me, Lou—and please admonish me if I'm being too forward—but have you and the Vengeance Queen . . . uh . . . slept together?" She turned to him and fluttered an eyelid. "And I don't mean *slept.*"

Chapter 8

Prophet had just taken the last sip of his whiskey.

The blatant impertinence of Phoebe's question nearly caused him to spit the bourbon across the table at her. He managed to swallow it down after a few seconds wrestling with it, then glanced toward Louisa once more.

It was as though Louisa herself had heard the question. She met Prophet's glance with a glance of her own, and a raised eyebrow.

Prophet looked back at Phoebe Dahlstrom and, blushing again, said, "If Ma Prophet taught this ole possum-poker one thing it was to not go around talkin' out of school."

"Oh, come on," Phoebe said, pooching out her bottom lip in a feigned pout. "I let you see the dust under my rug."

"You didn't need to."

She studied him, frowning. She glanced once more at Louisa, who had returned her own attention to Jonas Ford. Turning back to Prophet, Phoebe gave a whimsical half smile and said, "I had a feeling . . ."

Prophet sipped his beer, set it down, and fiddled with the handle. "About what?"

"You love her, don't you?"

Prophet sighed. He felt a wall going up inside him. A protective wall. He felt as though he was not only protecting himself from an eccentric young woman who knew few bounds, but Louisa, as well.

"Cat's got your tongue again, Lou."

Prophet yawned. "I must be gettin' old," he said, glancing toward the windows. The sun was getting low but was not yet down. Long, dark shadows leaned out away from the buildings on the north side of the street. "I do believe I'm going to have a smoke and roll into the mattress sack. We'll be getting an early start after Butters."

He leaned back and reached into his pants pocket.

"I'll get this," Phoebe said. "My treat."

"Not a chance. You pay me the five hundred for Butters, and we'll be more than square."

"Lou." She leaned over the table again, pinning him with a lusty, smoky gaze. "I'd like you to spend the night with me."

Prophet frowned. "Mrs. Dahlstrom, your husband hasn't been dead . . ."

"I lied." Phoebe looked down at her hands in her lap. "I didn't love him. I married him for the very obvious reason that I knew it would hurt and infuriate my father. Here's another little bit of truth for you."

Prophet literally braced himself in his chair.

"I didn't love Erik, either. I just hated my father while at the same time admiring the tyrant that he was and wishing I could be more like him. More like him and Max and the General. I wanted to make my own way. I wanted to dominate and crush and build things in my own vision of how they should be built. Then burn it all down if I so chose. That's hard when you're a woman. So I wanted to marry Erik. When he was taken from me, I married the next best thing. In fact, marrying Max was an even sharper, deeper sword in my father's heart."

"So . . . why are you so incensed that . . . ?"

"That my father had Butters kill Max?"

"Never mind," Prophet said. "I'm a little thick, but I think I can see it."

She leaned back in her chair. "Tell me."

"Killing your husband was an assault against you. He was invading your territory. Now you want to lash back at him. Make him pay. Exact the final revenge for your mother."

"There you have it." She gave a dry half smile.

"Please don't tell me I'm smarter than I look," Prophet said. "I get that all the time and it hurts my feelings."

"Sleep with me tonight." There was a definite, firm urgency in her voice. "You will not regret it." She blinked slowly. "I guarantee you."

Prophet glanced at Louisa. Doing so, he caught her glancing at him. She looked away quickly. Too quickly.

To Phoebe, Prophet said, "You're beautiful as all hell, Phoebe . . ."

"If she wasn't here, you'd do it, wouldn't you?"

"Like I was sayin', you're beautiful as hell, but I don't think I'm up to it tonight. I've been feelin' like a black cat's been loungin' around on my grave all day, and for some reason the cat hasn't gone away." In some ways, the feeling had gotten worse. "Besides,

I've always found trouble in mixing business with pleasure."

Phoebe pursed her lips, nodded. "All right, then. I hope you realize what you're denying yourself. I hope you wake up in the middle of the night with one hell of a . . . craving." Her cheeks dimpled as she smiled.

"No doubt I will."

"If so, and you decide to remedy your mistake, I'm in room eight. The end of the first-floor hall on the left."

Prophet chuckled. "You sure know how to ride roughshod over a fella, don't you?"

"I've built a life around it."

Prophet rose, tossed a couple of silver dollars onto the table, stuffed his hat on his head, adjusted the holstered Colt on his thigh, and said, "Good night, Phoebe."

"Good night, Lou."

Prophet did not look at Louisa and Jonas Ford before he turned around and walked out of the dining room.

Prophet had a cigarette out on the hotel's front veranda. As the sun drifted out of sight, taking its light with it and sending a refreshing chill along the main street of Carson's Wash, Prophet walked up to his room and had another drink.

Then he went to bed.

It took him a good, long while to get to sleep. A lot had happened this day. Men had tried to kill him for reasons he wasn't sure of, and they'd likely try again. They might even make a play this very night.

But he was accustomed to that.

What was really bothering him, he realized as he lay there in the dark, staring up at the pressed-tin ceiling, was Phoebe Dahlstrom. She bothered him even more than Louisa and Jonas Ford. Phoebe's words were like ghosts haunting him though he wasn't sure why. He'd known plenty of folks driven half-mad by life's circumstances. Hell, he often put himself in that category.

Something told him he'd find out soon why the young woman had disturbed him. Maybe before he was ready.

He wasn't sure when he'd nodded off. He realized he'd fallen asleep only when several light taps sounded on his door, hoisting him out of a shallow slumber.

Instinctively, he jerked his head up off his pillow and slid his Colt from the holster buckled around the right-front bedpost. He clicked the hammer back as he tossed the covers aside then, clad in only his longhandles, rose and walked to the door.

He stood to one side of the doorframe to avoid a possible shotgun blast through the door panel.

"Who is it?" he said, tipping his head close to the door.

"Me," was the quiet response from the hall.

Prophet set the Colt on the dresser. He twisted the key in the lock, and, frowning, opened the door. He crossed his arms, leaning against the doorframe.

Louisa stood in the hall. She wasn't wearing a hat. Her hair spilled messily across her shoulders. Prophet could see her silhouette by the dull lamplight slanting through a window at the hall's far end.

"Are you alone?" she asked, keeping her voice low in the dark hall.

"Yeah." Prophet gave the door a tug then released the knob and let the door's momentum open it. The hinges chirped faintly.

Louisa stepped inside. She appeared a little wobbly on her feet.

Prophet closed the door.

Louisa looked toward the bed. "Was she here?"

"Just left."

Louisa jerked her right hand back and flung it forward. Her fist glanced off his left cheek. She flung another punch and another. Prophet halfheartedly held his arms up to ward her off as she silently punched at him. She punched mostly air and his shoulders and chest. She wore out quickly, breathing hard.

"You're a skunk," she hissed.

"You're drunk."

Prophet stepped around her, wrapped his arms around her waist, picked her up, and threw her onto his bed.

She grunted as she hit the mattress. When she stopped bouncing, she pushed up onto her elbows and looked at him through the mussed blond hair hanging in her face. Her words were slurred and garbled with emotion. "You're still a smelly possum."

"I lied." Prophet sagged into a ladder-back chair by the dresser. "She was never here. We parted in the dining room, and that was it."

Louisa just stared at him. It was too dark in the room for him to see her expression, if there was one.

"Where's Jonas?" he asked her.

"In his room." A pause. She swept her hair back with both hands. "He kicked me out."

"Kicked you out?"

"The man's a gentleman," Louisa sobbed. "He said I was inebriated and that it would be beneath us both to continue on our current course. He did *not compromise the honor of young women not at their best.*" She smiled, sobbed, shook her head, sniffed. "He said that."

"Ouch."

"The skunk's a gentleman."

"I'm sorry."

"Yes, well . . . Do you have something to drink?"

"Fresh out of sarsaparilla."

"I want whiskey."

"It looks to me like you've had more whiskey tonight than you've had in your entire life. No more whiskey."

She lay back against Prophet's pillow. "I want to get good and drunk."

"Why?"

"I just do."

Prophet rose from his chair, walked over to the bed, slid his hands beneath her back and legs, and slid her over, making room for him. He lay down beside her and hooked his arm behind his head and stared up at the ceiling.

"Why?"

Louisa drew a deep breath. She turned toward him, drew her knees toward her belly, and pressed her forehead against his side. "You see the damnedest things on this job, Lou."

"Tell me about it."

"The last savage I hauled in didn't have a bounty on his head. I stopped at his place, a little tumble-down ranch just south of Amarillo, near Palo Duro Canyon, to water my horse and buy a little parched corn. A white man, middle-aged. Short, chubby, grizzled little man who seemed sort of bashful. He invited to me to stay for supper and to bed down in his barn. He had a wife. Half-Comanche. And a daughter. They seemed nice enough though the wife and daughter didn't say anything. They served me a nice meal.

"I heard strange sounds coming from beneath the floor. Groaning, whimpering sounds. I asked about it and the man only chuckled and shook his head. The wife and daughter stared down at their plates. I got up and walked over to a cellar door, and the man tried to come up behind me to bash me over the head with the locking plank for his cabin door. I laid him out with the barrel of my Colt, then lit a lamp and went down into that cellar."

She stopped, pressed her forehead more snugly against Prophet's side.

Lou reached down and ran his hands through her hair. "What was down there?"

"A dozen girls," Louisa said in a little-girl voice of her own, voice quavering slightly. "A dozen girls of various ages. Some white. Some Indian. One black girl. All chained up. Filth all around. He'd been holding them there. Two of the oldest ones were pregnant."

"Jesus."

"Turns out that girls had been disappearing from around Amarillo for years. He'd been taking them. Him and his wife."

Prophet sighed.

"What makes people do such things, Lou?"

"I wish I knew."

"Now, will you give me a drink?"

"No."

She hardened her voice. "You're rotten."

"I know. Jonas isn't. When we're done with Butters, you stay here with Jonas. Settle down, finally. Settle down with a man who dresses nice and don't stink."

"You're jealous."

"Just the same, you do it."

Keeping her forehead pressed taut against Prophet's side, she said softly, "Yeah."

Chapter 9

Birds woke Prophet early the next morning.

He lifted his head from the pillow, blinking groggily and looking around. The pale light of false dawn was pushing through the room's two windows. In the dim light he could see Louisa beside him, turned away from him, curled in a tight ball, her head on the second pillow.

Her breath was soft, raspy. Her shoulders rose and fell slowly, steadily as she breathed.

Prophet rose slowly. It was still early. He wanted his partner to get all the shut-eye she could before they hit the trail after Butters. He'd never seen her drunk before last night, let alone as drunk as she'd been last night.

He winced, imagining how her head was going to grieve her when she woke. Then his upper lip curled a devilish smile. Now she'd know how he often felt. Having now sinned herself, maybe she'd finally get off her high horse about Prophet's bad behavior.

As he rose from the bed, Louisa stirred a little.

Groaned. Then she must have fallen back asleep, for her deep, steady breaths resumed.

"That's right, darlin'—you just sleep," he whispered. "I'll wake you in another hour."

First, he'd go out and get a jug of water and one of coffee.

She'd need plenty of both.

Prophet dressed quietly and wrapped his gun belt and holstered Colt around his waist. He glanced at Louisa once more. She lay curled as she'd been before. He moved to the door, unlocked it, and stepped into the hall. He'd just started to draw the door closed behind him when he stopped suddenly and dropped his hand to his revolver.

A man stood before him.

"Mornin', Lou," Jonas Ford said. "I figured you'd be up by now."

Prophet became all too aware of the half-open door behind him.

"Uh . . . mornin', Jonas."

"I was just wondering if . . . uh . . . you'd seen Louisa yet this morning. I just stopped by her room to see how she was feeling, but she didn't—"

Behind Prophet, the bed squawked as Louisa moved on it. Her sleep-ragged voice: "Lou?"

Ford's lower jaw dropped an inch. His mouth opened but it took a second before he said, "Oh . . ." He canted his head slightly to look into the room, toward the bed. "Oh . . ." he said again.

"Lou, you're not starting after Butters by yourself, are you?" Louisa yelled, gravel-voiced.

Prophet winced as he reached behind him for the doorknob and drew the door closed.

"It's not what you think, Jonas," he said, keeping

his voice low. "She stopped by my room last night. She was embarrassed about—well, you know. She was pretty tipsy. I've never seen her drink anything but cold milk or sarsaparilla. Doesn't take much to get her pie-eyed. She was awful embarrassed and just wanted to unload on me about it. She crawled into my bed and fell asleep. Fully clothed. All night long."

"She feels pretty comfortable around you, doesn't she, Lou?"

"Well, we've been partners a long time."

"I see." Ford looked troubled standing there in his impeccable suit and black Stetson, thumbs hooked behind his black leather cartridge belt. "I guess . . . I guess riding together . . . doing what you do . . . would draw you pretty tight."

The door opened behind Prophet. He swiveled his head to see Louisa standing in the doorway. She looked as though she'd been swept up by a Texas tornado and deposited somewhere in the wilds of western Minnesota.

Her hair was a tangled mess, matted in places. Her face was drawn and sallow. She looked a specter of her former self. Her blouse was half-unbuttoned, showing a good bit of cleavage below her disheveled, white cambric chemise.

She stared past Prophet at Jonas Ford.

None of them said anything for nearly thirty seconds.

Louisa stared in mute horror at Ford.

"Oh God!" she finally yowled, and slammed the door.

Running footsteps sounded inside the room. They were followed by sounds of raucous vomiting.

Prophet turned to Ford, who stared in shocked silence at the door. Lou chuckled his embarrassment and said, "Like I was sayin', Jonas—she's more accustomed to cold milk and sarsaparilla."

"I think I get your meaning, Lou."

Prophet canted his head and walked a few steps away from the door, until Louisa's vomiting was appropriately muffled. Ford followed him.

"Look, Jonas, Louisa sets store by you a lot. I can tell."

"Well, I guess it's no secret I fancy her, too. I didn't want to offend her last night, but—"

"Well, heck, you would have offended *me* if you *hadn't* kicked her out of your room, the state she was in!" Prophet said with a laugh. "I hope you won't hold this against her. She's a good gal, Louisa is."

"I know she is."

"But she's got a lot of green in her, Jonas. She's a broomtail mare. Been runnin' wild in the wide-open for a long time, mostly alone. It's gonna take some time . . . and patience . . . to get her gentled, if you catch my drift. But she does want to be gentled. Maybe not tamed but gentled. And trusted. She'd make a good husband a good wife someday. And she'd make a passel of sprouts a good ma. But, like I say . . ."

"It's gonna take some time."

"That's right."

"I understand." Ford gave a sheepish smile. "Now, I guess I've just embarrassed her further. Not quite sure what to do about that . . ."

"Just give her some time. She'll feel better once she's on the trail after Butters."

Ford nodded.

"About that, Jonas . . ."

"About Butters?"

"Yeah. I got an idea about how to start trackin' him. Why don't we go down to the dining room and palaver over mud?"

Later that afternoon, Prophet lay prone atop a sandy butte roughly ten miles south of Carson's Wash.

It was hot. Cicadas buzzed. A hot, dry breeze caressed the bounty hunter's cheeks like sandpaper.

Prophet trained his spyglass across the wash that twisted around the base of the bluff, toward a shabby collection of mud-brick shacks and shanties roughly two hundred yards away. They slumped in a scattered stand of dusty mesquites.

A few horses moved in a corral. That was the only movement that Prophet could see. There was a main shack—a long, low, L-shaped cabin with a front veranda propped on fieldstones, and a fieldstone chimney climbing the far-left wall. No movement around the shack, either, but tack and other gear were piled on the veranda. That and the horses meant the place was likely occupied.

Prophet lowered the spyglass. He turned to his right and gave a low, clipped whistle through his teeth. Faintly, he heard the crack of Louisa's hand against the rear of Tom Lowry's horse.

He stared forward, toward the humble ranch yard, until footsteps rose off his right flank. He glanced over that shoulder to see Louisa climbing up the narrow trail from the wash, holding her Winchester in her right gloved hand. She had two canteens slung over her shoulders. She'd been drinking water like a parched she-lion all day, but she was still a little green around the gills.

Crouching, she strode quickly up to Prophet, breathing hard from the climb, and dropped belly down beside him. "This has got to be your most lamebrained scheme so far, and that's saying a lot."

"You're just another Prophet doubter, Miss Bonnyventure."

"You know there's no *y* in my last name. You say it that way whenever you feel threatened by my superior intelligence."

Prophet chuckled as he watched Lowry's claybank trot out from the base of the bluff and into his field of vision, heading in the direction of the Lowry ranch. Tom Lowry's blanket-wrapped body was tied belly down across the dead man's saddle. It moved stiffly beneath the blanket as the horse climbed up out of the wash and trotted straight toward the ranch headquarters. It likely smelled home as well as hay and water.

Pale dust rose from the dirt it churched with its shod hooves.

"You hide an' watch, Miss Bonnyventure," Prophet said, raising his spyglass to watch the horse as well as the L-shaped shack it was heading for.

The horse was a hundred yards away from the ranch yard, and closing.

To Prophet's left, Louisa took a long drink from one of her canteens. She wiped her lips with a gloved hand and said, "What did you tell Jonas?"

Until now, she hadn't spoken a single word about last night or this morning.

Prophet shrugged. "I told him you'd had better nights."

"I mean about him finding me in your room. In your bed."

"I told him it wasn't your fault you couldn't resist my charms."

"Lou!"

Prophet chuckled. "Oh, don't get your bloomers twisted. I told him how it really was. You kept your clothes on all night. I told him you fancied him and I hoped he'd give you another chance."

"What'd he say to that?"

Prophet stared through the spyglass. The clay was just now entering the Lowry yard and swinging past the house's left-front corner. It was heading toward the corral. One of the horses in the corral saw the newcomer and strolled slowly over to the gate. Prophet saw the corralled horse's left wither ripple. The greeting whinny drifted to his ears on the ratcheting breeze.

The clay approached the corral gate, stopped, and lowered its head. It gave its tail a single sharp switch.

Prophet glanced at Louisa. "Ford's gonna give you another chance."

He peered through the spyglass toward the house.

"Damn," he said.

"What is it?"

"Nothin'. Not a damn thing."

"I told you."

Prophet stared at the house. No movement. The clay stood statue-still in front of the corral. The horse that had greeted it stood facing it from only a few feet away, its head also lowered in the still, silent, mysterious communion of horses.

"If someone's there, surely they'd have come out and checked out that hoss," Prophet said in frustration, lowering the spyglass and staring toward the ranch yard with his naked eyes. "How does a hoss that is obviously carrying a dead man waltz into your yard and you don't come outside and check it out?"

"Maybe because they know it's a trap."

"But it ain't no trap! I just wanna get some sense of who's there. How many. And if Butters is there!"

"We should have ridden into the yard with Lowry. That would have gotten a reaction."

"It likely would have gotten the same reaction I got just outside of Carson's Wash yesterday afternoon. I avoided *that* bullet. Odds are gettin' steeper and steeper I'm going to *keep* avoiding all the ones that get tossed my way!"

"Just because you think Lowry was sent to bushwhack you by Butters doesn't mean Butters is here at the Lowry ranch. Besides, how would Butters even know you were on the way to run him down? We're ten miles from town!"

"Word travels fast even this far out in the wild an' woolly," Prophet said, peering again through the glass. "An' Jonas said himself he didn't see any reason to keep it a secret. Besides, folks have been seein' you in Carson's Wash for a week, followin' Jonas around all daisy-eyed. Someone who knows we ride together might have figured I'd be there sooner or later, an' sent word to Butters."

"I wasn't following Jonas around all *daisy-eyed*!"

"I don't know, when I first seen you and Jonas together in his office, you sure looked daisy-eyed to me." Prophet winged a brow at her. "You are gonna stay on here, aren't ya? After this is done? I mean, if I tucked my tail between my legs every time I embarrassed myself, I'd . . ."

"Lou?"

"What?"

"Shut up. Let's just get this done."

"That's what I'm tryin' to do, damnit!" Prophet looked through the spyglass again, adjusting the focus.

"Give me that."

Louisa grabbed the glass away from him. She lifted it to her right eye. She stared for ten seconds at the ranch house then slid the spyglass to and fro, inspecting the entire yard.

Finally, she handed the glass back to Prophet. "No one's there. Someone's living there, but they're not there now. We'd have seen some sign by now."

"How much you wanna bet?"

Louisa rolled her eyes. "Five silver dollars."

"Done." Prophet extended his hand. She rolled her eyes again as she let him shake hers.

"Let's not get in no hurry, now," Prophet said, crabbing back away from the lip of the butte.

As Louisa followed suit, Lou said, "I'll ride around to the south side and move in slow-like. You come in from the north. I'll go in first and check out the shack. You cover me from the corral area."

Prophet followed the trail into the wash in which he and Louisa had tied their horses out of sight of the ranch yard. As he approached Mean and Ugly, Louisa said behind him, "Lou?"

Prophet untied Mean's reins from a gnarled ironwood and turned to her.

She untied her pinto's reins and said, frowning down at the reins in her hand, "Were you really jealous of Jonas?"

Prophet grinned. "Bad enough to wanna shoot him in both knees."

Louisa's cheeks flushed as she continued to stare down at the reins in her hand.

"What about you?" Prophet asked her. "Were you jealous of Phoebe Dahlstrom?"

Louisa looked up at him with cool insouciance. "No."

She toed a stirrup and stepped into her saddle.

Chapter 10

"Polecat," Prophet grunted as he watched his partner ride off down the wash, heading north.

The bounty hunter stepped up onto Mean and Ugly's back and also rode off down the wash. His direction was south. The bed of the wash was cut deep enough that he didn't think he could be seen from the ranch house two hundred yards away, but he held his hat and crouched just to make sure.

When he'd ridden at least a hundred yards south, he turned Mean up out of the wash and, keeping thick chaparral between him and the house, rode east toward the ranch. He started to be able to see the mud buildings after about ten minutes of riding.

Stopping the horse in a thick tangle of brush and cactus, he dismounted, looped the reins around a sotol stalk, and removed his spurs. He left his sawed-off shotgun hanging from the horn of his saddle. He dropped the spurs into a saddlebag then shucked his Winchester from its sheath.

Slowly, he walked toward the house, its south side

taking shape before him through the brush. There were two windows on the facing side of the house.

Still no movement.

The only sounds were the crunch of the gravel and mesquite beans beneath his boots, the breeze, desert birds, and cicadas. The pulsing hum of the cicadas seemed to match the pulselike throb of the sun hammering the house's bleached adobe bricks across which the breeze slid the shadows of bobbing brush and tree limbs.

Prophet moved up to the house. He was out in the open now, in plain view if anyone was watching from a window. Quietly, he levered a shell into the Winchester's action, mounted the three rotting steps of the moldering front veranda, and stepped up to the front door.

The two windows to each side of the door were covered with heavy flour sack curtains. He tried the door latch. Locked. Probably barred from within.

He stepped to the window right of the door and rammed the butt of his Winchester through it, loudly shattering the glass. He stepped back from the window and pressed his back to the cabin's front wall, waiting for possible bullets. When none came, he slowly turned to the window, slid the curtain aside with his gun barrel, and peered inside.

His breath caught in his throat when he saw a blond young woman of maybe sixteen standing against the brick wall to his right, between a cupboard and a range. A stooped, spidery-looking woman stood beside her. The blonde, dressed in a plain wool dress, had an arm draped protectively around the old woman's spindly shoulders.

The blonde's blue eyes were sharp with fear as she looked at Prophet and said, "He ain't here!"

"Who?" Prophet said.

There was a thud and a scrape of door hinges somewhere in the back of the shack.

Crouching, Prophet stepped through the window. "You two stay here!"

Prophet pushed through a curtained doorway and ran down a short hall. A door was open on his right. He turned to peer into a bedroom. A brass-framed bed nearly filled the room. The covers were thrown back. The sheets were bloodstained. The room smelled like a neglected slop bucket.

He continued down the hall and ran out an unlatched door. He stopped just outside, near a clothesline and several piles of split stove wood and an old black, sheet-iron stove. Beyond, a man was running away from Prophet, straight out between two ancient cabins sitting side by side in tall brush and prickly pear.

Hoof thuds rose to Prophet's left. He turned as Louisa galloped past him, grabbing the coiled riata from her saddle horn. "I got him."

Prophet jogged after Louisa and the man she was chasing. Just as Prophet ran out from between the two ancient cabins and into the open, Louisa twirled the riata about a hundred feet beyond him. She let it sail. The running man screamed and fell. Dust rose.

A minute later, Louisa trotted her pinto toward Prophet, dragging her quarry behind her.

She dragged the man up beside Lou and stopped her horse. Her quarry lay writhing belly down on the ground.

He was a grisly spectacle, his right arm in a bloody

sling. Another bloody bandage was wrapped around his belly. He'd been wearing only the bottoms of a pair of longhandles, the top having been hacked off. The dragging, however, had nearly stripped the longhandles off him. One side was bunched around a knee. The other side dangled off his right ankle.

One sock was gone. The other was hanging from his big toe.

He was so dirty that Prophet probably wouldn't have recognized him if he'd been lying faceup.

Deciding to find out, Prophet hooked his boot under the man's left shoulder and turned him over. The man groaned, gritting his teeth. "Easy, easy—I ain't . . . I ain't in a good way here!" he cried.

His hair was shorter than Prophet remembered. He wore about three days' growth of beard on his severely, crudely chiseled face with broad cheekbones and spade-shaped jaw. A bull-horn tattoo with the name *Audrina* in smeared blue letters marked his throat, behind the beard stubble. From his chin hung a goatee with a six-inch braid hanging down the middle of it, dangling toward his chest.

"Charlie Butters, you handsome dog," Prophet said.

Butters lay on his back, groaning. "I . . . I ain't in a good way here at all, Lou."

"I couldn't feel sorrier for you, Charlie."

"You don't understand," Butters said, glaring up at Prophet and showing his teeth like a feral dog. His eyes were the frosty blue of the northern sky in January. An eerie shade of blue—a wild, demented hue. Prophet had thought so the first time he'd met the man, and he thought the same again now. "I'm hurt real, real bad. What's more, I didn't deserve none of it!"

Louisa said, "Tell that to the family of the six-year-old boy and eighty-year-old retired schoolteacher you killed in Alva. Tell it to the families of everyone in the bank you slaughtered just so they couldn't identify you!"

That last part she yelled, drawing one of her pretty Colts and clicking back the hammer.

"Easy, now," Prophet said, holding up his hand. He knew that once Louisa's fuse was lit, the powder keg would likely blow. "I know it's tempting as hell, but we're not out here to fill this demon so full of holes he'll rattle when he walks. We don't have a dead-or-alive circular on this one, partner. Besides, he already rattles. We just have to get poor, misunderstood Charlie back to Carson's Wash. *Alive.*"

The realization carved deep gullies across Louisa's forehead, beneath the brim of her Stetson. "Oh." A hard pause, a deeply consternated expression. "That's right." She quirked an ironically frigid smile. "Did you just feel the devil tickle your toes, Butters? You were sure close to hell there for a minute."

"Damn," Butters said. "That's Bonaventure, ain't it?"

"Forgive my rudeness," Prophet said. "Charlie Butters, meet Louisa Bonaventure, otherwise known as the Vengeance Queen. Louisa, meet Charlie."

"Hello, Charlie."

"She's crazy!" Butters cried as Prophet hauled him to his feet. "I heard tell she's crazier'n an owl in a lightnin' storm!"

Running footsteps sounded. Louisa's horse gave a start.

Prophet shoved Butters back down to the ground and planted a boot on his chest as he unholstered his Colt and turned back toward the cabin. The girl from inside the shack was just now running out from between the two moldering shacks. For the first time Prophet saw that her belly bulged behind the threadbare apron she wore over a shapeless gray, crudely sewn dress.

The girl was at least a few months pregnant.

She ran hard, breath rasping in and out of her lungs. She didn't appear to be carrying a weapon, so Prophet depressed his Colt's hammer and lowered the piece, throwing up his other hand, palm out.

"Hold on, now, girl."

"Please, don't hurt him!" the girl cried, half sobbing, as she stopped a few feet away, staring down in worry at Charlie Butters. "Please, don't hurt him! He didn't do what they said he did, Charlie didn't. Charlie ain't like that no more!"

"Jackie, go on back to the cabin," Charlie said. "You shouldn't be runnin' like that. It ain't good for the baby."

Louisa had a tight rein on her jittery pinto. In her other hand she held her Colt, barrel up. She glared down at Butters as she said, "Is that child yours, Butters?" Prophet heard the hard, menacing edge in her voice.

Ah, hell, he thought. *She's gonna kill this buzzard yet and it ain't that he don't deserve it but we got other fish to fry . . .*

"Louisa, holster that damn pistol," he ordered tightly. He slid his gaze between Butters and the girl, Jackie. "Let's all just settle down. Butters is goin' to town to stand trial for the murder of Max Dahlstrom, an' that's all there is to it."

"Charlie ain't like how he used to be," Jackie said, pleadingly, to Prophet. "He ain't that man no more. He didn't kill Dahlstrom—did you, Charlie? Please, let him go, mister. Charlie deserves a second chance!"

"He's gonna get a fair trial," Prophet said, adding for emphasis, "this time."

"You can't take him all the way back to Carson's Wash. It's too far. Look at him—you've opened up his wounds. He'll bleed to death if you make him ride that far."

Prophet looked down at Butters. Fresh blood stained the already-blood-spotted bandages. Butters was pasty pale, his face shrunken. He stared up at Prophet, who kept his boot pressed down taut against the man's chest. Butters's eyes were pain racked, but a faint, mocking smile twitched his lips.

"Oh, Charlie!" Jackie cried, and dropped to her knees beside Butters. "Look what they've done to you! Are you hurt bad?"

Butters didn't respond. He just stared up at Prophet with that same, vaguely jeering look.

"All right," Prophet said, removing his boot from the killer's chest. "We'll take him back inside. Miss Jackie, you can tend to those wounds, get the bleedin' stopped, put on some fresh bandages if you see fit. But then Charlie is comin' along with us back to Carson's Wash."

The girl scowled up at Prophet. "My pa and brothers are not gonna like that one bit, mister!"

"Where are your pa and brothers?" Prophet asked, glancing around. The whereabouts of the Lowry men had been a nasty thorn poking around in the back of his brain ever since he'd entered the cabin to find only the two women, and Butters skinning out the back door.

"They went to Mexico for fresh stock, but they'll be back just any day now. Might even be today. Charlie's kin. We Lowrys and Butterses are close blood!"

"Yeah, I see that," Prophet dryly quipped, glancing down at the girl's bulging belly. "Tell me, sweetheart, did you really let this mangy cur spew his foul seed into you?"

The girl bunched her lips and glared so hard at Prophet that the corners of her eyes danced. Butters only laughed and, rolling onto his belly then rising to his hands and knees, said, "She sure did! An' it didn't take much convincin', did it, Jackie-girl?" Butters grunted as the girl helped him to his feet and hooked his good arm around her neck. "She sees the good in me, Jackie does."

"I do see the good in you, Charlie Butters," Jackie said as she began leading Butters back toward the cabin. "Because there *is* good in you. It just took some peaceful livin' an' hard work at the ranch with Pa an' me an' the boys an' the old lady to make it come out."

"We shouldn't be shilly-shallying around here, Lou," Louisa said. "We should get that killer on a horse and get him on the trail back to Carson's Wash. Like the girl said, the Lowrys could be back anytime."

"It ain't gonna do much good to let Butters bleed to death, since your boyfriend needs him alive—now, is it?" Prophet snapped at his partner as he began following Butters and Jackie toward the cabin. He glanced again at Louisa and said, "Why don't you make yourself useful and fetch my hoss? While you're at it, cut Tom Lowry down from *his* horse and saddle a *fresh* one for Butters."

"Any other orders?" Louisa said tightly as she turned the pinto wide around the two ruined shacks and gave it the spurs.

"That'll do for now!"

Prophet slowed his pace. Jackie and Butters had stopped just ahead of him. They were both staring toward the corral in shocked silence. The girl said in a pinched, quavering voice, "I thought I recognized Tom's horse."

Butters looked over his right shoulder at Prophet. "Did you go and kill my cousin Tom, Lou?"

"No, I didn't kill him," Prophet said. "Whoever sicced him on me with that Henry repeater is the one that killed him."

Jackie wheeled to glare teary-eyed at Prophet, and yelled, "You'll pay double for that, you big, ugly lummox! Tom Lowry is my brother!"

"Sooner or later we all pay double, sweetheart," Prophet said. "Just get the proud father of that bun in your oven back into the cabin and get those wounds tended or we'll forgo the doctorin' altogether, an' I'll tie him belly down over his horse and gallop him all the way back to Carson's Wash!"

"I can't wait for my pap and my brothers to get back from Mexico," the girl said, shaking her head slowly at Prophet, narrowing her eyes. "There'll be nowhere you can hide they won't run you down!"

Chapter 11

"I'm sure your kin will know where to find me," Prophet told the enraged girl. "And if they're anything like your beloved Charlie here, I'll enjoy shakin' their hands and kickin' 'em out with cold shovels. In the meantime, kindly move your ass!"

Jackie told Prophet to do something physically impossible to himself then continued helping her beloved Charlie Butters to the cabin. Prophet followed them through the back door, aiming his Winchester at the pair's backs.

As the girl started to help Butters into the room with the bloody bed, Prophet said, "Nuh-uh. We're all gonna get cozy in the main room with Grandmom."

"What I need to tend his wounds is in here."

"Fetch it quick. I'll be watchin'."

The girl eased Butters back against the hall's right wall then cast Prophet another hard glare before striding into the bedroom. Butters was breathing hard and sweating. He turned his mocking grin on Prophet one more time.

"Ain't she a caution?"

"She's somethin'," Prophet said, keeping an eye on Jackie as she gathered some strips of flannel in her arms then swept up some bottles from a dresser.

The girl glared at Prophet once more as she stepped out into the hall and then, having gathered up the bottles and bandages into her apron, helped Butters into the main part of the cabin. As Prophet stepped through the curtained doorway, he saw the old woman sitting at the table, holding a small, copper crucifix in her gnarled hands that appeared swollen and purple with arthritis. One elbow rested on a large family Bible. She was so sun seared that she looked vaguely Indian. Her light brown eyes were milky with cataracts. Her coarse silver hair was swept straight back and up into a tight bun.

The old woman looked up as Prophet and the other two entered. Her eyes didn't focus. She turned her head this way and that, trying to pick up sights and sounds. Nearly deaf and nearly blind. Badly disoriented and worried. She didn't say anything. She just sat staring into space.

When Jackie had eased Butters into a chair at the table, she turned to the old woman and said loudly, "Go to your room, Gran. Everything is gonna be all right!" The girl's voice broke on this last, and she turned her gaze to look out the window at the horse packing her dead brother, Tom Lowry, standing by the corral. Louisa was over there now, tying Mean and Ugly to a corral slat.

The old woman turned her head slowly toward Jackie, grizzled brows beetled.

"Go to your room, Gran!" Jackie yelled.

Prophet walked over to the old woman, placed a hand on her forearm. He squeezed it gently, reassuringly, silently offering help.

Outside was a hammering explosion. It made the entire shack jump.

Jackie gasped.

Prophet jerked away from the old woman, raising his rifle in both hands and loudly racking a cartridge into the chamber. He peered through the window left of the door. The yard had suddenly gone dark. Rain like silver dollars plopped into the dirt, making small craters. He could hear it pelting the roof.

Prophet's heart gradually slowed. He'd expected to turn to the window to face a hail of hot lead.

Behind him, Butters laughed. "Damn, Lou, you look like you thought my uncle and cousins was home!"

The girl, crouched over Butters, laughed then, too.

"You know what, Lou?" Butters said, smiling out the window. "I don't think we're goin' anywhere today!"

"Don't bet on it," Prophet said. "Rain never lasts that long out here, and you know it. I 'spect the sky'll be clear in fifteen, twenty minutes."

He turned to the old woman again, and helped her up out of her chair. Jackie told him which room was Gran's, and, letting the old woman hold his arm, walked her to the door in the shack's far right wall. He opened the door, led the old woman into the small but tidy room, then turned away. He heard a faint clink, saw a thick shadow move on the floor to his left.

He whipped around as the old woman lunged

heavily toward him with a knitting needle sequestered in both her knobby hands. Prophet raised his left hand and wrapped it around the old woman's two hands clutching the needle, and saved himself a nasty poke.

"Law!" the old woman hissed, staring at Prophet but not seeing him through her wide, angry, milky eyes. Her breath was hot and fetid. "Filthy law scum!"

Behind him, Butters and Jackie laughed.

Prophet plucked the needle out of the old woman's hands. He knew she probably had more in her room, but he held on to this one, anyway. He gave her a gentle shove onto the edge of the tightly made bed, the woman still glaring at him, flaring her nostrils at him like an angry dog.

Then he walked back out into the main part of the shack and drew the old woman's door closed behind him.

Butters and Jackie were still laughing, jeeringly, as Jackie removed the bloody bandage around Butters's right arm.

Prophet sighed.

He looked outside again. The rain was hammering violently down. Already the yard was a bog. Louisa ran up onto the narrow front veranda, water sluicing off her hat brim. She opened the door, bolted inside, and slammed the door quickly behind her.

She was soaked, her clothes hanging on her supple frame. Her blond hair was pasted to the shoulders of her wet blouse. Leaning back against the door, she looked toward Prophet, her gaze fateful, and said, "Gully-washer. All-nighter, looks like."

"That's all right," Butters said with mock good cheer, glancing around the cabin. "Plenty of room here. Nice, tight cabin. And my Jackie-girl can cook a right tasty stew!"

Another thunderclap rattled the windows.

The rain was like the symphony of some angry, malevolent god being played on the roof.

"Look at him sleepin' there . . . just like an angel," Jackie said much later, well after dark.

The storm had stopped, circled back, dumped another load of rain and hail, and was now drifting off to the northeast. It was grumbling into the distance, lightning flashing, like an angry dog after a violent fight over a particularly tasty bone.

The night air was cool in the cabin. Prophet had laid a small fire in the hearth. It crackled and popped softly, sending the tang of mesquite into the shack.

Now, sitting at the kitchen table with Jackie, rolling a cigarette from his makings sack, Prophet followed the pregnant girl's gaze to her "angel," Charlie Butters, who lay on a worn leather fainting couch near the fire, on the parlor side of the cabin. He lay on his back, a tattered star quilt drawn up to his chin. His eyes were closed. He was snoring softly, thin-lipped mouth opening and closing with each audible breath. The little braid dangling from his chin trailed over the edge of the quilt—a grisly-looking thing.

A little devil's tail.

"Angel layin' there, huh?" Prophet grunted, rolling the quirley closed in his thick, red-brown fingers. "That ain't the comparison I would have made. I would have called him a big, fat, poisonous snake, but I reckon you see ole Charlie through different eyes than me."

Jackie turned to Prophet. The bounty hunter sat with his back to the kitchen, where he could keep his eye on the front door and front windows. Jackie sat across from him, her back to the door. Her eyes were hurt, angry. "I know Charlie better than you—now, don't I?"

"How long have you known him?"

"All his life. He grew up around here. His pa and my pa is cousins. They was raised out east."

By "out east," Prophet assumed she meant East Texas. Texas was the world to most born-and-raised, dyed-in-the-wool Texans.

"How long you been . . . ?"

"Goin' on a year now. We got to fancyin' each other when Charlie rode over to here to listen to Gran preach to us all about the Bible Sunday mornings, and pray over our bowed heads."

"Yeah, Gran seems real pious." Prophet glanced at the knitting needle lying on the table, near both his Winchester and sawed-off Richards, which lay there as well, within easy reach.

"Gran thinks you're the law, and she hates the law. The law has never been kind to a West Texas Lowry. When it comes to us Lowrys, the law always shoots first and asks questions later."

"Oh, why is that?"

"You tell me."

Prophet sighed. That angle of the conversation wasn't getting him anywhere. He already knew the Lowrys were considered a bad bunch, which they no doubt were. Border toughs who only played at ranching. What they mainly did was survive any way they knew how, many of those ways being illegal as hell.

Charlie Butters smacked his lips and muttered in

his sleep. Prophet looked at him. "How much older is he than you?"

"Twelve years. That ain't much. My pa is eighteen years older'n my ma . . . may the good Lord have mercy on her soul."

"So, Charlie came back here, to the country around Carson's Wash, right after that fool judge set him free. And you took up with him."

"That's right. But that judge weren't no fool. He knew the law. He set Charlie free because it was the right thing to do. He gave Charlie a second chance, and Charlie was makin' good on that chance. He was workin' for Mr. McReynolds out to the Rockin' R spread, huntin' wolves an' mountain lions, Charlie was. Makin' good wages. Then that damn fool Marshal Ford and his two damn fool deputies rode out there to arrest him."

"They rode out there to arrest him for shooting a high roller in these parts—Max Dahlstrom."

"Charlie done told you he didn't shoot Max Dahlstrom. He was tellin' you the truth, Mr. Prophet."

Prophet struck a lucifer to light on the bottom of the oilcloth-covered eating table and touched the flame to the quirley. "Charlie's a killer, Miss Lowry. He started killin' when he was thirteen years old. Robbin', rapin', holdin' up stagecoaches and trains. He killed every poor soul in that bank up in Alva just so no one could identify him. Thank God his partner did!"

"All that is true," Jackie said, defiantly holding her chin aloft. She had a round, waifish face with eyes the same color as her grandmother's but without the cataracts. "But Charlie saw the judge's ruling as a chance to turn over a new leaf. To live a better life.

So he found him good, honest work . . . and me," she added with a smile.

"Have you ever seen him with George Hill?"

"Never."

"Has he ever talked about Hill to you?"

"No. Why would he?"

"Because some folks in Carson's Wash believe Hill hired Charlie to kill Dahlstrom. In fact, two of Dahlstrom's men saw the whole thing. They identified Charlie."

"That's an out-and-out lie!" Jackie intoned, slapping the table and rising to her feet.

On the settee, Charlie groaned and shifted but kept his eyes closed. Louisa was sitting in a leather chair opposite Butters. She'd kicked out of her boots and curled her long legs beneath her hip. Her hat was hooked over her left knee. She'd been reading a little book with a yellow pasteboard cover, seemingly captivated by the yarn, but now she lowered the book and looked at Jackie skeptically.

Jackie glanced at Charlie and Louisa and then returned her passionate gaze to Prophet and repeated, lowering her voice, "That is an out-and-out lie, Mr. Prophet. Charlie would never do such a thing. Maybe earlier in his life he would have. But Charlie's a different man now, like I've been tryin' to tell you. He is not that man anymore. He is a good man. Bad men can become good men, Mr. Prophet, though I know you're too jaded to be convinced!"

"You're right—I am too jaded," Prophet said, taking a deep drag from his quirley.

Louisa raised the book again to her face, frowning in concentration at the page before her. Vaguely, Prophet wondered what story had her so absorbed.

She hadn't said a word for over an hour, since they'd dared let Jackie serve them bowls of beans cooked with onions and bacon.

"I been in this business long enough that zebras don't change their stripes, and men like Charlie don't become good Christian men." Prophet dropped his gaze to the bulging belly of the girl standing across the table from him. "Or good fathers, let alone good husbands. Sorry to bust your bubble. But there it is."

"You're wrong," Jackie said tightly, shaking her head slowly and easing down into her chair.

"If Charlie didn't shoot Dahlstrom, why did he start shootin' at Ford and the deputies when they rode out to that line shack he was holed up in on McReynolds's range?"

"Charlie said Ford's men fired first. Charlie was just protectin' himself. Besides, he knows that Jonas Ford isn't going to listen to a word Charlie had to say. Ford already had Charlie convicted of Dahlstrom's murder and hangin' from a gallows. Everyone in West Texas knows how close the General and Dahlstrom were, and that Dahlstrom . . ."

She let her voice trail off, flushing slightly and lowering her gaze to the table.

"Dahlstrom what?" Prophet asked.

"Never mind."

Prophet glanced at Louisa. She was so involved in her book that she hadn't heard one word of his and Jackie's conversation. Just now she slowly turned a page, sliding her eyes from the previous one to the new one. She shook her hair back and continued reading, pink lips slightly parted.

Of course, she probably wouldn't have listened to anything Jackie had to say even if she hadn't found the book in one of the back bedrooms. Louisa wasn't one to listen to excuses espoused by the lovers of killers. Louisa was as pretty as any debutante, but over the years since her family's massacre, her skin had grown as thick as that of a wild bull pawing the scrub in the south Texas Brasada country.

Jackie placed one hand atop the other atop the table and leaned over them, pinning Prophet with a direct look. "If you take Charlie back to town, he's going to end up dead. One way or another. They'll kill him."

"Who'll kill him?"

"You just mark my words. Someone's gonna have to take the blame for Dahlstrom's killing. Charlie just happens to be handy. Now she can finally run George Hill out of this country for good—or watch him hang."

"Who do you mean by 'she'?"

"You know who I mean by 'she.'"

"You know a lot about Carson's Wash, Miss Lowry. How so, livin' way out here?"

"Everybody within a thousand squared miles knows everything about Carson's Wash, Mr. Prophet. Word spreads fast. Especially *those* words. Carson's Wash is a favorite topic of conversation from El Paso clear up to Amarillo. Especially after how everybody knows that . . ."

Again, Jackie let her voice trail off. Her country-pretty, heart-shaped face acquired that sheepish look again.

"Doggone it, will you stop bein' so damn mysterious, Miss Lowry?" Prophet said in frustration, mashing out his quirley in his empty coffee cup. "You're obviously no shrinking violet, so why don't you stop pretending to be one and say what's on your mind? No one here is gonna wash your mouth out with soap. I can hear Gran snorin' in the room way over yonder."

Jackie looked at Gran's door, almost as though the girl really were scared the old woman would hear her talking out of school. She looked at Charlie. Then at Louisa, who had lowered her book and was staring with interest at Jackie. She'd apparently heard enough of the conversation to have gotten interested in something other than the yarn.

Jackie turned back to Prophet, crossed her arms on the table, and leaned over them. She spoke to the table as she said, "Phoebe's father nearly killed her lover. Dahlstrom's son. Later, he went to Mexico and was shot by rurales."

Prophet scowled at her. "Well, hell, I know that much myself!"

"I don't," Louisa said from her leather chair.

"Yeah, well, my date last night must've been a little more informative than yours." Prophet turned to Jackie. "Besides, I don't see what—"

"That ain't all of it," Jackie said.

Prophet studied her, waiting.

She let him wait, obviously relishing the drama she was building. There probably wasn't much drama out here. At least, not the kind to keep a girl entertained when she wasn't cavorting with the likes of Charlie Butters.

Jackie said in a devilish, conspiratorial tone, "Did Mrs. Dahlstrom also tell you that after George Hill beat Erik Dahlstrom nearly to death, he raped her?"

A three-second pause as Prophet absorbed the word *rape.*

"Raped who?" Prophet and Louisa said at the same time, in tones of hushed awe.

"Her," Jackie said. "Phoebe."

Prophet sank back in his chair, knees turning to putty from shock. He glanced at Louisa, who had lowered her book to her thigh. "Hill raped his own daughter?" Prophet said.

"That ain't all, neither." Jackie turned her head slightly and gave a teasing little half smile.

"Pray tell," Prophet said, half ironically.

Jackie glanced darkly at Gran's door once more. Then, hearing the old woman's muffled snores, she turned back to Prophet. "She had a baby. That ain't just a rumor. The old woman who works with Doc Collins in Carson's Wash let it slip to someone who let it slip to someone else."

Prophet and Louisa shared another dark glance.

"What happened to the baby?" Louisa asked Jackie.

"That's what everybody east of Lubbock would like to know," Jackie said.

Chapter 12

When Prophet had absorbed that last piece of grisly information from Jackie, he said, "I don't see what any of that has to do with your boyfriend over there *not* killing Dahlstrom."

"How do you know it wasn't Phoebe who killed her own husband . . . that old, dried-up gourd of a man, Dahlstrom . . . and then blamed Charlie because he was an easy one to blame? After all, everybody knows about what Charlie did up in Alva and the second judge turning him loose. Everybody around here's been layin' for Charlie ever since. All except his own kin and Mr. McReynolds, that is."

Prophet shook his head. "I know you believe in Charlie, Miss Lowry. But you're buildin' way too big of a story to support him. Phoebe's foreman and one other man saw Charlie shoot Dahlstrom."

"Oh, and you can say for sure they ain't lyin'!" the girl castigated him, planting a fist on her hip and firing lightninglike daggers at him with her gaze.

Charlie Butters lifted his head from his pillow with a start, his eyes wide and fearful. "Wha . . . *huh*?"

"Oh, easy, darlin', easy!" Jackie said, rising from her chair and hurrying over to where Butters lay on the settee. "I'm sorry I raised my voice and gave you such a start. That was so inconsiderate of me. You go back to sleep, sweet Charlie."

She sat on the edge of the settee, cradled Butters's ugly head in her arms like some grisly infant, and smoothed his short hair back from his temples, rocking him, cooing to him gently. "There, there . . . hush, hush, sweet Charlie."

Prophet rolled his eyes as he slid his chair back and gained his feet.

He looked at Louisa. She'd gone back to reading her book.

Prophet opened the front door and stepped out onto the front veranda and looked around. The rain had turned to a spitting mist. The storm's rumbling was growing fainter, the lightning more distant, its brief umber flashes silhouetting clouds in the far northeast. If Butters's relatives were on their way back from Mexico, they were likely holed up out of the rain. Every arroyo in the storm's path would be flooded until morning.

Still, Prophet wouldn't be getting much sleep. Any one of the three in the cabin was a threat, and Prophet didn't have it in him to tie up the old woman and Jackie. He supposed he could tie Butters but what was the point if he didn't tie the women, too?

He might catch a few winks, but he and Louisa would have to take turns staying awake so they didn't end up with a knitting needle or anything else embedded in their persons.

Prophet yawned and went back inside. Jackie was still cradling Butters's head in her arms. She sat back against the wall, her eyes closed, one leg outstretched along the edge of the settee. On the opposite side of the room, Louisa slowly turned a page of her book.

Prophet walked over to her. "What the hell you readin', anyways?"

She kept the front of the book pressed up against her raised knee. "Nothing."

"Let me see."

"No." She was about to pull the book away, but he grabbed her right hand and held the book at an angle he could read it by.

Across the top of the cover were the words BEADLE'S DIME NOVELS.

Beneath those words was a detailed sketch of a pretty, saucy-looking, long-haired young woman dressed entirely in buckskins and with fringed buckskin boots and two pearl-gripped Colt revolvers in her hands.

She was shooting one of the Colts at a big, burly gent hulking up before her. He had a hatchet in his hand and a look of shock on his bearded face. The girl was slashing the barrel of her second Colt toward the man's left temple. The two were in a saloon, men and painted ladies sitting or standing around, watching the festivities.

Beneath the sketch was the title of the featured yarn: LOUISA BONAVENTURE.

Beneath that was the tale's subtitle: THE VENGEANCE QUEEN GIVES NO QUARTER!

Louisa jerked the book from Prophet's grip. Her cheeks colored a little as she looked vaguely sheepishly up at him, curling a wry smile.

Prophet snorted.

"Give no quarter, huh?" he said.

"They got that part right, anyway."

"They mention me in there?"

"Not one time," Louisa said smugly.

"Since you're so involved in your own story, you can keep the first watch. I'm gonna catch thirty winks. Wake me when you get sleepy."

"The Vengeance Queen will never rest until she has attained the justice she rides for, Lou."

Prophet gave another snort and then walked back to the table. He sat down and rolled another smoke. When he finished the quirley, he dropped it into his coffee cup, doffed his hat, and laid his head down on the table. Instantly, soothing slumber washed over him. He woke later to what felt like a large, hot hand squeezing the back of his neck.

He lifted his head from the table with a groan, and, blinking, saw the Vengeance Queen sitting across the table from him, raising a cup of steaming coffee to her lips. Pale light shone in her hazel eyes and painted the steam rising from the coal black surface of her coffee.

"Ow," Prophet groaned again, rubbing the back of his neck and hipping around to peer out the windows. "You mean to tell me it's mornin'?"

"Close."

He turned back to Louisa. "Why didn't you wake me?"

She hiked a shoulder as she sipped her coffee. "You were dead out. I thought you needed sleep more than I did."

Prophet groaned again as he rubbed the fist-sized knots out of his neck. "Yeah, I know—the Vengeance Queen don't need sleep. All she needs is justice."

He looked around. The cabin was all smeared

shadows and blurred gray edges. A ray of pale light streamed over Butters and his girl on the settee. Jackie was curled up close against Charlie's side. Charlie snored softly. Jackie had one arm draped over his belly.

"Look at them two lovebirds," Prophet said, yawning and scrubbing a hand down his face, trying to get awake.

Louisa followed his gaze. "What about 'em?"

Prophet frowned at her. "You think there's any chance she might be right about Charlie?"

Louisa sipped her coffee again and set the cup down. "You saw what he did in Alva. You tell me."

"You think a zebra can change his stripes?"

Louisa glanced at Charlie again. "Not that zebra."

Prophet slid his chair back, rose, hearing the bones in his back and knees pop. He yawned as he headed for the big coffeepot steaming on a warming rack of the range. "I'm gonna have a cup of mud. Then I'll fetch the horses."

"Arrestin' the son of Emmett Lowry's cousin is one thing," Charlie Butters said. "But killin' his boy is somethin' else altogether. When you killed Tom Lowry, you really grabbed the devil by the tail, Proph."

"I been grabbin' it a lot lately, Charlie."

Prophet, Louisa, and Butters were riding between two eroded buttes, following the trail back north, toward Carson's Wash. It was midmorning, the sun high and hot, gradually burning off the humidity after last night's downpour.

All of the arroyos that Prophet's threesome had

crossed so far had been merely muddy. Water drained fast in this sandy country.

Prophet stopped Mean and Ugly. Butters's blue roan, which the bounty hunter was leading by its bridle reins, stopped just behind him. Prophet turned Mean and rode back until he sat stirrup to stirrup with Butters, who rode with his boots tied together beneath the roan's broad barrel.

"You sent Lowry after me, Charlie," he said. "You got word that Ford had sent for me. So you sent your cousin out to wait for me. To bushwhack me. I put them bullets in him, sure. He was needin' 'em, sure enough, a long time ago. But you're the one who killed him when you sicced him on me, Charlie. So don't sit there like you don't have as much of Tom's blood on your hands as I do."

"Nuh-uh," Butters said, shaking his head slowly. "You got it wrong, Proph. I didn't send Tom after you. I didn't know nothin' about Ford sendin' you after me. Hell, I didn't even know your purtier half was in this country." He smiled seedily at Louisa. "Hell, why wouldn't I have sent Tom after her, then, too?"

"Maybe I was next," Louisa said.

"Maybe," Butters said. "Maybe not. No, sir, Prophet. You grabbed the devil by the tail when you shot Tom. Tom was Emmett's favorite boy. Him and the other half dozen—Cal, Randall, Bad Frank, Les, Willie, and Little Steve—will be ridin' into Carson's Wash just as soon as they return from Mexico. Should have been back by now, matter of fact. They'll be gunnin' for you soon." He looked at Louisa. "Both of you."

"Stop, Charlie," Louisa said. "You're scaring me."

Butters's little eyes sparked with anger, and he

hardened his jaws. "You two got it all wrong, damnit. I didn't have nothin' to do with Dahlstrom's killin'. I was in McReynolds's line shack, baiting a panther! I'm gonna be a poppa, damnit! I'm gonna marry Jackie and do it up right!"

"Even if you didn't kill Dahlstrom," Prophet said, raising his voice in frustration, "you blew your chance of that happening when you shot Ford's two deputies."

"I didn't know they was Ford's deputies. They didn't identify themselves. I just heard someone sneakin' up through the brush, and when I looked out, one of 'em leveled a Winchester on me. So I fired back. What would you do, Lou?"

He stared at Prophet as though awaiting an answer. When Prophet didn't have one, Butters just stretched his lips back from his teeth and said, "Oh, goddamnit all, anyway!" His quavering voice cracked with what sounded like genuine emotion.

A tear oozed out of his right eye and dribbled down his severely, crudely chiseled cheek.

Prophet studied him for a moment, then reined Mean back around and headed on up the trail. "Let's go," he said.

After a few minutes' hard pondering, he glanced at Louisa riding beside him. "Tell me I'm a fool for starting to wonder if he's not tellin' the truth."

"It's already been established that you're a fool," Louisa said, glancing over her shoulder at Charlie riding with his eyes closed beneath the brim of his old hat, head lolling on his shoulders. "And it's already been established that Butters is a killer. You've seen his carnage yourself. He's working you. Him and that girl were both working you."

"Do you think she's lyin' for him?"

Louisa glanced back at Butters once more, a look of disgust on her mouth. "No, I think she believes in him. Which makes me hate that viper even more."

She paused as they rode a few more yards along the meandering trail. A deep line of consternation was carved between her brows.

She said, "What difference does it make, anyway? If he didn't kill Dahlstrom, he's killed plenty others."

"If he didn't kill Dahlstrom—who did?"

"It's not our jobs to worry about that. Jonas is only paying us to bring in Butters. The rest of it is up to him . . . and a judge and jury."

"And an executioner for Butters," Prophet grumbled.

"High time."

Prophet glanced back once more at Butters, who still rode with his head wobbling as though broken on his shoulders. But now his eyes were open. He stared at Prophet without expression.

Lou turned his head back forward. "Reckon."

Chapter 13

Prophet, Louisa, and their sullen prisoner rode into Carson's Wash around noon, the sun high and hammering straight down, blindingly, making Prophet yearn for the Colorado high country and a cool lake to take a dip in.

Something besides the heat and the sun was bothering him, though.

This whole thing with Butters was nettling him. It should have been such an easy job. Just bring a man in as a favor for a lawman friend with his wing in a sling. But it was more complicated than that. At least, it was more complicated in Prophet's head. Maybe it really shouldn't be.

But it was.

What he needed was a drink and a tussle with a woman.

As they rode down the main street of Carson's Wash, Prophet looked at Louisa. She glanced back at him and frowned curiously. His ears warmed, and he turned away.

"What is it?" she asked.

"Nothin'."

"Lou, what is it?" she prodded as Ford's office shifted into view dead ahead and on the street's south side.

On both sides of the street, people were stopping what they'd been doing to eye the two bounty hunters riding into town with the alleged killer of one of the county's most powerful men in tow. Charlie rode sulkily in the saddle, head down, sort of groaning and snarling like a cowed dog that had been caught with a mouthful of chicken feathers.

"Nothin'," Prophet said again.

He pulled Mean and Ugly up in front of the hitch-rack fronting the marshal's office. Louisa pulled up on his right and gave him a direct look.

"You're needing a woman . . . or a girl . . . and a bottle," she said, as though she were merely telling him what time it was. "Suit yourself. Then why don't you ride on out of here? You have nothing to hold you here. Look for some other owlhoots to chase. Winter'll be coming on, and you're gonna need a good stake to get you down to Mexico."

Prophet felt a little like how Butters looked—like a bad, cowed dog. Louisa knew him too well.

"You're stayin', then?" he asked her.

"Why not test the waters?" she said.

Ford's office door opened and the young marshal walked out, his arm in a fresh sling. He donned his black hat and smiled when he saw the two bounty hunters and Butters. "Well, I'll be doggoned," he said, sliding his gaze from Butters to Prophet and

Louisa. "You found him out at the Lowry ranch, didn't you?"

"Sometimes you guess right," Prophet said, swinging down from his saddle. "Sometimes you don't."

"I couldn't be more grateful, Lou." Ford looked at Louisa, and an extra light glinted in his eyes. He dipped his chin and pinched his hat brim. "Louisa."

"Jonas, how are you?"

"Me? Hell, I'm fine. Even better than fine now."

He winked, and Prophet thought he was going to have to look around for that slop bucket again. Lou gave a ragged sigh and cut Butters's feet free, then helped the outlaw out of his saddle. Butters didn't protest. He didn't say a word. He knew his ass was in the loop and his head likely would be soon, as well.

When Prophet had led Charlie into the marshal's office, nudged him into a cell, and closed the door, Ford turned the key in the lock.

"Thanks again, Lou." Ford hung the key ring on a spike in a ceiling support post then opened a desk drawer and removed two slender envelopes. He handed one to Prophet, the other to Louisa. "And here is my thanks to you again—cash on the barrelhead."

"Thanks, Jonas," Prophet said.

"Yes—thank you, Jonas."

"I hope you won't be running off," Ford said, hiking a hip on a corner of his desk. He kept his gaze on Louisa. "I could use a deputy . . . at least until I can get a couple more hired."

"Hmm, that might be right up my alley," Louisa said. She leaned back against the support post and lowered her eyes, demure. "About the other night, Jonas . . ."

Prophet interrupted her with: "If you two will excuse me, I think I'll pull foot, look for some whiskey that's in bad need of freein' from a bottle . . ."

As he headed for the door, boots thudded on the veranda. There was no knock. The door opened too quickly for Prophet not to slip his Colt half out of its holster before Phoebe Dahlstrom walked in, flanked by Melvin Handy and another man who wore a blond beard and deerskin chaps. He had a long, hooked nose and close-set eyes beneath the brim of his weathered, bullet-crowned black hat.

He was Handy's size—around six feet, slightly pot-bellied, rough and mean-looking. Also like Handy, he wore two pistols and a bowie knife. His sleeves were rolled up to his biceps. His arms were pale and mottled with freckles.

He and Handy sized up Prophet like the third dog in a possible alley fight.

Phoebe stopped before Prophet, as well, but her sizing up of the bounty hunter was of another strain entirely. Her coquettish gaze flicked across his broad chest and long, corded arms, and then it brushed across his mouth before sinking into his eyes. A smile stretched her lips. "I saw you bring in my husband's killer."

Her voice was thick, raspy . . . not so vaguely sexual.

"*We* brought him in," Louisa said. She'd turned to face the newcomers, also always alert for a threat. Both her hands were still closed over the pearl grips of her Colts.

"You her?" asked the blond-bearded man standing

beside Handy. His lusty eyes raked across Louisa. "The one they call the Vengeance Queen?"

"Phoebe, would you mind keeping your dogs on their leashes?" Ford said, rising from the corner of his desk and glowering at the pretty young widow.

Mrs. Dahlstrom glanced at the bearded man and then indicated Butters's cell with her chin. "This is Lars Gunderson. He was with Handy and my husband when this killer murdered Max."

Gunderson brushed past Prophet, who let his Colt slide back down into its holster, and strode over to the jail cell. He stared in at Charlie Butters, who sat on the cot, leaning back against the wall. His eyes showed the pain of his wounds, which had likely been aggravated by the ride from the Lowry ranch. He peered dully through the bars at the stocky man staring in at him.

"Yep, that's him," Gunderson said. "I seen him gallop off with that Winchester right after he blew the boss out of his saddle." He glanced at Phoebe and added, "Uh . . . sorry, ma'am."

"It's all right, Lars. You'll testify to that at the trial?"

"You betcha."

"I wouldn't know this ugly galoot from Adam's off-ox," Butters said, snarling. "Never seen him before in my life. He's lyin'." He raised his voice in bitter frustration, squeezing his eyes closed. "I never shot Dahlstrom, an' if you hang me for it, you're hangin' an innocent man!"

The man's voice echoed around inside the office.

"No, no—that's him, all right," Gunderson said, smiling mockingly at Charlie through the bars.

"Sure is," Handy said, determined not to be left

out, hooking his thumbs behind his cartridge belt. "I was there, too. Seen the whole thing."

Butters glowered at Phoebe's foreman. "Yeah, well, you're a liar, then, too, Handy—you lip-peckered son of a bitch! You come from a whole family of liars!"

"Why, you—!"

Handy lunged at the cell, gripping the bars of the door in his fists as though he thought he could rip them from their moorings.

"Hey, hey, hey!" Ford said, grabbing Handy's left arm.

"That's enough, Mel!" Phoebe yelled.

Ford said, "The sheriff, the county prosecutor, the judge, and the public defender are all on their way. Should be here day after tomorrow. Butters will have his day in court."

Prophet sighed, opened the door, and stepped out onto the veranda. He'd had enough. He had his five hundred dollars. Now it was time to see about a cheap whore and a cheap drink, maybe a little poker. After a good night's sleep, he'd pull his picket pin. He'd start makin' his slow way down to Mexico before the first chill winds of winter blew over the Rockies.

First, he'd stable his horse, grain and feed the ugly mug.

He dropped morosely down the veranda steps and untied the dun's reins from the hitchrack. He turned the horse into the street and was about to toe his stirrup when a voice rose behind him: "You get him?"

Prophet dropped his left boot into the street and turned to see George Hill and his four beefy bruisers walking toward him, in the same formation as before—Hill inside the box the four hardtails formed the corners of.

"Did you bring in Butters?" Hill said, clad in his top hat and shabby ice-cream suit that made him look like a well-dressed ape.

Prophet loosed a wry breath. *Here we go again.*

"You know I did or you wouldn't be here."

Prophet raised his foot to toe a stirrup again but stopped again when the marshal's office door opened and Phoebe Dahlstrom walked out onto the veranda. Handy and Gunderson were right behind her.

Prophet set his foot back down in the street and groaned.

Hill turned to Phoebe and snarled around the fat stogie clamped in his teeth. "So your dog fetched your bone for you, did he?"

"He's a reliable dog," Phoebe said, turning her taut, vaguely taunting smile on Prophet. Sliding her gaze back to Hill, she said, "He did, indeed. You and your, uh, bone will be swinging together soon. Jonas tells me that the mucky-mucks from the county seat are on their way as we speak."

Hill turned to Prophet, his flat eyes hard and angry. "Did Butters tell you he did what this polecat says he did?" He jerked his chin toward his daughter glaring down at him from the veranda.

"No," the bounty hunter said. "He said he was in McReynolds's line shack at the time, baiting a calf-eatin' wildcat."

"Don't worry," Hill said sarcastically, "his story will change. Jonas will change it for him. He'll offer Butters a deal. Ford is another of Phoebe's loyal dogs. She has a lot of loyal dogs in these parts. With a pair of breasts like that, and her husband's bankroll, a girl gets a whole pack of loyal dogs hot on her heels, sniffin' an' snarlin' and grovelin' like curs in a trash heap."

Hill threw his head back and laughed briefly before glaring at the men flanking his daughter, including Jonas Ford, who had walked out onto the veranda, Louisa at his side. "Look at 'em all!"

"Shut up!" Melvin Handy barked, pushing past Phoebe and dropping down into the street, his fists bunched at his sides. "You got no call to talk to her that way. I won't have it!"

"Ha!" Hill roared. "There's one of 'em now, showin' his teeth and raisin' his hackles!"

"How dare you talk about your daughter like that!"

As Handy lunged toward Hill, the bruiser nearest Prophet leveled his sawed-off shotgun at him. Automatically, Prophet took one step toward the bruiser and smashed his right arm down against the shotgun, which exploded.

One barrel of buckshot blew a foot-sized crater out of the street. Prophet smashed his left fist into the man's face, laying his nose sideways. The bruiser screamed and staggered backward, holding both hands over his nose. Blood ran out from between his fingers.

He tripped over his own feet and fell to his butt, cursing and spitting blood out his nose and mouth.

The shotgun blast had caused everyone, including Handy, to freeze. They stared toward Prophet, who shucked his Colt, clicked the hammer back, and aimed it straight out from his right side. Hill's other three men were all aiming something—either a pistol or another sawed-off shotgun—at him, waiting for their boss to give the order.

Hill glowered at Prophet.

"What the hell did you come over here for, Hill? You tryin' to start a war on the street? Who in the hell you think's gonna win that war?"

Hill extended an enraged finger at his daughter, curling a delighted half smile from where she stood atop the veranda. "She's here, ain't she? Spewin' her lies! That's all she does is spew lies, and he and everyone else around here listens, because the General was well liked in Carson's Wash, and Ford's the General's son!"

"That's enough, Hill!" Ford stepped around Phoebe to hurry down the steps. He stood in front of Hill and said with quiet equanimity, "What would you have me do? Those two men saw Charlie Butters gun down their boss."

"And what does Butters say about who put him up to it?"

Hill probed the vaguely sheepish Jonas Ford with his gaze.

Hill chuckled, rolling his cold cigar from one corner of his mouth to the other. "Denies it, don't he? Well, if he denies it, it's his word against theirs. And, without Butters involved, you can't prove I was involved."

He glared at Phoebe, who returned the glare with an even more hateful one of her own. "Always listenin' to her lies—aren't ya, Jonas? After all these years, still listenin' to her *lies* . . ." He took special care to emphasize that last.

Meaning what? Prophet wondered.

A particular lie?

Hill removed his cigar from between his teeth, spat in the dirt to his right, then wheeled and lumbered back in the direction from which he'd come. The three uninjured bruisers followed.

The other one glared at Prophet from over his bloody hands. He cursed loudly, angrily, spat blood in the street, and gained his feet heavily. Holding one hand over his nose, he started toward his shotgun, which he'd left near the crater it had blown in the street.

"Leave it," Prophet said.

"The hell I will," intoned the bruiser, squaring his shoulders at Prophet.

Mean and Ugly, who'd been flanking its owner, gave an angry whinny and lunged forward, bulling the man over. The bruiser gave another shrill scream, hit the street on his back, and rolled. Mean lowered his head before the enraged man and pawed the dirt like a bull.

"Come on, Mean," Prophet said, walking over and grabbing the horse's bridle. "He's finished for today." He looked at the bruiser staring up in silent fury and more than a little fear at the horse. "Ain't ya, pard?"

"Yeah." The man climbed heavily to his feet. As he slogged away, he shot a furious glare over his thick right shoulder, blood still dripping from his smashed nose. "For *today*."

Prophet plucked the bruiser's shotgun out of the street. He tossed it over to Ford.

"Thanks, Lou," Jonas said.

"Don't mention it."

He glanced at Louisa. She stood beside Phoebe, regarding him dubiously, one fist on her hip, head canted to one side. Phoebe glanced at Louisa then walked down the veranda steps to stand before Prophet.

She ran her hand down Mean and Ugly's scarred snout. "At least someone's looking out for you."

"A good hoss . . . even a mean and ugly one . . . is all a man needs."

"A hoss can't buy a man a drink. I can."

"Nah," Prophet said. "I got me five hundred dollars here in my pocket, and it'll just burn a hole if I don't spend it on a cheap woman and some cheap whiskey." Prophet finally managed to swing up onto his horse without further delay. He pinched his hat brim to Phoebe Dahlstrom, who frowned up at him skeptically. "Obliged, though."

He touched spurs to Mean's flanks and headed for the livery barn and the oblivion of store-bought love and who-hit-John.

Chapter 14

The Five Card Stud was a seedy, rat-infested watering hole that sat on the far northern outskirts of Carson's Wash. It catered mainly to Mexicans, but gringos favoring a brief walk on the wild side frequented the place, as well.

The building was one of those remaining from when the town was a Mexican *pueblito.* Long, slender, cool, and dark, it was a sun-faded, thick-walled, brush-roofed adobe with an adjoining stable, and whores' cribs on the second story. Several other adobes sprawled around it and a battered wooden windmill and stock tank. Some of the adobes were occupied, some were not.

The Stud, as it was locally called, was run by a half-breed Apache ex–cavalry tracker whose name was Alfredo Diego. When Prophet had visited the establishment the last time he'd ridden through Carson's Wash, Diego had appeared in the latter stages of alcoholism—deeply drunk, potbellied, swollen-faced, thin-legged, and cloaked in the stench of a slop bucket badly in need of emptying. He sat, semiconscious, head perpetually sagging, on a stool behind his bar. When he was awake, he swatted flies or tended a pot of beans on his range.

Always smoking.

Always sipping pulque from a crock jug.

He was dressed in a ratty cotton shirt and deerskin breeches. He wore no shoes or even sandals. On his head was a palm-leaf sombrero with a badly unraveling brim.

Diego appeared in no better condition now on Prophet's second visit to the place. He managed to keep pouring the drinks, however, and that's all that Prophet cared about. All Diego served was tequila and pulque. Prophet didn't mind. Pulque, the milky, sour-tasting drink of Old Mexico, was a cheap way to get and stay drunk, as long as you could hold it down, which Prophet had learned to do after several visits to southern Sonora, where the pulque flowed like fresh snowmelt in the northern Rockies.

When Diego's two plump Mexican whores were not upstairs moaning while some jake grunted between their spread knees, they tended bar or swamped out the place or hauled in firewood that kept the pot of beans perpetually bubbling atop the small range that occupied a little closetlike alcove behind the counter.

Prophet had never seen many customers in the Stud at one time, and he didn't over the next two days he spent in the pleasingly grim, liquory shadows, drinking pulque, eating beans, smoking, conversing with Diego, and gambling with whoever came in—mostly local ranch hands who stayed for a couple rounds of stud or red dog and a mattress dance or two.

He'd intended on having his own ashes hauled, but there was a blandness and distractedness in the eyes of Diego's two whores that he didn't find enticing or even welcoming. He didn't blame them for not enjoying their jobs, but he preferred whores who did.

Or maybe it was just a blandness and distractedness in himself that kept him from getting the itch to take one of the girls upstairs.

So he drank and gambled to numb his confusion about Butters and Phoebe Dahlstrom and her dead husband and George Hill and, last but not least, Louisa and Jonas Ford.

After the first afternoon and night in the Stud, Prophet staggered back to his room at the Rio Grande. The next morning, he checked out of the Rio and took up temporary residence in the Five Card Stud.

Despite the unappetizing whores, he liked it there. It was cool and dark and the pulque was freely flowing as well as cheap, and if he did decide to partake of a mattress dance—well, you couldn't get any cheaper than Diego's whores. He didn't care for the phony frills of other parlor houses.

He could have left Carson's Wash and ridden south toward Mexico, but he felt compelled to remain in town until the matter with Charlie Butters was resolved. He preferred to be hidden away here at the town's seedy edge where he was anonymous and most of the more respectable folks didn't wander. He'd always felt most comfortable on the wrong side of the tracks. He'd eventually learn, one way or the other, of the outcome of Butters's murder trial.

Then he could ride on.

The second night, Prophet played stud poker with seven Mexicans fresh off the range. He didn't play with all seven at once, because two were usually upstairs making the whores squeal and moan with a little too much vigor. They were all getting along just fine until the pulque had flowed a little too much like that Rocky Mountain snowmelt in the springtime, and one of the Mexicans started to give Prophet the woolly eyeball.

Prophet tried to ignore the dark, threatening stare until the Mexican said with low menace in deeply accented English mixed with border Spanish, "Señor, if you would be so kind as to roll up your left sleeve for me . . . ?"

Prophet turned to him and smiled. "Say what again, partner?"

"If you would be so kind as to roll up . . ."

"I heard you the first time, Pancho," Prophet said, though he hadn't learned the man's name. In his own drunken state, he was growing contentious, as well, and not feeling as given to smoothing feathers as he normally would have been. "Why do you want me to roll up my sleeve? You think I got cards up there, do you, *Pancho*?"

The Mexican blinked beneath the brim of his steeple-crowned sombrero. Smoke from the cornhusk quirley sagging from the right side of his mouth caused him to narrow one eye.

The other Mexicans stopped playing to look at him curiously.

"*Por favor, señor,* do not take offense. But if you would be so kind . . ."

"Go ahead and say what you're thinkin'," Prophet said, hardening his jaws and staring drunkenly at his drunken opponent sitting almost directly across the table from him. "If you think I'm cheatin', go ahead and tell me, straight up, you think I'm cheatin'."

Prophet's sawed-off Richards lay on the table to his right. He dropped his cards to the table and laid his right hand over the neck of the shotgun's stock.

"There you are, you old devil!"

The exclamation was as loud as it was unexpected, coming as it did from a female. It shattered the menacingly masculine and grave key of Prophet and the Mexican's conversation. Lou turned to his right and removed his hand from the Richards in time to catch Phoebe Dahlstrom in his arms.

"I'd heard you were still in town!" the girl said, wrapping her arms around his neck as she squirmed around in his lap. "I checked every watering hole in town. Then I remembered this place, and here you are, you trail-worn reprobate. No surprise at all! Have you missed me?"

She nuzzled Prophet's neck and then turned to the Mexican, who frowned at her curiously, apprehensively. "Who's this fella?" Not waiting for Prophet to say anything, she flung her right hand across the table. "I'm Phoebe Dahlstrom. The former *Mrs. Maxwell Dahlstrom . . .*"

"*Sí, señorita,*" said the Mexican who'd had the beef with Prophet. He gave a slow, respectful dip of his chin. "I know who you are." He glanced at the other Mexicans sitting around him. They had a brief, silent conversation and then started swiping their coins and silver certificates off the table, casting quick, anxious glances toward the beautiful woman in Prophet's arms.

"Are you leaving?" Phoebe asked with mock disappointment.

"Forgive us, señorita," said the Mexican who'd tangled with Prophet, and threw back a cup of pulque, the milky liquid dribbling down from the corners of his mouth. He ran a grimy sleeve across his mustached lips and rose from his chair. "We are due back to the rancho by midnight." He gave a wobbly, drunken bow, doffing his sombrero and holding it over his heart.

"Wait," Phoebe said, frowning and sticking her fingers up Prophet's left sleeve. "What's this?"

She pulled out the ace of hearts. She looked at Prophet, who gave a sheepish grin and a shrug. Phoebe flicked the card to the Mexican. It bounced off the buckle of his cartridge belt and fell to the floor.

The Mexican snarled a Spanish curse at Prophet. He tipped his face to the ceiling, from which the sounds of feral coupling emanated, and yelled, "*Nos vamos!*"

He and the others stumbled out the batwing doors. Leather creaked and bits and bridle chains rattled as the Mexicans mounted their horses.

Diego sat his stool behind the counter, his perpetual quirley dangling from one corner of his mouth, lips quirking a wry grin at Prophet, who sat with the beautiful Widow Dahlstrom in his lap.

Phoebe turned her gaze from the still-swinging batwings to Prophet, pressing her full breasts against his chest. "I hope I didn't interrupt anything."

"As a matter of fact . . ."

"Don't be a wet blanket," Phoebe admonished. "Those men are hardtails from one of the oldest Mexican spreads around, and they consider this their territory. Besides, it was five against one. I likely saved you from a cut throat and a deep ravine. Or was that what you were wanting?"

"Just a little diversion."

Prophet glanced toward the batwings. Two hatted figures stood, one on each side of the door, silhouetted against the starry sky behind them. A candle flickering on a wall identified Melvin Handy and Lars Gunderson, both cradling Winchester carbines in their arms.

The two Mexicans who'd been fornicating in the second story ran down the stairs at the back of the room and, tucking their shirttails into their pants, hurried toward the doors. They looked around, incredulous, frowning curiously at Prophet and the woman and then halted briefly, cautiously, before Handy and Gunderson.

Muttering to each other in Spanish, they brushed past the two Dahlstrom riders and headed outside. Soon, the thuds of their horses were fading into the night.

Phoebe looked around Prophet to her two men standing by the doors. "Mel, Lars—leave us, please."

Handy stepped forward, scowling. "What . . . what do you . . . ?"

"I said, leave us, please, Melvin."

It was as though the foreman couldn't believe his ears. "Where would you like us to go? We can't leave you here alone, Mrs. Dahl—"

"As you can see, I'm not alone," Phoebe said, her

voice growing louder, steelier. "And I don't care where you go. Just make it not here." She gave him a wide-eyed glare.

Handy stared at her for a full five seconds. Then he gave a caustic grunt, turned, and stomped out of the cantina. Gunderson followed him.

As their spurs chinged into the distance, Phoebe smiled at Prophet. "I can think of a better diversion than a stiletto in your belly."

Footsteps sounded at the back of the cantina. The two whores were coming down the stairs in their skimpy cotton dresses, hair disheveled. They were both barefoot. Like the men who'd abandoned them upstairs, they looked around incredulously, dark eyes fixing with mute fascination on Prophet and the woman in his lap.

They walked around behind the bar to stand in silence near Diego.

Prophet looked at Phoebe. She was a warm, supple weight in his lap. He felt her breasts pressing against him. Her breath puffed against his lips. It smelled like wine.

"What are you doing here?" Prophet asked her.

"I'm bored at the Rio Grande." Phoebe looked around. One of the whores had started sweeping in a desultory way, keeping one eye skinned on the two gringos who were now the only customers. "I went to your room. When you weren't there, I inquired with the manager, Dressler, and he said you'd checked out. He didn't think you'd left town, however."

She slid her head to his and kissed him. Her lips were plump, sensuously yielding. "Very mysterious, Mr. Prophet. Very, very mysterious."

"Nothin' mysterious about wantin' a little time alone," Prophet said. "To drink, gamble, an' whore."

"Oh, have you been with the whores?" Phoebe arched a brow and turned to the two girls of topic. Returning her gaze to Prophet, she asked, "Which one?" She waited. "Both?" Again, she waited, and when a response wasn't forthcoming, she said, "Or . . . neither?"

Prophet's heart thudded as her eyes probed his. Her mouth was perfect, her nose a fine, straight line before him. He could see fine bits of copper, like gold dust on the bed of a pure, shallow stream, glinting in her irises. Her lush brown hair fell loosely over his hands on her shoulders. He thought he could feel the beating of her heart ever so slightly nudging her body from within.

"Like I said," she said, just above a whisper, "I can think of a better diversion than a long, cold sleep at the bottom of a deep ravine."

Prophet reached around her for his shotgun. He slung the lanyard over his right shoulder and then, sliding his right hand under her legs and wrapping his left arm around her back, he rose from his chair.

She drew a deep breath as he lifted her against him. She pressed her lips to his once more.

He kicked away his chair, walked around the table, and strode to the back of the cantina. He climbed the stairs with the young woman in his arms. She smiled up at him as he gained the second story, walked down the dingy hall that smelled like sweat, sex, and cheap tobacco, and nudged open his door.

He walked into the room and tossed the pretty widow into his bed.

Chapter 15

Prophet woke when she rolled against him, groaned, and pressed her cheek against his chest. He opened his eyes, saw gray light pushing through the room's single window. It was touched with the gold of an imminent sunrise.

"Hell," Prophet said, clearing sleep from his throat, raking a hand down his face, then tenderly slapping her shoulder. "We're burnin' daylight. We'd best get movin', part—"

He stopped himself.

Phoebe turned her head on his chest to stare up at him from over his chin. She arched a brow. "Partner?" Her lips shaped a rueful smile. "You're getting your women mixed up, cowboy."

Prophet flushed.

"It's okay," she said. "I don't mind."

It was true. He'd woken up thinking that it was Louisa snuggling against him. He'd wanted it to be so, though he hadn't been fully conscious of the thought. He'd also half imagined that it had been

Louisa he'd been making love to the night before. Sometime later, Phoebe asked, "Any regrets?"

Prophet gave a ragged sigh and relaxed against his pillow, half sitting up against the headboard. "Nary a one." Suddenly, it was true. Louisa was with Jonas Ford, after all.

Phoebe chuckled with satisfaction as she cleaned him with a corner of the sheet.

He reached down and tucked a sleep-mussed lock of her hair behind her right, china-white ear. "I bet Melvin Handy's not feelin' near as good about you bein' here as I am."

She asked, "What does that mean?"

"It occurred to me last night, when we were still downstairs. You and Handy . . ."

He knew he didn't need to finish the sentence.

She shrugged a shoulder, blinked slowly. "A minor dalliance."

"When your husband was alive?"

"Sure." Again, she arched a brow. "Are you judging me, Lou?"

"I'm no one to judge, believe me."

"I believe you. I'm the one who found that card tucked up your sleeve, remember?"

Prophet smiled. "How do you feel about Melvin?"

"I told you," she said, her voice growing taught with annoyance. "He was a minor dalliance, Lou."

"Is that how he sees it?"

She scowled, as though the question were absurd. "I don't care how he sees it!"

Prophet studied her. He wanted to ask her about the baby, as well, but he could tell that he'd probed far enough for one morning. Besides, the lies she told or didn't tell . . . the child she'd had out of wedlock . . . were none of his affair.

He had the very poignant feeling that after last night and this morning, the lovemaking as well as the impertinent question, he'd worn out his stay in Carson's Wash. If only in his own eyes. It was time to ride on.

He'd done what he'd come to do. He had most of the five hundred dollars in his pocket. It was time to head to Mexico.

Prophet leaned forward, took her gently in his arms, and kissed her.

"It's been nice knowin' you, Mrs. Dahlstrom."

He dropped his feet to the floor.

"Are you going?"

"High time."

As he rose and, wincing against the dull throb of a pulque hangover directly behind each eye, began stumbling around for his clothes.

"You're not going to stay for the hanging?"

Prophet chuckled. "I've seen enough hemp stretched." He sat on the edge of the bed to pull on his longhandles. "I tell you what I will do, though. I'll send over a jug of coffee from the Rio Grande."

She smiled with genuine surprise and delight. "You'd do that?"

"Hell, after last night, what I *want* to do is follow you around for the next three months like a loyal puppy dog, wanting more of the same. You do know how to please a man, Miss Phoebe."

She watched him with that same serene expression, in silence, as he dressed. Just before he left, he drew the covers up over her legs and planted a parting kiss on her temple.

Groaning and working the kinks from his neck, loaded down with his gear, Prophet headed downstairs. He stumbled through the empty, semidark cantina, which smelled like stale smoke, spilled pulque, and scorched beans. He could hear Diego snoring in a back room.

He let himself out the front door, shifted the gear on his shoulders, and ambled south along the winding street that was turning salmon now as the sun lifted its molten orange head above the eastern desert.

Hoof thuds rose on his left. He turned his head to see two horseback riders walking their horses past a wide gap at the rear of two abandoned adobe hovels on that side of the ragged street. They were silhouetted against the sun, so Prophet couldn't see any details. He'd caught only a brief glimpse of them, anyway. They'd ridden out from behind one building, crossed the far end of the break, and disappeared again behind the next building to the north.

Probably a couple of ranch hands heading home after a night in a whore's crib.

Prophet walked into the lobby of the Rio Grande a couple minutes later and set his gear on the floor against the wall, keeping his shotgun slung over his neck and shoulder. The Rio's manager, whose named was Mort Dressler, was down on one knee, running an oiled cloth over the desk's oak facade.

He gave Prophet a dubious look. "It doesn't appear to me that Diego treated you nearly as well as we did here. If you'll forgive me, Mr. Prophet, you look like hell."

"You're forgiven."

Prophet stood in the entrance to the dining room,

quickly scanning the tables. There were only three customers—two together, one alone. None was either Louisa or Jonas Ford, or both together. For that he was grateful. He didn't care to see either one of them again for a while. He wanted to make a clean break from Carson's Wash.

He turned to Dressler. "Have the judge and the other mucky-mucks from the county seat pulled in yet?"

"Due in any time. Stage usually arrives from LaVerne between seven and eight in the morning. The rainstorms the past few nights have probably played hell with the trail, so who knows?"

"Right." Prophet started to walk into the dining room.

"Everyone's waitin' on the stage, it seems."

Prophet stopped, half turned. A worm of unease turned in his belly. "What's that?"

With a grunt, Dressler heaved himself up off the floor and made his way over to the clock ticking inside a heavy wooden cabinet leaning against the lobby's far wall, near the front doors. "You're not the only one who's been askin' about the stage. A couple of my customers inquired not fifteen minutes ago."

"They didn't happen to be part of the Lowry family, did they?"

"I'm new in town, Mr. Prophet. I wouldn't know the Lowrys from a bar of soap."

Prophet wouldn't, either, but as his pulse quickened, he said, "Have they been around long?"

"They were here all day yesterday, mostly holed up in two rooms upstairs. I brought up four bottles of whiskey and several platters of steak and beans. If I hadn't known which rooms they were in, I could have followed the stench. They obviously have not made use of Mr. Taylor's bathhouse—pity the poor Chinaman who washes our bed linens."

Dressler turned to Prophet and, expressionless, pinched his nose.

"An older man and a half-dozen younger ones?"

Dressler nodded as he climbed a chair, opened the clock's glass door, and began polishing the inside of the window. "One older man and *six* younger ones. Out-of-work ranch hands, I 'spect. A surly lot."

Prophet's heartbeat increased by a couple more notches. "Has anyone asked about me? Like, where they might find me?"

"They haven't asked me."

But they could have asked the night clerk. By now, word could easily have gotten around Carson's Wash that Prophet had been holed up in the Stud. Handy and Gunderson might even have mentioned it themselves.

Warning bells tolled in Prophet's ears. He wasn't sure what the bells were warning him about, exactly, but something told him to get back to the Five Card Stud pronto. He hurried to the door.

"What the hell's wrong?" Dressler said, scowling down from his chair.

"I hope nothin'!"

Prophet ran outside and retraced his footsteps back toward the Five Card Stud. He kept remembering the two riders who'd ridden past the break between the two abandoned buildings. They'd been heading toward the Stud, as well as the countryside. Why hadn't they been on the street? The only reason you rode behind buildings like that, sticking to the back alleys, was if you didn't want to be seen.

When he hit the first cross street, Prophet broke into a run.

He ran through an empty lot being used as a trash dump, around a lumberyard, and into the street that led north toward the Stud. He ran hard, holding the Richards in his right hand, the lanyard flopping against his thigh. He startled a mongrel sampling the trash outside a little Mexican eatery, closed at this hour. The dog barked and lunged for his ankles before turning tail and whining off into the brush.

Prophet stopped in front of the Stud. All was quiet.

Still, his heart was beating like a war drum, and he didn't think it was because he was out of breath.

He jogged around behind the place and stopped when he saw Alfredo Diego standing outside the cantina's rear door. Diego wore a ratty red robe and a frayed sleeping sock on his head, the tail dangling to his shoulder. Barefoot, his eyes badly red-rimmed, he was smoking a quirley and tipping his head back to stare up at the building's second story.

An outside stairs, rickety and in need of paint, ran up the building's rear wall to the door on the second floor. The door sagged about six inches open.

When Diego saw Prophet, a look of extreme sheepishness instantly clouded the cantina proprietor's face.

Diego turned away abruptly, limped into the cantina, and closed the door behind him.

"Dang," Prophet rasped as he lunged toward the stairs.

He took the steps three at a time, trying to ignore not only the crackling of the steps under his boots but the precarious and dizzying sway of the entire staircase. The contraption moaned like one of Diego's plump whores, as though it were about to break loose from the cantina wall.

Prophet gained the top of the stairs, jerked the door wide, and lunged into the building. He turned to his right. Two men were just then milling outside the door of the room in which Phoebe Dahlstrom was likely slumbering in hers and Prophet's love-rumpled bed.

The men were moving lightly on their feet, trying to be quiet.

They each had a pistol drawn and cocked.

Chapter 16

One of the men in the hall raised a leg and started to thrust the heel of his right boot toward the door behind which Phoebe Dahlstrom slept.

Prophet yelled, "Hold it!"

The man lowered his leg.

The men both swung toward Prophet, their lower jaws hanging in shock.

The taller man yelled and raised his pistol.

Prophet tripped the Richards's right trigger, filling the hall with concussive thunder that seemed to lift the entire building off the ground for one fleeting second and then slam it back down. The shorter of the two men was picked up and thrown backward down the hall.

The other danced around, triggering his pistol wildly as the widely scattered buck chewed into him.

Prophet squeezed the Richards's second trigger.

The building leaped once more. So did the second man.

He was swept back as though by a tornado. He landed atop his dead partner—probably his dead *brother*, if these were two Lowrys, and Prophet thought they were—and rolled three times before piling up against a rail post at the top of the stairs.

Prophet ran down the hall.

"Phoebe?" he called as he pushed open the door to his room.

She stood on the far side of the bed, wrapped in a sheet. She stared in mute shock toward Prophet. Her voice was husky from sleep. "What in hell was that all about?"

Prophet opened his mouth to speak but then closed it.

Distant popping sounds rose from somewhere outside. The din sounded like a Fourth of July celebration. But it wasn't the Fourth of July. Not even close.

Horses screamed. A man shouted. More guns popped, and then there were the hiccupping, belching reports of a rifle.

Another horse screamed. There was a crazy clattering sound.

The cacophony was originating from the heart of town.

The stage . . .

Prophet quickly broke the Richards open, plucked out the spent wads, and replaced them with fresh from the lanyard's loops. He closed the Richards, slid the savage popper behind his shoulder.

"Lou, what the hell is going on?" Phoebe asked, moving quickly around the bed.

Prophet was heading for the door. "I think the Lowrys are hitting the stage!"

"Oh no!" she gasped, cupping a hand to her mouth.

"Stay here!"

Prophet ran out of the room. He saw no reason to retrace his steps down the falling-down outside stairs when the front door was just as close to the main street. He leaped the carnage that was once two Lowry brothers and hurried down the stairs. He could still hear some gun reports, muffled by distance, but they were dwindling fast.

Alfredo Diego stood behind his bar in the main drinking hall. He stared sullenly toward Prophet as the bounty hunter strode toward him, kicking chairs out of his way.

Diego was the only person in the place. The two whores were probably cowering in their rooms upstairs.

"Sometime soon, Diego, you an' me are gonna have us a talk about why you told those two scumbags which room was mine!"

"They told me they'd burn the place!" Diego barked raspily in heavily accented Spanish.

"Yeah, well, maybe now I'll burn the place, you yellow-livered son of a bitch!"

"You're not welcome here no more, gringo!"

The words reached Prophet from behind as he pushed out the front door and began running south along the street. The only sound now issuing from anywhere around town was the fervent barking of several dogs.

Anxiety turned to ice the sweat basting Prophet's buckskin tunic to his back as he ran harder, faster. He gained the main street and skidded to a stop, looking around. He swiveled his head toward the west, and his racing heart hiccupped twice.

"Goddamnit!"

He ran toward the town marshal's office on the street before which half a dozen men lay strewn in bloody piles, as though they'd fallen from the high façades of surrounding buildings. Several townsmen were just now moving sheepishly out of the shops and saloons and walking tepidly toward the scene of what appeared to be a small, bloody massacre.

One man lay writhing against the veranda steps. As Prophet approached the office, he glanced at the seven men on the ground out front of it. Two were dressed in dust-soaked trail garb. They were the stage driver and the shotgun messenger. The messenger's coach gun lay near his outstretched hands that were still now in death. He'd taken a bullet through his left ear. His lips were stretched back from his teeth in a silent agony.

The five others lay in a close group near the veranda, but they were just as bloody and just as dead as the other two. These five were dressed in suits. One gray-haired, gray-mustached, middle-aged man wore a five-pointed sheriff's badge. Another, younger man, dressed in a cheap suit, wore a deputy's star. He was the only one of the dead men on the street who'd drawn a pistol.

The Schofield still lay in his slack hand. The deputy had taken a bullet through his right cheek and another in his neck.

They'd all been hit hard and fast, taken totally unexpectedly, it appeared.

Groans rose from the man writhing with his back against the steps.

"Jonas!" Prophet said, and dropped to a knee beside the marshal.

"Lou!"

"Take it easy, Jonas."

Prophet winced. Ford had been hit in the upper-left thigh and belly. He was losing blood from both wounds fast.

Prophet glanced at the townsfolk, mostly shop-keepers, some still with brooms in their hands, closing in a ragged circle around the marshal's office. "Someone fetch a sawbones!"

"The sawbones is here!" called a man approaching from behind Prophet, to the east. He was a tall man hefting a black medical kit.

As the medico sort of skip-walked toward Prophet, the bounty hunter looked around for his partner, dread biting him. He didn't see Louisa anywhere. He wasn't sure if that were good or bad.

A hand closed around Prophet's left forearm, and squeezed.

"They got her, Lou," Ford said, staring up through pain-racked eyes at Prophet. "They got Louisa."

Prophet's heart hiccupped again. "The Lowrys?"

Ford nodded. He chewed out a curse as he continued to writhe.

He'd lost his hat, and his thick, wavy hair was mussed and dusty. "Christ—I hadn't seen that coming. They were forted up around the office and when the stage pulled in and the sheriff and the judge and the others got out, the Lowrys came running and shooting. Mowed the judge and the sheriff down first, then the deputy and the county attorney and the prosecutor, Mossman. Louisa ran off the veranda, returning lead, but one of the Lowrys clipped her with a bullet and ran her down with his horse. Knocked her unconscious. When they busted Butters out of his cell, they threw Louisa over the back of one of the horses, and they all busted tail out of here!"

"Which way'd they head?"

"East," said the doctor, dropping to a knee beside Prophet.

Prophet looked east, beyond where the town straggled off into the sagebrush and cactus and scattered mesquites. He could see the stagecoach lying on its side maybe a hundred yards beyond town. The team must have spooked at the gunfire and bolted. The horses had obviously torn themselves free of the hitch and dumped the coach.

"Jonas!" The woman's worried exclamation had come from behind Prophet. He glanced over his shoulder to see Phoebe run out from the far side of a women's clothing shop. She was dressed in her skirt and blouse from the night before. Her hair was still mussed from love and sleep. "Jonas, my God—what happened?"

Ford looked at the young woman and opened his mouth to speak. No words came out. He froze, staring at her, the light slowly leaving his eyes.

Prophet's innards clenched. He'd seen that look too many times during the war and afterward.

Ford's lips moved. In a barely audible rasp, he said, "I'm sorry, Phoebe. I'm sorry . . . I never measured up . . . to the man . . . you wanted me to be. A man . . . like the General."

Ford's eyes rolled back in their sockets. His head dropped back against the veranda steps, tipped slightly to one side. His eyelids drooped. His body fell still.

"Oh, Jonas!" Phoebe cried, and lowered her head over the marshal's chest, sobbing.

Prophet rose to his feet. It was as though a spring had been tripped in his body. He staggered backward, mind reeling from grief and exasperation. He hadn't realized until that moment just how much he had liked Jonas Ford. Suddenly, he felt foolish and contemptible for the jealousy that had racked him.

Ford had been a good, decent man. Now he was dead. His blood soaked the veranda steps.

Phoebe sobbed over him. It was as though she felt many of the same things Prophet was feeling.

Adding to Prophet's horror was the fact that the Lowrys had Louisa.

Prophet swept his hat from his head, ran his hands through his hair. He had to settle down. He had to organize his thoughts, figure out how he was going to run the Lowrys down and retrieve his partner.

"Now, look what you did!"

The deep, pugnacious voice jerked Prophet's head west.

George Hill and his four toughs, one with a white plaster bandage over his nose, stood in the middle of the street, ten yards away. The shopkeepers were all moving out of Hill's way, cautious casts to their gazes.

Hill stared down at his daughter, sobbing over Jonas Ford.

Phoebe turned to him, her tear-filled eyes bright with grief.

"You got all these men here killed because you wanted to see your old man hang. Ha! Everything you do turns out just like you turned out, Phoebe."

Hill bent slightly forward at the waist, his fat, crude face puffed viciously. "Post stupid, poison mean, and a whore to boot!"

Phoebe rose from Ford's slack body and lunged, screaming, toward Hill. Prophet grabbed her around the waist, spun her around.

"I'll kill him!" Phoebe screamed. "Let me kill him!"

"Hold on, girl," Prophet said gently in her ear, holding her taut against him. "He ain't worth it. He's done everything to you he can . . . unless you let him do more."

"God, I want so much to kill him!" she sobbed against Prophet's chest.

"I know you do." Prophet glared at Hill over the young woman's right shoulder. "I don't blame you a bit. But you gotta let him go. You're better than he is. He's nothin'. He's dirt. Nothin' but dirt," he bit out tightly through clenched teeth.

"Dirt, is it?" Hill said, glowering at his daughter sobbing in Prophet's arms. Turning slowly away, he said, "She's just like her mother. Miss High and Mighty. I never could do enough for either one of 'em."

He started walking away, his bruisers turning as though they were attached to the same hidden rope as Hill was. He snapped his head back to shout, "That girl never did have one nice word to say to me. Not one nice word . . . after all I done for her!"

Her voice breaking, Phoebe screamed, "You killed everything good in me when you killed my mother, you brutal hornswoggler!"

She sobbed against Prophet's chest.

"What the hell's goin' on?"

Prophet looked over Phoebe's head to see Melvin Handy and Lars Gunderson approaching from the corner of a cross street to the northwest. They both had the red eyes and pasty complexions of badly hungover men. Prophet supposed he himself appeared the same way. They looked to have just rolled out of bed. Handy was knotting a bandanna around his neck and yawning.

He and Gunderson both stopped at nearly the same time and looked around, wide-eyed, at the strewn dead men.

Gunderson whistled. "What . . . the . . . ?"

"Where've you two been?" Prophet asked.

"Sleepin'," Handy said, tightly, glaring at Prophet. "Like you, we had a long night." He looked at Phoebe, and his expression instantly turned to concern. "What's wrong with her?"

"Take her," Prophet said, gently shoving Phoebe into Handy's arms.

"Where are you goin'?" Handy called.

Prophet didn't respond. He glanced once more at Jonas Ford slumped in death against the steps, surrounded by muttering townsmen, including the doctor.

He cast his gaze east, beyond the overturned stagecoach.

Louisa.

He cursed and headed for the livery barn.

Chapter 17

Prophet had led Mean out of his stall and was throwing the saddle onto the mount's back when he saw through the open double doors Phoebe, Handy, and Gunderson approach the barn. The woman's face was tear streaked but her eyes were hard now, determined.

So was her stride.

"We're going to help you track them," she said, walking past Prophet and down the hay-strewn alley between the stalls in which horses blew and fidgeted.

"No," Prophet said, punching Mean in the side so the stubborn horse would let out its held breath. Then he tightened the latigo and threaded the strap through the cinch.

"What do you mean, 'no'?" Phoebe glanced at him as she approached one of the near stalls. "There are five Lowrys left. They might be headed for Mexico."

"I don't think so," Prophet said. "They just came back from there. Besides, those five might think I'm dead. They'll soon know otherwise, but for now they think that nearly every damn lawman in the county is wolf bait."

"You're still going to need help. Even you, Lou!" Phoebe opened the door to her horse's stall.

"Forget it." Prophet glanced over his shoulder. Handy and Gunderson were holding back in the barn alley between Prophet and their employer. Both men looked uncertain, vaguely guilty.

Prophet turned to both men and said, "Where were you two when Ford and the others were ambushed?"

"*What?*" Handy said, though he'd heard the question.

"Where were you?" Prophet repeated.

"Mel told you," Gunderson said. "We were asleep. Had us a long night."

"You didn't hear the gunfire?"

"Sure we did," Handy said with a caustic chuff. "But gunfire ain't all that uncommon in West Texas, amigo!" He was flushed with anger, leaning slightly forward at the waist.

Prophet continued with: "Who told the Lowrys where I was?"

Both men studied him in stony, narrow-lidded silence.

Phoebe stood in the barn alley, holding her cream gelding's halter rope. "Lou, what's this about?"

"I think Handy and Gunderson told the Lowrys where they could find me." Prophet glanced at Phoebe. "*Us.*"

"That's absurd," Phoebe said.

"Yeah," Handy said, canting his head toward his boss. "What she said." He laughed. "Why would I pull a stunt like that?" He glanced at Gunderson and laughed again, too loudly and without an ounce of genuine humor.

Gunderson didn't laugh. His flush only deepened. The muddy pores in his ruddy face seemed to be opening wider, oozing sweat.

Prophet had been following a vague suspicion. Judging by both men's fishy demeanors, he was on the right trail.

He glanced at Phoebe. "You know what I think? I think your husband's killer has been under your nose this whole time, Mrs. Dahlstrom."

The possibility must have just occurred to Phoebe, as well. She stared suspiciously at Handy, the skin over the bridge of her nose deeply wrinkled. She didn't say a word. She just stared.

"Oh, go on!" Handy said, trying to laugh again. "Get out of here with your fool talk! You must've had too much of that Mexican's busthead over to the Five Card Stud!"

He glanced at his employer and frowned. "You don't believe a word of that, do you, Phoebe . . . uh . . . Mrs. Dahlstrom . . . ?"

Prophet kept his voice low, taut, as his own anger began to build. "You shot Dahlstrom out of jealousy. You thought that by killing him, you were making Phoebe your own. You blamed Charlie Butters for the killing, because he was an easy blame. Everyone knows what a killer he is, and that he should have been in prison. But he wasn't in prison. He was in the county."

"Bull!" Handy said, taking one step forward and pointing an arm and enraged finger at Prophet.

"That's pure garbage and you know it. You stop poisonin' Phoebe's mind with such accusations!"

Prophet kept his voice calm while his heart was turning somersaults. "Maybe you figured she'd blame the killings on her father, maybe you didn't. I'm betting you probably did. And in all the confusion, and with Gunderson backing your play, you figured you'd get off scot-free. Butters would hang for the murder. And the man Phoebe hates the most in this world—George Hill—would swing, too."

He smiled angrily. "And you were just stupid enough to believe that with Dahlstrom out of your way, Phoebe would be yours—a forty-a-month-and-found cowpuncher."

"And then Lou came along," Phoebe said in a voice that matched Prophet's for taut calm. "And you saw that I was attracted to him, because I've always been attracted to big, rustic men. Free-living men. And you knew you didn't stack up."

Handy merely stared at her in hang-jawed shock.

"Did you really send Lowry's men to the Stud hoping they'd kill both of us, Melvin?" she asked in a voice teeming with hushed awe.

Handy stared at her for several seconds without saying anything.

Then, slowly, he nodded. "Yeah," he whispered. "I was hoping they'd kill both him and his whore!"

With that, he slapped leather.

Handy didn't get his pistol even half out of its holster before Prophet's own Colt came up. It bucked and roared. The bullet took Handy through the neck and threw him back against a stall partition. As it did, Gunderson bellowed a curse and raised his own

Russian revolver but not before Prophet's Colt spoke once more.

Both men piled up at the base of a stall on the opposite side of the barn alley, groaning, dying hard and fast.

Up and down the barn, horses whinnied fearfully and stomped the stall partitions.

Prophet lowered his smoking Peacemaker and glanced to his right. Phoebe held her hands to her head in shock, staring at the fast-dying ranch hands. "What have I done?" she rasped. "Oh, good Lord in heaven . . . what have I done?"

She turned to Prophet.

"Jonas . . . the judge . . . all those men . . ." she said, saying the words slowly and with utter disbelief in their meaning, ". . . dead because of me."

What could Prophet say?

He holstered his Colt and walked out to where Mean had bolted when Prophet's gun had roared and the men had died. He grabbed his reins, mounted up, and galloped east out of town, keeping a close eye on the tracks etched into the sand and gravel beneath him, slowing occasionally when he lost the sign.

Quickly, his keen man-hunter's eyes picked it up again.

When the tracks told him the horses had slowed, which meant the gang might have been preparing to stop, he turned Mean into a notch between two low hills and swung down from the saddle. The tracks had led him first east and then south. He ground-tied Mean, pulled his spyglass out of his saddlebags, slid the Winchester from its sheath, and climbed the hillock rising in the southeast, dropping down well before the crest and doffing his hat.

He crabbed to within a few feet of the crest.

Keeping his head low, he stared straight out away from the rise, into a shallow bowl of desert in which lay a few scattered rocks and three mesquites growing up around three boulders half the size of wagons. The first thing he saw of the Lowrys was the nervous switch of a horse's tail among the mesquite branches.

He raised the spyglass, adjusted the focus.

The boulders and the three mesquites clarified in the sphere of magnified vision. Several men in rough trail garb were milling around the mesquites. More horses milled, as well, grazing on mesquite beans, tugging at the branches. One person sat on the ground, her back against one of the boulders. The blond hair and slender figure with all the right curves told Prophet he was looking at his partner.

He tightened the focus a tad. A red bandanna was wrapped around Louisa's upper-left thigh. She wasn't wearing her hat. She'd probably lost it during the dustup in town.

Now she raised her right knee, rested her arm atop it, leaning forward to inspect the bandage.

One of the Lowrys stepped away from the others. He had his arm in a sling. Charlie Butters moved better than Prophet had remembered. Butters stood in front of Louisa. He was looking down at her, saying something. Probably taunting her, threatening her.

Leaning forward, he grabbed his crotch. His head was jerking. He was giving Louisa an earful, probably telling her how much fun he and she were going to have later.

Louisa slumped casually back against the rock, having none of it.

Prophet ground his molars.

He resisted the urge to pick up the Winchester and plant a bead between Butters's shoulder blades. It would be a long shot, almost an impossible one, but he could hit him from here. It would have been easier with a Henry or a Sharps. A Big Fifty, for sure. But he'd made a Winchester shot that long before.

Once or twice . . .

Blowing a chunk of lead through Butters's spine would make Prophet feel a whole lot better but it would likely only get his partner killed.

The others kept glancing along their back trail as though waiting for someone. As though to confirm the speculation, hoof thuds rose from over Prophet's left shoulder.

He jerked a startled glance behind him. Phoebe rode her cream gelding into the notch where Mean stood ground-tied and craning his neck to look back at the newcomer, twitching his ears and giving his tail an incredulous thrash.

"Goddamnit!" Prophet bit out.

Phoebe swung down from her saddle and jogged up the low rise. Prophet gestured to her anxiously with his arm, and she dropped to her hands and knees, swiping her hat from her head. She crabbed up beside him.

"They might have seen you, goddamnit!" he wheezed at her.

"I'm sorry," she said, looking at him gravely, eyes

grief stricken but also determined. "I had to do something. I had to do something . . . helpful."

"You're not helping me."

"Goddamnit," she hissed, hardening her jaws. "Let me try!" Her voice broke. "I couldn't stay back there . . . with all that carnage I caused!"

Prophet picked up the spyglass again, stared through it.

Butters stood leaning against the same boulder Louisa sat against. Charlie appeared to be rolling a quirley from a makings sack. The others were milling about, conversing. Prophet could see their jaws moving.

Relief touched him. They hadn't seen Phoebe.

"What are they doing?" she asked Prophet as he continued to stare through the glass.

"Waiting."

"For what?"

"Those two rats I exterminated back at the Stud."

"What happens when they don't show?"

"That's what I'm waiting to find out." Prophet lowered the glass and stared into the bowl with his naked eyes, squinting against the sun. "They're too out in the open for me to try getting Louisa away from them. They'd see me comin' as soon as I left this hill. They'd have plenty of time to shoot her."

When the other two Lowrys didn't show, they'd probably figure Prophet would show up sooner or later.

What would they do then? Where would they go?

"Lou?" Phoebe's voice was small beside him.

She was staring at the ground in front of her.

"What is it?"

"I need someone to apologize to and . . . you're all I have."

"I'll tell you you're forgiven when I have my partner back."

"Why don't you call her what she is? Your lover."

"Whatever," he said, annoyed.

Prophet turned to her. He no longer considered the question nearly as impertinent as he had before. "Did Hill really rape you? Did you have his baby?"

All the color drained out of her face. She stared at the ground again.

"He did rape me. But I didn't have his baby. I told people it was his, because he'd raped me in the past. And no one has felt so much anger toward any man as that which I have felt toward George Hill." Shaking her head slowly, Phoebe looked demurely up at Prophet. "It was Erik's baby boy. When it was born dead, I wanted it to be my father's . . . to help take away the pain of losing it . . . of losing Erik."

"Did Dahlstrom believe it was your father's?"

"Yes. He would have believed anything I told him."

"I got a feeling there's a lot of men around here who would believe anything you told them. You got a way about you that goes deeper than your pretty face and well-filled blouse. I got a feeling there's a lot of men in these parts in love with you. Including Jonas Ford."

Phoebe drew a deep breath. When she released it, it rattled in her throat. A sob bubbled out, as well, though her blanched face was averted, expressionless. "Poor Jonas."

"Yeah," Prophet said, returning his attention to where the killers milled among the mesquites. "Poor Jonas . . . and six other men back in Carson's Wash."

"Are you going to kill Butters?"

"Of course I am."

"Even though I'm responsible for all the bloodshed?"

"Ah, Phoebe," Prophet said, grimacing. "You're not responsible for all this bloodshed. Melvin Handy got the ball rollin'. Your father or whatever you want to call George Hill got it rollin' before that. He's as much to blame as anyone. Butters was, is, and always will be a killer, and so's his Lowry kinfolk. Charlie's the one I'm sure sent the first Lowry after me with that Henry rifle. Innocent folks got caught in the whipsaw. It's the way of life. The way of people. Been happening since we beat each other with clubs and lived in caves. We can cry over it all we want and berate ourselves for our own parts in it, but all we can really do is vow to live better in the future. We probably won't but we can say we will, and that's something, anyway."

A distance-muffled but all-too-familiar voice came to Prophet's ears on the sandpaper breeze: "*Proph-et?*"

Chapter 18

"Shit!"

Prophet dropped his head. He shoved Phoebe's down as well.

"Prophet, you out there?" Butters shouted. His voice, thin with distance, was pitched with mockery. "Oh, come on—I know ya are! You gotta be! My cousins didn't show. So you had to!"

He dragged the "had to" out like the last words of a long refrain. The way his voice changed pitch ever so slightly, at times growing reedier and thinner, told Prophet that he was turning his head, looking around as he yelled. Which meant they hadn't spotted Prophet and Phoebe up here.

Butters was guessing.

Of course, he was guessing right. But guessing just the same.

Butters's voice rose louder, angrier. "You show yourself, Prophet, or we'll cut her throat right now!"

To Prophet's left, Phoebe gasped.

"It's all right," he said. "They don't know we're here. They won't kill her. Not yet. They'll use her to draw me in so they can kill me. Then they'll kill her," he added, mostly to himself, trying to figure out what to do.

Phoebe turned her head to look up at him, keeping her left cheek pressed against the ground. "What are you going to do?"

He jerked his head slightly and began snaking his body back down the slope. Phoebe did the same. Ten yards from the crest, Prophet rose to his knees and donned his hat.

He said, "They'll pull out soon. When they do, I'm gonna follow 'em. I'll wait till dark to make my move. Me an' Louisa have been through this before. She knows I'm here. She senses it. And she can take care of herself . . . until I get there."

Despite the certainty of the bounty hunter's words, he was far from certain. His heart thudded heavily, by turns racing and slowing. The anxiety must have been written on his face. Phoebe pulled up close to him, sandwiched his face in her hands, and pressed her lips to his.

"I want to go with you," she said. "Maybe there's nothing I can do to help. But I'd like to be there, just the same. If only to tend your wounds, if it comes to that." She paused, then urged quietly, almost desperately, "Please, Lou . . . ?"

Prophet looked at her, thought it through. It couldn't hurt to have her there. Like she'd said, he . . . or Louisa . . . might need someone to tend their wounds.

Prophet nodded once. "All right. You stay here with the horses, try to keep 'em quiet. I'm gonna go back up and keep an eye on them killers. I want to know when they pull out, and I want to know which direction they head."

"I will," Phoebe said, nodding. "I'll keep the horses quiet."

Prophet doffed his hat again and snaked back up to within a few feet of the crest of the rise. Again, he raised the spyglass. The gang was milling around the mesquites, conversing. Prophet could tell by their quick, fidgety movements that they were nervous. They were angry about the two men, cousins to Butters, brothers and sons to the Lowrys, they'd left in town.

Prophet identified the Lowry patriarch by his stooped shoulders, heavy gut, and gray sideburns dropping down from the frayed brim of his canvas hat. He wore a red calico shirt with the tails out, a brace of pistols belted around his impressive girth. At the moment, he stood staring into the distance over Prophet's left shoulder, along the gang's back trail toward town.

His feet were spread wide, fists on his hips. Long, gray hair danced across his shoulders.

He was grieved, angry.

He stood like that for nearly five more minutes while the others kowtowed around behind him, glancing at him skeptically.

Finally, Emmett Lowry turned and walked back toward the others. As though with a quick second thought, he switched course over to Louisa, leaned down, and cracked the back of his right hand against her right cheek. The blow jerked the Vengeance Queen's head sharply to her left, hair flying.

Prophet jerked as though with the force of the

blow. He must have imagined it, but he thought he could hear the smack of the man's hand against his partner's face.

He ground his teeth, felt the blood boil in his cheeks. "You're gonna pay dearly for that one, Lowry," he raked out. "In spades!"

Louisa righted herself, leaned back against the boulder, holding her hand to her bruised cheek. Suddenly, her left leg shot upward. Prophet couldn't tell for sure, but he suspected she'd buried her right, pointed-toed boot into the old man's crotch. Emmett Lowry hadn't seen it coming. The fool.

"Ooh!" Prophet grunted, grinning, as Lowry crouched forward over his smashed oysters, taking mincing steps backward. "Now, you see," Prophet said to himself, "you don't mess with the Vengeance Queen. When she's wounded, she's even more dangerous than when she's healthy. I coulda told you that."

He chuckled again as old Emmett Lowry remained bent forward, both arms pressed against his balls.

Prophet's delight was short-lived.

As Butters and the others gathered around old Lowry, a couple exchanging grinning glances, Prophet saw through the spyglass Emmett straighten and pull both his pistols from their holsters.

"Ah, shit," Lou said, holding the spyglass taut against his right eye.

Emmett aimed both revolvers at Louisa's head. Lowry was shouting. Prophet could hear the enraged pitch of the yells but not the words. He could see the quick, angry jerks of Lowry's head as he aimed the pistols threateningly at Louisa.

Prophet's heart lurched into his throat. He braced himself, then reached for the Winchester.

"Don't do it, you son of a bitch," Prophet gritted out. "Don't . . . even . . . think . . . about it!"

He crawled a little higher on the slope, raised the Winchester, pressed the stock against his right shoulder, and pumped a cartridge into the action. He peered through the spyglass once more. Lowry was still aiming both pistols at Louisa's head. His whole body was jerking, enraged.

Louisa smiled challengingly up at him. Through the glass, Prophet could see her bat her lashes at him, as though daring him to blow her pretty head off.

As though egging him on to do it . . .

"Damnit, Louisa, you cork-headed fool! He's gonna do it now whether he wants to or not! Now he's *gotta* do it!"

Prophet tossed the spyglass aside.

"Lou, what is it?" Phoebe asked, crawling up behind him.

Prophet snugged his cheek up against the Winchester's stock.

Emmett Lowry was only about the size of Prophet's thumbnail from this distance. But Prophet had made a similar shot before with the same rifle. It had been a while, but he'd made it.

Almost two hundred yards.

It might not have even been a lucky hit . . .

Prophet lined up the sights on Lowry's slightly humped back. Then, allowing for the distance, he raised the forward bead and slid it into the V atop the rifle's breech, placing both on the brim of the man's hat. He held his breath, took up the slack in his trigger finger.

Crack!

"Lou!" Phoebe said with a gasp.

Prophet lowered the rifle, grabbed the spyglass, raised it to his right eye.

Lowry jutted both pistols at Louisa. She was still smiling up at him. He clicked both hammers back, thrust the cocked revolvers straight forward and down.

And then he tensed.

Louisa's smiling face suddenly turned red.

He did it! Prophet thought, his heart a cold stone dropping into his belly.

The sonofabitch killed her . . .

He was about to slam the spyglass to the ground, but then he saw old Lowry stumble forward, lowering his pistols, firing both into the ground near his boots. Louisa threw herself to one side as Lowry fell forward against the boulder she'd been leaning back against.

Butters and the other Lowrys whipped around, grabbing pistols from holsters. The report of Prophet's rifle had probably reached their ears a second or so after they'd seen the bullet blow the old man's heart out his chest and onto the rock he was leaning against, like a drunk pissing against a tree. Prophet rose quickly, racking another round into the Winchester's breech, said, "Stay here, Phoebe!" and started running toward the horses.

"Lou!" she cried.

"Stay here!"

Prophet gained the crease between the hillocks, grabbed Mean's reins, and leaped into the saddle.

"Come on, partner!"

He didn't need his spurs. Mean knew the stakes.

The horse wheeled, jogged out of the crease and onto the trail. He swung right and lunged into a ground-eating gallop away from the rise and into the bowl. Prophet took the reins in his teeth and raised the Winchester in both hands, ready to start flinging lead before Butters or the other Lowrys could drill Louisa.

He no more than got the long gun pressed against his shoulder, however, before he lowered it.

Louisa must have grabbed both of Emmett Lowry's pistols. Two pistols were in her hands, and, leaning back against the boulder beside Lowry, who remained leaning forward against the boulder like that pissing drunk, she was going to work with both poppers, calmly, methodically shooting one at a time the men dancing around her.

Butters and the Lowrys had apparently been distracted enough by Prophet's assassination of Emmett that by the time they'd remembered Louisa, she'd already had Emmett's guns.

Two Lowrys were down. One of the two was down and writhing. The other was down and still.

Two others were exchanging lead with Louisa.

Despite her wounded leg, Louisa had the steadier hands. One of the last two Lowrys stumbled backward, twisting around and firing his pistol into the air before dropping to his knees and falling forward against the ground. The last man standing fired his own pistol then screamed and grabbed his left knee.

As he did, Louisa extended one of her pistols at him again and fired. The man's head snapped back with such violence that Prophet, who was within fifty yards now and closing fast, could hear the pistol-like pop of his neck breaking. Lowry crumpled, dead before he kissed the sand.

Prophet galloped up to within ten yards of Louisa, who was sliding back down against the boulder, beside Emmett Lowry. He looked around, frowning, then turned to his partner.

"Where's Butters?"

Louisa hooked a thumb over her left shoulder.

Prophet looked behind her. A horseback rider was just then pounding to the crest of a low, steep butte maybe two hundred yards away. Butters rode low in the saddle, hatless, his right arm tucked against his chest. He glanced behind him a half a second before his horse gained the crest of the butte. Then the horse plunged down the opposite side, and horse and rider were gone.

"I wounded that dog," Louisa said, curling one half of her plump upper lip. "Shot him in the cheek."

Prophet looked at her. "How bad you hit?"

"You've hurt yourself worse falling out of bed drunk," she grunted, leaning forward and tightening the bandanna wrapped around her leg. She glanced sidelong at Prophet, worry in her eyes. "Is Jonas . . . ?"

"Dead."

Louisa glanced over her shoulder again toward where Butters had fled. She turned her hard gaze on Prophet and flared a nostril. "Run him down and kill him, Lou."

Prophet heard hoof thuds behind him and turned to see Phoebe approaching on her cream. He was glad she was here. He wouldn't have left Louisa alone otherwise.

"I'll be back," he said, and nudged Mean with his spurs.

Horse and rider vaulted into an instant, rocking lope.

They flew around the mesquites, across the open flat, and then up and over the butte, following Butters's trail. Prophet didn't need to keep an eye on the man's hoof prints. He knew where he was headed.

The Lowry ranch was just over the next dyke rising like a toothy dinosaur jaw dead ahead and straight south.

Prophet crested the dyke fifteen minutes later and dropped down the other side and into the broad flat in which the shabby ranch slumbered. Ahead, Butters was just then galloping into the ranch yard, lifting a fine plume of tan dust behind him. He sagged, head hanging miserably, in his saddle.

A blond-headed, feminine figure stood in the cabin's open doorway, holding the door half-open. Prophet saw Jackie's plump belly behind a pale apron, her eyes drawn wide with concern.

Butters halted his horse, slid gingerly out of the saddle. He was holding his left hand against his bloody cheek. He ran shamble-footed to the porch, mounted the steps, pushed the girl inside with his body, and drew the door closed behind them.

Prophet urged Mean into a faster gallop. The horse snorted, lowered its head, and stretched its stride.

As the horse approached Butters's mount standing

wearily in the yard before the cabin, Prophet leaped off Mean's back and, leaving his rifle in its scabbard, ran up the porch steps. He knew Butters would have barred the door, so he drew his Colt and threw himself through the window left of it.

The cacophony of breaking glass was followed by a girl's scream.

Prophet hit the floor at the end left of the eating table, between the kitchen and the parlor part of the cabin. He rolled as two shots barked loudly. Bullets chewed slivers from the table edge.

Lou rose onto his left shoulder and hip, window glass still tumbling off his hat and his shoulders, and aimed his cocked Colt up at Butters. Jackie screamed as the killer grabbed her and pulled her in front of him. He stood behind the eating table, near the range. He held his cocked pistol against the girl's jaw.

His left cheek looked like hamburger. Blood dripped down from the ragged hole, trickling over his jaw, coating the little braid hanging wormlike from his scraggly goatee, and into his shirt.

"Drop the Peacemaker, Lou," Butters shouted, spitting blood, sounding as though he had rocks in his mouth, "or I'll blow her fool head off!"

"Charlie!" Jackie screamed.

"She's carrying your child, fer chrissakes!"

"Charlie!" Jackie screamed again.

Butters rammed the barrel of his pistol up hard again the girl's jaw, tipping her head up and back. She screeched in pain. "Lose the Colt, Lou, or I'll paint the ceiling with this pregnant bitch's brains!"

"All right, Charlie." Prophet depressed his Colt's

hammer and leaned forward to set the gun on the table. "All right, Charlie . . . there you go."

Prophet grinned.

"You think this is funny?" Butters barked.

"Yeah, Charlie," Prophet said. "I do."

Just then the blind old woman, who'd been stealing up behind Butters, raised her arthritic right fist and sunk a knitting needle into the back of Charlie's neck.

"Trash!" the old woman cawed like a dying crow. "Butters barn trash!"

That last was nearly drowned by Charlie's agonized wail.

He dropped his right hand and stumbled backward, reaching up with his left hand for the needle sticking out of his neck. Jackie dropped to her knees, sobbing.

Charlie yowled again, and then realizing he wasn't going to be able to dislodge the needle, he pivoted back around and extended his pistol at Prophet.

Lou had already swiped his Colt off the table.

The Peacemaker roared.

The bullet punched a quarter-sized hole through Butters's forehead, a little right of center. Still, a good shot, though. It did the trick.

Charlie's head snapped back sharply. He dropped his pistol with a thud to the floor.

The killer's ugly, bloody head wobbled, Charlie's eyes losing their focus and rolling back in their sockets. The head sagged back again and the rest of Charlie followed it to the floor.

The old woman stood over him, snarling and rasping and shaking her head.

Prophet strode around the table and helped the sobbing Jackie to her feet. She stared down in horror at the dead father of her baby.

Prophet held her close against him. "That, Miss Jackie," he said with a fateful sigh, "was Charlie Butters."

Epilogue

Two weeks later, Prophet held his hat down against his belly as he watched Louisa set a spray of wildflowers over the freshly mounded dirt and rocks that was Jonas Ford's grave.

The heat had broken finally, portending the cool breezes of autumn. Blackbirds cawed in the cottonwoods and mesquites that lined the cemetery that lay across the side of a low hill southwest of Carson's Wash. Mean and Ugly and Louisa's nameless pinto were tied to the shabby picket fence that surrounded the boneyard.

Louisa remained on one knee for a time, staring down at Jonas's grave. Prophet wondered if she was praying. The girl she'd once been would have said a prayer. The woman she'd become, however, likely wouldn't. The woman she'd become would have vowed revenge if Ford's killer hadn't already gotten his due.

Someone else would pay, though. Some other deserving killer would get the bullet she herself had wanted to punch through Charlie Butters's brisket.

Louisa straightened with a wince against the pain in her left thigh.

She should still be in bed or at least be on crutches, as the sawbones had advised. Neither was Louisa's way. She sure as hell shouldn't be riding yet, but that's what she intended to do though she'd promised Prophet she'd stop often and early and change the bandages frequently.

Prophet doubted she'd do either one.

Just wasn't the Vengeance Queen's way. There were men out there . . . and some women . . . who needed to die for their sins. That was more important than Louisa's health. At least, in her eyes.

She turned to Lou. The cool, fresh breeze buffeted the blond hair tumbling to her shoulders.

"He was a good man," she said.

"He was a good man," Prophet said. "I'm sorry, Louisa."

"It wasn't meant to be." She'd turned her head to pensively study the grave once more. "Just wasn't meant to be."

"You'll find another man. You'll get another chance at a normal life."

"The question is," Louisa said, "is that what I want?" She looked at Prophet. "A normal life?"

"Yeah," Prophet said with a sigh, setting his funnel-brimmed hat on his head.

He turned and started walking slowly toward the horses. "Well, I'll be seeing you down along the trail somewheres, Vengeance Queen. You keep your hooves clean and your tail free of cockleburs, you hear? And avoid them sidewinders. They make for venomous sleepin' companions."

Prophet chuckled to himself as he strode between the graves.

"Where you headed?" Louisa called after him.

Prophet stopped, half turned, narrowed one eye in question.

Louisa hiked a shoulder, crooked a half smile. "You want company? Down in Mexico?"

Prophet pointed an admonishing finger at her. "You're too bossy for Mexico. And you'll scare off the señoritas."

Louisa pursed her lips, nodded. "Right."

"We might make it halfway, though. Before one of us piss-burns the other an' we fork trails again." Prophet spread his arms, smiling. "You never know what we'll do."

"No, you don't." Louisa walked toward him. She allowed herself to limp only a little. She flicked his hat brim back off his forehead, rose onto her toes, and pecked his lips. "That's the thing about us—isn't it, Lou?"

"That's the thing about us." He continued walking toward the horses. "Come on—I'll buy you a beer and a shot for the trail."

"Make mine a sarsaparilla," Louisa said.

Keep reading for a special excerpt of the next LOU PROPHET, BOUNTY HUNTER *novel.*

BLOOD AT SUNDOWN
by Peter Brandvold

On sale in January 2019, from Pinnacle Books

"Gonna get yourself killed, Prophet, you no-good crazy Rebel!" Lou railed at himself, his words whipped and torn by the wind.

With a determined grunt, he scrambled on hands and knees, keeping his head down against the headwind, to the second train car's front end. He stopped a few inches from the edge and peered at the passenger coach from which young Fairweather had fired at Little Fawn.

"All right, you devil!"

Prophet scrambled down the ladder running up the front of the stock car and dropped to the vestibule at the rear of the passenger coach. He bent his knees, letting his feet and hips take the brunt of the landing.

Rising, he grabbed the knob of the door facing him. It turned. He threw the door open and lunged inside. He was a bull barreling through a chute, his heart thudding, the fire of his rage fighting back the cold that had so mercilessly assaulted him.

"Lou!" the countess screamed, rising from a chair somewhere to his left.

Prophet didn't look at her. He didn't look at anyone except the senator's son, whom he'd picked out of the crowd sitting or standing in the posh parlor car, warmed by a small, ornate iron stove, the second he'd entered the coach.

Several Russians leaped from their over-stuffed leather armchairs, exclaiming their astonishment at seeing the big, red-faced bounty hunter so unceremoniously entering their private domain.

"Good lord, man!" Senator Fairweather exclaimed, frowning at the intruder. He sat smoking a fat cigar with the old count.

Rawdney Fairweather was leaning over the rifle stretched across a table before him, on an open, fleece-lined scabbard, lovingly running a cloth down the polished stock while holding court with several men standing around him, some still chuckling or laughing over Rawdney's kill shot. Rawdney's face was still flushed from his own boastful laughter. A smile still played across his thick-lipped mouth as he turned to see Prophet striding toward him.

Prophet stopped three feet away from the murderous young dandy, yelled, "Kill-crazy fool!"

As he raised his fist, Rawdney screamed, *"Help!"*

He started to duck but couldn't avoid Prophet's large, clenched fist, which smashed into his left temple, knocking him back against the table.

"Help!" Rawdney screamed again. *"Help m—!"*

Prophet slammed his fist against the kid's mouth and instantly felt the wash of warm blood as Rawdney's lips exploded like ripe tomatoes. Lou slammed his fist against the kid's mouth two more times—powerful, savage blows laying waste to the kid's mouth and shattering both of his front teeth—before two or three Russians grabbed him from behind.

Prophet turned, head-butted one and punched another, shrugging out of the grip of the third, who tripped over one of his fallen comrades. Prophet turned back to his quarry, who lay back atop the table, his hands over his face, screaming. Rage a living, breathing beast inside him, Prophet commenced throwing one blow after another at the dandy's face, driving the mewling urchin to the floor.

Prophet followed Rawdney to the carpet, both fists like pistons.

Wam!

Wam!

Wam!

Wam-Wam!

"Get him, for God's sakes!" he vaguely heard the senator yell. "For the love of God, get that man off my son!"

Several men grabbed Prophet from behind. One grabbed his hair and jerked his head back sharply. Still, he managed to shrug from their grips long enough to land two more hammering jabs to Rawdney's face, which was by now a mask of pulp and blood.

One of the big Russians launched himself onto Prophet's back, grunting as he wrapped his arms around Lou's neck and rolled over onto his own back, pulling Prophet over on top of him, belly up. The other two and then yet another big Russian surrounded them, dropping to their knees and punching Prophet's face while others kicked him in the ribs, hips, and thighs.

Lou tried to fight back but the big man beneath him, holding him fast against him, pinned his arms behind his back.

Prophet stared up in frustration, grunting and groaning as the Russians' big fists smashed into his face—one hammering blow after another. He felt his brows and lips split. Thick, oily blood ran down his face only to be smeared against his cheeks and jaws by more savage blows. Meanwhile, the Russians' boots were like railroad spikes hammering his ribs and belly, his hips and his legs . . .

Vaguely, as though she were standing atop the deep well at the bottom of which he lay, being pummeled by the Russians, Prophet could hear the countess screeching out protests and crying. Just as vaguely, he could see someone, probably her father, holding her back away from the fray.

The room was beginning to fade around Lou when a man, probably Senator Fairchild, bellowed in perfect English, "That's enough. You're making a mess of the place. Get him the hell out of here!"

Prophet was fading fast when the beating suddenly stopped.

Several hands brusquely pulled him to his feet. His boots dragged across the thick carpet as two men, each holding an arm, half-carried him across the rail car and out onto the windy vestibule. The cold, cold wind and bright sunlight braced him a little, at least enough that he opened his eyes in time to see Rawdney's assistant, the immaculately tailored and barbered Leo, step out through the door behind him and the Russians.

"Hold on!" Leo yelled into the wind.

The two Russians dragging Prophet to the top of the vestibule steps stopped and turned him around.

His short, dark, carefully cut hair sliding around his head in the cold wind, Leo stepped up to Prophet and curled a menacing smile. With a pale, beringed hand, he removed the cap from a six-inch stiletto with a jewel-encrusted, obsidian handle. The nasty, slender blade glistened in the new-penny sunshine.

Leo snarled again and gave a prissy little grunt as he lunged forward, sinking the blade into Prophet's belly. Prophet felt the blade's sharp bite, like a snake sinking its teeth into him, just above his cartridge belt.

"There!" Leo shouted. "Now rid this train of that Dixie vermin!"

The Russians stepped around Prophet, each holding him by an arm then gave him a shove.

Prophet flew backward off the vestibule. His arms flopped out around him. He watched in an absent-minded sort of horror his moccasins leave the iron platform and dangle in midair. For a long, cold moment he hung there in the air beside the train, glimpsing the snowy, gravelly ground rise up around him.

The snowy ground engulfed him like a firm pillow.

"Ohhh!" The exclamation was punched out of his lungs in a burst of wind.

He went rolling, rolling down a long hill, the snow biting into him like a million cold teeth while the train's whistle blew somewhere beyond him.

"*Oh!*" he heard himself say. "Oh, oh, oh . . ."

In the periphery of his blurred vision he watched the train slide away . . . away . . . away along the tracks until there was only silence and a bed of ice around him and a cold night enfolding him in its black wings.